SAVING CHRIST

STARWAY SEVEN

FRANCIS T PERRY WILLIAMS

Kravitz & Sons

INNOVATORS IN PUBLISHING, MARKETING AND ADVERTISING

Kravitz and Sons LLC
1301 Farmville Blvd, Suite 104
Greenville, NC 27834

Contributing Editor: Kathryn Tedrick

Published by Kravitz and Sons LLC.

ISBN: 979-8-89639-170-8 (sc)
ISBN: 979-8-89639-169-2 (e)

Library of Congress Control Number: 2025909246

SAVING CHRIST

TABLE OF CONTENTS

WHAT IF WE COULD?

In A.D. 70, Roman Emperor Vespasian sent his son and future emperor Titus to stop the Jewish takeover of Jerusalem. Titus had over 60,000 troops at his command, along with 16,000 support personnel. The Jewish rebels, estimated at around 23,000, held control of Jerusalem for over three years. Vespasian needed to maintain control as this was an insult to Rome and its power, especially to him as Romans did not look kindly upon Jews in outright rebellion to Rome.

It is estimated that between half a million and a million people were killed, mostly Jewish. One of the reasons so many Jews were killed was because many of the troops were Roman soldiers from Turkey and Syria. They had a long history and inbred hatred for the Jews and didn't care who they killed. Old, young, women and children, no one was safe. They wanted all Jews dead. They massacred much of the remaining Jewish population without mercy.

At first, Titus wanted the Temple to be spared, but his soldiers wanted the complete destruction of Jerusalem and ultimately, the destruction of the Temple was complete down to the last few bricks, along with almost every important structure in Jerusalem. Nothing was spared, no libraries, no history, and no religious institutions. Thousands of Jews were enslaved and sent to the mines in Egypt. Thousands of other young Jewish men were sent to the arenas to be butchered for the amusement of the Roman Public. To put it simply, Rome had no respect for Jews or any form of Jewish history. To them, it needed to be destroyed.

The reason I bring this up is that it shows that a vast amount of history, especially about Jesus, was destroyed and everybody who knew about it or him were probably killed. I had to read as much as I could to make educated guesses as even the Bible was rewritten, and no one really knows who did it. In all reality, all we have are bits and pieces. So yes, in this book I did the best that anybody could. I tried to be open and not swayed. Many, many hours of thinking, reading, and trying to be logical went into this, because most of the truth is no longer known.

So much history was lost forever and only because Jesus was such a strong figure was anything left of him. Luckily for us it was. Jesus gave us faith, and faith can never be truly lost. So, if we could go back in time, what would we find? A love for Jesus and his words that will never be lost, along with faith. Please enjoy my version. I almost feel like I didn't write this story. I'm just telling history.

Francis T. Perry Williams

PROLOGUE

"It's a thing of wonder. Is it not?" Dr. Daryl Hathaway asked the man standing beside him.

"It is indeed," the Secretary of State replied. "Why so big?"

"There will be six people going on this mission."

"Do you really need that many observers? It seems to me that the chances of someone doing something that could change history would be awfully risky."

"They originally wanted to send 25, if you can believe it."

"Unfortunately, I can."

"I told them, the more people who know about it, the greater the chance of this top-secret project being exposed." Dr. Hathaway turned and looked at the Secretary full on. "To tell you the truth, Connor, I agree with you completely. But that's the orders I received from the military."

Connor McDougal's eyebrows went up. "What? Were they planning on sending a strike team? That would be eleven to thirteen special forces members."

Hathaway sighed. "That's what I feared. It took a lot of negotiating and haggling to get them down to six. Funny thing is, there will be seven seats on it."

"Seven? That just sent a shiver down my back. It's almost like they want one in reserve to bring someone back."

"That's what I thought. But they denied it. Said it was in case someone important last minute needed or wanted to go," Daryl replied.

"So, who makes up the six?"

"No one has been named yet, but it will include a pilot, an FBI agent as the commander, two scientists and two military observers."

"I was told the military observers would make sure no one steps out of line and if necessary, keep the team safe," the Secretary said.

The two men turned back to the time capsule. Made of Aerospace Aluminum, the time machine was circular, and looked like a flying saucer with four windows made from aluminum silicate glass and fused silica glass—the same type used in the old space shuttles. There were no wheels and the only thing that broke the surface was a port on the bottom where the anti-gravity engine was installed. A three-inch nozzle, and a small touch plate on one side would be used to open and close the door. The inside was fitted with seven comfortable seats and a control panel was centrally located in front of one of the windows, where the pilot would sit. The technology was state-of-the-art, the computer so advanced that there were only two in existence. The power source was so top-secret that only the Secretary of Defense, Harold Winston and the scientists, who built it, knew what it was. "How does it work?" Connor asked.

"I'll tell you what," Dr. Hathaway said with a smile. "We're doing a test run tomorrow. Since the only observers allowed are those who know about the project, and the scientists and engineers who built it, why don't you come watch?"

"Just tell me the time, and I'll be here."

"Make sure you're here before 9:00 P.M"

"Once last question," Connor asked. "That thing is going to stick out like a sore thumb in the past. How do you plan to hide it?"

"Easy." Daryl pressed a button on a remote control, causing the time capsule to look like an ancient home for lepers. "Several holograms have been designed to disguise the capsule to look like something no one would want to go near, depending on the timeline they are in—like a leper colony." "Sweet."

The time machine had been moved outdoors to an enclosed area made of reinforced concrete, like the kind used in NASA launch pads. The observers were allowed to tour the capsule so they could see that it contained nothing but what should be there, including a large empty leather bag and a small video camera that had no footage on it. The excitement felt almost tangible.

"Would everyone please head over to the observation area now? We're about to start the test run," Dr. Hathaway said.

One of the two Captains trained to operate the capsule was wearing Colonial garb and entered the area, using the pressure plate. He reopened the door of the time capsule. Before he did, he looked over at Dr. Hathaway and gave him a grin and a thumbs up.

"Good luck, Captain Wagner. God speed," the scientist called out.

Bracing for they knew not what, the observers arranged themselves in a designated space 40 feet away. Since this was its first mission, no one was sure about the noise level or heat they would have to deal with. History was about to be made, or at least they hoped so.

"Captain, you have a go," Hathaway said through a microphone like the ones actors used on stage.

"See you when I return," the Captain replied.

The silence that followed was complete as everyone held their breath to see what would happen.

Then the time machine fired up, surprisingly causing no more noise than a diesel engine would. As it rose up three feet from the pavement, one observer stated, "I hope this works. If it explodes, I doubt any of us will survive."

"I assure you. That will not happen," the Secretary of Defense said. "At least it better not."

"Here we go," Hathaway said excitedly. This project had been his baby for the past ten years. No one was more anxious and excited to see it succeed than he was.

Then the sound of the engine grew noticeably louder and the time capsule shot straight up into the sky, leaving Earth's atmosphere in a blink of an eye with a loud sonic boom. High above the Earth, a swirling black wormhole formed and closed so quickly, anyone seeing it would not have been certain it had actually occurred. For those in the know, a loud gasp came from several people, followed by a round of cheering, clapping, and slaps on the back. A moment later, the portal opened once more and the capsule reappeared, quickly slowing to a stop and landing on the exact spot where it had taken off.

"What happened? Why is it back already?" Secretary McDougal asked.

There was no one to answer him as everyone rushed toward the capsule, which the pilot was shutting down. He opened the door, and seeing the anxious faces of those standing before him, he grinned before stepping out with the large leather bag that was quite clearly no longer empty.

Dr. Hathaway stepped up to the Captain and shook his hand. "I take it you have the evidence I asked for, Johann?"

"Yes, sir, I do."

"Excellent!" He turned to the others and said, "Let's go inside to the meeting room where it's more private."

As they walked inside, Secretary McDougal showered the scientist with questions.

"Patience, my friend," Dr. Hathaway said. "I will explain everything inside."

Once everyone was seated, Hathaway took the evidence bag and stood at a podium facing the others, who found seats at two long tables.

"I know you must have lots of questions, but I promise that I won't bore you with a physics lesson. Yes, that was a macroscopic wormhole the Captain created from the ship, which allowed him to travel back in time. Unfortunately, I can't give you the details of how we were able to do it because…."

"It's Top Secret," everyone said, finishing his sentence.

"Well, yes," Hathaway said with a smile.

"But how do we know he actually went back in time?" the Secretary of Defense asked. "He wasn't gone more than a few seconds. And what's in that evidence bag?"

"He was gone a few seconds in our time, but I assure you. It was much longer for him. He spent two days in the past."

"Two days? Where's the proof?" the Secretary of Defense asked.

Hathaway opened the evidence bag, extracting two things: the camera and a musket.

"Is that…?"

"A musket, yes, circa the 1700s." Then Hathaway set the video camera up so that whatever was on it could be seen on a wide flat screen, hanging above and behind the podium. When he turned it on, everyone in the room rose to their feet in astonishment as they watched a scene with George Washington and his troops battling the English Red Coats. It was indeed George Washington, and no one doubted the proof before their eyes.

"Stole that gun off a dead Red Coat," the Captain said.

"And with that conclusion, it's time to christen the time capsule *Starway Seven* and celebrate."

PART

ONE

CHAPTER

ONE

At the White House, President Jim Peck and his family were almost finished eating dinner. The dessert, a flaky cherry strudel with a scoop of French Vanilla ice cream, was placed before the three members of the family and their coffee refilled.

First Lady Madeline Peck took a bite and briefly closed her eyes as she enjoyed her favorite dessert. "I swear, Jim, every time they make this, it tastes even better than the last."

Both her husband and son, Ian, who was the spitting image of his mother smiled.

Ian was tall and slender like her with the same baby blue eyes and winning smile.

"As long as the dessert is cherry, Mom, you're guaranteed to love it," Ian said, teasingly.

"Too true," she admitted. "Although I do love other fruit, cherry is my favorite."

The family finished dessert, exchanging small talk as they ate. Afterwards, they retired to the sitting room, where the President, a man of medium build and height with dark brown hair, slightly flecked with gray, a firm, dimpled chin, and hazel eyes, made his wife a martini and himself a bourbon on the rocks. Settling into their favorite chairs, they relaxed and talked about their day.

"How's that new committee coming?" Jim asked his wife.

"I am very pleased with what we have come up with so far," Madeline replied. "It's exciting to think about all the good we'll be able to do to help the abused women and children in this country."

"A worthy cause indeed," her husband said. "You're making quite a name for yourself as First Lady."

"I don't care about making a name for myself. I just want to use the power I have in my present position to help as many good causes as I can."

"Knowing you, Mom, if you could do it without your name being involved, you would," Ian said. "But in this case, you need to be openly involved as that brings in more rich and famous people to help the cause."

"I know, and that's fine," she admitted. "I just don't feel that people should go around advertising their good deeds. That's not what the Lord wants us to do, but in this case, there's no way around it."

"That reminds me. How did your interview with Ed Shultz go today?" Jim asked his son. "Goldsmith, Hamilton, and Shultz is a very prestigious law firm that will give you a great head start in your career."

Ian did not answer right away. He knew his father would not like hearing it, but he had made up his mind, and that was that. "I cancelled it." He was right.

"What!" His father set his glass of bourbon down a bit too hard, spilling some. "Why not? Do you know what kind of favors I had to call in to get you that interview?"

"I changed my mind. I'm not sure what type of law I want to go into yet. Besides, I don't want the job just because you happen to be good friends with one of the partners."

"That's the most ridiculous thing I have ever heard," Jim said angrily. "You know the old saying, 'Don't look a gift horse in the mouth'? Well, you just did, and it might come back to bite you."

Ian looked at his mother. "I told you he would react like this."

The President's eyes flashed as he turned his attention to his wife. "You knew about this? Why didn't you say something?"

"It wasn't my place to say it. You keep pushing him towards the kind of law that would lead to politics. Ian isn't interested in politics, and there is no reason why he should have to go into a profession he isn't interested in. This is his decision, and to be frank, I can see his point," Madeline said calmly.

"Point? What point? The only way to get ahead in this world is through connections, knowing the right people in the right places. What's wrong with that? Do you think I would have been elected president, if I didn't have connections?"

"That's okay for you, but I don't want to be president or a senator, or anything else. I want to stay as far away from politics as I can. Besides, what kind of man would I be if I went through life hanging onto the shirt tails of people in power? If I am going to make something of myself, I want to do it on my own merit, not because of some big shots that owe you something or have traded favors with you. I don't want people saying that the only reason I got where I am is because of you."

"I never took you for a fool before, but now I wonder," Jim said.

"Aren't you being a bit too hard on him?" Madeline asked her husband. "It may take him longer, but when he reaches the goal he has in mind, he will have earned it all on his own. And that's something to be proud of."

"That road is filled with pitfalls that will slow you down. Why deal with them when you don't have to?"

"When 99% of the rest of the people have to, why shouldn't I?" Ian asked.

"Because you don't have to!" Jim shouted angrily.

"That's the difference between you and me. I want to earn my merits based on what I do, not have everything handed to me on a silver platter." Ian was angry now, too. "And that doesn't make me a fool!"

"And just what is that supposed to mean?" his father asked, growing angrier by the minute. "Are you saying that's how I made a name for myself, by gliding in on someone else's shirttails?" "You said it. I didn't," Ian said.

Jim rose to his feet. So did Ian and Madeline. She quickly stepped between the two men, fearing this would lead to physical blows.

"That's enough, both of you!" She did not shout, but her voice was firm and authoritative.

"Don't worry, Mom. I'm leaving. I knew I should have left right after dinner. These so-called talks always end up this way. He doesn't care about what I want. He wants me to be a carbon copy of himself. Well, no thanks!"

Ian stormed out of the room and left the White House, speeding away in his BMW Z4 Convertible, and making his Secret Service guards scramble to follow him in their own vehicle.

*****

"Mr. President."

Jim Peck roused from a light sleep, blinked, and switched on the lamp on his nightstand. He looked up at the man who woke him. "Brian?"

"Yes, sir," his Chief of Staff replied in a quiet, solemn voice.

Madeline also awoke. "What time is it? Has something happened?"

"It's 2:25 A.M. I'm sorry to disturb you both, but there has been an accident. It's Ian."

Jim and Madeline both sat up.

"What kind of accident? Is Ian okay?" Madeline asked, trying to keep the panic from her voice.

"Your son's Secret Service agents called from George Washington University Hospital. He was in a bad car accident." "Were they hurt as well?" the President asked.

"No, sir. Ian took off without them. They were following behind in their vehicle." "Have my car readied," the President said. "And call Father Murphy. Have him meet us at the hospital."

"Already done, sir." The Chief of Staff left the bedroom to give them some privacy.

Thirty minutes later, the President, the First Lady, and the Chief of Staff entered the limo and headed off to the hospital.

"How much do you know?" Jim Peck asked.

"Not much, I'm afraid. According to the Secret Service, he was speeding and lost control of the car before slamming into a tree. They said he had been with friends at a local nightclub for most of the evening." Madeline's breath caught in her throat.

"Was he drinking?" the President asked.

"He was in a nightclub, so he probably was, but they don't know how much."

Jim reached over and took his wife's hand. "I'm sorry. This is my fault." "No, you can't blame yourself. You are both hot-headed," she replied.

"Yes, but I should not have pushed him. It's just that he can't seem to make up his mind, so I pushed him, maybe a little too much."

Madeline squeezed his hand. "We can worry about that later. For now, just pray that he will be all right."

When they arrived at the hospital, the President and his wife were escorted to a private room to wait for word about their son, who was still being treated. Father Murphy was already inside.

"Have you heard anything?" the President asked him.

Father Murphy shook his head no.

Fifteen minutes later, a tall, slender man with brown hair and eyes entered the room. "Mr. President, Mrs. Peck, I'm Doctor Austin, Chief Neurologist here at George Washington."

"Neurologist?" Madeline asked. The color drained from her face.

"Please sit down, and I'll tell you what we know so far," the doctor said. "After swerving around several cars, your son's car slammed headon into a tree, ending up on the wrong side of the road." "Had he been drinking?" Peck asked.

"His alcohol limit was .09, which is over the legal limit. So, yes, he was. He sustained two fractured ribs, cuts and contusions to the face and head, and a head injury to his frontal lobe, which has caused bruising to his brain."

"What can be done for him?" the President asked.

"Right now, he isn't showing any signs of a brain bleed, and that's good. But I have ordered a CT scan to be sure."

"Other than a CT scan, how would you know he has a brain bleed?" Madeline asked.

"Blurred vision, severe headaches, a stiff neck, and weakness on one side of the body. If the CT is good, then there is nothing to worry about. His other injuries should heal just fine," Dr. Austin assured her.

"When can we see him?" the President asked.

"As soon as he's finished with the CT, we'll take him to a private room, where you can be with him."

"Thank you, Doctor," Madeline said.

Once the doctor left the room, Father Murphy prayed with them and offered comfort, telling them that it was in God's hands and all would be well. He couldn't have been more wrong.

*****

Three days later, Ian was still bothered with a persistent headache that was getting worse. His mother was constantly at his side. His father could not shirk off his presidential duties, but he came as often as he could.

Around 2:00 P.M., Ian looked at his mother, who was sitting in a chair close to the bed. "When are they going to bring my lunch?" he asked.

His mother looked surprised. "You already had your lunch over an hour ago."

"I did? I don't remember."

This worried Madeline. "Are you still hungry? Should I try to get you something else?"

Ian pondered his answer. Was he still hungry? Why didn't he remember eating lunch? "Maybe not. If I could just get rid of this headache. I feel like my head is going to explode."

"Let me call the nurse and ask if you can have something more for the pain," his mother said. This would also give her a chance to ask the nurse about his forgetfulness. She pushed the call button.

A moment later, his nurse entered the room. "Do you need something?"

"I…." He looked at his mom. "I…don't remember."

Madeline stood up, more alarmed than ever. She turned to the nurse. "His headache is worse. Could he have something more for the pain? And a few moments ago, he asked about lunch, forgetting that he'd already had it."

Concerned, the nurse checked his vitals. "It's normal to have some forgetfulness with a head injury, but this is concerning." She checked his eyes. "Follow my finger with just your eyes."

Using an index finger, she went from left to right, and his eyes followed. Next from right to left with the same result. However, when she went from up to down, something changed.

"I can't see," Ian said. "I can't SEE!" he cried more alarmed. "Why can't I see? Everything looks grey."

Madeline stood next to him and took his hand. "It's all right, Ian," she tried to soothe him, but it was difficult keeping the fear out of her voice.

The nurse made an urgent call for Doctor Austin, who arrived within moments.

As he rushed into the room, Madeline asked, "He can't see, Doctor. What's going on?"

"And he started having short-term memory issues a few moments ago," the nurse told him.

As Dr. Austin made a quick examination, a second doctor entered the room—a third-year resident.

"I don't like the looks of this." He turned to the resident. "Book an O.R." The resident ran out of the room, and Dr. Austin turned to the First Lady.

"I believe he is having a brain bleed."

"Can you stop it?" she asked worriedly. "Do you have to cut open his head?"

"I have no choice. I have to stop the bleed now. I'll do everything I can, but I suggest you call the President."

As Ian was wheeled from the room, Madeline called her husband on her cell phone. "Jim, you had better get to the hospital now," she said as tears rolled down her face. "Ian has developed a brain bleed, and they are rushing him into surgery. Better ask Father Murphy to come, too."

*****

President Peck, a firm believer in God, had the priest meet him at the hospital. "Father, pray for my son and that his doctor can stop this brain bleed." He was worried, but firmly believed that because he was the President, God would save his son. "You must convince God to save my son."

The priest nodded.

In the operating room, the doctors did everything they could, but it did not look good. When Ian was returned to his room, Dr. Austin did not sound hopeful.

"We managed to stop the bleed, but he is not out of the woods yet. The main thing now is to wait for him to regain consciousness." "When will that happen?" the President asked.

"There's no way to tell for certain. It's all a waiting game now."

After the doctor left the room, Father Murphy asked, "Would you like me to give him his last rites…just in case?"

"Yes," Madeline said. "Please do. Even if he pulls through okay, it's better that he has them."

*****

Ian remained in a coma for a week. The doctors had done everything they could, but his condition only worsened. He never regained consciousness, and eventually the son of the President died, taking his father's hopes and dreams for his son with him.

"WHY?" Jim Peck shouted at Father Murphy. "Why did God abandon me? Why did He take my only son…my only child? I'm the President of the United States—the most powerful country in the world. Am I not doing a good enough job? Haven't I helped the people here have a better quality of life?"

Father Murphy tried to calm him. "You have been an excellent president, sir."

"Well, that certainly is good to hear, Father. So why is God punishing me?"

"God isn't punishing you, Mr. President. He did what He felt was best for your son."

"Really? And what about me? Because He sure didn't do what was best for me!"

"The doctor said that Ian might have irreversible brain damage. He could have remained in a coma and never regained consciousness," Father Murphy said.

But there were no words to console Jim Peck. And as his grief overwhelmed him, he grew angry—angry at the doctors for their failure to save Ian, angry with the people trying to console him, but most of all, angry with God. He thought about going back to the White House and breaking the news to his wife. It broke his heart. She would be devastated.

When he told her thirty minutes later, she collapsed in his arms, sobbing hysterically. How do you console a mother who has lost her only child? As he held her in his arms, his mind turned to revenge.

Something must be done, he thought. But what? How can you seek revenge against God?

He didn't know, but he would find a way. Somehow.

CHAPTER

TWO

FBI Special Agent Jennifer Mary Williams was 5'7" tall with medium blue eyes and tawny brown hair. At the age of 30, she still had an athletic body like a gymnast and was strong, independent, intelligent, and proficient in jujitsu and tai kwon do. She had a degree in Comparative Religion—a systematic comparison of the practices and doctrines, migration, and impacts of the world's religions, which led to a deeper understanding of the fundamental philosophical concerns of religion.

With hate crimes on the rise, concerning not only people of color but those of specific religions, her degree made her a valuable asset to the Bureau. Jennifer, however, did not want to be known simply for her intelligence. She had a strong competitive nature in whatever she did, be it games, sports, work, and just about everything else. Although more and more women had become agents in not only the FBI, but the CIA, AFT, and Homeland Security, the men still outnumbered them greatly.

Assigned to Quantico in Washington, D.C., she trained constantly, and late one afternoon as she put herself through the obstacle course, she was approached by the FBI Science and Technology Branch Executive Assistant Director, Gerard Barnett. He had been watching her from the sidelines on several occasions and when she finished the course and used a towel to dry the sweat from her face, he called out to her.

"Agent Williams. I'd like a word with you."

Jennifer was puzzled when she realized who he was. What would Assistant Director Barnett want with her? Walking over to him, she replied, "Director Barnett. What can I do for you?"

"Actually, it's what I can do for you, Jennifer," he said with a smile.

Still wondering what this was all about, she cocked her head slightly and waited for him to continue.

"I've been watching you, and I must say that I am impressed with your physical performance. You're small and fast, and I believe that very thing that many might overlook, could be of great service to you."

"Thank you, Director. What do you have in mind?" Jennifer was more curious than ever and it showed as a spark of interest in her eyes.

"The agency is organizing a top-secret assignment that requires a very special, special agent. I think that agent could be you. But in order to make that determination, you will have to enter an obstacle course competition…and win." Barnett watched her carefully and believed that he saw exactly what he was looking for. "Of course, your background will also help, but we need both physical and intellectual attributes. It could also mean a big plus for your career. Are you interested?"

Jennifer knew there might be a woman or two also competing, but that did not concern her. She wasn't interested in competing against women. She found that too easy. It was the men she wanted to compete against. In part, that was where the FBI came in. She was a stunningly beautiful woman, her looks almost exotic, and she knew how to take advantage of that beauty. It was a valuable asset she made good use of, because too many men saw her only for her good looks. They made the mistake of thinking that she couldn't possibly have the intelligence or physical stamina to go with it. Her male counterparts might think she would be a pushover, but none of them could ever make the claim of haven gotten to first base with her.

Most of her competitors would be men, who were bigger, faster and stronger. She would have a huge disadvantage. Jennifer had learned that whenever she competed against men, she needed to find the 'weakest link' among them. There always was one—just a little bit less than the others, and this one she could beat. Normally, as long as she accomplished that and did not come in last, she was satisfied. This time, however, was different. She would have to beat them all. Could she do it? She wondered.

The Director told her that she would have to win. Did she even stand a chance? Was this a joke being played on her? She studied the serious look on his face and somehow, came to the determination that no, it was not a joke. Impossible as it might seem, she could not pass up the challenge. Besides, she was intrigued about what this so-called top-secret assignment was all about.

"I accept your challenge, Director Barnett. Just tell me when and where, and I will be there to do my absolute best." Was it just her imagination? Or did the Director actually look pleased?

"Excellent, Agent Williams. The day will be two weeks from this coming Saturday at 9:00 A.M. Take all the time you need to practice until then."

"Thank you, Director."

"And Jennifer, I expect you to win. This assignment is of the utmost importance, and while there are others I could use, you are the one I want. Good luck."

*****

The two weeks that followed went by as a blur, except for one strange thing. Not overly religious, lately Jennifer found herself drawn to everything religious. She would see a church and stare at it without knowing why. And she became fascinated by anything that resembled a cross, especially if it was an actual cross or crucifix. One night, it was nearly midnight, but she could not sleep. Something was on her mind, but she couldn't figure out what it was. Changing from her nightshirt into a sweatshirt and pants, she put on her running shoes and went outside to her back patio. The night was quiet, except for a dog barking in the distance and the sound of a single car driving past.

Closing her eyes for a moment, she took a couple deep, cleansing breaths, using them to relax her body and open her senses. The air was fresh and clean from a brief rain that had passed over the area a couple hours earlier. Looking up, she noticed that the moon wasn't much more than a sliver, which made the stars shine even brighter. She stared at them in wonder. Something was there, but she just couldn't figure out what. Still, Jennifer kept looking, and as she did, in her mind, the stars appeared to form into a cross. This startled her, and she blinked a couple times, but the image would not go away.

Then she thought about this special competition she would be competing in—top-secret. Jennifer shook her head. *No, that couldn't be it. Could it? The director did mention about my background being important. Is that what triggered all this weirdness? Nah. It has to be something else. But what?*

She did not know, but she knew she had a purpose in life, and she felt that something special was about to happen. She just didn't know what or when.

✶✶✶✶✶

On the day of the competition, Jennifer arose at 6:00 A.M. and ate a protein bar. Normally, she would have had something more substantial, but she did not want a lot of food rolling around her insides and weighing her down. Changing back into her sweats from the night before, she padded down the hallway to her spare bedroom, where she kept her own workout equipment. After a light workout to warm up her muscles and work out the kinks from a night of too little sleep, she rolled out her yoga mat and went through her normal morning routine. Afterwards, she headed into the shower.

She was ready by 8:00 with 30 minutes to kill before the competition. Jennifer decided to spend it in meditation. She wanted to be totally relaxed and ready. When she arrived at the obstacle course where the competition was to take place, she discovered that she was up against only one man, Agent Robert Winfield, and she did not know him, except by reputation. This surprised her. He certainly wasn't at the top when it came to physical competition, and she could not help wondering why they had chosen him. Did they want her to win? The director had made it clear that he expected it.

Although there were only the two of them, several other agents, both male and female were there to watch. The women to cheer her on. The men all knew that her competitor was normally the weakest link among them. This puzzled them, and there were whispers that the whole thing was rigged. It wasn't. Whatever the reason, they did not want him to lose. They crowded around him, giving him tips and encouragement, until the Director signaled the observers to take their seats. Director Barnett wasn't the only top man there. He was joined by the Chief Director Gately as well.

The agent conducting the competition called out, "Agents Williams and Winfield, please take your starting positions."

They would both be on the obstacle course at the same time.

"On your mark. Get set. Go!"

Both agents took off at a run. After making their way through a field of tires, they approached a 30-foot-tall rope ladder with poles at the top to climb over. Jennifer was behind at first, but she managed to catch up by dropping the last 10 feet on the down side.

Because of his weight, her male competitor could not risk injuring himself in a drop, which cost him precious seconds. Jennifer being lighter, landed with no problem, taking full advantage of her slim lead.

It did not last, though. She fell behind during the rest of the competition. But there was one area where they had to crawl. Although Winfield arrived there first, Jennifer arrived seconds later, and she had the advantage. Because she was smaller, she was able to crawl very quickly under the barbed wire obstacle. Her competitor, because of his larger size, got tangled up for precious moments in the barbed wire, giving Jennifer a small lead. After that, the only thing left was a hundred-yard dash to the finish line in mud a foot thick. Every movement was a struggle, especially for Agent Winfield, who slipped and fell, getting mud all over himself. Once again, because she was lighter in weight, she could move faster. Jennifer carefully maneuvered through the mud. Her competitor ended up a muddy mess. Jennifer was muddy, too, but not as much. She maintained her slim lead and just barely won. But a win was a win, and she was pleased. The female agents surrounded and congratulated her.

"Way to go, Jennifer!" one agent hooted.

"Now that's what I call woman power!" another cheered.

The 'weak link' was ridiculed by the other men.

To Jennifer this was a total victory.

"If you agents will excuse us, I want to congratulate Agent Williams." They turned and saw Chief Director Gately and Assistant Director Barnett standing there, smiling.

Once everyone else was gone, the Chief Director spoke. "Congratulations, Agent Williams. That was quite a performance. When Director Barnett told me about you, I had my doubts as to whether you could physically fill the bill. I was wrong."

"Thank you, Director Gately," Jennifer said. Guess I showed you.

"As for that special assignment, you certainly earned the right to become a team member. There will be a meeting in my office next week, where I will give you all the necessary information, so that you can decide whether or not to take this assignment. My secretary will fill you in on the details."

"Thank you again, sir. Both of you."

As the two men left, Jennifer looked back with pride at the obstacle course she had run and practiced on so many times. It had all been worth it, and she could not wait until she found out what was behind it. Whatever it was, she was certain it would be something out of the ordinary.

CHAPTER

THREE

Filled with anger over his son's death and the need for revenge, President Peck had no idea what to do. *How can I get revenge against God?* The question plagued him unmercifully. Scenario after scenario ran through his mind day and night, even distracting him from his presidential duties. He became depressed, even surly to the point where the people around him began to notice the change in him. Concerned, Madeline invited Father Murphy over for dinner one evening. The atmosphere was a bit uncomfortable, with the President saying little, leaving the First Lady to do most of the talking. But she was determined to see this through. Jim needed counseling, and who better than Father Murphy?

After the meal was concluded, she ushered the two men to her husband's private sitting room and made sure they had liquid refreshment. Then, making the excuse she had decided upon earlier in the day, she left the two men alone. At first, neither man spoke. The President took a hefty swallow of his brandy and set it down on the table next to his chair. "I suppose my wife asked you to offer me some comfort. To be honest, I don't think such a thing exists."

"I understand your thinking, but God loves you and should you seek it, He will console you," Father Murphy said. "And there are other professionals, who can help as well."

Peck let out a nasty laugh. "Really? How can you say that, Father? If He hadn't allowed my son to die, I wouldn't need comforting—His or anyone else's."

"Then you blame God for the loss of your son?" he asked in a quiet voice.

"Blame? Yes! I blame Him. I'm the President of the United States. With all that I do and have done for this country, He should never have allowed this to happen in the first place."

"So, you're saying that He should have taken away you and Ian's free will." "If that's what needed to be done, then yes. I do." Jim took another sip of his drink.

"Are you listening to what you're saying, Jim? That is something that God will never do. He gave us brains, intelligence, free will, and the ability to figure out how to use them. To take that ability away, would leave us nothing more than automatons," the Priest said.

Peck remained silent for a few moments before saying, "I guess you're right. But I still think He could have done something to save my son's life. He seems to do it for others. After all, miracles happen all the time," he concluded bitterly.

"We can't know the reason why Ian was chosen to go home to God. Had he lived, he might have been left in a vegetative state, paralyzed, or so disabled that life would not have been worthwhile. His brain injury was severe."

The President thought about Father Murphy's words. And he had to admit that they made sense. He still believed, however, that Ian could have been saved and healed, but God had not wanted to do it. Was he being punished? For what? He decided to come at it from a different angle. "Let me ask you this, then. I'm sure you saw the story on the news about the mass shooting at a synagogue in New York."

The priest shook he head sadly. "I did. It's a terrible thing when people cannot even be safe to worship in their communities."

"I agree. The men that did that, who do they hate? The Jewish people?"

"Yes."

"What about the members of other churches who have been shot and murdered by white supremacist groups? Is it the people they hate? Or is it God?"

Father Murphy was startled by the question.

"It can't be God. Could it?" Peck asked. "Those people claim to belong to other Christian faiths."

"Ah, but even among the various religions, there are those who hate people who don't belong to their particular sect," Father Murphy said. "Christ taught forgiveness, and tolerance, and turning the other cheek. Unfortunately, man often gets caught up in his own version of what he thinks is right, forgetting what God wants and the most important thing that Jesus taught us—Love. What God wants goes out the window in favor of human desires."

"Do you think that these attacks on churches and synagogues are a form of punishing God?" the President asked.

"That's an interesting question. In some minds, maybe they are." "And are they correct in that thinking?"

"I don't believe so. God undoubtedly is angered by it and feels sorrow and compassion for His people. But in the end, the only ones who suffer are the people."

They talked another hour, before Father Murphy had to return to his parish. Had this talk done anything to help Jim Peck feel any better. Unfortunately, not. He was still angry and just as determined to get his revenge, but how?

✳ ✳ ✳ ✳ ✳

The following week, the President and his Chief of Staff attended a top secret meeting that included Dr. Daryl Hathaway, the head scientist for Project Starway Seven, the Secretary of Defense, Harold Winston, and the Secretary of State, Connor McDougal.

Secretary McDougal was very excited about disclosing the project to Peck. He believed that it could be the one thing to snap the President out of his funk. When the President and his Chief of Staff, Brian, entered the Situation Room, everyone already inside stood up.

"Sit. Sit," Jim Peck ordered as he and Brian walked over to their chairs and sat down. On the table in front of them were folders marked *Eyes Only*. Opening the folder, he saw the name of the project, Starway Seven. "What's this, Harold? Another *Star Wars* program?"

"No, sir, something totally different," the Secretary of Defense replied with a smile. "Starway Seven is a time ship, so named because it uses the position of the stars to find a time period, then opens a macroscopic wormhole to travel there. The stars also tell the ship the exact location of the period we want to travel to, and uses a newly developed anti-gravity system to move and travel through time."

For the first time in weeks, Jim Peck was riveted to every word the Secretary of Defense said. He looked at the faces of every man in the room, and his heart pounded wildly in his chest. "Time travel…time travel? Does it work? Have you tested it yet?"

"It works perfectly, sir," Secretary McDougal answered, cutting in. He laid the English musket on the table in front of Peck and turned on the overhead projector. "That, sir, is an authentic English musket taken off the body of a red coat by the Captain of the time ship. And if you'll watch this clip, I believe you will have no doubt as to its authenticity." He hit enter on the laptop computer.

Jim Peck watched intently, and when he saw George Washington, his mouth dropped open. "Is that…?"

"General George Washington. Yes, sir," McDougal replied, grinning from ear-to- ear.

When the clip ended, the President picked up the musket and examined it thoroughly, running his hands over it like it was the most precious thing he had ever touched.

"Let me introduce Dr. Daryl Hathaway, the lead scientist, who developed Starway Seven," McDougal said.

Hathaway stood up and walked over to the President. The men shook hands. "It's an honor to meet you, Mr. President," he said. "This project has been my baby for the past 20 years. I can't begin to describe how exciting it is to present it to you."

"The honor is all mine, Dr. Hathaway. Please, return to your seat." Daryl did so.

"You say this machine can go back in time, and by the evidence I have been presented with, I believe it. But can it also go into the future?" Peck asked.

Dr. Hathaway smiled. "I get that question a lot. But no. It cannot go into the future, because the future hasn't happened yet. It can only go back in time."

"I see. Still, think of what we could learn about past historical events. The truth, not just the way whoever wrote the history books say it happened."

"History is written by the victors," Dr. Hathaway agreed. "Or the way others wish it to be perceived. Hence, you can understand why this must be kept so top-secret. The ability to go back in time can be a powerful learning tool, but it can also be a weapon, used by the unscrupulous to change or even destroy the future. It is important that while visiting the past, we go there not to change, but to observe."

"I agree," the President said. But mentally, his mind was going in a totally different direction. What if? "And has there been a destination… a timeline picked yet?"

"I believe we have an excellent time and location to visit, if you agree, Mr. President," Hathaway said. "For our first real mission, I would like to send a team back 2,000 years to the time of Christ. Can you imagine the impact it would have if we could actually show people that Jesus was alive and did everything the Bible says He did? What it would mean to those who believe and others who don't or aren't sure it was just a fairytale?" Hathaway was clearly excited about the prospect.

"Yes. It could change everything," Jim Peck agreed. His mind raced. *Could this be? Have I finally found a way to do the unthinkable and somehow punish God?* "But wouldn't that also change the future?"

"Possibly. Who's to say. There will always be those who refuse to believe the truth."

"Agreed. So, what needs to be done yet?"

"We'll need to pick a crew of six people to make the journey," Secretary Winston said. "Which will take some time."

"Yes, I can see why," the President said. "We'll want to be certain that we have the very best people we can trust on board to do what is needed, and protect the timeline." "Yes, sir," Winston agreed.

"Then let's get started."

CHAPTER

FOUR

President Peck had spent most of the previous day going over pages of information about possible candidates and interviewing them for the position of mission leader. A file was created on each individual that included education, background, personality, accomplishments, interviews with family, friends, and coworkers, military or law enforcement affiliation, and two pictures—a full-length and a head shot.

All but two were men. And although every candidate would have made a good leader, Peck was looking for someone special. He interviewed all the men, seeming almost bored or impatient to dismiss them. That left the two women. One was a CIA operative, and although she was attractive and fit the bill in what he was looking for, she was a woman of 45 years. He wanted someone younger.

"Thank you for coming in, Agent Sauder," Jim Peck told her as he shook her hand again. "I have one more person to interview before I make up my mind. However, I will tell you that thus far, you are the best candidate I have interviewed."

"Thank you, Mr. President. I am honored, and if I am chosen, I promise that I will do my best to fulfill your every expectation."

The agent was escorted out. Thirty minutes later, his secretary brought in the last and final candidate, Jennifer Williams.

The President stood up as she entered the room. "Good afternoon, Agent Williams. Please have a seat in front of my desk."

"Thank you, Mr. President."

Peck walked around the desk and shook her hand, and then returned to his chair and opened her folder. He didn't really need to. He knew everything inside by heart, having read it over and over. She was the one he had decided on in the beginning, but to be fair, he decided to interview her last, just in case he discovered some negative qualities that would disqualify her.

"You come highly recommended by your superiors. And they tell me that you are a proven leader."

"Thank you, sir. I'm very competitive. Always have been. I believe that there is always room for improvement, and I am willing to do whatever it takes to achieve that goal."

The President continued with his interview, and by the time he was finished, he knew she was the one. He'd had plenty of time to plan his revenge over the past week and had decided he wanted a woman to head the mission, especially one as attractive as Jennifer, who also had a great personality. Peck believed that Jesus would be more receptive to a woman.

"Congratulations, Agent Williams. I want you to head up the team of a very important mission."

"Thank you, sir. Can you tell me anything about the mission?"

Peck's eyebrows lifted. "They haven't told you yet?" He paused briefly. "Of course, they wouldn't have. It's a Top-Secret assignment. They would not have told anyone, until the team leader was chosen." His eyes twinkled. "I believe you're about to have your socks blown off."

As the President explained the mission, Jennifer's eyes went wide in shock and surprise. "But how is that possible? I thought time travel was strictly science-fiction."

"And up until now, your belief would have been correct. Not anymore. Tomorrow, you will be flown to the secret facility where the time machine was built to meet the head scientist, Dr. Hathaway, and see the machine for yourself. You will also be shown a video clip and a souvenir from the past. Afterwards, your doubts will disappear."

Jennifer sat in her chair dumbfounded. "I don't know. And even if what you say is true, I can't believe that you want *me* to command a mission into the past. If this some kind of joke?"

"I assure you. It is not a joke. If you agree, you will be taking a team back into the past to observe and learn the truth about what happened. And not just any past," he told her with a grin. "You and your team will be going all the way back to the time of Jesus." "What? How, how is that possible? I'm not sure I even believe in His existence."

"Ah, well then, this will be the trip of a lifetime. It will prove to you that He does exist. And that what the Bible says about Him is true!" "That…that would be earth shattering," she said in soft voice.

"And just imagine what it would do for the people around the world, if they could actually meet Jesus and see for themselves that He is indeed the son of God."

"I…How is that possible? You said the machine only holds seven people." Are you planning multiple trips back in time? But even so, there are millions…maybe billions, who don't believe in Him."

"Which is why you are going to convince Jesus not to die on the cross and to come back with you to the present. Seeing is believing."

"Not necessarily," Jennifer said. "Look at how many refused to believe back then. The same thing would happen now."

"Ah, but people the world over know the story of Jesus. All He has to do is a few miracles, and they will believe."

Jennifer wasn't sure she liked the President's idea. "What if He doesn't want to come back?"

"Simple, we'll kidnap him."

His suggestion shocked her. "But doesn't He have to die on the cross in order for Christianity to be born…in order for people to believe?"

"So, we'll take Him back after a few months. But think about how much more He could do for the people of the world, if he didn't die on the cross?"

"What if we don't get Him back in time?"

"Time is different when you cross the barrier. On the first mission of Starway Seven, the Captain was gone only a few seconds. When he returned, he told us that he had spent two days in the past. So, why wouldn't the reverse be true? Jesus could spend a few months in the present, and still return to the past in time to do what He needs to do." *And if necessary, I have people who will kill him. The most important thing is that he doesn't die on the cross.*

*****

The next day, Jennifer visited the site and stepped inside the time machine. The Captain who went on the first mission, and Dr. Hathaway explained everything, how the controls worked, the gauging of the stars, opening the wormhole, etc. Jennifer listened to every detail. Then the scientist took her to his office and showed her the video and the musket. She began to believe in the impossible and became fascinated at the thought of meeting Jesus. The crosses and churches now meant even more to her, and she couldn't help wonder if it had been a sign. She agreed to make the voyage.

"Great!" Dr. Hathaway said eagerly. "Then I would suggest that you go home and pack your bags. Starting on Monday, you will be attending our training camp here for the next two weeks. Among other things, I want you to know how to pilot Starway Seven, in case something unforeseen happened to our pilot while you're in the past."

*****

Jennifer had four days before she was to report back to Dr. Hathaway for training camp. Her thoughts whirled in her mind. Time travel— going back nearly 2,000 years. Even though she'd had an extensive education in religion, she could never fully convince herself to believe in God. There had always a little bit of doubt in her mind. But that was about to change. She hadn't slept well last night and spent the day doing errands. After lunch, she felt a slight headache coming on, so she decided to lay down on her bed, hoping that she would be able to turn off her thoughts and actually sleep. As her eyes closed, she felt like something was reaching out to her. Something that wanted her to believe. But what?

In a matter of seconds, she fell asleep, looking peaceful and calm for a few hours. Then she went into REM sleep and suddenly, Jennifer began to twist and turn, at times violently. She did not wake up but continued to jerk, twist, and turn in small sudden movements, caught up in a very serious and intense dream:

Jennifer was attacked by strange men, coming at her from several positions. But everything and everyone was slightly blurry. She could not make out who her attackers were, but they were dressed in strange clothing, and she bravely fought back.

"What is this? Halloween? Who are you guys and what do you want?" she yelled. No one answered. Every time she defeated an assailant, a new one ran up from another direction to take his place.

"This is crazy." She could not understand why her attackers only had knives and small swords, nothing modern. She reached for her gun, but neither it nor her holster were there. "Where's my gun when I need it?"

She continued fighting, but there seemed to be no end in sight. "Is this part of my training for the mission? But how the heck did I get here?" Again, no one answered. Then a thought occurred to her. She was dreaming. She had to be. Everything was strange— strange land, strangelooking structures and a sky that was dark and blue with an abundance of dark clouds. Jennifer continued fighting, wondering that if she died in her dream, would she die for real? She did not know, but something told her that she couldn't give up. She had never had such an intense dream like this before. Somehow, it seemed more real than life itself. "This is like the worst obstacle course I have ever been on."

Jennifer was growing fatigued. She did not know how much longer she could continue fighting. After defeating yet another opponent, she looked up, and in the distance, she saw a white light that seemed to call to her. Puzzled, she stared harder, and in this light, she saw hope, salvation, and love. Then, she heard a voice.

"Jennifer, come to the light."

"I can't. They won't let me!" Her words nearly broke her heart. For the first time in her life, she wanted something so badly, it affected her entire being. "Jennifer, they are evil. You must defeat them and come to the light."

"I will try!"

"You will succeed because your heart and body are pure. Come to me now." Suddenly, Jennifer was filled with renew vigor and strength. She lashed out at her attackers and punched them as each one appeared, slowly driving them back.

"Jennifer, I need you to come to me. I need your strength," the heavenly voice called. "Come to me, and I will protect you."

Creating a break in the attack, she ran to the light. The closer she got to it, the more her emotions ran through her. Love, admiration, hope, trust, and most importantly, the feeling of being protected. As she closed in on the light, she could see a figure standing within it. It was a man. The image was still fuzzy, and she could not make out his features, but she knew without a doubt that he was amazingly beautiful. The most beautiful person she could ever imagine. An incredible feeling of power and good engulfed her, with not one feeling of evil, except for the attackers.

When Jennifer finally reached the image, she knelt before him and put her arms around his legs.

Then in a loud, commanding voice, the man looked out at her attackers and spoke. "Evil, be gone!"

Suddenly the attackers were quickly swept away. Now it was totally quiet and calm. Jennifer looked up at the faceless man. The light around him was so pure and full of love. And she felt herself swept up and embraced by it. Fear, anger, and all negative emotions disappeared as though they did not exist.

"Who are you?" she asked in a voice filled with awe.

"I am the way, the truth, and the light—the one you have been looking for all your life. I am the reason for you, and I am pleased. I need all the good that is in you."

"I don't understand."

"You don't have to. All you have to do is to find me. Come and find me. I am waiting."

Her soul ached with need. "Where? Where can I find you?"

"Deep within your heart and soul."

"I want to find you. Please help me."

"You do not need my help. The pureness and goodness inside you are all that you need. It is so great that even I need to borrow some of it."

"Are you God? Are you Jesus? I didn't know for sure. I have always hoped, but I never really knew for sure."

"Come find me. Come find me. Come find me."

His words seemed to echo and grow lighter as Jennifer emerged from her dream, peaceful and calm. Her eyes slowly opened, and she smiled. Looking at the clock, it read 3:00 P.M. Earlier that day while doing errands, she had gone into a store and for no reason at all, except for her sudden fascination of crosses, she bought a small wooden cross with an image of Jesus on it. Reaching over to her nightstand, she picked up the cross and with both hands laid it on her chest. She quickly fell back to sleep peacefully and calm.

CHAPTER

FIVE

Madeline Peck entered Holy Trinity Catholic Church to attend morning mass. She didn't attend morning mass that often during the week, as it created a lot of hassle for everyone, although not as bad as when the President came. Unfortunately, he had not been to church, since the loss of their son. After mass, the First Lady was escorted to the office of Father Murphy, having made an urgent appointment the previous day.

"Good morning, Mrs. Peck," Father Murphy said as he stood up from his desk chair and walked around to greet her with a handshake.

"Good morning, Father."

His expression was one of concern. He knew she was still grieving for the loss of her son, but from her anxious telephone conversation yesterday, he sensed that what was troubling her was something more serious and deeply disturbing to her. Escorting her to a chair in front of his desk, he asked, "Is there something I can get you? Coffee? Tea? Water?"

"Thank you, Father, but no. I'm good." She turned to her Secret Service agent and said, "Would you mind stepping outside and closing the door, Bryan? This conversation is private and deeply personal."

Bryan nodded. "Yes, ma'am. I'll be in the hallway if you need me."

"Thank you, Bryan. I appreciate your consideration."

The agent left the room, softly closing the door behind him.

Turning back to the priest, she said, "On second thought, I believe I would like some water."

Father Murphy left his office and went to a refrigerator in another room, returning with a bottle of water and handing it to her after closing the door behind him.

Madeline accepted it gratefully, opened it, and took a sip.

As the priest returned to the chair behind his mahogany desk. Madeline looked around, taking in the efficiently setup office that was neat and tidy and very much a man's room. A picture of the current pope, Pope John XXIV, hung on the wall behind his desk. And an ornate golden crucifix had been placed on the wall facing the window.

"What can I do for you, Mrs. Peck?"

"Before I begin, I need your word that you will tell no one but the appropriate person, who will pass this on to the Pope. It is top secret, so it's crucial that you do as I ask."

Father Murphy was disturbed by her words. "If it's top secret, maybe you shouldn't tell me. I'm not sure I want to be involved with state secrets."

"Normally, I wouldn't. But this has to do with something that could permanently affect the Church, Christianity, and the entire world. Please, Father. You need to hear this and act appropriately."

"Very well. If we make this a confession, I am bound by oath not to repeat it," he said.

"But can you add a codicil that it can be passed on to…I don't know, the bishop or a cardinal, who will then tell the Pope?"

"Considering what you say this involves, I will give you my solemn oath that no one else will hear of it, except those who can pass it onto the Holy Father. Priests are bound by their oaths, which is why we don't give them lightly. However, by what you're indicating, this seems like an appropriate time."

She sighed. "Thank you, Father." Madeline composed herself, organizing her thoughts on how to present the problem to him and praying that he would believe the fantastic tale she was about to unfold.

"As you know, my husband took the death of our son very hard. What you may not have realized is that he became so full of despair, so angry that the only thing he could think about was vengeance."

"Vengeance? Against who?"

"God."

Father Murphy leaned back in his chair. "He believes that God should have saved his son. He told me so himself. Your husband believed that since he is the President of the United States, God had to save his son as a reward for the work he has done. Okay, that part I understand and knew about. Many people who lose a loved one often become angry and blame God. But tell me. How does he plan to get vengeance against God?" The priest blanched. "He's not planning on attacking Rome or Israel. Is he?"

"No, he would never start a war, especially against innocent people. And although in some respects, one might think they were punishing the Lord by directly hurting his people, Jim doesn't. He's going straight to the source."

The priest shook his head in amazement. What she said did not make sense. "I don't understand…unless…. Dear Lord, he isn't planning on assassinating the Pope, is he?"

"I fear it's much worse than that. As you know, the Pope, although the head of the church, is only God's representative on Earth. He isn't God."

"Then I don't understand. He doesn't believe that he can go directly after the Father in Heaven. Does he?"

"He does. And he can."

Father Murphy had mixed emotions. Disbelief was followed by dismay. It would seem that the President had become somewhat deranged by the death of his son. Why? Was it guilt because of the argument they'd had that sent Ian storming out into the night? The First Lady had said that whatever he was planning was top secret. Still, he couldn't figure out how the President could have found a way to get back at God. "How is this possible?"

"You won't believe me at first. But let me assure you. It's not only possible, it has already been done." She took a deep breath before going on. "A group of scientists have created a time machine."

The priest smiled and shook his head in disbelief. "If this is a joke, Madeline…."

"Believe me when I say it is not. I only wish it was. The machine was built to go back in time. And they have already tested it. The pilot took it back to the Revolutionary War and came back with not only an authentic 1700s British musket, but a video of George Washington leading his troops in battle. It's been authenticated, and before he left, he had nothing more with him than a camera and an empty bag for souvenirs."

This wiped the smile off the priest's face. If what she said was true… But how?

"They are currently putting together a special team to go back to the time of Jesus. They are supposed to observe and photograph only, hoping that this evidence will convince more people that Jesus really exists, and that he died on the cross for us. But I overheard my husband speaking with someone about the mission. It's being commanded by Special Agent Jennifer Williams of the FBI. Of the six people going back, two are army commandos, supposed for the protection of the team. Agent Williams is unaware of the real reason for this mission. But the commandos have orders to bring Jesus back to the present with them. And failing that, to kill him before he ever makes it to the cross."

Father Murphy was so stunned, he was speechless. "If they do that, the President really will have his revenge against God." He crossed himself with shaking hands. "It would destroy Christianity in every sense. The world would be taken over by other religions, even paganism could return. It would destroy history as we know it. When they came back, everything would be different. We would all be different. I don't suppose he realizes that when they return, Jim Peck might not even be president any longer."

"No, I'm sure he hasn't thought of that. He thinks that everything will be the same, except for Christianity," the First Lady said.

"He hasn't taken into account that all the things that have happened through time because of Jesus and the growth and spread of Christianity. People like Joan of Arc and others would have no reason to lead the army in the Hundred Years' War and become a heroine of France as well as a saint. And…and speaking of saints, many would cease to be so, ending up as nothing more than ordinary men and women. There is no end to what would come undone, or how it would affect the world."

Madeline sighed. "I'm glad you understand the repercussions of what he is about to do, even better than I did."

"When is he planning on doing this?" "I believe it isn't scheduled to happen for another two or three weeks. There are still things to be done before they are ready to go."

"Then we still have some time. Not much, but some. I must speak to the bishop. From there, he will contact the Cardinal, and the Cardinal the Pope. I don't know what His Holiness will do, but he will try and find a way to stop it, somehow. I don't think that excommunicating your husband at this point would make any difference. If he is this angry at God and willing to sacrifice his very soul for vengeance, there is no saving him."

A tear slowly rolled down Madeline's cheek. "I feel terrible that I am the cause of my husband's downfall with God."

The priest stood up, walked around his desk, and sat in the chair next to her. He took her hand. "That's not true. This has nothing to do with you. You are trying your best to save, not destroy him. If successful, the President will be the only one to blame for this. I fear that his heart is so hardened that nothing will stop him. As for his soul, only God can make that determination. We must pray for him and that the Pope will be able to prevent this madness from happening somehow. If not, I fear we are all in for a very bad time."

"I will never stop praying for my husband, or that his plan will fail. I know that God does not like to interfere, but I'm hoping that this time, He will."

The two stood up and Madeline gave the priest a hug. "Good luck, Father, and God speed."

"The moment you leave, I will get on the phone and request an urgent meeting with Bishop Erinson. It will be unusual, since I am not the head pastor here, unless you feel I can include him." He looked at her questioningly.

"Only if it is absolutely necessary. I know that like anything else, you have a chain of command. The thing is, you have to convince them that this is real and must be stopped," Madeline pleaded.

"I will pray that the Lord will give me the strength and correct words to do so. I promise to do everything in my power."

"Can you somehow let me know if you are successful?"

Father Murphy thought a moment. "Make sure you come to the 11:00 mass. Afterward, I will either shake my head no, or say that it is done."

"Thank you, Father. The world is counting on you."

CHAPTER

SIX

Father Murphy was experiencing a conundrum. Normally, if he had a problem, he was supposed to go to the head pastor, Monsignor David Campbell for a possible solution. And it wasn't that he didn't trust his superior to handle it. But he believed that the fewer people, who knew about this 'top-secret' development, the better. At the same time, he did not want the Monsignor to think he was trying to go behind his back. After praying about it for the rest of the day, Father Murphy decided to present the problem to his superior, hoping he could convince him of his need without saying too much about the content.

He had the secretary schedule an appointment for him the next day. Normally, he would not do this so formally, but he figured that it might take a while to handle the problem and wanted to be sure they would not be interrupted.

At 2:30 P.M., Father Murphy entered the Monsignor's office and closed the door behind him.

Monsignor's right eyebrow raised. "Are you in need of confession, Father Murphy?"

"No, sir, but I have an urgent matter to discuss that cannot go beyond these doors," he said as he took a seat in front of the walnut desk. "I'm intrigued. Please continue."

"I was approached by a parishioner yesterday morning and told a story that, frankly, I did not want to believe, until she convinced me it was true."

"Can you tell me who the parishioner is? Or was this in confession?"

"It wasn't in confession, but I gave her my solemn oath that I would keep this secret and tell as few people as possible, while doing everything in my power to see that her concerns were delivered to… the Holy Father."

Monsignor Campbell was taken aback. "To the Holy Father? That's quite a promise. Of course, if this is as important as you say, you would have to inform Bishop McAllen, who would pass it on to Cardinal Valenza, who would tell His Holiness."

Father Murphy nodded. "Yes, those people would have to hear her story."

"I hate to say this, but before I can allow you to take this to the bishop, I need to know more, maybe not all of it, but definitely more."

"I kinda figured that. So, let me give you a few details, without telling you everything and see if that will suffice."

"Go ahead."

"I'm sorry, but I will have to ask you make a solemn oath that whatever I tell you goes no further than the bishop and so on." The Monsignor frowned.

"You know I trust you, Monsignor. But this is a matter of national security." Campbell studied the priest a moment before making up his mind. "In that case, I give my solemn oath. Since you said this came from a woman, I assume we're not talking about the President."

"That is correct, but you're close. It came from the First Lady, who through information she received from her husband and overhearing a private telephone conversation, became alarmed."

"Top secret, huh? I understand the need for secrecy then. Please continue."

"As you know, after the death of President Peck's son, Ian, he became an embittered man. Normally, you are the one to take care of the President and First Lady's spiritual needs. But you were out of town when it happened, so I stepped in."

"Yes, if I remember correctly, I was on vacation, visiting my sister and her family in Montana."

"Because of that," Father Murphy continued, "Mrs. Peck and I have developed a close spiritual bond. And I believe that's the reason she came to me, instead of you."

"And I'm grateful you were able to help her in her time of need," Monsignor said. "So why does Madeline feel the need to pass this onto the Holy Father?"

Father Murphy rubbed the stubble on his chin. "The President believes that God let him down—deserted him. And he wants revenge."

Campbell grew alarmed. "He's not planning on attacking the Pope or Vatican City. Is he?"

"No, sir. It's much worse than that. He is going after the Lord himself."

"I don't understand. How is that possible? There's no way to go after God."

"I'm afraid there is."

The Monsignor shook his head. "I know you want to keep from adding another person into this equation, but if you believe that what Jim Peck is about to do is viable, and with the full might of the United States Military behind him… I'm sorry, but I need to know everything."

"I was afraid that would be the case." Father Murphy went on to tell him about the time machine and the President's plan to go back to the time of Jesus to stop the crucifixion.

He did not want to believe that such a thing was possible, but David Campbell was a man of science, and he knew that if this project had the backing of the American government, and a successful test run had already been performed. He had to take it seriously.

"I'll make an appointment with the Bishop as soon as possible."

*****

The meeting with the bishop happened two days later, resulting in a flurry of action. Bishop McAllen immediately requested an urgent meeting with Cardinal Valenza and took the next flight available to Rome. Although he wasn't happy about the need for his meeting with the Cardinal, he was excited about the trip to Italy and Vatican City. He had not been there since he was ordained a bishop. He would give the message to the Cardinal, but he hoped he would be able to see the Pontiff, however briefly, as well and receive a blessing.

The flight was long, taking nine hours and 40 minutes, plus stopovers. And when he arrived in Vatican City, it was late. His appointment with the Cardinal was for 2:00 P.M. the next day. McAllen was to stay in the Vatican Guest House, Casa Sancta Marta—(St. Martha's House), a 1996 building designed as a hotel for clergy visiting the Vatican.

Since they were expecting him, a late supper was prepared, which he ate with several American and English-speaking bishops and priests, who were eager for news about the States, and he caught them up on everything he thought would interest them. That night, even with the heavy burden he carried, Bishop McAllen slept deeply, knowing that soon this burden would be taken from him and passed along to the one who might actually be able to take action.

The following day, having time to kill, the bishop did a little sightseeing before heading over to his afternoon appointment. He would stay in Rome for a week. He did not have to worry about renting a room or meals, unless he chose to eat out, so the cost for his trip was minimal.

When it was time for his meeting, Bishop McAllen was escorted into the Cardinal's office. They exchanged greetings before getting down to the reason for his visit. After carefully retelling the entire story, the Cardinal, who like everyone else did not want to believe that such a thing was possible, was stunned. He requested an urgent meeting with Pope John XXIV.

Later that afternoon, Cardinal Valenza entered the papal office to deliver the most critical and frightening news he had ever heard.

"Welcome, my son. I understand that you have news that requires my urgent attention from the Americas," the Pope said in greeting. "Please take a seat and unburden yourself."

Valenza did so, after performing the ritual greeting. "Thank you, Holy Father. I came to you with a heavy heart about a matter so hideous, it is hardly to be believed."

Pope John buzzed his personal secretary, one of the priests that worked at the Vatican.

Taking a few steps in the office, he waited for the pontiff's request.

"Please close the doors to this room and make sure that I am not interrupted in any way, neither by person nor by phone." "Yes, Holy Father." The priest did as he was told.

Pope John turned his attention back to the Cardinal. "The office is sound proofed. So, feel free to unburden yourself, Pablo."

Cardinal Valenza began to speak, starting with the revelation the First Lady made to Father Murphy and so on. When he finished speaking, the Pope had several questions.

"Is Bishop McAllen still in Rome?" he asked.

"Yes, Your Holiness. He is staying in one of the guest suites."

The Pope buzzed his secretary on the intercom and asked him to locate Bishop McAllen. Fortunately, he was currently in his room, and the bishop hurried over and was escorted into the pontiff's office.

"I have heard the story from Cardinal Valenza and would like your take on it," Pope John said. "After speaking to Monsignor Campbell, do you believe this to be real?"

"Yes, Holy Father. I do. I also spoke to Father Murphy and was quite convinced that not only does the President of the United States has the ability to send a team back in time, he is determined to get his revenge against our Lord."

The three of them spoke for another hour with the Pope asking many questions and looking at the situation from every aspect. When the bishop and cardinal left, Pope John sat and contemplated his options.

He would have to take the heads of the church into his confidence, so they could come up with a way to stop this horrendous act from happening. It would not be easy, and it wouldn't happen overnight. First, he needed additional information, like the exact date and time of launch. He also needed the names of the other crew members assigned to the mission.

He had never tried to thwart the actions of a world leader, although other popes in the past have not had a choice. But he was determined to stop this mission, no matter what it took. And he prayed to the Father in Heaven for guidance and strength to do the job.

CHAPTER

SEVEN

Pope John quickly set up a special meeting with security and the heads of the church, telling them that he had been informed by a secret contact in the White House about the Starway Seven mission to go back in time, and save Jesus Christ from dying on the cross. "This has to be stopped, no matter the cost. If this mission is successful," he said after explaining the situation to everyone in the meeting. "Everything about religion will change. There will be no Christianity, no Pope, and no Vatican."

The room filled with murmurs of distress.

"In all likelihood, all of us here might not even exist anymore. The results would be disastrous for the entire world. At this point, nothing else matters. Unlimited funds will be made available. This is the most important mission in the history of mankind. No matter what the price, or how many lives have to be sacrificed, Jesus must die on the cross, as he was meant to. It was the will of the Father, and ours as well. This is our number-one priority."

"What do you suggest we do?" one of the German Cardinals asked. "It's not like we can force President Peck to stop the mission."

"From what you have said, Holy Father, I don't think we could convince him of the error of his ways," one of the Italian Cardinals said.

"I understand that he a strong-willed man, and once he makes up his mind...."

"If I believed it were possible to change his mind, I would speak to him myself, even threaten to excommunicate him," the Pope said. "Unfortunately, he appears to be beyond that point and simply does not care. It would also inform him that I plan to do everything in my power to stop him."

"I hesitate to ask this, but if...Peck were no longer president, would it stop the mission?" a member of the security team asked.

The Pope thought the question over. "It's difficult to say. I believe the mission would still go forward, but without Peck, it may become what it was truly meant to be, simply observation."

"Surely, the President has already assigned people to make sure they do as he wants. And if he has convinced them that it is the right thing to do, it might not make any difference," the same German Cardinal said.

"We dare not risk it," a French Cardinal concluded.

"If I may, Your Holiness," an English Cardinal began. "I believe we should find all the religious members of the Starway Seven team and convince them to sabotage the mission at all costs—even if it means their lives."

"Agreed. Our number-one priority will be to stop the mission. However, I would be interested in finding out things unknown to the church. That would be very valuable information," Pope John said. "Find out if any of the crewmembers are women, aside from the commander, Jennifer Williams. They may be easier to turn to our side." "What about Jennifer Williams?" the English Cardinal asked.

"Leave her to me," the Pope replied. "I have something special in mind for her. I just learned that she purchased a ticket to visit Jerusalem." "One last question, Your Holiness."

The Pope turned to look at the security member, who had spoken up earlier. "How far should we go?"

"As far as it is deemed necessary. While I normally do not condone murder, if it is necessary in order to make sure that our Lord completes his mission, then so be it."

*****

It was a long flight, especially in coach. Jennifer was lucky enough to get a window seat where she could lay her head against the window and sleep. The woman next to her had a small baby. At first this worried her, but the good news was that in between bottle feedings, the baby slept the entire time. The other good news was that the woman didn't speak English, which meant she couldn't converse. And as far as Jennifer was concerned, that was a blessing. Acutely aware of her body, she had learned to control it, training herself to sleep whenever she needed to. She slept most of the flight. She only had four days in Jerusalem and wanted to make the most of them. Even if it meant no sleep, she didn't care. She knew she wanted to make this trip the second she found out about the mission and her new command. Actually, she had dreamed of visiting Jerusalem since high school, when she had decided her course of study. Now, it finally was coming true.

The first call she made the morning after she found out, was to her travel agent, a woman she knew and trusted for the last several years. For more reasons than one, she was very excited to see the land of Jesus. In her mind, she kept imagining who Jesus was, and who he would be. Was he short, tall, good looking, average looking? Actually, she didn't care. Whatever he was would be more than enough, just as long as he actually existed. And let's face it. That was the biggest reason for the trip back in time. She would finally discover the truth and settle her mind.

Did he exist or not?

She looked forward to when the plane landed. Being able to stretch her legs and walk around would be heaven. She didn't have much luggage other than a carry-on bag and a large purse. Unlike most women, she didn't use or need a ton of makeup. In fact, most of the time, she didn't use any makeup at all. She was blessed with a natural beauty that didn't need enhancements. Looking out the window, Jennifer saw that it was sunny with a few clouds. Even from high up in the airplane, it looked hot. The weather report stated that the average daytime temperature would be in the low 90s, which made her smile.

She might even get a tan.

The landing at Ben Gurion airport in Tel Aviv was smooth. The first thing she noticed after debarking the plane was the number of guards with guns all around the airport. A lot of security, and these guards didn't have just one gun but two and three. Jennifer had a vast knowledge of weapons and knew everything about them. She had trained her whole adult life in shooting and was considered one of the best and most accurate shooters in the FBI. Beauty, brawn, and brains, she had it all.

It was different, hearing the various languages being spoken around the airport. For the first time, she felt like an outsider. Fortunately, almost everyone knew English, whether they admitted it or not. Her agent got her a deal with the Abraham Hostel, which was located within easy walking distance to the old city. That was perfect as it was where she would spend most of her time. As part of the deal, the Abraham Hostel sent a shuttle to pick her up.

The ride to Jerusalem was fabulous, the old and the new all blended into one. She quickly realized that this was a very old land with a long history. Basically, the history of religion as we knew it. Upon arrival, she found the hostel to be simple, but very well maintained and super clean. Jennifer was happy about that. She had a private room all to herself with a bathroom and a shower and a small TV, which was more than enough. She wasn't going to spend much time in her room anyway. And the best part was that it was private. Jennifer quickly unpacked her carry-on and put everything in its place. Everything was organized, and she kept her camera secure in her purse. She even had a special attachment on her purse. If anyone tried to steal it, they would find it securely attached to her. Should that happen, she would punish that thief with pleasure.

As she grabbed a city map from the front desk, she knew the very first place she wanted to see. There were a few tourists in the lobby, but two stood out. Sitting together at a small table were two Catholic Priests. They both waved at Jennifer, and she politely waved back, thinking they were just being friendly. She was so excited that she forgot which way the doors opened and almost broke them. Luckily for her, there was no damage. She smiled at the people at the front desk.

"Sorry!" she apologized. "I'm just excited to be here."

The people at the front desk smiled back and waved her on. Jennifer was on her way to the Via Dolorosa or the Way of Suffering. This was the path that Jesus had taken with the cross to the hill where he was crucified. For some reason, the realization of what Jesus had gone through, enthralled her. To carry a heavy cross to the place where you would die was both cruel and ironic. It fascinated her as it seemed to captivate all visitors.

And the locals had a smart way of making the most of that fascination, which earned them a good living. They made wooden crosses in various sizes for the tourists, who would rent one to carry along the supposedly same path as Jesus had gone. There were tourists carrying crosses everywhere. It was extremely popular and amazing to see. Jennifer stopped to watch a woman pick out a cross. There were at least ten wooden crosses, all in various sizes, and one very large one that nobody wanted to touch. The woman kept picking up the smaller crosses to see how heavy they were. Ironically there was always one person in the crowd who liked to egg people on. That man pointed to the big cross.

"Hey, lady, this is the cross that Jesus would want you to have. You need to feel his suffering," he said, goading her on. "This is the one for you."

"That's a little too big and heavy for me. I think I want the smaller one," she replied.

"You think Jesus had a choice? Do not disgrace him," he continued goading her. "You need to suffer just like he did."

She continued checking out the smaller ones, trying not to show her irritation. "I don't want to suffer too much."

"Are you kidding? This is called the Way of Suffering, not the way of having an easy time. Jesus would want you to suffer a little bit."

Jennifer was so happy, and she laughed at the scene taking place before her. She decided to talk to the man. "Why don't you take that big cross? You're a big guy. You could handle it."

"I would, but that cross is reserved for this beautiful lady. I would not take that privilege from her."

"That may be far too heavy for her. Have some compassion."

"What, you think I am weak?" the woman asked. "Just a helpless woman, who can't do anything on her own, like my stupid husband is always telling me."

"I didn't mean to interfere," Jennifer apologized. "I was only trying to help. I just think that cross is too big for you." "You mean too big for Jesus," the man said.

"That's it! Give me that big one. Now!"

The woman pointed at the big cross. After being paid, the owner of the shop put the cross on the woman's shoulder, and she began her march. The cross was heavy, and it was obvious that she was definitely going to suffer. Even so, she was determined to make it all the way to the end.

"Good luck," Jennifer said.

"I'm proud of you."

"Thank you."

As the woman dragged the cross, the man said, "I think I'm going to follow this one. You know, to make sure she makes it. I might even help her, a little."

The woman gave him a sideways glance. "Bastard."

Jennifer watched for a while, taking pictures and having a grand old time. *Jesus took his last walk right here,* she thought, becoming serious. She couldn't get Jesus out of her head as she wondered what was in store for her. Taking out her map, she planned her next adventure. Of course, where else but the Western Wall. After figuring out which way to go, she began walking and truly enjoyed being a tourist. She got a big kick out of the Hasidic Jews with their funny hats and beards—at least, they seemed funny to her. It did not take long for her to realize one thing about them though. They did not want their picture taken. In fact, they hated it. As soon as they spotted Jennifer with a camera, they turned around or crossed the street to the other side. This frustrated her a bit.

She yelled out to one, who was crossing the street. "I have zoom."

Jennifer then noticed a group of young adults, marching in uniforms, and carrying a gun. She had to remind herself that all Jewish people were required to serve their country. And like the airport, there were guards with guns everywhere.

"Maybe I am really in Texas," she said to herself. She laughed at her remark and walked past a small, hometown restaurant with a large picture in the window of an older man, probably the owner with his six cats. Below the Hebrew writing were the words 'Cat Café.' Feeling a little hungry, she decided to try some Jewish food. Peeking inside, she noticed that the customers were mostly old people. *Must be good,* she thought. She entered the restaurant, and the owner, the same man in the picture with the cats, spoke to her. The six cats were all around the restaurant, and nobody seemed to care. Jennifer didn't say a word. She just smiled.

"Hello, beautiful American. Welcome."

"Is it that obvious that I am an American? I didn't say a word."

"Oh, I knew the second you walked in. In fact, we all did." The people in the restaurant all nodded in agreement.

"Absolutely. No mistake," one customer said with a smile.

"One hundred percent," a second added.

"So easy to tell," chimed in a third.

"What can I get you, beautiful lady?" the owner asked. One of the cats was now rubbing against Jennifer's legs. "Moses! Stop that," he told the cat. "She is our guest."

"I don't mind. I love cats, and Moses is such a big boy," Jennifer assured him. "Please, have a seat."

Jennifer sat down at an open table, and the owner brought her a glass of water. "I would like anything Jewish. Anything."

"You're in luck, then," the owner said. "That is all we serve here."

Jennifer's lunch consisted of falafel, served with a great-tasting hummus, and a glass of pomegranate juice. Everything was delicious, and when she finished eating, she thanked the owner and petted all of the cats. As she was leaving, the same two priests, whom she saw in the lobby earlier, came in. They waved at her again. Jennifer nodded her head in response and exited. The Western Wall was waiting.

It was already in the nineties, but she did not care. She was approaching probably one of the most religious sites in the world. She knew what it was the moment she saw it. The pictures she had seen did not do it justice. It was magnificent. The history here was amazing. And she was pleased to be so special that she was actually going to be able to compare the old with the new. She would be the first person to have such an experience. There were over a thousand people in the courtyard, and she watched all the Jews bobbing their heads in prayer in front of the wall. People were on their knees praying everywhere, not just in front of the wall. Never in her life has she seen so much faith. It overwhelmed her, and she remained rooted to the same spot for almost an hour, observing everything. She even forgot to take a picture, believing that no picture could do it justice.

She turned to look at the place, where the original Temple Mount used to be. She knew that was the spot, where Jesus had become angry and said the words, "My house is a house of prayer, but you have made it a den of thieves." After which he had cast out the money changers and dove sellers. Thinking about all this, she didn't fully understand her feelings, but the fact that she was actually going to be an observer to that event, filled her with excitement. She felt so amazed that she was going to witness everything as it happened, or so she hoped. The sun was setting as she walked back to her hostel. It was a beautiful, tranquil walk, and she realized how much she loved this place and the people, who were so friendly. Were they as friendly two thousand years ago? She would find out. Entering the hostel, the same two priests were in the lobby, and of course, they waved.

Being a trained FBI agent, she thought it was a coincidence that she kept running into them. But she did not believe in coincidences. What was going on? She wasn't sure and eventually shrugged it off. Feeling hungry, she headed into the hostel restaurant ordered some onion soup with bread, wondering if they would follow her inside. They did not. Afterwards, she went to her room and watched Israeli TV on a small

18-inch television. Nothing was in English, but it didn't matter. She was still entertained. After an hour, she yawned. *Time for bed.*

Turning off the TV, she changed into her night clothes, brushed her teeth, drank some water, and cratered into the small bed. She quickly fell asleep, even though she was eagerly waiting for tomorrow. Tomorrow was going to be a full day at the Church of the Holy Sepulcher.

CHAPTER

EIGHT

Jennifer was up and dressed the next morning, when she heard the sounds of the shofar horn, which had been used for centuries, being blown in the old city. Made from a ram's horn, the shofar was blown in the morning during services, after the Torah was read. The hostel, like almost all hotels, had a breakfast special included in the price of the room. Jennifer had a glass of orange juice, and a bowl of oatmeal with some strange-tasting milk.

Needing to exercise, and being the best time to do it with hardly any people around, she took off for an hour run, going up and down stairs and occasionally stopping to do a few squats and pushups. It felt wonderful and exhilarating. Just what the doctor ordered. Jennifer was used to working out almost every day. But since this was a small vacation, mostly for research, she had put that routine aside for a while. She returned to her room, took a quick shower, and headed out the door. As she left the lobby, the same two priests were there, waving. Her suspicions from the previous day deepened. Something was going on, and she had a feeling it had something to do with her upcoming trip back in time. She would need to keep alert, which for her, was automatic.

After a twenty-minute walk, she reached the Church of the Holy Sepulcher just as it opened, so she was one of the first ones to go inside.

It was old, and beautiful. She could feel the history in it, which she knew from her studies in college. The Romanesque, Baroque, and Byzantine architecture could all be seen. And somehow, she felt the presence of Jesus, knowing that he had been here two thousand years ago. After all, it was built on the ground where Jesus was crucified and buried. Jennifer tried to imagine this spot as open land, during that time, because the church was built in 335 A.D., long after the death of Jesus. This place attracted millions of people from around the world. Tourists and the loyal religious streamed in, walking through four beautiful arches with lintels that were decorated with Crusader crosses at the entrance to one of Christianity's most sacred sites.

Jennifer had never seen so many different types of clothing, or even knew they existed. Once again, like when she had been at the Wall, she felt an amazing amount of faith. People were praying everywhere. Nothing like this existed in the United States, as the country was too young to have this kind of history. That would take time, lots of time. Looking around and taking in every inch of this magnificent structure, she glanced at one corner and to her amazement, spotted the two priests again. If she still had any doubt, it was erased. She definitely knew that something was going on and that she was being followed, although completely in the open, as if they didn't care…as if they wanted her to know.

Determined, she decided not to allow it to spoil her visit here. She wanted to spend the entire day soaking up the energy. So, she turned away and focused on the beauty and meaning of this church, feeling the spirit of Jesus all around her. It was important and necessary for her to do this. She didn't know why, but she knew she had to. Finding a corner, she watched the people for hours, taking only a small lunch break, and then returning until closing. So many people from so many different places. It was a new kind of education. She returned to the hostel, had a large steak dinner, watched TV, and made herself fall asleep. Every day was one day closer to her amazing adventure. Every hour spent here, soaking in the ancient wonders, the beauty, and most importantly, the powerful faith that seemed to permeate everyone and everything, made her even more excited to take that trip back in time.

Tomorrow, she would take another run before moving on to the Mount of Olives.

*****

Once again, Jennifer was up before the sun. She was looking forward to another run even before the day had begun. She walked past the lobby and of course, there they were, sitting at the same table. Jennifer wondered if they even slept. She decided to talk to them soon, but not today. Maybe tomorrow, if they were there again. With her luck, probably not. So much the better. During her run, some locals actually joined Jennifer. She decided it was time to show a little more speed and quickly left them behind. They didn't even try to keep up with her. Jennifer was a very good runner, actually good at almost everything. Afterwards, her shower felt great, cooling her down, and making her feel fresh as she dressed for the day. After a quick breakfast, she was out the door and onto the line one tram, which got her to the base of the Mount of Olives in three minutes. She could have walked it just as easily and decided that maybe she would on the way back.

It was another clear sunny day, and her first stop was at the Garden of Gethsemane, where Jesus spent his last night and prayed, knowing that he was about to undergo a horrible ordeal that would end with his death. When she looked at the old olive trees, she knew that Jesus had been here and wondered how it had looked two thousand years ago. She took a deep breath and smiled, knowing she was going to find out. Overwhelming emotions ran through her, and she had to sit down on a nearby bench to chill out. She knew right then and there that she was going to see this place again. In her mind, she could almost see the image of Jesus, off alone a short way from his disciples, praying, "O my Father, if it be possible, let this cup pass from me: nevertheless, not as I will, but as thou wilt."

Being in this place, those words hit her harder than ever before. She could not imagine how hard that must have been for Jesus, how awful. Wanting to avoid the horror and pain of what he was about to endure, yet knowing that it was necessary in order to save His people, and submit to the will of his Father.

Jennifer walked up the hill to the actual Mount of Olives, looking at several churches built over the centuries. In a nutshell, you could describe the history of the Jews as tears and pain with a little bit of happiness thrown in for luck. She knew and felt that Jesus had walked this area many times on his way to Jerusalem. To her left, she saw the entire city of Jerusalem, and in the morning light, it was spectacular. To her right, she saw the Dead Sea. *What a strange name,* she thought.

She found a shady spot to sit and started thinking about Jesus, wondering what he might be doing at this exact time. She thought about the time ship and the time continuum. Could Jesus be alive right now, only in a different time? She kept thinking and then a vision came to her. Was it real or a dream? She did not know. But she could feel it. In her vision, she saw the ancient city of Jerusalem, and she focused on a small construction site. She didn't know what to expect. It was a sunny day, exactly as today, but everything felt old.

Jennifer saw a piece of wood being lifted into place by two wellshaped arms. It was the start of a roof being built on a mud-walled house, or at least it looked like a house. Slowly the piece of wood was lowered to reveal the gorgeous stunning face of Jesus. *What a work of art,* Jennifer thought. The face and hair were just perfect. Jesus was with two coworkers, who were friends and believers.

"Well, Jesus, we are almost done. Thank you very much for helping us. We needed a third person to finish the roof. I know you have other duties," one of his coworkers said.

"Yes, I do have to leave," Jesus replied. "I have a higher purpose and a calling that I must follow."

"We honor and love you very much," the other man said. "You are our savior."

"I am honored to have you not only as my friends but as followers of the one true God," Jesus replied.

All three hugged each other, but at that same moment, two Roman soldiers entered the scene, making fun and ridiculing them.

"All right, what kind of a party do we have here? I am sure your elders would not want to see this," one of the soldiers said.

Jesus, who knew this particular soldier, said, "We are just saying goodbye, Tiberius. Nothing more."

"I don't know, maybe we should report this. Just look at how pretty Jesus is. I can definitely see some awkward things happening. The elders might want to know about this," the other soldier jeered.

"What can I do to make peace?" Jesus asked Tiberius.

The soldiers were having fun, giving Jesus a hard time. They weren't about to stop, unless he made it worth their while.

"I don't know. Maybe you could sweeten the deal with something," Tiberius suggested.

"How about some fine wine for your thirsty tongues?" Jesus asked.

"That would work," the second soldier said. "But I don't see any fine wine here. It's been a while since I've had some. And because you brought it up, if I don't get some, I might get angry and turn you in."

"Fine wine coming up," Jesus said walking back to where the water containers were. He grabbed a large one. His two coworkers followed him.

"Jesus, we have no wine, only water," the first coworker said. "This will make the soldiers even angrier."

"Have faith," Jesus replied calmly. Walking back to the soldiers, he handed the container to Tiberius. "Drink."

Tiberius drank, and to his amazement, it was the best wine he had ever tasted. "That is good! Here try this," he said, handing the container to the other soldier, who drank it and also was amazed.

"Where did you get this? It's great!"

"It's a secret. Please take it with you and enjoy it as my gift."

"Thank you, we will," Tiberius said.

The soldiers walked away with the container.

"There was nothing but water in that container. I know. I filled it myself," his coworker said. He was flabbergasted.

"I know. But the soldiers think it's fine wine. It is still water, no matter what they believe. They will not get drunk." "This is a miracle," his friend declared.

"I bid you farewell," Jesus said. "I will see you in heaven."

The coworkers knelt, and Jesus gave them a blessing and walked away.

As Jesus and the vision began to fade, Jennifer woke up from her vision. "Wait! Stay!"

Realizing that she was talking to herself, she felt somewhat embarrassed. Jennifer stood up and walked back to the hostel. In her mind, she now knew what Jesus looked like and how to find him. At least, she thought she did. All she had was faith, and it was growing stronger all the time. As the sun began to set, she walked past several old structures, the shadows making them look even older.

Jennifer looked at her map and realized that one more site was close by that she just had to see—the complex of Mount Zion and the room of the Last Supper. There was no stopping her. Jennifer didn't even bother to inspect the ancient structure but went right to the room of the Last Supper. She felt an amazing love encased within this room and wondered if it was the same as it was two thousand years ago. What was the food like and what did Jesus eat? This just made her more excited to start her journey back in time. She realized now how lucky she was to be the one chosen, and she was going to make the best of it. She walked out turning around for one last look. Well, maybe not the last look.

I will see you again, she thought with conviction.

Arriving back at the hostel, she grabbed a salad and roast chicken for dinner. Afterward, she retired to her room to watch some foreign TV for a little while, before going to sleep. To her amazement, when she turned on the TV, one of her favorite old shows was on. It was actually in English with subtitles. That didn't matter. It was in English, and she was overjoyed. It was her favorite show called *Rome,* and she used to watch every episode.

*****

Morning came early this time, but Jennifer was up before five. Breakfast didn't open for another hour. And for some reason, she didn't feel like a run, which was rare for her. She actually wanted to see if the two priests were there in the lobby again. She kept thinking they wouldn't be. But sure enough, there they were, sitting at the same table. It was time.

Jennifer approached them. "Hello, boys, what's going on? What can I do for you?" "Actually, it's what we can do for you," the priest, who was average looking in every way. "You are the big winner. You have been chosen."

"Chosen? For what? And why are you following me?"

"You have been selected to visit the Pope," the second priest, who was taller and more muscular, said as if announcing the winner of a game show.

"Are you guys insane?" Jennifer asked. "This is Jerusalem. The Pope is in Rome." "Of course, he is. And we will fly you there for the day and fly you back, all in under eight hours. You will not miss your flight home."

"You guys are wasting your time. I'm not Catholic, and I'm not that interested."

"The Pope, however, is interested in meeting with you," the first priest said.

"You know, maybe some other time. But thank you," Jennifer politely replied, and began to walk away.

"Maybe we can sweeten the deal," the taller priest said. "I don't think so. It would take quite a lot."

"How about if we add a private viewing of the Sistine Chapel?" the average-looking priest asked.

"What?" Their offer surprised her and stopped her forward progress.

She turned around and walked back to them.

"Yes, a totally private viewing of the Sistine Chapel just for you," the tall priest said.

"Your tour guide will be the Pope." The average-looking priest gave her a look, daring her to refuse.

"That is an offer I think you can't refuse," his partner said. "Yeah, I've heard that before in a movie." She was about to move off but stopped. She had always wanted to see the Sistine Chapel. But she knew there would be thousands of tourists, and a lot of the time, it simply closed down. She didn't know if the offer was good or not, but what the hell. This indeed was an offer she could not refuse. "When do we leave?"

"Right now," the tall priest said. "The limo is waiting just outside."

"Limo?"

"Yes, right outside. We'll drive you to the airport and from there, we will fly on a private jet. We'll be there in just over two hours," the first priest said. "Can I get something to eat first?"

"No need," he replied. "Breakfast will be served onboard the jet. Let's go." "Don't I need anything for the airport? My passport, clearance, or something?"

"No, just you."

They exited the lobby and sure enough, a black limo was waiting for them. The average-sized priest opened the door, and Jennifer entered the vehicle. They arrived at the airport in twenty minutes. No security or checks, nothing, just drove right in. It was strangely eerie. Driving to a private hangar, Jennifer spotted a brand-new Gulfstream G700 private jet. The fastest private jet on the market. It could travel at Mach 0.99, or 759 miles an hour. Jennifer quickly entered the jet and took a seat. It began moving in a matter of seconds. No waiting in line, no guards, no nothing. The jet taxied to the runway and was in the air in just under two minutes. "That was fast. I wish all my travel was like this."

Jennifer now had time to look at the inside of the jet. It was like a five-star hotel and her seat was as comfortable as a cloud, maybe even better. She wanted to take this seat home with her. It was that good.

After a few minutes a man in a white uniform, pushing a cooking cart complete with a grill, stopped in front of her.

"What can I make you, young lady?" he asked.

Jennifer looked at the cart and pondered. "I don't know. What do you have on the menu?"

"Anything you want."

She thought for a moment before saying, "How about a chili omelet, hash browns with grilled onions, sausage and rye toast with butter and peach jam."

"Coming right up."

Jennifer turned in her seat to look at the two priests, who had followed her. "Can you tell me what's going on?"

"We cannot. We don't even know. Only the Pope knows. He will tell you, after your private tour of the Chapel."

After a truly wonderful breakfast, Jennifer sat in her seat with another glass of pomegranate juice. This juice was really good. The best she had ever had. The jet was amazingly fast. In just over two hours, they were preparing to land at Leonardo da Vince International Airport. It was the smoothest ride she had ever been on. Once again, there was no waiting in line. They landed and taxied to a nearby hanger, where another limo was waiting. Jennifer walked off the jet with her two new friends and entered the limo. No security, no guards, just walk right in. This was amazing. Jennifer finally knew how the super-rich lived and traveled. The limo drove off and exited the airport without stopping for anything. Then seemingly out of nowhere, four policemen on motorcycles drove up and surrounded the limo to form an official escort. Once again, Jennifer was impressed.

"We have some extra time before we reach the Chapel. How about a little road tour of Rome? What do you think, Jennifer?" the first priest asked.

Jennifer had never told them her name, but then she should not have been surprised, as they had been following her, since her arrival in Jerusalem. "Thank you. That would be nice. Especially since I've never been here, and I only have a few hours."

The first priest spoke to the driver in Italian. The driver nodded and took them past all the main sights, especially the Colosseum and the Arch of Constantine.

Jennifer gazed in wonderment at the Colosseum. "I can't believe they built this over two thousand years ago. It's so big!"

They drove past the Roman Forum, Trevi Fountain, Circus Maximus and of course the Pantheon.

"The pictures don't do them justice," she said, unable to take her eyes off the wonders she had read about but until now had never seen.

The final part of the drive was Saint Peter's Square, then finally, the Sistine Chapel. Jennifer was so excited. She saw thousands of people standing and waiting outside the Chapel. As they drove closer, however, she noticed that most of them looked pretty angry.

"Why is that crowd so angry? They are in one of the greatest cities in the world."

"They are waiting to enter the Sistine Chapel," the tall priest said.

"Unfortunately, it has been temporarily closed down. They will have to wait, some until tomorrow."

"Why is the Chapel closed?"

"For your private visit, of course," the first priest told her.

"For me?"

"Yes, for you," the tall priest said.

Jennifer stared at all the angry people—angry because of her.

"Whoops!"

CHAPTER

NINE

Jennifer continued watching the crowd as the limo pulled up in front of the building containing the Sistine Chapel. Examining the architecture, she was slightly disappointed, noting that it wasn't anything fancy—kind of like Catholic and Roman all mixed up in one. She knew, however, that the inside was what really counted, especially the two Michelangelo masterpieces. That's what everyone wanted to see when they came here. The greatest art in history was right there inside that building. Stepping outside the limo, she was immediately surrounded by four Vatican guards.

"Please follow me and stay close," one guard instructed her.

Observing the crowd, Jennifer had no intention of doing anything but what she was told, knowing that the crowd would grow even angrier if they learned that she was being allowed in, and they weren't. "Absolutely. Lead on."

Jennifer did not want anyone to know that she was the reason for their super-long lines and wait time—a wait for her. The guards took her to a door on the side of the Chapel, opened it, and escorted her inside. It opened onto a hallway leading to the Chapel. Naturally, it was full of religious artwork. But of course, this was the Church of the World. To Jennifer, this art was no big deal. All she really cared about were the two major paintings by Michelangelo. That was what she wanted to view.

The guards stopped at a large door, which was the entrance to the Sistine Chapel, and opened it.

"Please, you may enter. And I hope you enjoy and appreciate this special treatment," the guard who had spoken to her earlier said. "Not many ever get a private viewing."

"Yes, thank you. I feel very fortunate."

Jennifer entered the room, and the guards closed the door behind her, leaving her all alone. Looking up at the ceiling of the Sistine Chapel, what she saw nearly put her in a state of shock. They were the most amazing pieces of artwork she had ever seen. She moved closer to examine the paintings on the wall of Moses and Jesus, then strained her neck as she looked up at the ceiling. Everything was beautiful and amazing all in one. There was art everywhere, no wasted space. She took out her camera. Even the tapestries were stunning. All were very religious. The pictures in the books just could not do it justice. No way. The real thing was the way to go. She looked around some more, finally seeing all the signs that prohibited photography and put her camera back in her bag.

"Aw, shoot."

It was very quiet, and Jennifer could only hear her own footsteps as she walked to the center of the Chapel. Then she heard a voice. "It is okay," Pope John XXIV said. "You will be allowed to take all the pictures you want."

"Really?" Jennifer asked, not knowing who was speaking to her yet." "Yes, really," Pope John assured her, stepping out to reveal himself.

Jennifer was taken by surprise. She had already met the President of the United States. Could this be any different? Stepping in front of Pope John, she went down on one knee. "Your Holiness, I am honored to meet you. What a wonderful place you have here. So much beauty."

"Yes, there is much here, but most people only care about the Michelangelo's. Please get up, young lady."

Jennifer stood up in front of the Pope. "Well, look at these two masterpieces. Can you blame them?"

"Yes, Michelangelo painted the ceiling from 1508 to 1512. It is considered the greatest piece of art in all of human history. It changed the course of Western Art and is the major artistic accomplishment of human civilization."

"Probably even more than the Mona Lisa."

"Are you kidding? Leonardo Da Vinci was nothing more than a common street artist comparted to Michelangelo—a total amateur. Not even close. The Mona Lisa is a very distant contender. Just look at this. There is nothing to compare it to."

"Everything is so beautiful here. Look at the frescos of Moses and especially of Jesus." She paused in her admiration to ask a question. "Your Holiness, may I ask you something? I'm just curious."

"Of course, anything for you."

"Do you think Jesus looked like the Jesus depicted in these paintings?" "I understand that people often ask that question," the Pope said. "But why do you want to know?"

"Just wondering."

"Well, young lady, you wonder with great interest. In answer to your question, I don't think anyone really knew what Jesus looked like. The only way to find out would to be able to go back in time, and of course, we can't do that. It is impossible. Or is it?"

Jennifer hid the shock his question caused. "No one has done it yet." She quickly changed the subject. "Can I take a picture from the floor? I know exactly where I want to take it."

"By all means, enjoy."

Jennifer laid down in the center of the Chapel underneath the *Creation of Adam* painting with God touching the finger of Adam. "It is so gorgeous, more than I thought it would be. There are no words to do it justice. How did the Pope back then get Michelangelo to do this? It took four years."

"We have our ways."

"But how?" Jennifer insisted.

"We got you here. Didn't we?"

"This is just for a few hours." She pointed at ceiling.

"That took four years."

"We simply told him that if he wanted to paint past the gates of heaven, he had to paint in front of them first. He couldn't turn it down. Being admitted to heaven was pretty important in those days. In his day, everybody wanted heaven. Now, not so much. Then he came back later in his life to do The last Judgement, the one right in front of you. That was done from 1536 to 1541. It took longer than the ceiling. Though to be fair, he had some help with the ceiling."

Jennifer took a picture of The Last Judgement. "The history of modern man and art all in one place, and you live here. How lucky you are."

The Pope laughed at that remark. "Yes, I am lucky. In fact, I was chosen to be the Pope right here in this very chapel. All the Popes since 1492 have been chosen from here. And someday, another one will be chosen here to replace me when I am gone."

"I hope not too soon."

"Only God knows that. God knows a lot of things we don't know or should not know. Some things need to be protected."

There it was again, another reference to her upcoming trip. Jennifer quickly changed the topic and stepped next to Pope John with her camera. "Do you mind? I mean, I have to prove to my friends that I was here."

"You want a selfie with the Pope?" he asked amazed.

"Please, if you don't mind."

"All right, but just keep it between you and me."

Jennifer took several selfies with the Pope. "Thank you very much, Your Holiness. Thank you."

"Good. Now, I think it's time we headed to my office."

"Can I have five more minutes here alone? Just me. I won't touch anything."

After a moment of thought, Pope John nodded. "Follow me through this door in five minutes. I will be waiting for you in my office. Remember, there are a lot of people who also want to see this place. None are being treated as special as you. I can tell that you are very special. I think God brought you here. Do you believe in divine intervention? Do you believe in fate?"

"Not yet, but I am leaning in that direction. A lot of things are happening to me in a very short period of time. Things I don't quite understand yet."

"I believe there is more to come. A lot more. Do you believe that?" the Pope asked.

"Yes, but no one knows the future. They only know the past. Or at least the past that was told to us whether it is true or not. Yes, it would be nice to be able to find out the actual truth, no matter the consequences."

"That is the ultimate question to be decided later. Please enjoy your five minutes. I will be waiting."

"Thank you, I will."

The Pope left, closing the door behind him and leaving Jennifer all alone in the chapel. She wanted to take it all in, and it was a lot. It came at her from all angles. Things were happening so fast. Never in her wildest dreams had she ever thought she would be here, especially for a private tour. What was in store for her? Did God have a plan just for her? Three months ago, she never would have dreamt that such a thing was possible. Now everything was happening. The Pope wanted to see her. Jennifer knew why. What else could it be? It was obvious by his inferences that he had found out about the time machine. How much did he know? And how did he find out? That was the mystery, one she was determined to discover if possible.

Jennifer knew back in Jerusalem that something was wrong. At first, she didn't believe it but when they said the Pope wanted to speak with her. She had to find out why. She decided to play dumb and act like a tourist. For the sake of her mission, she needed to know everything, especially what the Pope was planning. She knew she had to be careful about what she said. The Pope was very smart. She had to be ready. That was the real reason why she needed five minutes alone, to think of all the possible answers she might need.

The Pope wanted to interrogate her, and she had to be prepared for anything, even a possible escape plan if things got out of hand. He seemed like a very nice man, but he was fighting for his church and two billion Christian believers, with Catholics making up the largest group at 1.3 billion. She felt nervous and almost trapped but decided to play along. She would tell him only what he needed to hear. As far as she knew, they were not going back in time to change anything, just to observe. Nothing would change.

Looking at the paintings of Jesus, she said, "I hope he looks like that." Taking one long last look at the chapel, Jennifer exited through the door used by the Pope. Then stopped and turned around one more time. "Bye."

Outside the door, the same four Vatican guards were waiting for her. They surrounded her once again.

"Please follow us."

Jennifer was now on high alert. Although they seemed like simple guards, they were part of one of the oldest and most skilled armies in the world. Their training, however, did not include espionage, and they could never imagine what she was capable of. She figured the Pope would not do anything drastic, but what worried her was that no one knew she was here. No passports, guards, just the church. What did he want? And if he wasn't pleased with what she said, would she suddenly disappear?

The guards stopped at an office door and quietly opened it.

"You may enter. A seat is waiting for you in front of His Holiness. Good day."

Jennifer entered the office, and the door was closed behind her. Pope John sat behind a huge exquisitely carved wooden desk that had to be ten feet across. On the wall, crosses and crucifixes were hung everywhere, especially crucifixes with the image of Jesus on them. This place was meant to intimidate people, although it wouldn't work on her. She was now prepared for anything, and she needed to take control. She wasn't a highly trained agent of the FBI for nothing.

"Please, have a seat, a seat of honor," the Pope said.

"Thank you." Jennifer sat in the chair and like the one in the jet that brought her here, it was very comfortable. She wanted to take this one home, too.

"Can I get you something to drink? Anything? Coffee or tea perhaps?"

"How about some hot Earl Grey tea? That sounds pretty good right about now."

The Pope pushed a button and ordered the tea. "Let us…."

"You know, let's wait until the tea arrives."

Pope John's right eyebrow raised slightly. He wasn't used to someone overriding him. Still, he decided to play along. "As you wish."

For the next several minutes, the two played a pleasant waiting game. No words were spoken, but they kept looking at each other. Occasionally, the Pope smiled, and Jennifer politely nodded back. Jennifer studied the Pope, and he studied her—old on one side, young on the other. She looked all around the office, knowing that the Pope knew more than he should. This mission was top secret.

How did he find out? She also realized that he would never tell her. She would have to figure that out on her own. But just how much did he know? That was the next step. Finally, an assistant brought in the tea on an ornate wooden tray, placing it in front of Jennifer along with sugar, milk, cream, honey, and spoons.

"Can I put anything in it to your liking?" the priest asked.

"No, thank you. I like it just the way it is." She took a small sip.

"This is good. One thing about this place is that the food is great. I mean five stars or better. Especially on the jet."

"Now may we get started?" the Pope asked as his assistant left the room.

"Yes, of course. I like to start by finding out what the other side knows first. You wanted me, and I allowed you to bring me here. I also need some information. It's my job, you know."

"Your president was indeed wise in choosing you. You have it all. You even had me fooled for a while," Pope John said.

"Sometime you have to play the game to find out the rules. Tell me what you know?"

The Pope folded his hands on the desk in front of him. "Your name is Jennifer Mary Williams, thirty years old, and an FBI agent with a degree in Comparative Religion. You are one of the best if not the best. You do, however, have one flaw."

"And what is that?" Jennifer asked intrigued.

"No man has ever been good enough for you." She shrugged.

"The search continues."

"And you are the Commander of Starway Seven with the purpose of going back to the time of Jesus."

Jennifer was unpleasantly surprised. *How did he know, and who spilled the beans?* "If what you say is true, why does that concern you? What better way to prove that Jesus actually existed?"

"Because your president wants revenge against God. And to get it, he wants to change the course of religious history by not having Jesus die on the cross as he did and has to."

"If such a thing were possible, I mean time travel, I assure you. It would only be to observe, not change the course of history."

"If Jesus does not die on the cross, none of this will be here. It would be a whole different world with a whole different way of thinking. I definitely would not be here if that happened, nor billions of Christians. It would be the most dangerous threat to the history of what we know."

"What if there was no Jesus and none of the events happened? No cross, just nothing but a made-up story by a group of men who wanted to form a new religion based on the stories in the Torah," Jennifer asked.

"I know for certain that it did happen, and you are the one who will find out the ultimate truth. You are the chosen one. The one who is going to meet Jesus. What an honor and yet, a heavy burden to bear."

"Maybe if Jesus had lived, he could have accomplished even more good deeds. Think about that," Jennifer said.

"God knew what He was doing. It could only happen this way. You can't question God."

"Then there is nothing to worry about. Everything will go according to God."

"Sometimes the devil likes to interfere. He does his best work through subterfuge, and he has to be stopped."

"The mission is to observe. The President did not tell me to interfere, and even if he did, I wouldn't. We don't even know if we can go that far back in time. We may all disappear." She hated lying to the Pope, but if she told him of Peck's plan to kidnap Jesus for a while, things would go very wrong. Even though she was not sure she wanted to go along with the plan.

"Do you want to meet Jesus?"

"With all my heart and soul. And of course, I will always do the right thing."

"I am pleased that you are neutral. Now let me tell you this."

"Tell me what?" Jennifer asked.

"No one knows you are here. I had all the cameras turned off both outside and in before you arrived. There is no history of you being here. No passport, nothing."

"What is the significance of that?" she asked, wondering if her earlier thoughts might actually happen.

"If you really want to meet Jesus, you will keep your visit here a secret. If your government finds out that you were here, they would immediately replace you. Then you would never see Jesus. Do you understand?"

"Right or wrong, you are still right. I can see that now. Things would change and not for the better. Yes, they would quickly replace me, thinking I was compromised."

"For you especially, but you are the chosen one. How do you choose?" Jennifer took out her camera.

"What are you doing?" Pope John asked, wondering if this talk had all been in vain.

"Erasing all the pictures I took here. This one of you and me is so darling. Goodbye, pictures." She began deleting the pictures. "You will have to remain nothing but sweet memories."

"It was a pleasure meeting you. My guards will take you back to the limo where your two new friends are waiting. You will return back to Jerusalem the same way you came. I know your flight home is early tomorrow morning. Please have a pleasant flight, and God be with you." "Thank you, Your Holiness."

As Jennifer left the office, the Pope kept looking at the door she used to leave. "We need to be sure."

It didn't take long until Jennifer was in the jet, flying back to Jerusalem. The same man in a white uniform pushed his cooking cart with a grill towards her. "How can I please you again, young lady? Tell me what you want."

"It's going to be tough this time. I'm hungry." "Tell me," he said with a smile.

"I want lobster and a filet mignon with lyonnaise potatoes, creamed spinach, Caesar salad, and strawberries with whipped cream for dessert. And some cranberry sauce."

"Coming right up. How to you want your steak cooked?"

"Medium, thank you."

After a wonderful meal, pleasantly full, Jennifer relaxed in her seat and looked out the window at the sky. She could not help wondering how she had gotten picked. Or was she truly chosen? One thing for sure, she was going to make the best of it. The landing was once again very smooth. Later, the limo dropped her off at her hostel, and the two priests waved goodbye to her.

"Thank you. We had a wonderful time being with you and greatly enjoyed our visit here. God bless," the average-looking priest said.

Jennifer waved back at them and went to her room. The shuttle was going to pick her up at five A.M. the next morning. So, except for the flight home, her journey here was over. She changed into her night clothes, brushed her teeth, and got into the bed. There was so much going on in her mind, but she knew she needed sleep. With the hope of getting sleepy, she decided to watch TV for a minute or two. Turning it on, she was surprised to see that the movie *The Passion of the Christ* was just starting. Unfortunately, the movie was too long to get involved in. "No, I better not this time, I will have plenty of time for Jesus later."

Picking up the remote, she turned off the TV, pulled up the cover, and closed her eyes. "It's time to sleep," she told herself. Jennifer lay quiet and peaceful, not moving for a few moments. Then her hand grabbed the remote, and she turned the TV back on. *The Passion of the Christ* had gotten her attention. She decided to watch it to the end.

"I'll sleep on the airplane."

CHAPTER

TEN

Six people would make the journey back in time aboard *Starway Seven*. This included three men and three women: the pilot who had journeyed back to the time of the Revolutionary War, two security officers, one male and one female, two scientists/historians, one male and one female, and their commander, Agent Jennifer Williams. They were only supposed to observe, not interfere. But the powers that be, both secular and religious had other ideas. President Peck needed people who would stop Jesus from dying on the cross, even if it meant kidnapping him and bringing him back to the present. But he had decided that he would rather have Jesus killed before he ever made it to the cross. Whichever way it happened; it would have to take place before the Last Supper.

On the other hand, Pope John XXIV needed people on that team, who would make sure that Jesus was allowed to follow the script—so to speak, ending with His dying on the cross. He was determined that history remain the same, that God's plan be followed to the letter, and with Jesus' dying and rising from the dead, the creation of the one true church would reach fruition. To his way of thinking, the destruction of the Christian way of life, even before it had a chance to take root, would mean the loss of billions of souls, and the rise of paganism on a scale that made him shudder with dread. It could NOT be allowed to happen. Fortunately, he had over 414,000 priests, 456 bishops, and 227 cardinals to help him, if he needed them, although that extreme seemed unlikely.

The President, however, had no one but himself to put his devious plan into motion. He knew that he would have to recruit one or two people on the team who were as devious and uncaring as he had become. To that end, he inserted himself into the program to oversee each person to be chosen. After going over the files on each candidate, he came to a decision. He would have to be careful, so as not to attract suspicion by the scientists and those members of the team whom he realized he could not turn.

Peck spoke with Jennifer on several occasions, and after her return from her visit to Jerusalem, he decided to visit the facility where the time capsule was located, where he knew she was spending most of her time before the journey. Upon his arrival, he asked for her and was taken to a room where the pilots trained on simulation modules. He found her hard at work.

"How is she doing?" Peck asked her instructor.

"I believe she was born to do this. If she wasn't with the FBI and set in her career, I would recruit her in a heartbeat as a permanent team member."

"That's great," the President said, but his praise did not reach his eyes. "Nice to know that if the pilot became incapacitated for some reason, she would be able to bring everyone back to the present."

"Yes, sir, she could do that quite easily."

"How much longer will she be in this session? I would like to speak to her about the mission," Peck asked.

The instructor looked at his watch. "She should be finishing up just about now."

As he finished speaking, the simulator shut down, and Jennifer opened the door to exit it.

"If you don't mind, instructor, we need a few minutes alone," the President said. "Not a problem, sir. She is finished up here for the day, and I was just on my way out to grab some lunch." The instructor, an

Air Force pilot, saluted and left the room. Jennifer stepped through the door and climbed down a short metal staircase to the floor. When she realized that the President of the United States was waiting for her, she hurried over to him, wondering why he was here and what he wanted.

"Good morning, Jennifer. Or should I say afternoon," Peck said, glancing at the expensive watch on his wrist.

"Good afternoon, Mr. President. To what do I owe this surprise visit?"

"Before I get into that, how about some lunch?"

"The food in the cafeteria here is pretty good," she replied.

"I'm sure it is, but I have a much nicer place in mind."

They walked out of the facility to the parking lot, where the Presidential limousine was waiting. Seeing the President and two Secret Servicemen exit the building, a third left his post by the limo and opened up the rear passenger door. Peck indicated the car to Jennifer, but she had other ideas.

"If you don't mind, sir. I would rather follow along in my own car. I have a few errands I need to run before my trip, and time is of the essence," she said smiling. While what she said was true, she suddenly realized that she did not want to remain in his presence any longer than necessary. Her trip to Rome had opened her eyes about Peck and what he had in mind, and she wanted no part of it. If the Pope was correct about the president wanting revenge against God, she would have to remain on alert, especially when it came to those making the trip with her. She had no doubt that he was trying to turn the others to his way of thinking. She only hoped he would not succeed. For now, she would keep her guard up whenever she was around him. At least until she left the present for the past.

"Very well," Peck said. He knew Jennifer well enough by now to realize that once she made her mind up about something, there was no changing it. Still, he had to try one last time to bring her to his side. If nothing else, he wanted her impression of the Holy City, and whether or not seeing it had made her more of a believer. "You don't know where we're going."

"It's pretty hard to lose a limousine," Jennifer responded dryly.

"Of course, you could tell me the name of the restaurant."

"I could." Without saying another word, Peck turned and entered the limo.

If he thought that would upset her, it didn't. Jennifer shrugged and headed for her car. Naturally, she had no problem following the limo or the other two cars in the Presidential procession. When they arrived at a small family restaurant, she was surprised. It featured homecooked meals. Somehow, she had not figured him liking anything less than fancy, expensive restaurants with even more expensive food. Naturally, the place had been cleared out even before Air Force One had touched down at the airport. Fortunately for the owners, they were being well compensated, and having the President of the United States eat there was one that would bring in lots of business.

Neither the President nor Jennifer said a word until they were seated at a booth where the Secret Service could cover all the exits and surround the President from a discreet distance. The owner, himself, approached their table and after the President thanked him for the use of his establishment, took their orders.

"Are you surprised by my choice of restaurants?" Peck asked Jennifer, after the owner left with their orders.

Instead of answering his question, Jennifer replied with her own question. "How did you learn about this place?" "I have my ways," he replied cannily.

"So, tell me. How was your trip to Jerusalem?"

"Interesting, informative. I enjoyed visiting all the sacred places, and the food was wonderful. There is a feeling about the city that you just cannot ignore."

"Like what?" Peck asked.

"I guess I would have to call it faith. I've never seen so many people praying—Christians, Jews, and Muslims alike. Whatever their religion, you could tell they were true believers."

"And what about you? Have you become a true believer?" The question was asked simply, but Jennifer picked up on the undertone.

She knew she would have to carefully measure her words. Fortunately, two waiters came to the table, bringing their drinks, salads, and rolls.

When they left, she shrugged nonchalantly. "It would be easy to do there, but I still haven't made up my mind."

"Seeing is believing?"

"Maybe."

The President continued to question her throughout the meal, but when they parted ways, he was still in the dark about her thinking and decided not to push her any further. It was time to approach someone else.

*****

The following day, after reading a thick folder about Captain Wagner, the President met with the pilot of the mission in the suite of his hotel room. Naturally, the rooms had been swept for bugs, and the Secret Service were stationed all around to make sure that no one could overhear the meeting taking place inside. Peck had a pretty good idea of what kind of man the Captain was, but he wanted a personal interview to seal the deal.

"Come in, Captain Wagner, and take a seat. Johann, isn't it?"

"Yes, sir. Thank you, sir."

The Captain sat down on the loveseat the President had indicated.

The President took the chair stationed across from it.

"With a name like Johann Wagner, I take it you are of German descent."

"Yes, sir. Second generation born here. My grandparents came over back in the fifties."

"I see. And what made them decide to change countries?"

"WWII. After the war, things were pretty bad in Germany, especially East Germany once the commies took over and built the Berlin Wall. My great-grandfather was killed in the war, and my great grandmother was left with three children to raise and very little to keep them going. After one of the boys died of starvation, she took the other two and escaped from East Germany with machine guns firing at them, and came to America."

"Then your great-grandfather was a member of the Nazi party?" Peck's question was asked slyly but without any sense of accusation.

It did, however, put the Captain on alert. "I'm not sure. Not everyone fighting for Hitler were Nazis. And since I never met him or my great-grandmother, I can't be sure." "Understandable. But surely your grandparents knew."

"Forgive me, sir, but I'm not sure where you are going with this. I can assure you that I am a red-blooded American, who has served his country with distinction and honor."

"And I'm not saying otherwise, Captain." The President took a sip from his coffee mug. "I'm sorry. Would you like some coffee or tea perhaps?"

"No, thank you, sir. I'm good."

"Are you a religious man, Captain?"

"Because of my affiliation with this project? Not necessarily. My family has never been into church or anything religious. As far as I'm concerned. I believe in God, but everything else is a waste of time, especially organized religion. As for my being with this project, I'm here because I am the most qualified person to pilot Starway Seven. They didn't ask me what missions I would or would not go on. Only if I was willing to take the risk of venturing into the past. And I am."

"Excellent. Speaking of your current assignment, how do feel about it?"

"I am excited, naturally. Going back to the Revolutionary War was a thrill beyond compare."

"Was it dangerous, other than the actual trip? Were you at risk of being killed?" Wagner thought it was an odd question, but he figured an understandable one.

"Yes, sir. I was, especially with a war going on."

"And this trip? Will the danger be less, since you won't be visiting during wartime?"

"Not necessarily. We have no idea what we will be walking into there. Between the Roman soldiers, and the Jews stirring up a ruckus, I suppose anything could happen."

Peck smiled to himself. There it was. The trigger he was looking for. Captain Wagner might pretend not to know about his great- grandfather being a member of the Nazi party, but he did. And with the information he had gleaned from Wagner's folder, the man's feelings about religion, and his prejudice against Jewish people, the President knew he had a winner.

"Will you still feel the same when you meet Jesus? Or will you become a believer?"

"Does it matter?"

"It does, but your answer will not change anything. You will still be the pilot on this mission," the President assured him.

"In that case, no. So, what if he's there? That doesn't prove anything, other than the fact that there was a man named Jesus, who went through everything they say he did. However, it does not prove that he was the son of God."

"What about the miracles?"

"What about them? There's no proof they actually happened. Everything he did has a logical explanation. People were pretty stupid back then. It could all have been a setup just to make people believe he was who he said he was."

President now smiled openly. "In that case, I would like to discuss with you a secret mission of my own."

*****

While the President was busy doing his best to make sure the mission went his way, the church was also busy. The church had many priests who were accomplished scientists, engineers, astrophysicists, computer technologists, and so on working for them. The Vatican also owned its own Advanced Technology Telescope (VATT), located on Mount Graham in southeastern Arizona. Having the right personnel, it was a simple matter to hack into the American government's computer to discover who had been chosen to make the journey to the past.

The Pope would have loved to turn all six to his way of thinking, but he was smart enough to know that would be impossible. Accessing the same information the President had, he decided that the pilot and the male security agent could not be turned to his way of thinking. Jennifer, he had already spoken to, but he was still up in the air because of her uncertainty. The male scientist/ historian, Dr. Leo Garnier was another wash. Although technically a good man, he was too wrapped up in science to have any real faith. Maybe that would change once he actually met the Savior. The female security guard, Winifred Scott, was not a certainty either way.

Then the Pope discovered the female scientist/historian, Elizabeth Johansen, who was deeply religious. "Yes," Pope John said with a smile. "I believe we can turn her very quickly."

The task proved easier than even the Pope had thought it would be. On the Saturday morning before the mission was scheduled to leave, Elizabeth made an appointment with her priest to receive the sacrament of penance. Upon arrival, she was surprised and a little disturbed to find not only her priest, but the Bishop McAllen of the diocese waiting for her in the head pastor's office.

"Oh, I'm sorry," Elizabeth said as she stepped into the office. "I did not mean to interrupt."

"Elizabeth," her Priest called. "Please come in. The Bishop and I have been waiting for you to arrive."

"I don't understand. Why would the bishop be here for my confession?" McAllen stepped forward to greet her, a warm smile on his face. "I know about your mission to the past, and I wanted to give you a special blessing."

"You know Your Excellency?" she asked, bewildered.

"But how? That mission is top secret!"

"We have our ways," he told her, indicating that she should come in and have a seat in a chair in front of the desk. "Do you think that Pope John would not find out that you could actually travel back to the time of Our Lord?"

"Well, I...."

"Of course, he would. And he has sent me to give you his blessing and a warning," Bishop McAllen said.

Elizabeth blushed with pleasure that she would have the Pope's blessing. Then the second part of what the bishop said hit her. "What kind of warning?"

"There are things happening here of which you are not aware," the bishop began. "President Peck has been very angry with God, and he has decided to take revenge by not allowing Jesus to die on the cross."

"He what?" Elizabeth could not have been more shocked if the bishop had told her that the President was the devil himself. "I…I don't understand. Why would he do that? Doesn't he realize what it would do to Christianity, to the Church, to…everyone?"

"I'm glad you understand the depth of this problem," Bishop McAllen said, relief in his voice. "His Holiness believes that one or two members of your team have been convinced to do the President's bidding."

"That's terrible. It's unthinkable. How could they?" She stopped speaking and took a moment to get her thoughts in order. "Do you know who they are? They must be stopped. What do I have to do?"

"Unfortunately, we don't know for certain, but we suspect it could be the pilot and the male security guard. You must do everything in your power to make sure that Jesus dies on the cross." His words hit her like a ton of bricks, and she was glad she was sitting down. Otherwise, she may have fallen to the floor. "I…. Do you know what you are asking?" Both men nodded.

"Every year before Easter, I attend all the services: Ash Wednesday, Holy Thursday, Good Friday, the Easter Vigil on Saturday night, and Easter mass again on Sunday morning. The hardest day is Good Friday, when we have the veneration of the cross. Every year, when I walk up to that wooden cross and kiss it, I cry—hard, uncontrollable tears that shakes me to the core. I think about the suffering and pain our Lord went through, and it crushes my soul."

"And that proves how much you love our Lord, Elizabeth. You understand why He had to go through all that horror," McAllen said.

"Yes, I do, and I love Him even more because he was willing to sacrifice Himself to save all of us. But it still hurts so badly," she said, bowing her head. Tears streaked down her face.

Bishop McAllen walked over to her, knelt on the floor in front of her, and took her hands in his. "Then you understand why Jesus has to die on the cross. Your love will give you the strength to make sure it happens."

"Yes," she softly replied. "I promise to do whatever is necessary. Even though it will rip my heart in two to see it happen in person."

*****

On the same day that Elizabeth received her mission from the bishop, the President had a meeting with the male security guard, Keith Smith. Peck chose him because he was a known killer, a highly trained mission specialist for the army, who believed himself to be an All-American good old boy, liked his work a little too much, and blindly followed orders without question or conscious. More importantly, he was such a strong atheist, that he wished that Jesus had never existed. He hated all religions, regardless of their beliefs.

Peck did not beat around the bush with Keith, but came right to the point. "I have a very special mission that I want you to handle when you arrive in Jerusalem."

"I have to admit, Mr. President, that I'm not keen about going on this mission. I am a tried-and-true atheist, and I don't believe in any of that crap they try to sell people."

"That's exactly why I want you to go," Peck told him. "If you think this is going to change my mind about…"

"That is not what I think or want, and you will listen to what I have to say before making any more comments!" Peck said angrily.

"Yes, sir."

"Your mission is that under no circumstances, will you allow Jesus to die on the cross."

Keith smiled. "Really? What about the others? They won't be happy about my interference."

"I'm sure they won't, except the pilot, Captain Wagner. He'll be on your side, but the killing is your job and your job alone. That means that even if you have to kill the crew, except Captain Wagner, but including Agent Jennifer Williams, you are authorized to do so."

"Not to worry. I want Jesus to die before he gets on the cross to prove that he was not the son of God, just another person. And I will gladly kill him and anyone else to prove my point."

Keith Smith stood up and smiled. "Thank you, Mr. President, thy will be done."

President Peck shook his hand and smiled.

CHAPTER

ELEVEN

A small theatre was located within walking distance of where Jennifer was staying that occasionally had special showings of old movies. She noticed that tonight, on the last evening before she was scheduled to go back in time, they were playing *Jesus Christ Superstar*, the hit musical from 1973. Actually, she had never seen it, but when she saw the word Jesus on it, that was all it took. She had heard the music from it, but until now, she had never made the effort to see the movie. It was a fitting movie for her last night before the mission. With popcorn and soda in hand, she was in her own personal heaven. It made her think about Jesus, and what was in store for her. At this point, Jennifer still did not know for certain if Jesus was real or not. But with all her recent dreams and events, he had to be real. Right?

She really enjoyed the movie, especially the main song, *Superstar*. And afterwards, Jennifer stayed in the theatre to watch all the end credits. She saw the names of people she never knew or would ever know. She didn't care. She just liked looking at the names. It was a fun time.

"I never get tired of this movie," the person sitting behind her in the theater said. "I love it more every time I see it."

"How many times have you seen it?" Jennifer asked, turning in her seat to look at the woman.

"Thirty or forty times, and I still cry every time."

"Why do you cry?" Jennifer asked, puzzled. "Because Jesus died for us. So, we should cry."

"Do you love Jesus?"

"With all my heart," the woman replied, her hands held over her heart.

"If Jesus were alive and in front of you right now, what would you say to him?"

"I would get down on my knees and thank him for his sacrifice. Without that sacrifice, there would be no belief, no heaven, and no redemption," the woman said. "He loved us so much."

"Without Jesus, it would be a different world. Do you think Jesus is still alive?"

"Of course! He is with his father and mother looking down upon us from heaven. Jesus is even looking at you right now. Maybe even looking after you."

"I hope so," Jennifer said with more feeling than she had ever felt.

"Guaranteed! Good evening."

*****

As Jennifer left the theatre, she hummed the main song, which she couldn't seem to get out of her mind. She thought about calling an Uber but looking around, she decided it was a good night for a walk. It didn't matter in what direction, just a walk. The night was warm, and she didn't even need a jacket. She wore a short-sleeved shirt that showed off her well-toned arms. Just by looking at her, it was obvious that she was in good shape. She walked by two men sitting on a bench, who looked her up and down and grinned.

"Hey, babe, you look lonely," the first man said. "How about joining us? You look like you could use a couple friends."

"Thank you, but no thank you," Jennifer replied. "I have a very busy and early day tomorrow."

"Ah, come on. Why can't you be a little more friendly?" the second man asked.

"I told you I'm busy."

"Not even for a little while?" the first man asked.

"I have someone I have to meet. It's very important."

"You would think she had a date with God," the second man scoffed.

"Yes, actually, I do!"

"Thank you, that's good enough for us," the first man said. "Never get in the way of God."

"I don't want God angry at me, especially if he's waiting for her," the second man said. "Let's go."

The two men got up and left.

Jennifer crossed the street and continued walking until she spotted a small but beautiful church. It was old and made of stone, but very well maintained with the perfect amount of landscaping. The front door was open, and she saw a priest talking to some people inside. He was handsome, probably in his late sixties or early seventies, and he had a full head of striking white hair. Jennifer didn't know why, but she instantly liked this priest, even though she knew she would never meet him, or so she thought.

She fought the urge to go inside the church, even though she really wanted to. Winning that round, she continued walking past it. At that moment, four teenagers still in high school—three boys and a girl between seventeen and eighteen years old, walked right past her. The tallest one purposely bumped into Jennifer.

"Hey, watch out, lady! Watch where you're going," he sneered. "You could get hurt."

"You walked into me. You should apologize," Jennifer said, her eyes narrowing.

"Listen, lady, just keep moving and mind your own business. You don't want us angry. I guarantee it. Especially not now. We are on a mission and nothing will stop us," the second boy said.

"What mission could you possibly have? I'm sure you guys are up to no good." "Look, my advice is to move on," the girl said. "Go home and have a nice simple life."

"Come on, guys," the third boy urged. "Don't worry about this idiot. This church needs some paint and a lesson. Let's do what we came for."

Checking their hands for weapons, Jennifer noticed the cans of spray paint they were holding. "What are you doing with those spray cans?"

"We are going to make the world more beautiful," the tall boy said. "Let's go. We are artists looking for work."

Jennifer watched them as they walked away.

"Stupid, young idiots, you need to wake up." Jennifer continued on her way.

The four teenagers headed over to the front of the church and pulled out their spray cans. Then they covered their faces with devil masks. One painted on the door 'God is dead.' Another painted on the side 'Religion is control.' A third painted 'Jesus never lived.'

The priest was about to step back inside the church, when he saw what they were doing and ran over to stop them.

"What are you doing?" Father Davis asked, horrified. "Stop this! Leave at once!"

"Oh, no, you started this, old man," the tall teenager said. "You came to our school and tried to teach us. You tried to control the way we think. We won't allow that. None of this is real, and you are nothing but an old man who can't see the truth."

"I was just trying to teach you the love of Jesus," Father Davis said. "Is that so bad? I didn't force anyone to listen to me. You had a choice."

"No," the second teen said. "You and the way you think are dangerous. All religions should be destroyed. It does no good. Actually, we should get rid of all the old people, too."

"Since when is love not good? And don't worry, because either you become old or you die. There is nothing else."

"But we are young and that is a long time away," the second teen said. "Nothing to worry about for a while."

"It will happen long before you realize it," Father Davis said. "It won't take long. God takes care of everything."

"Listen, old man. There is no God, and Jesus was never real," the tall teen said.

"It was all a lie to trick us into submission—the biggest trick of all time just to control us!

But we won't fall for it anymore. We are going to fight back and prove that God is not real."

"God is real. Just look at everything around you. How is all this possible without God? Even you are not possible without God." "Prove it!" the third teenager shot back. "You know you can't."

"That is the mystery and true power and glory of God," the priest said. "You don't need to prove it, having belief is proof enough."

"Just another old man who doesn't know what he's talking about. You and your kind are nothing more than cowards who are afraid to die," the tall teen said. "I don't fear death. I am not afraid of religion. Death means nothing to me."

"In time, it will," Father Davis warned.

The third teen held up his can of paint and forced Father Davis back inside the church. The other teenagers followed. They looked at the people in the church.

"Everybody leave! Now!"

The people in the church were mostly elderly.

"Everybody, please leave. I don't want anyone getting hurt," the priest told them calmly. "Just leave. I'll handle this."

The parishioners exchanged glances. Had there been younger men among them, they would have stepped up and forced the teenagers to leave. But there weren't, and being elderly with their own fragile conditions, they did not want to risk injury to themselves. They rose to their feet and quietly left, saying a silent prayer for Father Davis and the church's safety.

As soon as they were gone, the priest looked at the tall teen, who seemed to be the one in charge. "Now what do you want?"

"I…. No! We want you to never try to convert us again. Never come to our school. Stay in your church. We don't want you spreading your lies. Do I make myself clear?"

"Yes, you do. But I will never allow people like you to get in the way of our Father and his Son. Never! Especially someone who hides behind the mask of the devil. It would seem that you love the evil one. What else could it mean?"

"Looks like this guy needs a lesson," the second teen said. He sprayed the front of the priest's vestments with paint.

Father Davis calmly took it, even though he knew it was ruined and would have to be replaced.

"Oh, no, just like Jesus, he turns the other cheek," his attacker said, his voice filled with scorn. "What a coward. Oh, wait, I forgot, Jesus was never real. Just a fake, nothing more, yet still a coward."

"Yes, there's no fight in him. How pathetic," the tall teen said.

"I have chosen a life of non-violence," Father Davis said calmly. "It's something you young people should consider."

"No," the second teenager said. "Violence is too much fun. Who needs love? Let's teach this coward a lesson. He won't even fight back. Just a stupid old man with no common sense."

"Just who are the ones with no common sense, me or the ones with the spray paint?" the priest asked.

"Come on, guys," the girl urged. "Let's go. We've made our point."

"Let's paint the inside of the church first." They pull out their spray cans again.

"No, no more damage. Get out! Leave!"

The tall teenager balled up his fist and pulled back his arm, preparing to attack Father Davis. But before his hand could reach the priest's face, another hand grabbed it and jerked it down to his side. That hand was Jennifer's, who had decided to come into the church after all.

"Just who is the coward here? The one who won't fight back? Or the one who attacks the one who won't fight back?" she asked.

"Not you again!" the tall teen said angrily. "Listen, old lady, get out before we really hurt you."

"Old lady? Are you kidding? I'm only thirty!"

"That's really old in our world," the female teen said. "Still, please leave. I don't want them to hurt you."

"These teenage idiots are not going to hurt me," Jennifer shot back as she stepped in between the teenagers and Father Davis. "They need a lesson. If you want the priest, you'll have to go through me. After that he's all yours. What do you say, boys and girl? Are you afraid of a Godfearing woman? And by the way, you guys are terrible artists."

"Please, just everybody go," Father Davis pleaded. "Please, young lady, this is a house of peace, not violence. Someday, God will punish these miscreants for their misdeeds."

"Yes, that day is today and right now," Jennifer assured him. "Dinner will be served, and it will be hot."

"You stupid old lady! I'm going to enjoy this," the tall teen said. "One old lady going down the drain. You'd better pray that your God will save you. By the way, that never works. God will not protect you." "I'll sit this one out and wait for the leftovers," the girl teen said as she calmly stepped out of the way.

"Get ready, old lady," the second teen said. "The young shall inherit the earth." "Don't ever call me old lady again!" "Or what?" the tall teen sneered.

With lightning speed, Jennifer slapped him, knocking off his devil mask. The other two watched, but they, too, were caught unaware, and their masks were quickly knocked off. Jennifer was so quick; they never saw it coming.

"There is no place for the devil in this house," she told them.

Seeing how fast Jennifer demasked the boys, the teenage girl said, "You got a point there." She took off her mask, revealing a very pretty girl underneath.

"You look much better now," Jennifer said. "Don't worry, I'll come back to you."

"Thank you, but no need to hurry."

The tall teenager rushed Jennifer, but to no avail. She gave him a quick chop to the neck that instantly choked him. He fell to the floor gasping for air. Then she kicked him in the head, knocking him out. The other two boys remained standing a few feet apart, facing Jennifer.

"This is too easy," she said, mocking them.

The second teen had his fists raised up to hit her. Before he realized what was happening, Jennifer slapped him in the face five times. He stood there stunned.

Confused and a bit dizzy, he said, "Ouch! That hurt! What are you, anyway?"

"What do you think? I'm an angel from God, sent to teach you boys a lesson—a lesson in how to be humble." Jennifer slapped him two more times.

"Please stop!" the boy begged.

Jennifer approached the third teenage boy, who, like the other boy, just stood in front of her.

"Oh, are you now like Jesus? Do you want to turn the other cheek? Please let me help you." Jennifer slapped him five times before he could react.

"That hurts!"

"Trust me, I know," the second teenage boy said.

"Let me help you some more."

Jennifer round kicked both of them in the head, sending them crashing to the floor.

"Now hear this. If any of you boys get up, I will break you in two. Any takers?"

"No, ma'am," the tall teen, who had just woken up, assured her.

"I'm down," the second boy said.

"Believe me. I am not moving," the third said adamantly.

The teenage girl looked at Jennifer and her friends on the floor. Jennifer looked back at her.

"I think it's your turn now. What do you think? Leftovers?"

"I'm actually okay. I'm full. I don't need any leftovers. Girl power! You rock!" she said, punching her fist in the air.

Satisfied that she would not receive any trouble from the girl, Jennifer's eyes went from one to the other. "Now listen to me! You need to understand that you don't control anything. Other people have feelings, too. You don't control them just because they don't agree with you. Whether you believe in God or not, you have to believe in love. There is just too much hate in this world, and I want to find out why. God is not dead. He is simply watching to see which way we're going to go. Love or hate, you each chose the direction. God may not be what you think he is, but one way or another, he still exists. I believe his son exists, too."

Her eyes continued passing from one kid to the other as she spoke. "Trust me, if he didn't, we would have destroyed ourselves long ago. He is the only thing keeping us alive, and you must realize that. You kids have to feel the pain of others, before you can truly feel your own pain. But I have a better idea. Try feeling the love of others and see what it does for you. Now get up and leave. And remember, the damage you did here belongs to you. It is your responsibility to make it right. I expect you to be back here bright and early tomorrow with brushes and cleaner to remove that paint. If you have hate, you won't care. If you have love, you will. Go in peace, and I forgive you."

The three boys slowly got to their feet and walked to the front door of the church along with the girl.

The girl turned around and looked at Jennifer. "Wow, girl power! I don't know about them, but I am sorry. Thank you." Jennifer nodded. "Please leave your spray paint behind." They put their spray paint cans down on the floor.

"Please come back anytime you want, even if it's just to talk," Father Davis said. "You are welcome here."

They all left. The girl softly closed the doors to the church behind them, leaving Jennifer and Father Davis alone facing each other.

"Well, young lady, you put on quite a show. I had no idea you could handle yourself like that. And for some weird reason, I truly think the Lord sent you to me. Does that sound funny to you? By the way, I'm Father Davis."

"I saw those kids as I was walking by. And I knew they wanted trouble. I'm Jennifer."

"Trouble seems to follow young kids nowadays," the priest said.

"What they need and aren't getting is discipline. And a lot of it."

Father Davis nodded, but as he did, he also studied her face. "I think you have questions for me, too."

"Yes," Jennifer admitted. "I'm still a bit confused."

"I can't tell you want to believe. You just need to see more evidence. Am I right?"

"I have been having these strange feelings and dreams about Jesus for quite some time now."

"In some ways, those kids were right," the priest said. "We have no proof, just a belief. I mean, it would be wonderful if we could somehow go back in time and find out the truth. Unfortunately, that is impossible, so we will never really know until we die. But it would be nice if we could."

Jennifer smiled at that one.

"Imagine having a time machine that could take you back to witness some of the greatest events in history. What a miracle that would be," the Priest said with wonder in his eyes.

"Miracles happen all the time. What if *we could* go back in time? Should we? Or should we just leave it alone, a mystery for all time."

"For better or worse, yes, I believe we should. Better to know the truth than live a falsehood. And another question. Where did you learn to fight like that? That was truly amazing."

"Oh, a little bit here and a little bit there."

"Well, young lady, just know that I believe in God and Jesus. I have no doubt. In fact, just you being here tonight proves my point. You didn't come here. You were sent here, almost like an avenging angel. I feel there is something special about you. Is there? I just can't shake the funny feeling that there is." Father Davis pointed to the front of the church at a large cross with a carving of Jesus on it that hung behind the altar. "I think you're looking for him." "Not that I know of. But I am very glad to have met you. Can I come back and visit?"

"Any time, and I know you will be back. Somehow, I believe that you are going to do something special and soon."

Not wanting to say anything more, she said, "I hope you're right. I wish you well, Father. Have a good night."

"Goodnight, and God bless you."

As Jennifer left the church, Father Davis remained where he was, staring at the door she had gone through. "Special mother," he said quietly, and then shook his head. Where did that come from?

Jennifer smiled as she continued her walk down the street, knowing that tomorrow would be the biggest day of her life, one she had been waiting for it seemed for a long time. She probably wouldn't sleep, and she decided to continue walking. Tomorrow, she would go on the adventure of a lifetime, many lifetimes.

"Jesus Christ, Superstar, do you think you're what they say you are?" she sang.

PART

TWO

CHAPTER

TWELVE

Jennifer stood in front of the time capsule, waiting for the door to open. Inside and out, a team was doing a last round of disinfecting to make sure that none of the modern germs went back in time that could potentially cause trouble. She hadn't been able to sleep at all last night. It wasn't for lack of trying; she was just too excited. She also wanted to be the first one in the capsule to watch the crew enter. Jennifer was dressed in her new outfit, a simple blue woven garment worn by peasant women during that time period. She had requested a hood to protect her from the sun as well as an additional large, full robe also with a hood. She was also supplied with a pouch filled with a whole lot of the local money of that era.

The lead scientist, Dr. Adams, walked up to Jennifer. "Looking very good, Jennifer. Very good indeed!"

"Are you kidding? These things make me look like a tramp."

"In that case, you are the hottest-looking tramp I have ever seen," Dr. Adams said, grinning.

Dr. Adams along with many others on the project had a secret crush on Jennifer. She was just so beautiful with a magnetic personality. Even some of the women longingly looked at her, wishing they would have been born so lucky.

"Okay, they're done, and it's ready to go," Dr. Adams said as the sanitation team gave him the thumbs up. "I'm already missing you, and you haven't even left."

"Thank you. It's nice to be missed." She gave Dr. Adams a light hug. "But you know, I won't really be gone that long, based on your test mission." "That's actually hard to say. You will be travelling further back in time than the initial mission to spend seven or eight days, depending on how accurate our computations are. So, we really don't know for certain. At any rate, I'll never wash these clothes again."

"You are too funny," she said smiling. "Wish us luck!" "God speed," Dr. Adams replied.

Jennifer headed for the open capsule. But before entering, she turned around and faced the camera that the President was using to watch the event from his office. She politely waved to indicate goodbye. After all, he was the President of the United States, even though she disliked and did not trust him now. Turning around, she entered the capsule. Finally, the time had arrived to make this historic trip. She thought about the last few months and how everything had worked out just right for her, even secretly visiting the Pope.

Sitting in her chair, which faced the open door, she waited for her crew, picking up a nearby writing tablet and pen, in case she needed to take notes. They were scheduled to leave in less than an hour, so they should be here soon. Finally, someone entered the time machine. It was her new best friend, Winifred Scott, one of the security guards. Winifred was plain looking, but very friendly. Like Jennifer, she was dressed in the outfit of a commoner. Now, she actually looked homely, but in a cute way. Jennifer had met her about a month ago, and they had instantly hit it off.

"Hello, Winifred. Welcome aboard," Jennifer said with a smile.

"Hello, Commander."

"For this trip, 'Jennifer' will do. You are to sit right here next to me. My protector."

Winifred laughed. "As if you really needed it. I think you could take us all out at the same time. I know all about you."

Winifred sat in her seat. A moment later, the pilot, Captain Johann Wagner, came in and sat in the pilot's seat, where he began his prelaunch checks.

Jennifer was taken aback, slightly, as he was dressed a little fancier, more like a rich man. "Welcome, Captain Wagner. You're looking good, maybe a little too good. I don't want you to become too noticeable."

"Well, someone has to be, or everybody will just notice you," Captain Wagner replied. "Besides, I want to feel special."

"Point well taken."

As they were talking, Jennifer heard someone else enter. It was Elizabeth Johansen, one of the scientists. In her fifties, she was slightly heavy but not too much. Like Winifred, she was dressed very common, and she fit right in. She had a loud voice but luckily, she didn't talk much.

Jennifer noticed that she wore a gold cross necklace, around her neck.

Jennifer pointed to an open seat. "Welcome, Elizabeth, please take that seat. I'm not sure, but that cross around your neck may be a little bit premature. I don't think it would be a good idea to wear it. At least until after Jesus dies."

"Oh, yes. I'm sorry, I just forgot to take it off. I will now," she placed it in a small compartment next to her seat. "Thank you."

"Thank you."

Dr. Leo Garnier, the other scientist, came next. The designers had really gone to work on his outfit. He looked like the poorest of the poor, a very good job. In his mid-forties, he was younger than Elizabeth, thin and slightly taller. Jennifer pointed to an empty seat.

"Welcome, Dr. Garnier. You look stunning."

"Sure, I do," he replied with a grin. "Let's get ready to rock and roll."

Dr. Garnier sat in the seat next to Elizabeth. There was just one more person to go. Everybody was quiet as they waited. Jennifer played with her pen and tablet, until they heard loud steps approach the time machine. To Jennifer's surprise, Keith Smith, the other security guard, entered the capsule in full dress as a Roman soldier, complete with a sword and knife. Jennifer held back her surprise, thinking, *Something doesn't feel right about this.*

Keith was well-built and muscular around six feet tall. From the first day she had met him, she had a strange feeling about him. His presence always brought up her guard. She knew that the President had personally chosen him, and maybe that was part of it. Still, she had decided from the very beginning to never let her guard down around him.

She just did not trust him.

Keith had a very fancy sword, and Jennifer knew that he was highly trained in all forms of combat, including swords and knives. There were modern weapons on board the time machine as well, but Jennifer made sure that she was the only one who could access them. In fact, thanks to Dr. Adams, she was the only one who actually knew they were onboard. It had been easy to convince him of their necessity, especially when she explained that they might be necessary to make sure that no one disturbed the timeline.

"Hello, Keith. What do we have here?" Jennifer asked. "Because of my build, I felt I would blend in better as a soldier."

"And since no one said anything to me about it, who approved that?"

"The President," he replied. His voice and attitude came across almost as a dare. Jennifer, however, was too smart to take the bait. "Where did you get that sword?"

"I had it specially made. It's perfect for me." "I hope you never have to use it," she said.

"Yes, so do I." His words, however, did not ring true.

Keith sat in his assigned chair. And Jennifer made a mental note to keep a close watch on him. A loose cannon in the time of Jesus could be very dangerous.

"Commander, it's time," Captain Wagner said, breaking through her thoughts. "The moment of truth."

Sitting in the commander's chair, Jennifer watched the time capsule door close in front of her. The windows were pretty small and thick, and it was hard to see much out of them. Strangely, she felt that they were more for decoration than function. Still holding the writing tablet and a pen in her right hand, numerous thoughts passed through her mind. Neither she nor anyone else, except the pilot, had any idea about what to expect next.

After a few seconds, Captain Wagner spoke again. "Commander Williams, we are ready to go anytime you say."

Jennifer thought, This is actually going to happen! The wait is over. Too late for anybody to change their minds. The big question was: What was going to happen? Would everything just disappear, with she and her crew forever lost in time? Or worse, forever erased from time as if they had never existed? Would she end up being chased and eaten by a dinosaur like in the movies, or tortured in a medieval torture chamber? Maybe being burnt at the stake like the so-called witches in Salem? Or how about on a totally whole different planet, never to see Earth or her home again. The thoughts raced through her mind and there was only one thing to do—the thing she had been trained for, and the thing that would bring meaning to her life.

"Engage," she said, using the term she had heard a certain captain use so many times on TV.

"Acknowledged," the pilot said. "Ten, nine, eight, seven, six, five, four, three, two, one. Engage."

At that moment, Jennifer dropped the pen and tablet she was holding and grabbed the arms of her seat. Everything was slowing down. She glanced out a window and saw a massive rainbow of colors. No sound just color and no sense of movement, just time slowing down. Turning from the window, she saw her pen and tablet floating in midair between her hand and the floor of the time capsule. Glancing out the window once more, she saw the most spectacular sight she had ever witnessed as a wormhole opened in a spectacular swirling black cloud that sucked Starway Seven inside. Jennifer closed her eyes for a few seconds. The next thing she heard was her pen and tablet hitting the floor. Opening her eyes, she realized that everything was back to normal. Then she looked out the windows and saw sunlight and some hills in the distance.

She looked around at her other crewmembers. After what seemed like only seconds, the time capsule shut down and was still.

"Everybody okay?" she asked.

The crewmembers nodded that they were fine.

"A little dizzy but okay," Elizabeth said.

"Commander, the computer indicates that we have arrived at our proper destination and time," Captain Wagner informed her. "At least, I hope it's right."

"Let's find out," Jennifer said, rising from her seat, releasing the door hatch, and stepping outside. Looking around, she shaded her eyes, wishing she had her sunglasses, and looked into the distance to find the walled city of Jerusalem. At first it didn't look real. The time machine had landed near a hill about half a mile away. To Jennifer, it looked more like a movie set than the real thing. It was like something out of a Bible movie. Then she wondered, was it real? She thought about the moon conspiracies and how some people said that everything was staged and phony. Was this the same? Had she been tricked into believing that this was real? Was time travel even possible? Or was this all a joke?

"Engage the hologram," she called back to Captain Wagner.

The ship took on the appearance of a house of lepers as programed.

"Commander, what do you see?" Captain Wagner asked.

"Everything." Everything looked so much smaller than she had thought it would be. Jerusalem was small with no tall structures, and the wall went all the way around it. She could see the tops of only a few things. She had studied the past, but being here was very different. Everything was limestone with not a lot of color. It still did not look real. Jennifer looked up into the sky expecting to see an airplane flying by to prove her point. There was nothing but a vast expanse of blue sky. Looking down she saw a lot of empty dirt everywhere. One thing was certain, the sky was the most vivid blue she has ever seen. It was so blue; she didn't know how to describe it. It was just so bright and the air was so fresh and clean, it almost tasted sweet.

So, this is what no pollution looks and feels like. Was she really here? And was it really two thousand years in the past? She saw nothing modern, no asphalt roads, not even a telephone pole, nothing. The sun was so bright, there just wasn't anything in the way. The temperature felt the same as it had when she had visited modern Jerusalem, just more intense now. It had to be real, no one could build this much in such a short period of time.

"Okay. Let's not waste any time. Time to get started. Everybody has their missions. Remember, do not interfere. Blend in and learn."

Winifred joined Jennifer outside the capsule. "All set to go, Commander, I mean Jennifer. Search and find. Wow, it feels so warm and just look at that city. The past is no longer the past. It is the present. This is the adventure of a lifetime, many lifetimes. More than I could have ever hoped for."

"Be careful that you don't call me commander here. It could create a problem." "I'll be careful, Jennifer."

"I, for one, would like a guide," Jennifer said. "Let's go." "Which direction?"

Jennifer noticed some people walking by with a donkey. They looked absolutely real. She approached them. "Sorry to intrude, but I am looking for the man called Jesus. Do you know where he is?"

The husband and wife look at Jennifer. They could tell that she was not from this region.

"No, we do not," the man replied. He grabbed his wife, and they quickly left.

"They know," Jennifer told Winifred. "They just don't trust me."

"We've only been here a minute. We have plenty of time. In fact, we now can control time."

"Let's begin our search. The sooner we find Jesus, the better."

They began walking, eventually spotting more people, whom they approached.

"Is Jesus here?" Jennifer asked. "Where can I find him?"

"He is not here. Search somewhere else," a woman in a red robe said.

"Please, I only want to meet him."

"Are you looking for a miracle?" the man next to her asked.

"No, only a man."

"Keep searching," the man said. "Just not here."

"If at first you don't succeed, try again," Winifred said.

Jennifer approached a young teenage boy carrying a cage full of doves. "Have you seen the man called Jesus?"

"There are a lot of people around here named Jesus," the boy replied. "Which one?"

"The one who people pray to."

"Not yet, but I keep hoping and praying he will appear soon. Good day, lady, and good luck in your search."

"Where are you off to with those birds?" Jennifer asked.

"To the temple, of course."

"Thank you and good luck to you."

"If he is here, we will find him," Winifred said reassuringly. "There really isn't much around here to hide him from us."

"I don't know. I just hope he really does exist." Jennifer looked around. "How do people live like this?"

"They didn't have a choice like we do," Winifred said.

"I mean the poorest, homeless person from our time would be considered living like a king over here. Look at this. No hospitals, no police, no stores, no water, no food, yet they all live. It's amazing."

"How about no public bathrooms, like I could use right now," Winifred said. "We don't know how lucky we have it."

Winifred's bathroom remark had passed right over her head. "I wonder if somebody, two thousand years in the future from our time, would say the same thing about us. It's all relative."

Jennifer shrugged her shoulders. "If you have a major injury out here, you're dead."

"They don't know what antibiotics are and won't for a long time," Winifred agreed.

"We have come a long way, even though we don't always think so."

"And remember, most of the people of Rome and even here are slaves of some sort or other."

"Yes," Jennifer agreed. "The history of mankind is surely slavery. Cheap labor. How else could Rome be built?" "Especially with no cell phones or phones at all."

"You know what's funny?" Jennifer asked. "Most of them seem happy."

"It's because they don't know that there's something else. We do and that's the difference between us and them."

"That is truly a gift from God."

Their conversation was interrupted when they heard a noise behind them. Two Roman soldiers on horseback approached them from behind.

"Get out of the way, peasants!" the first Roman soldier shouted. "Just your presence is insulting to my horse."

"You people smell like pigs!" the second one added.

"No, we do not!" Jennifer shot back as she turned to face them.

"What? You dare talk back to me?" the second soldier said as he pulled out his sword. "I will execute you for that!"

"You will what? I don't think so!"

"You common pigs, we don't need you around here," the first Roman soldier said. "You should all go away and die. We own this land, and you are nothing but slaves. It's simple. Disobey and die." He pulled out his sword.

Winifred knew that Jennifer could take care of both of these soldiers. But she did not want a problem right now. And she knew that Jennifer could get pretty angry and do some damage, which could cause future problems. This encounter needed to stop. All of the time travelers had been supplied with a serious amount of local money. She pulled out a goodly amount from her pouch. "Please forgive my friend, noble gentlemen, as she is new to this area and does not know the proper respect for a Roman soldier. Allow me to offer you this as an apology and ask for your forgiveness."

She gave the soldiers some money that for them, was a lot, more than a month's wages. They were surprised and impressed. The soldiers stared at the money.

"We forgive you and accept your apology," the first Roman soldier said. "Have a peaceful day."

"And remember, always show respect," the second one said. "We will, kind sir. All our respect to you. Thank you." The soldiers rode away.

Winifred turned to Jennifer. "I know what you wanted to do. But we need to be careful, especially in this time. Even the smallest change could affect the timeline. Being hit by a woman could change the history of mankind."

"Nitwits," Jennifer grumbled. "It would have been fun." She yelled at the soldiers. "Have you seen the man called Jesus?"

The first soldier stopped and turned in his saddle. "I have heard rumors. Look to the west."

The soldier pointed at some hills in the distance. The soldiers rode away.

They moved on, eventually coming upon an area near the small city of Bethany. They had been walking a couple hours. Jennifer constantly looked for any sign of Jesus. Everything seemed ancient because it was. This was vastly different from her trip to Jerusalem. Like a puzzle, she needed time to put things together. How was she going to find Jesus when everything was so different? They were about to give up for a while, when Jennifer looked at a nearby hill with the sun partially blinding her sight. When her sight cleared, she saw about twenty people looking up and listening to a man speak. In her mind, it was almost as if a light was emanating from the man.

She reached out and grabbed Winifred's arm to stop her. "I've seen that light before. In a dream." Something about this man was warm and felt good. Jennifer continued staring, until the dream came back to her.

"What do you see?" Winifred asked, knowing the commander's vision had turned inward.

"The answer to my dreams. Finally, it's all here and real." Jennifer couldn't explain why, but she knew without a doubt that this man was Jesus. Tears streamed down from her eyes, and she smiled, knowing what had to be done. She looked at Winifred. "You can return to the ship and start your surveillance mission. I will take over on this one. If there are any problems, I'll contact you."

All the members of Starway Seven were given special communication devices that looked like a simple bracelet, worn by almost everybody.

"All right," Winifred said. "If there is any trouble, you know what to do."

"Got it, but I don't think there will be. I'll see you in a week. We have little time and a lot to learn."

The mission that Jennifer was sent to do had just started. She was excited and eager to begin.

Winifred left. "Happy hunting."

At this time, Jennifer was wearing a hood that covered most of her face and hair. She joined the crowd, who were listening to Jesus. Tears still fell from her eyes. Her emotions were going wild. She felt such goodness in this man, who was speaking like nothing she had ever before experienced. Jesus was the most beautiful person she had ever seen. Yet it was more than that. It went beyond physical beauty to something pure and good. She stepped in front of the crowd.

Jesus spoke to the people, giving one of his parables.

Jennifer quickly realized from her studies that this was *the Good Samaritan* from Luke 10-25-37. She listened in wonderment at this amazing man.

"Teacher, what shall I do to inherit eternal life?" a man in the crowd asked.

"What is written in the law? How do you read it?" Jesus responded.

"'You shall love the Lord your God with all your heart, with all your soul, with all your strength, and with all your mind, and your neighbor as yourself.'"

"You have answered correctly. Do this, and you will live." "Who is my neighbor?" another man asked.

"As a man traveled from Jerusalem to Jericho, he was stripped of his clothing, robbed, beaten, and left half dead alongside the road," Jesus began. "A Jewish priest walked by and saw the man, but passed by on the other side of the road, so as not to be bothered. Later a Levite did the same. Although Samaritans and Jews despise each other, a Samaritan saw the Jewish man lying beside the road and took pity on him. He bound up the man's wounds and carried him to an inn, where he continued to care for the wounded man until he had to leave. Then, he gave money to the innkeeper to continue the man's care."

"He was a kind man," the second man said.

"Now which of these three do you think was a neighbor to him who fell among the robbers?"

"The Samaritan, who showed him mercy," the man replied. "Go and do likewise."

"I will, my Lord."

Jesus continued speaking. "To be the right type of neighbor with all those around us, we should show mercy and compassion to all."

All the people at this time knelt before Jesus, except Jennifer, who really didn't know what to do. Jesus looked up at her. Jennifer pulled her hood down, revealing her face and hair, and smiled at Jesus, who smiled back.

"You are not from around here. Are you? But from somewhere very far away." Clearly her presence puzzled him. "Why are you here?" "To learn the truth from the truth," Jennifer said honestly.

Jesus was fascinated by this strange and beautiful woman. She seemed unlike any other woman he had ever known, and he found himself drawn to her. "Let me teach you the truth," he told her.

"I would like that very much."

Turning to the crowd, Jesus said, "That is enough for today, my friends. Go in peace and love."

"We honor and love you," someone in the crowd said. "You are our savior and our father."

The crowd dispersed, leaving only Jennifer.

Jesus walked up to her. "You are indeed beautiful, unlike anyone I have ever seen. Where are you from?"

"A long way from here," she replied. "This land is mysterious to me. I feel so alone."

"Then let me guide you. You will be safe with me. Come. Let us walk and talk. I want to know all about you," Jesus assured her. "You are no longer alone."

"Do you live around here?"

"I live everywhere there is love," he replied.

"This land is amazing."

"How long will you be here?"

"Seven days, maybe more," Jennifer said.

"Then let us make them wondrous."

"I was hoping you would say that."

"This is strange, but somehow, I think you are here to help me learn. I hope so."

Jennifer shook her head. "I am just a simple country girl."

"Yet, I feel that there is so much more about you."

"Is there a public restroom around here?"

Jesus looked at her in surprise. "A what?"

"Never mind. I'll figure it out."

Jennifer and Jesus walked away, and the love affair began.

CHAPTER

THIRTEEN

Dr. Leo Garnier was shocked *and amazed that he had traveled back two thousand years in time. The people who sent me here do not even exist yet. So, it would be impossible to communicate with them. On the other hand, these people here right now have been long dead for centuries. Yet here they are, very much alive.*

After Jennifer and Winifred had left, he looked at the remaining crew members, especially Keith, who stuck out in his Roman outfit with his knife and sword. *That guy looks like a true killer.* But he figured it was best to keep that to himself. After all, he could be a great guy once you got to know him. Captain Wagner, however, was a different story. Dressed in his rich man's outfit, which was very, very red, he would not go unnoticed. *That's for sure.*

"Well, I guess it's time we went out to explore," Leo said. "After all, we are the first to experience this."

"This is even scarier than the Revolutionary War," Wagner admitted. "And that was an actual war."

"These people have no idea what's going on," Keith said. "They aren't much smarter than the animals they eat. They have no idea what the future will bring. Well, look out! Here it comes."

"Don't tell the Romans that," Elizabeth said. "Look, they built the coliseum, so, they can't be *all* bad. And just so you understand, they were experts at killing. Don't underestimate them. In this time and area, they were allowed to kill with almost complete impunity." "That's refreshing to hear," Keith said with a smile.

"Yes, I figured you would like that," Elizabeth said, frowning. "The only problem is that everybody was allowed to kill almost anybody. There was really no law enforcement or punishment. It was local law, and whatever you could get away with. I recommend that everyone watch out. Thieves are everywhere. They would kill you for a single shekel."

"I'm actually looking forward to that," Keith said, a little too enthusiastically. "As a Roman soldier, I can dish out a lot of punishment."

"Just remember, we are only here to observe," Wagner said. "If you kill someone who did not die from this time, it would send shockwaves throughout history that could change the world we go back to drastically." He looked around at the crew. "Ready? Activate your cameras."

Along with a wrist bracelet communicator, the clothing the crew wore had tiny cameras secretly hidden within the front folds of their clothing.

"Those cameras will record audio and video in super-high definition nonstop for up to a month." Wagner said. "Now remember the cameras are pointing straight ahead with wide vision."

"We definitely won't need a month," Keith said. He had no intention of staying any longer than was needed to accomplish the purpose the President had sent him to do.

"Keep a careful watch on your bracelet communicators," Wagner continued. "And if you lose one, use your ring finder to locate it. We can't let any future technology fall into the hands of these people."

"They wouldn't know what to do with it or what it was," Keith said, brushing Wagner's concerns off.

"Don't be so sure," Elizabeth said. "Maybe not now, but someone later in time might be able to figure it out. Even if it happened as late as the 1900s, it would still change time and accelerate the future." "I agree," Wagner said.

"Don't let anyone near you, and trust no one," Elizabeth added.

"You are carrying a lot of money, so keep it hidden at all times."

"They made that money very safe," Keith bragged. "It is securely, and I mean securely attached to my body. No thief is getting it. They would be shocked if they tried. Besides, they wouldn't dare touch a Roman soldier." "Yes, they would," Elizabeth warned.

"That will be an interesting test," Keith said. "Especially for my pretty sword."

"I can tell you're going to be trouble," Elizabeth said with a sigh. "Just be careful, and remember, kill someone from this time, and you screw up the future."

"Okay. Let's get going," Wagner said. "Leo, you're coming with me to explore the countryside. Bring water." "Yes, sir, got it," Leo said.

"Elizabeth, you and Keith can explore the old city of Jerusalem," Wagner said. "Should be fun."

"Yes," Elizabeth said happily. "I want to meet all the people in the Bible."

Keith was surprised by Elizabeth's remarks. He now knew for certain that she was super religious and could possibly interfere with his plans. The President had given him permission to prove that religion was fake—a control system for the masses. He had waited his whole life for this. His parents were religious and had taken him to church regularly. He hated it from the very beginning. He had never been abused, but he'd had friends that were. And once that had happened, they were never the same ever again. Like the President, he wanted to get even and would do anything, including kill, to get it. He looked at Elizabeth. *Although I'm not supposed to kill someone from this timeline, that remains to be seen. You, however, are a different story. Get in my way, and you're gone. And I will get away with it, too. Once you're dead, no one will ever remember that you had even been born.* To Elizabeth he said, "Yes, I want to meet them, too."

"Let's go," Wagner said. "Welcome to the great adventure."

"Yes, master of the red," Leo said. It sounded like he was kidding, but was he?

Wagner and Leo headed for open country, while Elizabeth and Keith began their short journey to the ancient walled city of Jerusalem. Leo found a small trail and headed towards some rolling hills. Wagner closely followed behind. Two Roman soldiers approached them.

"Good, Roman soldiers," Leo said. "Maybe they know where we can find Jesus." He addressed the soldiers, "Excuse me, kind sirs."

"Be silent, slave! Only your master can speak to us!" the first Roman soldier ordered.

"I am not a slave," Leo replied, indignantly.

"Oh, no, not another one. That's what they all say. If it looks like a slave, acts like a slave, smells like a slave, and talks like a slave, it is a slave," the second Roman replied.

"What can we do for you, and please keep your slave quiet," the first Roman soldier said.

"We are looking for the man they call Jesus," Wagner said. "Do you know of him?"

"Yes, I do," the first Roman soldier said. "By now, he is probably in the hills near Bethany. You should not be out here, especially dressed the way you are. You are nothing more than a rich target. Looking at your slave, I guarantee he would offer no protection." "I am not a...," Leo began.

"You slaves just don't get it! You were told to be silent! If you say another word, I will cut out your tongue."

"He will be silent," Wagner assured him. "When we get back to my camp, I will have him beaten for insubordination."

"That is a very good idea," the second Roman soldier said.

"Trust me. In Rome, he would learn respect or die."

"Thank you, sir," Wagner said.

"Which way is Bethany?"

The First Roman soldier pointed to the east.

"Good day."

The soldiers left, leaving Wagner laughing at Leo.

"I have to admit, especially the way you look and are dressed. You do look like a slave."

"Very funny."

After a half-hour of walking, they came across a goat herder tending fifty or more goats.

He smiled at them. "Good day, sir. You look wonderful in your red outfit. Can I get you some goat milk to quench your thirst? I can also give some to your slave."

"I am not a slave," Leo insisted. He was getting sick and tired of being called a slave.

"That is strange," the goat herder said with a puzzled expression on his face. "Because you look like a slave. Are you being disrespectful to your master? Because if you are, he should beat you."

"What is wrong with the people out here?" Leo asked, disgusted.

"Some milk would be wonderful," Wagner told the goat herder. He pulled some change from his pouch and gave it to the goat herder, not realizing that it was a lot of money to the goat herder. "This is amazing and truly generous," the goat herder exclaimed.

"You can have one of my goats if you want."

"That will not be necessary, but thank you," Wagner assured him.

The goat herder gave Leo and Wagner some milk. "Some for the master, and some for the slave."

"I am not a slave!" Leo shouted.

"You should be beaten. You are lucky your master is so kind and generous."

"Have you heard of a man called Jesus?" Wagner asked, after tasting his milk, which was warm and fresh.

"Of course, the man of miracles. The man who will save us."

"Where can we find him?" Wagner asked.

"If you believe, he will find you. Good day, sir."

"Well, Master Wagner, at least we now know that there is a man named Jesus." He started drinking his milk and made a face.

"Yeck! This is hot and awful."

Wagner laughed. "What did you expect? It's goat's milk. Actually, it's not bad. Better drink up. This is the desert. We'll need to stretch our water supply as far as possible."

Leo wasn't happy about it, but he realized that what Wagner said was right. He drank down the rest of the milk as quickly as possible.

They started off, but not before the goat herder yelled a warning to them. "Be careful of the wild boar hunters. The boars are big and dangerous, especially when they are hunted."

"Thank you." He turned to Leo. "What is a wild boar?"

"A big, nasty pig with tusks, huge tusks." "What do we do if we see one?" "Run," Leo said.

They continued their journey, and everyone they met was very friendly. After walking for nearly an hour, they met three men with short spears and long knives.

"These must be the wild boar hunters," Leo said. "Greetings!"

"Greetings to you," hunter one said. "Please tell your master to be careful. We are hunting a herd of wild boars and have wounded some of them. They are close and very dangerous."

"I will tell my friend that. Thank you," Leo said.

The second hunter frowned. "I hate it when slaves don't know their place." With a sense of humor, Wagner said, "Thank you, kind sirs. When I get back to my residence, I will have my slave beaten."

"Yes, you should," the third hunter said. "Be safe, kind sir."

"That makes me feel really good," Leo said sarcastically. "I am ready for my double beating, master." Wagner laughed.

The hunters left, talking among themselves in the distance.

"We should kill the rich man in red and his slave. I am sure it would be much more profitable than trying to kill a wild boar. I'll bet he has a lot of money with him," the first hunter said.

"Yes, we can do both," the second hunter said. "Let's herd the wild boars in their direction. Let them do the killing for us."

"I'll scare them from this end," the third hunter said.

"Good, let us begin," the second hunter said. "One less rich man will do the world good."

The three hunters shouted and ran at the wild boars, driving them in the direction of Leo and Wagner. There were about twenty, big and fast, and the males had large tusks that could do a lot of damage. They ran at full speed. Then the head boar, which was wounded and wanted to attack anything that moved, spotted the red-clothed Wagner, ran straight at Wagner, its herd following.

Hearing a noise behind them, Leo and Wagner turned around, and to their surprise and horror, the wild boars were charging them. Both were terrified.

"Find cover! Hurry!" Leo shouted. He looked at Wagner, seeing only red.

Wagner was frozen in fright, much like a matador holding a red cape for a bull to charge. Only this time, Wagner was the cape, and he had no sword with which to defend himself. He stood out like a homing beacon, and the boars headed straight for him. Leo jumped behind a nearby boulder and tried to grab Wagner, but it was too late. The large boar rammed into Wagner's side, knocking him down. Its tusks gored his legs, ripping out a chunk of flesh. Wagner screamed and fell to the ground, blood everywhere. "Oh my God, no!" Leo cried.

Wagner was seriously hurt and out of his mind with pain. "Call 911, now! I need an ambulance!"

"We can't! There is no 911!"

"Call anybody!" Wagner pleaded.

"I'm sorry, Johann. There is no phone here!"

Leo was helpless. He needed to contact the commander for instructions. This was an unexpected event that no one would have thought about. He brought his communication bracelet to his mouth. But before he could say a word into it, the wild boar returned and gored Wagner again. This time in the chest and belly. Leo heard bones breaking, and Wagner screaming and crying in pain. Near death, he sadly looked at Leo, who was looking around to make sure the wild boars were gone before he went to his fallen comrade. Covered in bright red blood, Wagner opened his mouth to say something, but nothing came out but blood and spittle. A moment later, he died.

At that precise moment, a giant but short sonic boom ripped through the wave of time. The time wave was felt everywhere, even in the present. Leo strongly felt the boom and looked down at Wagner.

There was nothing on the ground, and Leo could not understand why he was looking at the dirt. And there was the true paradox of dying in the past. If you die before you are born, everything about you disappears because you never existed. There was nothing to remember because the future had never happened.

Everything changed around the time wave. At that same moment, Jennifer, Winifred, Elizabeth, and Keith all forgot that Captain Johann Wagner had ever existed, because now, he never did.

Leo looked around and spotted the three hunters running toward him with the intent of picking the body clean of valuables, but then coming to a complete stop. They looked at each other questioningly. When Wagner died and disappeared, the reason for driving the boars there to kill him, disappeared as well. They remembered Leo, but not why he was there in the first place. After all, he was just a slave, and therefore, worthless. There was no chance a slave would have any money on him.

"What am I doing here?" Leo asked himself aloud.

"You should not be here, slave," the first hunter said.

"I am leaving." Because of his own confusion, for the first time he did not complain about being called a slave. He wished that he had a companion, even though he decided to go alone. With his memory of Wagner gone, Leo couldn't remember why he wanted to call the commander. He lowered his wrist. Then he wondered, who the pilot of their mission was, which was strange. Why don't I know that? He thought a moment longer. It's probably Jennifer. Yes, it must be Jennifer. Leo continued walking, passing the ground where Wagner's body had breathed its last, but nothing was left. It was as though he had never existed.

"I wonder why that slave was out here all alone," the second hunter asked his friends.

"Probably trying to hide from his master," the third hunter replied.

"Forget about him. Come, let us continue the hunt."

Leo continued his journey, a lonely man who looked like a lost slave.

*****

Elizabeth and Keith walked leisurely around the outer walls of Jerusalem. Keith, being large for a Roman, looked imposing, and people gave them plenty of distance as they believed that Keith was guarding Elizabeth.

Elizabeth was amazed as her eyes took in as much detail as possible. "I can't believe we are actually here. I mean we can touch the whole Western Wall, not just a part of it. This is where our religion got started. It's all here. Everywhere."

"You are very religious, aren't you?" Keith asked, even though he was certain what her answer would be.

"I mean just look at this! How could you not? I feel God everywhere, the most I have ever felt."

At that moment, she reminded Keith of Alice in Wonderland. "I guess we'll find out soon enough, Alice."

"What did you call me?" Elizabeth asked.

"Nothing. It was just a joke," Keith said. "Did Jesus actually exist, or have we been fooled for the last two thousand years?"

"He does, and he did." Remembering her promise to the church, she said, "I want to visit Caiaphas; he is the main religious leader around here. He needs to be told the truth."

"About what? Remember, we can't do anything that will change the timeline." Keith found this odd, since Elizabeth was the one who kept harping about not changing the timeline.

"I know. I know."

"Where are we going to find him, anyway?" he asked.

"He has a palace somewhere close. It should be easy to find. A palace would really stand out."

"What are you going to tell him?"

"Simply that he needs to trust his instincts." Seeing a woman carrying a large water jug, Elizabeth approached her. "Excuse me, but where is the Palace of Caiaphas?"

"Just around that wall. You can't miss it. Nobody can miss it," the woman with the jug replied. She did not try to hide the disgust in her voice.

"Why is that?" Elizabeth asked.

"It is the house of a very rich man. A man too rich to be in his status. He should be poor like all of us praising God. Instead, he is praising his money. Good day."

Elizabeth and Keith walked around the wall, and instantly spotted the palace. Even for this era, it was large, clean, well kept, and spectacular— bigger and fancier than anything else around. They walked up to the large front door, and Elizabeth knocked on it.

A servant opened the door. He had an angry look on his face. "What do you want? You should not be here!"

"I have important information for Caiaphas. I need to see him."

"No one sees Caiaphas unless he wants to see you first. No one!" the servant declared.

"This is very important. I need to see him," Elizabeth insisted.

"No! Leave now!" The servant closed the door in front of them.

"That wasn't very nice. Hey, Keith. You might have better luck." "Let me try." Keith knocked on the door and once again, the servant opened it, still upset.

"We need to see Caiaphas," Keith said in his most official voice.

"No Roman soldiers are allowed in here. That is the agreement. You and your lady friend are wasting your time. You will never see him. Never!" The servant slammed the door in their faces.

Keith wasn't happy about that. "Maybe I should convince him another way." He grasped the pummel of his sword, but he did not pull it out yet.

"No, no, no. There must be another way," Elizabeth insisted.

"Oh my God, of course there is," Keith said, releasing his sword and smacking the side of his head. "I am so stupid. I didn't realize where I truly was and the kind of people that live around here. It's so simple." "What do you mean?" Elizabeth asked.

"Look, this is the land of the Jews. Caiaphas is basically the King of the Jews, maybe the very first one. There is something they can't resist. It all started here. Make no mistake. This will work." Keith pulled out a gold aureus from his pouch—a coin of Ancient Rome. "This is a hell of a lot of money here, especially since it's gold. Try this."

Keith gave Elizabeth the gold aureus, and once again, she knocked on the door. The angry servant once again opened the door. But before he could say anything, Elizabeth showed him the gold coin.

"Maybe this will help."

The servant was astonished to see the gold coin. Only rich people had gold. He took the gold coin from her hand. "I'll be right back." A few seconds later, the door opened wide. "Please come in as our invited guest. Sit over here while I wash your feet."

Elizabeth and Keith entered the palace and sat on a bench next to the door. The servant washed their feet as was the custom for an invited quest. They were then taken to Caiaphas and seated in front of him. It was hard to tell his age, but he had a full beard, and his style of dress was distinctly Jewish. On the short side, he was five foot three inches tall with a lean build. He sat in a very impressive chair with food and fruit all around him. A servant helped keep him cool with a large feather fan. Two other men stood behind him—a guard and one of his assistants.

"Told you," Keith whispered to Elizabeth.

"I am impressed by your very generous gift to the temple. Not many people give gold. How may I help you?"

"We came here about Jesus," Elizabeth explained.

Caiaphas shook his head in disgust. "That troublemaker. I wish he would go away. He is a thorn in the side and doesn't understand the true ways of our religion. He wants to change everything."

"According to the Torah."

"He thinks he is the Son of God. The only problem is that no one told me. He is delusional."

"Could he be the Son of God?" Elizabeth asked.

"No, he is nothing more than trouble and must be dealt with," Caiaphas insisted.

"You might have more trouble than you think. Way more trouble than Jesus."

"Oh? How is that?" Caiaphas asked.

"He may be accompanied by a strange new woman. One that could make him even more powerful. She is beautiful but controlling. I have come to warn you about her," Elizabeth said.

"Who is this woman?"

"She is from my land. And she has a secret agenda to make Jesus even more powerful than you."

"Many have tried. Many have failed," Caiaphas said, shrugging off her words.

"This one is extra special," Elizabeth insisted. "Exotic and cunning."

"I appreciate your warning and will take it into account. Your gold is up, good day."

Keith and Elizabeth were led out the front door.

As soon as they were gone, Caiaphas spoke to his assistant standing next to the guard. "Keep a close eye on Jesus. If he does have a new friend, I need to know. She could be useful to me and my plans."

"Maybe we could lock her up and see what Jesus does about it. He is always so humble," his assistant suggested. "Maybe a lady might make him different."

"Yes, that could work. Find out. Maybe she is just the right temptress to make him act out in such a way that we can arrest him."

"Yes, my Lord. My Lord, is Jesus truly a danger? I have met him, and he seems to be a peaceful, loving man. I know he is different, but I know he is not evil. Maybe we should just banish him."

"Bah. You know nothing at all. Nor do you take into account that it is expedient that one man dies for the people, so the whole nation does not perish."

His assistant was amazed. "One man could do all that?"

"This Jesus is becoming too popular. I will speak with the elders and decide how to put an end to this madness called Jesus."

CHAPTER

FOURTEEN

Keith and Elizabeth walked into the city of Jerusalem. Compared to modern day, everything looked old and in need of repair. It was hot and dusty. Stopping in the shade of a nearby building, they drank a few sips of water from their water pouches. The city was busy with people going about their daily business, shopping for food, working, and other things.

"See, I told you it would work," Keith bragged. "Works every time, even two thousand years in the past. Guaranteed!"

"That's racist and stereotyping!" Elizabeth said in a huff.

"Actually, Jews are not a race. And yes, it is stereotyping, but it worked. Did it not? You were able to talk with Caiaphas."

"Yes, it did work. Thank you," Elizabeth admitted. "Now, let's go exploring. This is fascinating, and I want to see everything I can in the few short days we will be here."

They continued their exploration, walking down the main shopping area, where everything from goats to clothing, tools, cook pots, and various types of dried food and grains were sold.

"None of this food looks good," Keith said, making a face. "I'll eat when I get back to the ship. Actually, I looked at the supplies, and the food they sent with us is really good. I even saw some wine."

"I wonder how Captain Wagner and Leo are doing. Maybe we should contact them and find out."

At that precise moment a sonic boom ripped across now and the future times.

Keith and Elizabeth felt it, but it was over very quickly.

"Wow, what was that?" Keith wondered. "If I didn't know better, I'd think a jet had just flown past going faster than the speed of sound."

"It must have been some kind of shockwave, but what would have caused it? If you are correct, there is nothing in this time period that could have done that, except maybe a meteor. I sure didn't expect that."

"Nothing that is other than our time ship."

"You don't think…?" Elizabeth asked horrified.

"No. Jennifer would never leave us behind. Now, what were you saying?" Keith asked.

"I wonder how Leo is doing. After all, he decided to go it alone, which was pretty brave."

"Or pretty stupid," Keith said. "The way he's dressed, they'll take him as a common slave. I guess he'll be okay." Neither of them realized all the trouble Leo was having because he did look like a slave. Keith would have found it funny.

Though most people were avoiding Keith, because they thought he was a Roman Solder, a group of boys, ages fourteen through sixteen, appeared from behind and actually bounced into Keith and Elizabeth. Keith quickly surrounded Elizabeth to protect her in case of trouble. They hurried on, and Keith noticed three of them part ways with the others and head down a small walkway, slightly hidden by structures on both sides.

Keith checked himself. "Son of a gun!" His expression turned to one of anger.

"What happened?" Elizabeth asked.

"They took my knife. I love that knife. I had it especially made just for me."

"I warned you about them. We will find or buy you another."

"Oh, no, I want that one. What they don't know around here is that I have a tracer on it. I'll get it back." "You have a tracer on it? The sword, too?"

"Absolutely. I wasn't about to take any chances. Those two weapons cost me a fortune. Besides, you would not want the technology used in making them left behind. Someone might be able to figure it out and wham! There goes your timeline."

"You're right," Elizabeth said. "I didn't think of that. Just be nice. Show mercy and teach them the forgiveness of God."

"Yes, of course. I will teach them religion and the kindness and justice of God. Godly justice actually. Please wait here. I will be right back."

"I am starting to like you more and more. At first, I was a little concerned, but now I know what's in your heart." At least she thought she did, but she couldn't have been more wrong. Keith was a killer at heart, and he always would be. He would never show mercy, compassion, or forgiveness to anyone, especially if they had wronged him.

"My heart is full of God," Keith lied.

Keith entered the walkway and spotted the three boys sitting on a bench, looking calm and easy. As he walked toward them, the first boy whispered something in his friend's ear.

"Look how stupid he looks. Just big and dumb like all of them. We will get a lot of money for that special knife. His loss is our gain. He will never figure it out."

"We should have taken his sword, too, the second boy whispered back. He truly does look stupid." He laughed.

"Did you boys see the thief who stole my knife around here?" Keith asked when he finally reached their bench. "It has to be around here somewhere."

"No, sir," the third boy lied. "No one would dare take a knife from a Roman soldier such as yourself."

There was some space behind them, and Keith moved into it. "Are you sure?"

"Go ahead, search us," the first boy said.

"No need to. I trust your word. Do you swear by your God that you don't have my knife?"

"I swear," the first boy said, slightly laughing.

"You, too?" he asked the second boy.

"I swear."

"Me, too," the third added before being asked.

"That's good to hear. Do you also swear to your God that you do not know where it is, and if you are lying may he strike you dead?"

"This is ridiculous!" the first boy said, angrily. "We do not have your knife. You always try to blame us for your problems. We are not your problem."

"I just wanted to know. I don't want your God making a mistake. Swear on your lives."

"Fine, we do, now leave us," the second boy said.

The other two boys nodded their heads in agreement.

"This is where you find out that modern technology is a bitch!"

Keith pressed his ring and from a small pile of rocks right in front of the second boy came a loud beep from Keith's knife. Keith pulled out his sword and drove it down the neck of the second teenager, forcing it all the way down to the stomach. It killed him instantly. Keith pulled out his sword and reaching down, picked up his knife. The other two boys were horrified.

"We are sorry. Please spare us," the first boy begged.

"I want to," Keith said. "But my knife is upset that you took the Lord's name in vain. You lied."

Keith slashed the throat of the second boy, who crumpled to the ground. The third boy tried to run, but Keith threw his knife. It sunk deep in his neck, killing him.

"Vengeance is mine, saith the Lord." Would those words come back to bite him in the afterlife?

Keith retrieved his knife and wiped the blood off both the knife and sword on one of the boy's clothing before putting them back into their sleeves. He walked back to Elizabeth, who didn't suspect a thing.

"Did you teach them the ways of the Lord?" Elizabeth asked. Had she realized that he had taken her words and used them as an excuse to murder those boys, she would have been frightened and horrified.

"Yes, I did. They will never steal again. I even taught them about heaven."

"You know at first, I wasn't sure about you, but now I am. I know you are on my side. You and I have a lot in common. We will do great things together."

"Greater than you think," he grinned. The thought crossed his mind that he might have changed the future timeline, but he mentally shrugged it off. *Who cares? It won't affect the United States, only this region. Probably won't even notice any difference when I get back.* But it would have a very real effect, in more ways than he could ever imagine.

"What is that red stain on your sword?"

Oops! Must have missed a spot. "I think someone spilled wine on it. I'll clean it off later." He wondered if she could really tell the difference between blood and wine. They were two very different substances with blood being thicker than wine.

Apparently, she couldn't. Forgetting about the boys, Elizabeth went on to say, "I can't believe it all started here. There is where it all began."

"So do you really think that Jennifer could get in the way?"

"I'm not sure, but it's a good possibility. Why did the President pick such a beautiful, young woman to lead us?"

"So that Jennifer might change things?"

Elizabeth became vehement. "She cannot, and she must not! Jesus has a destiny, and it must be fulfilled!"

"Why?"

"Because Jesus died to save us. He paid the ultimate price, so we could have eternal life and a chance of redemption. I feel very sure that if Jesus didn't die for us, God would have destroyed the earth and started over again. He has that much power. He created us to be like him. Without Jesus dying, there would be no heaven for our souls everything would be as nothing. Jesus is everything, life, death, and rebirth." "What is heaven anyway?" Keith asked.

"Peace, calm, and love forever."

"Didn't God command his son to die on the cross? Where's the peace, calm, and love in that?" Keith asked.

"Absolutely not! God felt that it was necessary, but it was up to Jesus to make that decision. He had a choice. He even prayed: 'Father, if you are willing, take this cup from me; yet not my will, but yours be done.' Jesus also said, 'No one takes my life from me, but I lay it down of my own accord. I have authority to lay it down and authority to take it up again. This command I received from my Father.' God wanted to save us from a horrible death and only by his son dying a horrible death could we be saved. For that I am the most grateful person. I would do anything for Jesus."

"Would you give up your life for Jesus?"

If Elizabeth had known what was behind that question, she might have answered differently. "Many times over. I would do anything to make sure that Jesus fulfilled his destiny. Without that destiny, we as a race would be lost and ultimately destroyed. Destroyed by ourselves." "Why is that so important?" Keith pushed.

"Because we as humans need meaning. Meaning to our life and existence, and meaning to why we were created. It is so very important. Without meaning we would be lost and empty." "Why here and in this time?" It wasn't that Keith really wanted to know those answers for any spiritual reason. He asked them because it would help him decide if he had to eliminate Elizabeth and Jennifer.

"Because here and now is the tiny seed that grows into a massive tree. It needed to be at this time so it could keep on growing for the many billions to come in the future. Or if you want to be precise, our present as we know it. There is too much going on in our present, and if Jesus would have waited, it wouldn't have had the same impact. It had to start from the time Jesus was born, so it could affect everybody in the future, and it definitely had to be in this place and time, when the people were in desperate need of salvation. Anything else would not have worked. True faith and belief have to start small in order to grow into something big."

"Is God and Jesus love?" Keith asked.

"Not love as you know it. You don't fall in love with Jesus. You become saturated by the simple love he has for you, just because you are alive."

"Do you think Jesus could fall in love with Jennifer?"

"Right now, Jesus is still a man and to the best of my knowledge, he never had a girlfriend. Jennifer is amazing and magnetic and beautiful. Yes, I believe that she could tempt Jesus. But that must not happen."

"Would God stop Jennifer?" Keith asked.

"That's a good question, because God gave us free will. I think Jesus would know what he has to do no matter what. Still, Jennifer could be a temptation."

"What would happen if Jesus did not die on the cross?"

"Complete and utter destruction of religion as we know it. Something very evil would take its place, and we would be lost forever."

"I never had much faith in the human race."

"Maybe being here will change your mind."

At that moment, Keith knew for certain that he would have to eliminate both Elizabeth and Jennifer to fulfill his mission. Nothing would change his mind. He wanted to prove to the world that religion was all fake, and he would let nothing get in his way.

"I now understand what has to be done."

"This history will not let itself be changed."

"We will see. Come, let's have some fun and explore."

Keith and Elizabeth continued their exploration of Jerusalem. Elizabeth was fascinated by everything around her. She soaked it all up to keep in her heart for the rest of her life. Keith, however, just wanted to get back to the ship, where there was air conditioning and cold drinks.

It was hot as Jennifer and Jesus walked together along a dirt trail that, for the most part, was open ground with very few trees. Trees were special out here, especially in this time period. It was early afternoon, and Jennifer thought about how nice it would be to have an ice-cold beer. And while that would be possible, she would have to go back to the ship for ice, as there wasn't any ice in this region, just a lot of thorns.

They stopped and Jesus pointed to a hill. "Beyond that hill is Nazareth, my home, where my earth family lives. I have four brothers and two sisters."

"Oh, my gosh, I want to meet them!" Jennifer exclaimed. "This is exciting."

"That is good because it is important for me to see them."

"I love family, even though I don't have one of my own."

"Just so you know. None of them look like me, because we are from a different source. Not even my mother, Mary."

"Yes, of course, Mary."

"What do you mean?" Jesus asked her. "Do you know of her?"

Jennifer had to think fast. If she claimed to know her or of her, she would have to explain that she was from the future. And there was no way she was going to do that. "No, of course not. Because of you I want to know everything about you and that includes your family. What do you mean by earth family?"

"You may find this difficult to believe, but my father is not of this earth. He resides way above us."

"Like in the clouds?"

"Much higher." At her puzzled expression, he said, "Take your time. You will learn more later."

"Mary is your earth mother?"

"She is the vessel that bore me, and my mother in every sense of the word. She also gave birth to my brothers and sisters, but they were fathered by my Earth father, Joseph. Sometimes, they are jealous of me, but it is not my fault."

"This is going to be fun and educational."

"Then let us go. I must warn you to beware of what you say to them about me, especially to some of my brothers as they do not fully believe yet."

As they continued walking, some Roman soldiers approached them on the path. Jesus and Jennifer politely stepped aside. Even Jennifer fell in line this time, especially with Jesus by her side. They bowed their heads as the soldiers walked past them. As they passed, Jennifer looked up and noticed that the last soldier in line was carrying a large spear. The soldier carrying the spear was huge for a Roman, standing six foot two and weighing 235 pounds. She thought that was big for a Roman in this time period. She smiled and looked at the soldier carrying the spear. He looked back at her with a very sad look on his face. His spear almost looked like a work of art, very distinctive with a beautiful point. He probably had it specially made just for him, especially since he was so large. The point of the spear caught the sunlight and reflected right into her eyes. Jennifer could not get the spear out of her mind, and it caused a vision, a very strong one.

In this vision, she saw Jesus being nailed to the cross with three iron nails, one nail in each wrist and a single nail driven through both feet with the right foot over the left. Jesus cried out in pain with each blow of the hammer. The soldiers put the nails through the wrists because using the hands would not hold his weight. The nails would rip through the five metacarpal bones that made up the middle of the hand. Blood poured from the fresh wounds. Drops of blood fell on the ground. Jesus was now silent and looked up at the sky. He knew it had to end this way, but he could not figure out why his father had wanted it like this. His hands and feet grew numb, and the pain slowly eased. Earlier when he was beaten, the soldiers had placed a purple robe around Jesus and taking pieces of a small thorn bush that grew almost everywhere, wove a Crown of Thorns and rammed it onto his head. Blood poured from the wounds made by the thorns. Some of the blood fell into his eyes, and he shook his head to get it away.

The soldier with the large spear sadly looked on. His name was Longinus. Somehow and in some way, he had a special feeling for this man. He looked up at Jesus. "I do not understand why, but I know that what we are doing is wrong. I know you are my Lord, and you are greater than any king. Rome is the devil."

Looking down from his cross, Jesus said, "I forgive you, for you have to do what you are meant to do. Someday, you will be with me in heaven."

"It hurts me to see you suffer. I don't know why, but I feel a special love for you."

"Not for me, but for my father. His love is above all."

"There is still so much to learn from you," Longinus said, his voice and expression filled with loss and need.

"And you will," Jesus promised.

"This is not right. Why are we Romans so wrong? Why do we destroy love but not hate?"

"Forgive them. If you do not forgive others, then the Father cannot forgive you."

Longinus looked at Jesus and tears sprang forth from his eyes. He sat down and thought for a while. He now knew the truth and could see the amazing strength in Jesus and the terrible pain he was suffering. He could see the pain, but the one thing he did not see was fear. Jesus was truly amazing. For his whole life, Longinus had been a loyal Roman subject. Now, he had come to realize that Rome was truly evil, and the world would be better off if Rome were destroyed. Everything that Rome touched caused pain, misery, and death. One thing was certain, he would never follow Rome again. He looked up at Jesus and knew what he must do, what he had to do.

Jesus looked up to heaven and said, "Father, forgive them, for they do not know what they do."

Longinus stood up and picked up his spear.

"It is finished," Jesus said.

Longinus walked over and stood in front of Jesus.

Then he spoke his final words. "Father, into your hands I commend my spirit." "Truly, you are the Son of God." Longinus took his spear and stabbed Jesus in the side. Blood and water come out, covering the tip of the spear. Some of the blood reached his hands. From out of nowhere, lightning and thunder filled the air. He looked up at Jesus and saw that he was quiet and no longer suffering. Jesus was dead.

"You will suffer no more, my Lord. I am yours forever."

Longinus kept staring up at Jesus. All the bystanders, many of whom had mocked and jeered the Lord, were quiet except for Mary, who cried, her heart broken at the foot of the cross. The temple veil was torn from top to bottom. Darkness descended upon them from the sixth to the ninth hour, and a rare and strong rain began to fall. Longinus fell to his knees as the rain cleansed the blood from him. The other soldiers left to get out of the rain. What did they care? They knew nothing of the Lord or how great He was. Looking up at the dead body of Jesus, Longinus realized that he now had faith, and that he would see Jesus again someday. His faith would keep him strong. He gently touched Mary on the head. "Love."

With his spear, Longinus slowly walked away. He turned around for one last look, knowing where his life and future were headed. It definitely was not to Rome. Rome was now dead to him.

Jennifer snapped out of her vision, still looking at Longinus.

"Good day, young lady. I have never seen beauty such as yours."

"Thank you, kind sir," she replied. "I am honored."

"You are not from this place."

"That's correct. I am from somewhere far away from here."

Compelled by her exotic beauty, Longinus added, "You belong in a palace, not out here in the sun and dirt."

"I am where I belong," Jennifer assured him.

"For some reason, I feel that I will see you again. Be well."

Forgetting that the Romans did not believe in God, she said, "God be with you."

"I'll take all the help I can get." Longinus caught up to the other soldiers, and they continue their march.

Jennifer stared at the spear. "That soldier has a spear."

"Yes, they use them to kill people. Does that have any special meaning to you?"

"Not yet, and I hope never, if I can help it. I mean that was a really big spear."

"Yes, it surely was big. Let's give it a name," Jesus suggested. "How about the Spear of Destiny?"

"That is a good name. Done."

Jesus and Jennifer continued walking along a steep hillside.

A man with six goats easily walked past them, and just as Jesus had said, everyone knew him.

"Hello, Jesus, good to see you. Your mother will be so happy."

"Hello, San, good to see you, too. Be well."

They approached Nazareth, a small Jewish village of around 400 inhabitants.

"This has been my home for most of my life. Everybody knows everybody, and my earth family lives here."

"What about your father?"

"As I said before, my father does not live on earth. He is in a completely different realm. In fact, he has never even met my earth mother, Mary, although he knows everything about her." "How is that possible?" Jennifer asked.

"With my father, everything is possible."

Jennifer knew that he was speaking about God, but she was trying to straighten things out in her mind. "What about the father of your brothers and sisters?"

"He was a very good man but much older than my mother. He died a few years back, and I took over his responsibilities to the family."

They walked into the village where people were going about their daily business.

Jesus pointed to his house. Sure enough, everybody waved at Jesus, and he waved back.

"They will be both excited and disappointed to see me."

"How is that?"

"You will see."

As they approached one of the mud houses, Jennifer observed it with keen eyes. Before leaving on the time ship, she had studied this very same thing, but in books, not real life. She looked at it closely and knew exactly what it was and what was inside. The house was four two level dwellings made of mud bricks on a stone foundation. In the center was a courtyard, which was exposed to the sun. The courtyard was used for various tasks such as cooking, spinning, and weaving. It was also a meeting place to talk and discuss their plans for the day. An open fire with an oven filled another corner with a mortar and pestle for grinding next to it. Another corner contained stalls for their animals, especially one for the prized goat. Next to it was the family latrine, which was emptied every day at a public waste site.

Inside, the rooms were mostly dark, lit with oil lamps. Mats were rolled up and used at night to sleep on. The ceilings were made with wood that was expensive and sometimes hard to find. If it was really hot, everyone slept on the roof in the cooler night air. Jennifer remembered a verse from the Bible that now meant a whole lot more than it had when she had first read it. It stated, 'Isn't this the carpenter? Isn't this Mary's son and the brother of James, Joses, Judas and Simon? Aren't his sisters here with us?' She even remembered it was from Mark 6:3.

Jennifer could not believe that she was standing in front of the boyhood home of Jesus. Yet here she was, ready to meet the family. She hoped they liked her.

"Mother, are you home?" Jesus called out.

The door quickly opened to reveal Mary. She hugged Jesus. Jennifer looked at Mary and saw a small woman around five feet tall. Actually, Jesus towered over her. She was around 47 years old with graying hair, but still attractive for a woman her age. For this period in time, she would have been considered quite old. She looked strong and firm, with average body weight and a gorgeous smile, especially when she saw Jesus. Jennifer instantly took a liking to her.

"My son, how good to see you," Mary greeted him.

"It is good to see you. Mother, this is my friend, Jennifer. She is not from around here, and I am now her protector. Jennifer, this is Mary."

"She is truly beautiful, Jesus. I had no idea you knew someone such as her."

"I consider her a gift from my Father. For some unknown reason, I feel there is something special about her."

"Jennifer, what a strange name. I have never heard it before." "Hello, I am very pleased to meet you. Actually, my middle name is also Mary, just like yours."

"You have two names?" Mary asked, surprised. "How interesting."

"Actually, I have three, but who's counting?"

"Please come in out of the hot sun. You probably need some water. I will have it brought to you."

They entered the house where Martha, the youngest, was doing chores. She looked up, and when she saw Jesus, she was so excited that she got up and ran to him. "Jesus! My favorite brother! Don't tell the others, but I love you best!" Martha put her arms around Jesus. She looked a lot like her mother but much younger and was easily ten years younger than Jesus.

"Martha, this is my friend, Jennifer."

"I'm very pleased to meet you." Martha looked back at her brother. "She does not look like women around here. Only you could find such a person."

"Pleased to meet you, too," Jennifer said, smiling.

"Martha, get the others and tell them Jesus is here. Hurry! And bring some water."

"Yes, Mother."

Martha left to get the others.

"Jennifer, where are you from? You are so beautiful! I have never seen anyone like you. You are tall for a woman or even a man, for that matter. Amazing."

"I come from very, very far away and actually, where I live, everybody is tall. Well, not quite everybody, but it's quite common."

"What brought you here?" Mary asked.

"I am a student of history, and I am here to learn. You have a very special land full of riches."

"I doubt that. Everybody here is poor."

Miriam, the oldest daughter, entered the room. She politely hugged Jesus and kissed both his hands. "Jesus, my brother, I am honored to see you. You are becoming well known everywhere and that pleases me. Just don't become too well known because that could cause trouble around here."

Miriam looked at Jennifer. To Jennifer, Miriam was somewhat prettier than her sister. She was slightly taller than the other two women with lovely dark brown hair and large, full lips, which helped her look almost exotic.

"Who is this? Is she with you, Jesus?" Miriam asked.

"Yes, she is," Jesus replied. "Her name is Jennifer. Jennifer, this is Miriam."

"Pleased to meet you," Jennifer said.

"You don't know how happy this makes me. For the longest time, I thought that Jesus was a loner. Someone who did not want a woman. I am truly relieved. Thank you."

"Well, basically, we just met, but we are on the way of becoming very good friends, even now."

The brothers, James, Joses, Judas, and Simon, entered the house. Jennifer quickly noticed that as Jesus had told her, they did not even remotely look like him. Much shorter, darker with dark hair and quite ordinary looking. Compared to Jesus, they looked like mutts. Jesus was definitely the pick of the litter. James, the eldest, gave Jesus a hug. Jennifer stood back a little, so the brothers had not noticed her yet, as their focus was on Jesus. Joses, Judas and Simon surrounded Jesus and very lightly hugged him.

"The man of miracles has returned. I hear much of you. I only wish that the man of miracles could perform a miracle and make us rich," Joses said. "Now would that be so difficult? Especially for the Son of God?" "Joses! Do not mock the Lord your God. He is not concerned with wealth, but the riches of the soul," Mary said angrily.

"Well said, Mother," Jesus said. "Joses, you will never learn. Just being alive makes you rich beyond anything."

"Yes, you and your parables," Joses said. "They make sense to you but no one else. Still, it is good to see you. I hope you haven't done anything crazy yet."

"Give him time," Judas said. "I am sure something crazy will happen. Yet, it warms my heart to see you, brother."

"Mother, I still don't understand. Why is Jesus so tall, and we are not? Also why is Jesus so handsome, and we are not? Why does Jesus have beautiful hair, and we do not? Actually, the only thing we have in common is that we are all poor." "That we are," Joses agreed.

"My children! I am so happy that we are all together," Mary said. Clearly, she wanted to change the subject.

Jennifer looked startled as she realized that moments like this would never happen again. This was the last time Jesus and his family would be together. Nothing but pain, sadness, and misery would follow his death.

Joses finally looked at Jennifer. "Now who is this? Do my eyes deceive me? Or is my loving brother finally with a woman? And such an attracted one. Truly amazing."

"I never thought this was possible," Judas said.

"This is Jennifer, from a faraway land. She is here to learn about us. Jennifer, this is James, Joses, Judas, and Simon. In that order." "It is an honor to meet all of you," Jennifer said, smiling. "More than you think. I want to get to know all about you."

"Then let's give her what she wants," James said, grinning. "Come, let us go to the courtyard, light a fire, drink some wine, and talk. I want to know all about this very lovely Jennifer with the exotic name." "Yes, time for wine," Joses agreed. "I have been saving some for a special occasion. What better time than now?" "I'm just pleased it's a woman," Judas added. "Judas, mind your tongue," Miriam scolded.

"Actually, me, too," Simon said.

"Your brother, Judas, that name sounds familiar," Jennifer said. "There is another Judas in my life. You will also meet him. But I am sure that no matter what, he will not be friendly to you." "I make friends pretty easily."

"Not with him you won't," Jesus warned her. "Come, let us celebrate family."

They went out to the courtyard where water was given to Jesus and Jennifer. Jesus stayed very close to Jennifer. They talked for hours. Actually, they were a very happy family with many good memories. They laughed and made fun of each other, ate food and drank wine. Jennifer enjoyed their company and after a while, they discovered that they liked her, too, especially Mary, who thought she was a good influence on Jesus. She hoped that Jennifer would be the one to open his eyes to the idea of loving a woman.

Jennifer laughed a lot, but deep down inside, she knew that if only she could change things, maybe family gatherings could happen again. All she had to do was convince Jesus to live. She knew her mission was not to interfere but after meeting all these real people, it was proving to be more difficult than she had ever believed. She looked at the family and realized that they, too, had dreams just like her.

Later that night, Mary prepared sleeping spots for Jesus and Jennifer. She placed one mat down for Jesus in one corner of the room, and laid down another mat for Jennifer, as far away as possible.

"Goodnight to both of you."

"Goodnight, Mary. You really are an amazing mother and person. You should go down in history as the mother of all time."

"You are so funny, but I really like you," Mary said. "You are different, but at the same time, loving."

"Goodnight, Mother. We will leave early in the morning. Please don't get up for us."

"As if you thought that were possible," Mary said with a smile. "I will see you in the morning."

Mary left the room and Jennifer and Jesus laid down on their mats. Jennifer moved around a bit, trying to find a comfortable spot. It just wasn't possible, at least for her. She was not used to sleeping on the floor with only a thin mat to cushion her body.

"Oh, what would I give for a pillow top," she sighed. "A what?" Jesus asked from his mat.

"Never mind, just something from my land. It's not important."

"Goodnight, my new special friend. I am pleased that you are here."

"By the way, where are the facilities?"

"The what?" Jesus asked. Then it came to him. "Oh, yes, I understand now. Out in the courtyard next to the goat."

"Great, sounds exciting, especially for the goat. Goodnight, Jesus."

Jesus quickly fell asleep, while Jennifer was just too excited to even think about sleeping, maybe she would at some point, but it would be much later. The room was dark, but light from the full moon poked through tiny openings. Hanging on a wall was a small wooden donkey that might have been a toy when the children were young. *Wow. If they knew what toys were like for the kids in the future, it would drive them crazy.* Unable to find a comfortable position, she figured she might as well use the facilities. Getting up quietly, she headed out to the courtyard. She found the latrine and of course, the goat was right there looking at her.

She looked at the goat. "Do you mind? A little privacy would be nice."

The goat watched her for a while longer before getting bored and heading back into her stall.

"Thank you."

Jennifer finished her business and headed back inside to the mat. She laid down but still could not relax. She couldn't believe that she was actually here—two thousand years in the past. All these people were alive right now, and the people in the future did not yet exist. That was weird, unless we all existed at the same time. But that would mean we would have to die at the same time, too. Wouldn't it? Too much to think about. She didn't sleep the night before, so she figured she had been awake for at least 24 hours. Finally, her eyes closed, and she fell asleep. She awoke in the morning when she heard Jesus and Mary talking.

"I have these strange dreams about you," Mary was saying quietly. "You are on a hill with the sun beating down on you. I feel as though someone wants to harm you. You cannot let that happen."

"Mother Mary, my time has come. Soon, I will have to do the bidding of my father. No matter what."

"You are the Son of God. You can do whatever you want. You don't have to...."

Her words dropped off. While she did not know yet what was to happen to her son, her dreams had been filled with things of the past, sayings, more specifically the words that Simeon had said when they had brought the infant Jesus to the temple: "Behold, this Child is appointed to cause the rise and fall of many in Israel, and to be a sign that will be spoken against, so that the thoughts of many hearts will be revealed, and a sword will pierce your soul as well." Those words had troubled her for some time, before fading into the recesses of her memory. Lately, though, they had returned, and she feared they were about to come true.

"It must be done according to my father. I will love you always. This may be our last time together on earth. But later, you will be with me forever in heaven."

Jennifer got up, rolled up her mat, and placed it in a corner. "Ready?"

"Yes." Jesus hugged Mary.

"Goodbye, Mary, it was a pleasure," Jennifer said warmly.

Mary hugged Jennifer. Jesus took Jennifer's hand and was heading toward the door when a voice was heard behind them. Jesus turned around to find all his siblings there.

"Do you think you could leave without saying goodbye?" James asked. "I think not."

Jesus and Jennifer stepped outside into the dim morning light. The sun had not quite reached the distant horizon yet. Jennifer stepped back to give the family a chance to say a final goodbye. Sad and happy all at the same time, a tear formed in one of her eyes. Things were going to change really fast, and she could not help thinking that she did not want that to happen.

"We love you, brother," Miriam said. "We will love you to the end and beyond."

Mary and his brothers and sisters all surrounded Jesus for a family hug. It lasted for over a minute, until Jesus gently broke away. "And know that I am with you always—even to the end of time." Jesus and Jennifer walked away. Jesus looking forward.

"God be with you, Jennifer," Mary called out.

"Thank you. In this rare case, I think that he actually is."

Jennifer looked at Jesus as they walked and wondered what he was thinking.

CHAPTER

SIXTEEN

Jennifer and Jesus left his home and family, heading toward his next destination. It was sad as his family watched, for they did not know that this would be the very last time they would see him before he was crucified. Jennifer knew what was going to happen, and she felt sad. But at the same time, she realized that this was an amazing opportunity to learn from this wonderful man named Jesus. *I am actually with Jesus, the real deal,* she thought. Everything that she had gone through for the last few months had led up to this—all the preparation, studying, and reading had happened as it should have. Now, she was with Jesus. The pictures and paintings she had studied did not look even close to the real thing. No painting could capture the real image, the compassion, and the magnetism of Jesus. Who could compare to the Son of God? Who indeed?

It seemed crazy to her, but here she was, walking with the most important and celebrated person on earth. For over two thousand years, people have been wondering and arguing about what Jesus looked like. Now, out of the billions of people who had lived and died since his birth, she was the one who actually knew that his physical as well as spiritual beauty was beyond that of mortal man. In fact, no man could ever compare to him because he truly was one of a kind. She felt sorry for his brothers, especially having to grow up with him. They never had a chance. Yet Jesus loved them with all his heart. It made her wonder what God looked like. Was Jesus in His image or just what he wanted Jesus to look like, since he was going to have to live among humans?

She could see both God and human in this wonderful man named Jesus, or at least what she thought was God, because nobody really knew. And out of all the people on planet Earth, she, for some amazing reason, had been the one chosen to experience this golden opportunity. Had God planned this? Or had it just been luck? And of course, meeting the actual Virgin Mary, what an experience. She was positively the most loving, kind, and beautiful person she had even met. She was a true angel on earth and absolutely the right mother for Jesus. Jennifer now understood why God had chosen Mary as the vessel for Jesus. It was truly a great choice. Nobody could be better. True beauty did not change even after two thousand years. She would always remember her. Jennifer took one last look at the village as they headed toward Jerusalem. Looking up, she still could not believe how blue the sky was. When she returned to the present, she would never look at the sky the same way again, as this unpolluted purity had ruined her forever. Gazing upon Jesus, she smiled at him. Jesus smiled back.

"Have you ever met your father? I mean your real father?" Jennifer asked.

"You don't meet my father. Rather, you feel him. He is everywhere and always in view if you know how to see him. He has always given me the correct direction."

"I guess fathers are fathers, no matter what."

"Not really," Jesus replied. "At least, not in this case."

"I can always talk to my father and almost always, he is reasonable and sees my point of view. Actually, I think all fathers are like that. It's something they're born with."

"Ah, but my father was not born. He came into existence as he is and always will be. I promise you that you do not have a father like mine! No one does. My father is one of a kind! Therefore, I, too, am one of a kind."

"Okay. I get it. For the moment, no father talk. What were you like as a young child?"

"After I was born, one of our hideous leaders, Herod, ordered his soldiers to kill all the Jewish male children two years old and younger in Bethlehem and its surroundings. He was so cruel. It is strange that he was known as Herod the Great. He should have been known as Herod the Terrible."

"Why did he want to murder those poor children?" Jennifer asked.

"He did not know who I was, but he felt that I would become a serious threat to him and his way of life. He believed that someday I would replace him. He was a fearful man. He had many babies murdered, and there is no place in heaven for him, now or ever."

"Thankfully you survived."

"My earth father, Joseph, was warned by an angel in a dream to take me to Egypt to escape Herod's wrath. After Herod died a most hideous death two or so years later, an angel told Joseph to take me and my mother back to Nazareth. I was too young to remember much of Egypt, except that it was always hot. And of course, we were always on the move, seeking sanctuary from those who would have harmed us."
"Hotter than here?" Jennifer asked.

"Much hotter. When I was old enough, I learned carpentry, while I waited until my father informed me that it was time."

"Time for what?"

"Time to set his people on the road to being saved instead of being destroyed. They needed to relearn the Hebrew Bible, known as the Mikra or TaNaKh, in order to save themselves. They have forgotten so much. The religious leaders no longer know who they are or their purpose. I think humans, in general, are destined to destroy themselves, unless they are shown a way that gives them purpose, going all the way back to Cain and Abel. Is it the same in your land?"

"Even worse than it is here. You are needed everywhere and in every moment of time."

"I think you would call that a reset," Jesus said after a moment's thought. "Humans need to be reset, so they don't kill each other. I am afraid to think about the new weapons that will be developed over time. Everything is made to kill more efficiently. The Romans know so many horrible ways to kill and make people suffer."

"That will never stop as long as they are in power," Jennifer said. "I believe that someday, Rome will fall only to be replaced by something else."

"Rome falling would be a good thing. They have learned many terrible ways to kill people. Have you heard of crucifixion on the cross? It is a most horrific way to die," Jesus said.

"Yes, I have heard of it. Rome knows no mercy," Jennifer agreed. "Their greed reaches out for more and more, and they will never be satisfied, until their empire comes crashing down around them."

"I have seen men crucified, and it tears at my soul and angers me every time. And I am not an angry person. They nail your hands and feet to a wooden cross and wait for you to die. And while you do, they laugh and make fun of you as you hang there in agony, until finally, they break your legs. Left with nothing to support your weight, you suffocate and die. I truly wish my father would abolish this hideous form of death. It is not pleasant."

Jennifer wanted to change the subject, especially the talk of crucifixion. She could not bear to think of Jesus dying in such a manner. It was just too much to bear. They walked for several paces before she spoke again.

"But this is pleasant right now. Isn't it? Look at the beautiful sky."

"You are amazing. I see beauty in the sky and in all of the Father's creations. Not many people bother to look. Their lives are so full of their day-to-day struggle, they miss it. You, however, are different, and I am pleased that you can appreciate that beauty, too." "Everything is beautiful if you look at it the right way," Jennifer said.

"The secret is finding the right way. And you always seem to be able to do that. Is there someone special in your life?" Jesus asked.

"Nope, not yet. Maybe never, but I'm always looking, just not finding, maybe until now."

"Whoever that person is will be lucky, very lucky."

They continued walking along the road when they were approached from behind by two Roman foot soldiers. The soldiers all knew who Jesus was, but seeing him with a strange woman got their attention. They wondered why the woman was walking alongside Jesus, instead of behind him, as was the tradition at that time. In fact, she seemed almost to be leading him. In general, these soldiers liked to cause trouble just for the fun of it. If anybody needed a harsh lesson, they did.

"Jesus, you let a woman walk in front of you?" the first soldier asked. At that time, a woman had to walk six paces behind her husband.

"What do you mean?" Jennifer asked. "In my world, women are equal to men."

"That is crazy! Not in Rome," the second soldier said. "Woman, know your place, get behind him now!"

"Please, she is not from here but from a different place with different customs. She is a proud and strong woman, and we are not in Rome."

"For the King of the Jews, this is a disgrace," the first soldier said. "You Jews have no respect or pride. What kind of a woman is she? I've never seen anything like her. Her skin is so white. Pathetic!"

Jennifer pulled back her hood and gave the soldiers the finger.

"What is that? Is that supposed to hurt me? It doesn't," the first soldier mocked.

"I think it is a sign of trying to learn respect," Jesus offered. If he had known what it really meant, he would have been shocked.

"Blatta, blatta, blatta! Femina blatta!" the second soldier jeered.

The soldiers laughed hysterically.

Jennifer turned to Jesus. "What is he saying? What does this blatta mean?"

"I'm trying to be polite, but he is basically calling you a... cockroach."

Jennifer's anger boiled over. "A what?"

"Actually, it's worse. He is calling you a female cockroach. Not high praise around here."

Now, Jennifer seriously wanted to punish the soldiers. Jesus tried to calm her. But she kept staring at the soldiers in anger. Jesus had no idea what Jennifer's capabilities were. He just wanted her to stay out of trouble.

"Cover your head and look down, woman! Are you a harlot? Only harlots fail to cover their heads. How dare you! I expect where you came from your father did not teach you proper respect or manners. You need some serious lessons. Maybe I will teach you."

Jesus did not want any trouble, especially from Roman soldiers. Being from a different place, he feared that she did not realize what kind of trouble she could bring upon herself. He gently turned her to face him and looked into her eyes. "Please, cover your head and look down. Please. No more trouble today. I do not want Rome angry at me. They will show no mercy. They will hurt you and laugh, and they never get punished."

"You know, a few days ago I met some people just like them. They had to learn the hard way," Jennifer replied stubbornly.

"Please!" Jesus quietly implored her.

Jennifer slowly covered her head and lowered it as a favor to Jesus. "Thank you."

"Now that's much better," the first soldier said haughtily. "Maybe you can teach her some respect. At first I thought she was just stupid."

Jennifer's eyes lit up with anger. She stared at the soldiers, her hands becoming fists at her side.

"There it is again," the second soldier said angrily. "Now we are going to beat you."

Jesus stepped in front of Jennifer. "Please, if you are going to beat anybody, beat me. I won't resist."

"Where is the fun in that?" the first soldier said. "I want a little resistance. I hear you like to turn the other cheek. Not this time."

The soldier pulled his arm back to slap Jesus. Suddenly, Jennifer stepped in front of Jesus and sternly faced the two Roman soldiers. The soldiers looked at Jennifer and started laughing.

The first soldier said to Jesus, "You would shame yourself as a man and let a common woman defend you?"

"It is not me that she wishes to defend, but herself and her honor," Jesus replied.

"Look at her," the second soldier sneered. "She couldn't defend a goat."

"By the will of God, please leave us alone. Why do you always hate so much? Show some peace and calm."

"At first, I was going to let this go," Jennifer said. "But you have crossed the line. It's time for a little Roman stew."

"Jennifer, I will not let them harm you," Jesus insisted. "If I have to call upon the power of God, believe me, I will."

A reading from the Bible popped into her head. "You shall not put the Lord your God to the test."

Jesus was startled to hear his own words quoted back to him. "How could you possibly know about that?" He thought about the incident. After being baptized by John the Baptist, he had gone into the Judaean Desert and fasted for 40 days and nights. At that time, Satan came to him and tried to tempt him. After refusing each temptation, Satan departed, and he had returned to Galilee to begin his ministry. Very few people knew about it.

"I could never allow you to do that. If you wouldn't give in to the devil's temptations, you should not do so for me."

She was right, and as much as he wanted to protect her, he knew he would have to find a different way.

"I will show you how pathetic and weak you and your miserable God are," the second soldier said angrily. "Your God cannot compare to our mighty Roman Gods. After I rid you of this slug you call a woman, I will beat you so you will never hide behind a useless and pathetic woman again. What kind of a man are you? Have you no shame? What are you?"

"A man who understands peace, the meaning of life, and the power of love. We will leave, and you will not see us again, as my father has not given you the power over me yet."

"Really? No, that is not going to happen," the first soldier said. "I hope you love the beating you and your pitiful woman are going to get!"

The soldiers moved toward them. As Jesus tried to protect Jennifer, she moved as fast as lightning and kicked both soldiers in the head. Then she continued kicking them over and over again. The soldiers were helpless against her. She hit both men in the chest, knocking them to the ground. The soldiers were temporarily knocked out. When they regained consciousness, Jennifer went to each man and kicked them over and over, until one soldier raised his hand.

"Please show mercy!" the first soldier begged.

"Why should I? You never show mercy. How about this!" Jennifer slapped both soldiers numerous times in the head. Until, the second soldier screamed out, "We surrender! We surrender!"

"All right, I accept your surrender. My condition is that I never hear or see you again. Agreed? Or do you want to let me finish what I started, because I would love that."

"Agreed!" both men said at once.

"Good!" Jennifer said. "Now stay on the ground until we are a good distance away. Don't move."

"I can barely move. It is going to be a while before either of us gets up," the first soldier groaned.

"If you're lucky, you will never see me again. Ever!" Jennifer shouted.

"Nothing would make me happier," the second soldier said. "Please leave."

Jesus was amazed and speechless as they walked away from the soldiers. He had never seen a woman or anybody, for that matter, fight like that. She had taken out two Roman soldiers as though they were nothing more than children. He wondered, where and how she had learned to fight like that.

"We had better get out of here. They could cause us a lot of problems." She glanced sidewise at Jesus. "I am sorry, but they needed that lesson."

"I agree. You are truly a warrior. I have never seen such skill from a man or a woman. I do not believe, however, that you need to worry about those two. If those soldiers went back to their captain and told them they were beaten and knocked out by a woman, the Captain would whip them and then cruelly execute them as a lesson to the other soldiers. That is a shame no Roman soldier could bear. We will never hear from them again. I am so proud of you."

"I know you prefer peace, but sometimes it doesn't work."

"Where and how did you learn to fight like that?" Jesus asked.

"Oh, here and there. I am pretty good at picking things up."

"Maybe my father sent you as my protector. Another great gift."

"And maybe he sent you as a generous gift to me." Jennifer knew there was a bigger, more important reason for Jesus' presence on Earth, but right now she did not want to think about that, because in her heart, she really wanted it to be for the first reason.

"In the future, please try nonviolence first."

"That is always my way," Jennifer assured him.

"Still, it was wonderful and amazing to see. Although it was enjoyable, once is enough. I almost felt like cheering in glory. Maybe Rome will one day fall. Especially if they meet more people like you."

Jennifer shook her head. "No, it will be people like you that will teach us that there are better ways than violence. Unfortunately, some people never learn, and violence is the only way to stop them, for nothing else will."

"I am meeting you at just the right time," Jesus said. "Maybe you are more of a teacher than I am, although in a much different way." "No," Jennifer disagreed. "You are the main teacher, and there is much for you to teach."

"Then I am very lucky to have you as a student—a student who even knows how to fight. That is a bonus."

Jesus put his arm around Jennifer's back as they walked toward Jerusalem. As he headed into his final days as a man, he would be engulfed in things that were not going to be pleasant. And he had much work left to do.

CHAPTER

SEVENTEEN

Jennifer and Jesus walked into Jerusalem. She was still astounded that she was actually back in the same city she had visited only a few weeks ago. She had not expected this much change, but it was vastly different and a lot smaller. It reminded her of the story that big things often came from small beginnings. She knew the city currently had about twenty-five thousand inhabitants living within its walls. Seeing it, made it even harder to imagine that two thousand years later, it would hold over a million, but it was true. If only these people could see Jerusalem in the 21st century.

After passing the main gate, the first thing Jennifer noticed was the Temple, a wonderful magnificent building. It was definitely one of the wonders of the ancient world. Reconstructed by Herod the Great, it could accommodate thousands of people, and it was a powerful statement of the Jewish people. It didn't look ancient. It actually looked new. Then it hit her. *Of course, it looks new, I am back in time!* Servants were cleaning it constantly. The Temple was actually bigger than she had thought, for it took them over ten minutes to walk around it. Jesus had grown up with it, but it was new to Jennifer because in 70 A.D., the Romans had completely destroyed it.

Except for the temple, the rest of Jerusalem was plain and simple, small structures not well built and actually not very pretty and dust everywhere. There were a few larger structures but for the most part, everything was small. Jennifer guessed it was easier to build smaller. Then she thought, What a great movie set. For once, it wasn't too hot, and there were plenty of people doing various tasks, including selling anything that people might want to buy in a number of small shops and stands, almost like a future shopping mall. Just like in modern times, everyone needed to make a living. As a herd of sheep passed them, Jennifer reached out to pet one. And it actually didn't seem to mind. It rubbed itself against Jennifer, wanting more attention.

The sheepherder recognized Jesus. "Good day, Jesus, nice to see you. I hope you have more wonderful teachings planned for us."

"Good day to you, sir. I recognize you. You have listened to many of my teachings."

"In a world of confusion, you are the only one who makes sense," the sheepherder said. "I am truly honored for that. I look forward to your next lesson, and I plan on bringing more friends with me. You are becoming more popular every day."

The sheepherder looked at Jennifer. "Has God sent you a beautiful angel from heaven? I have never seen anyone like her. She is incredible. Where is she from? Definitely not from around here or any place I know."

"I think my Father may have. She is truly a gift," Jesus replied.

"Thank you," Jennifer said. "You're making me blush."

"Jesus, you are the son of God. This woman looks like the only woman who could be with you. Good day, Rabbi. I will see you again soon."

Jennifer looked at Jesus. "Everybody knows and likes you."

"Not everybody. The chief priests and elders have a problem with me and refuse to believe when I say, 'I am the light of the world. Whoever believes in me, even though he dies, will have eternal life."

Jennifer did not understand. "That is a powerful statement. Why don't they believe it?"

"Because they have forgotten the true meaning of the scriptures. I am trying to reteach them before I am no longer here to do so."

"What do you mean, no longer here?"

"My Father will soon call me to His side," Jesus said. "Can't you just go to him and visit but come back?"

"I'm afraid it's not that easy. I must give up my earthly body to go where he is." "In that case, don't be in a hurry. It took a long time for the chief priests and elders to lose their way, and it may take them a long time to find their way back."

"That is one of the reasons why I came here."

"I understand," Jennifer said. "You must help them find the proper path." Her eyes, however, had not been fully opened yet. Like the disciples, she understood his greatness, but not the full reality of who he was.

"Yes, but it is more difficult than you can imagine, because they believe that I am a danger to them and their ways. They have become more concerned with the ways of man, and have forgotten the ways of God."

"All you can do it try and leave it up to them. They have a choice, but sometimes people never make the correct one."

Jesus realized that Jennifer did not understand, partly because she was not Jewish. His people had lost their way. They needed a good shepherd. They needed him to guide them back to the Father. But his time on Earth was coming to a close. He would have to make the ultimate sacrifice. But even that would not be enough to sway them all. Many, both Jews and those of other faiths, or no faith at all would come to believe, and they would multiply like the stars in the heavens. Others would remain held fast by their closed hearts and false deities. Regardless, the Jewish people were still God's chosen ones.

"I need to speak with the elders in a place where you will not be welcome or allowed to enter. I hope that does not offend you."

"Of course not," Jennifer responded. "I know your customs here are different, and I would not wish to intrude upon them. I will be happy to wait for you."

"It won't take long. It's here in the temple. I need to stop some trouble before it begins." He gave her a weary smile. "Such is my life."

"Tell you what. I'll go exploring and meet you at the Temple gate. How long will you be?"

"Not more than an hour, maybe less."

Jennifer looked around. "Looks like that's about all the time I will need." "Please be careful. There is danger even here."

"You saw what happened to those two Roman soldiers. I'm very good at taking care of myself."

"Even I was impressed. But please don't hurt anybody. I still want to know where you learned how to fight like that. I have never seen such a thing."

"Like I said. I pick up things pretty fast. Do you want me to purchase something for lunch?" Jennifer asked.

"That would be nice." "What do you want?"

"How about some bread?"

"I thought you were going to say that. Tell you what. Let me decide and surprise you."

"You are already the most wonderful surprise I have ever experienced."

"Take care of your business. I'll be fine."

"Yes, I know. But I will still ask my father to watch over you and give you protection."

"Okay. That's an offer I can't refuse. Protection it is, no matter how it happens." "How is it that I have never met you before? It's like you are a part of me I have been missing my whole life. Where have you been?"

"Out of sight but not out of mind," Jennifer said. "You are also a part of me that has been missing my whole life. Be well and wise."

When Jesus entered the temple, Jennifer left to walk down a narrow road with street venders selling on both sides. She stopped and talked with one seller, who offered dried fruit.

"Where do the rich people shop, or is it here?"

"No, the rich have a special market near the east end of the Temple," the vender said. "You can't miss it because not many people can afford to go there, so it is never busy. They even sell beef there."

"Is the beef good?"

"They say it is very good, but only for Kings and the very rich. It's way too expensive for me. I have never tasted it. They even have eggs," the woman said. "Maybe you should shop over there. Someone as beautiful as you could just smile and get whatever she wanted."

"Thank you, but I think I like it over here better."

She purchased some fruit and continued walking until she spotted an old lady looking at the variety of food for sale. Jennifer could tell that she was hungry and from the way she was dressed, she had little to no money. She decided that the woman would not go hungry today and maybe for months. She removed a number of silver coins from her pouch and handed them to the lady. "Here, enjoy the food from this market. Do not go hungry."

The old woman stared in amazement at the coins in her hand. She had never seen that much money at one time. And she certainly never ever believed that some stranger would just walk up and hand it to her. She was overjoyed. "You are a gift from God. Thank you! Thank you! Thank you! I will pray for you. You are as beautiful inside as you are outside." The old woman kissed Jennifer's hand, after carefully placing the coins in a small coin pouch that previously had held only one small coin.

"Go shopping."

"By your love, I will."

The woman left, but Jennifer's kind gift had not gone unnoticed. Four men standing nearby had observed the whole thing. They surrounded Jennifer.

"You are not from here. We are starving, too," the first man said. "Maybe you can help us as well."

Jennifer gave them the onceover. "You are not starving and are dressed pretty well. You do not need my help. She did."

"It might be in your best interest to help us, too. If you know what's good for you," the second man said. "We would not want any harm to come to you."

"I still say no. Good day to you."

"You had your chance," the third man said. "You are not going anywhere."

"You want me to yell for help?"

"No one will help you out here. Nobody cares what happens to other people, even when it's one as beautiful as you. It's best to just give us what we want."

Jennifer stepped back, ready for a fight. "You're going to have to take it." "As you wish," the first man said with a grin.

Jennifer moved behind a large wooden pole, and the four men tried to surround her. Suddenly a spear sank into the pole, slicing into it like a knife through bread. Surprised, Jennifer looked at it. It was the Spear of Destiny. Glancing to her left, she saw Longinus, who easily pulled out his spear and faced the men.

"This lady is under my protection!" he shouted. "Anything happens to her, and you will answer to my spear. Leave and never bother us again. Now!"

The men were horrified. Longinus was a Roman soldier, one of the largest men they had ever seen, and his spear was huge.

"We greatly apologize! Please forgive us," the third man apologized. They bowed their heads and quickly left.

Longinus turned to face Jennifer. "I told you I would see you again. Greetings, beautiful lady."

"You are my protector. I am honored. Very nice to see you again. I see you are alone. Could we talk for a few minutes?" Jennifer asked hopefully. "Yes, there is some shade and seats over here. Come. Let us sit."

Jennifer and Longinus sat on some wooden chairs in the shade. The shop owner approached to see if they wanted anything.

"Two cups of your best wine for my friend and I," Jennifer said with a smile.

"Right away, beautiful lady."

The shop owner quickly left to fetch the wine.

Jennifer turned to her rescuer. "First of all, my name is Jennifer." She put out her hand for Longinus to shake, but he grabbed her wrist in the Roman greeting.

"Longinus at your service."

"When I first saw you on the trail, I felt a sadness coming from you. Was I mistaken?"

"No, you were right. I have never heard the name Jennifer before. Where are you from?"

"Up north. Way up north."

The shop owner brought the wine and set two cups down in front of them. Jennifer motioned for Longinus to drink, which he did, taking a healthy swallow.

She then handed the shop owner a coin. "Keep the change."

Impressed, the shop owner said, "Thank you! Thank you! Thank you!"

"This is good wine," Longinus said appreciatively. "Thank you. A very welcome surprise."

"You are very welcome," Jennifer said. She turned to the shopkeeper. "Longinus and I are grateful."

As soon as the man left to tend to another customer, Longinus said, "I know of the man you are with. He is very special. I have been watching him for a while. He is more than a man. I feel a godly presence about him."

"As do I. Which is why I want to learn from him."

"Be warned. There are people who would do him harm, to you as well if you follow him. And I'm not just talking about the Romans."

"But there is so much I want to learn about him."

"Listen, Jennifer, I am Roman, but this man tells me that he is truly the One. The One true God."

"Don't Romans believe in a lot of gods?"

Longinus shook his head in disgust. "It is all a joke. There are no Roman gods. Never have been. Everything was made up to give us meaning. This man has meaning."

"Won't you get into trouble with your fellow Romans?" Jennifer sipped her wine.

"I would not say this to anyone else, but for some reason I feel I can trust you. Soon I will no longer be a Roman. I need a different path. This man is the right path. I need to follow his way and his teachings."

"You are very special, and I feel that you and I have a purpose in all this. It's funny a woman on one side, and a Roman soldier on the other."

"When I first saw you, it wasn't just your beauty that drew my attention. It was something else."

"That's funny," Jennifer said. "We gave your spear a nickname." Longinus right eyebrow lifted slightly. "And what is it?"

"The Spear of Destiny."

"I like it. I really do. I had it specially made just for me." He smiled. "I need to get back to my duties, but it has been an honor to talk with you. The Spear of Destiny, very nice. Thank you again for the wine."

Longinus drank the remainder of his wine and set down his cup. Jennifer handed him hers, motioning for him to drink it, which he quickly did.

"I will watch over you, beautiful Jennifer. I know I will see you again."

"Same for me. You are my special protector. I believe that God is looking out and has a special purpose in mind for you."

Longinus left, and Jennifer continued exploring. She stopped at another vender and picked up some bread for herself and Jesus. Then she returned to the temple entrance to wait. Before long, she saw Jesus in the distance, walking toward her.

"How did your talk go?" she asked when he reached her.

"They are stubborn, but I won't give up. Instead of being willing to learn, they are too busy trying to trip me up—always looking for ways to persecute me. What did you get us to eat?"

"Fresh bread and dried apricots."

"Exactly what I wanted," he said to Jennifer. "Come. Let's find somewhere to sit and eat."

They walked a short distance before settling into a couple chairs. The same shop owner, still pleased with the money he had received from Jennifer, brought them two cups of wine.

"My gift to you."

"Thank you," Jennifer replied.

She and Jesus drank some wine.

"This is excellent wine. Just what I needed," Jesus said.

Jennifer handed Jesus some of the bread and apricots. "Bread sounds great. Better than beef."

"Trust me. No one here has ever had beef, except the wealthy," he told her. "Maybe it's about time they should. By the way, God did send me a protector, just as you said."

"Really, who?"

"The Spear of Destiny."

"Please tell me as we eat," Jesus said, tearing off a hunk of bread. "I hope you didn't cause any damage."

"Not to worry. Four men tried to rob me. That's when Longinus stepped in. He didn't hurt anything, except maybe a wooden pole. At least not much. Actually, it was a good day for me."

While they ate their food, Jennifer told him about Longinus.

CHAPTER

EIGHTEEN

After lunch, Jennifer and Jesus left Jerusalem, heading for the home of Lazarus, who lived in Bethany, a small village in Judaea located two miles east of Jerusalem. As they walked along a trail, Jennifer saw donkeys, horses, and camels, and realized that these animals were the main source of transportation. Cars, trains, and jets were a long way off in the future. Nobody here, except maybe Jesus, would ever be able to understand that. Walking was the number-one mode of transportation. She thought to herself that because of that, everybody should be in good shape. She realized that not many people were overweight around here. In fact, she could not recall seeing more than one or two people with even a mild weight problem. Of course, their diet also played a major part in keeping them at a healthy weight. And she also realized that those with a serious weight problem might only be found among the rich.

"Where are we going?" Jennifer asked.

"To my friend Lazarus' house, where we will spend the night. He and his sister Mary will be happy to see us and will treat us well. It's not much further to Bethany."

"It will be nice to relax for a while. Thank you, my new and special friend. You have treated me well, and I am pleased and grateful."

"Yes, especially after the way you handled those Roman soldiers," Jesus said teasingly.

Walking alongside a small lake with a tiny island in the middle, Jennifer thought it would be nice to feel the cool water against her skin. "Let's swim to the island." She stopped and looked at him. "You can swim. Can't you?"

"Yes, I can, but there is no need. We can walk to the island."

Jennifer was speechless, but knowing the stories of Jesus walking on water and not necessarily believing them, she did not want to embarrass him. "No one has ever walked on water, so far as I know."

"Then let me show you." Jesus picked up a rock about the size of his hand and threw it into the water. It sank as soon as it hit the surface.

"The rock has no balance and will always sink."

"The rock is too heavy and dense," Jennifer argued.

"No, it just has no balance. Weight is not the problem. Look at how heavy the ships and boats are that float upon the water. Even the smaller ones are heavy when they weighted down with a good day's catch. At times, the fish are so many that they come close to overbalancing the boat. Now watch this."

Jesus removed his sandals and stood still for a moment. Closing his eyes, he began a meditation process. He began breathing deeply through his nose, and then gently expelled it through his mouth. Reaching a calm state of mind, he stepped into the water. But to Jennifer's amazement, Jesus did not sink, but walked on top of it. He walked about twenty feet across the lake, turned around, and waved at Jennifer.

"Come on in."

What the heck, she thought. *I'll try anything once.* Jennifer copied Jesus, breathing deeply through her mouth and exhaling through her nose a few times. When she felt calm, she stepped into the water and quickly sank. Rising to the surface, she started treading water. "How are you doing that?"

"I have really good balance. Basically, I'm just floating on top of the water like a ship. I learned it very young. I am amazed that no one else has ever been able to learn how to do it. I am the only one so far." Jesus walked back to dry land followed by a wet Jennifer. "You are definitely one of a kind, so full of wonders. I think I'm beginning to fall for you."

Maybe it was the modern terminology that kept Jesus from understanding what she meant. When he replied, he said, "I think if I had more time, I could teach you. But my time is limited."

"Maybe not," Jennifer insisted. "Maybe you'll have more time than you think to teach me." At least she hoped so with all her heart and soul. She had finally found a man who respected her for who she was—and not only cared about her, but listened and respected her like she was worth listening to, and not just a pretty face. And now that she had found him, she did not want to let him go. She especially did not want him to die on a cross.

"What is written in the stars cannot be changed," Jesus said sadly.

"I used to think like that, but things are very different now."

"I'm just happy and pleased to have this time with you. You are unlike anyone else I have ever known and actually, I find that I am also learning from you. You are so brave and fearless, and so confidant."

"Then let's be brave together."

Jennifer hugged Jesus, and he did not want to let her go. Without even trying, Jennifer had had quite an effect on him. They walked for another hour until they reached the home of Lazarus. For the time period, it was a very nice house, owned by a slightly wealthy man. Jesus knocked on the door. Lazarus, an older man with a full beard, opened it and smiled broadly. Lazarus owed Jesus a great debt.

"Jesus, my friend and savior, welcome!" He enveloped Jesus in a bear hug. Lazarus had been waiting all day for his arrival. And he could not be more thrilled to see him.

"Greetings. This is my friend, Jennifer."

"She is welcome, too, and a beauty for the ages. Like no other," Lazarus declared.

"Yes, she hears that a lot," Jesus replied.

Jennifer greeted him with a smile. "Hello."

"Please come in and sit. You must stay the night, my friends. I don't get to see you as often as I would like, my Lord, but I know you have important work to do. I will tell my sister, Mary, to prepare for you." Jesus and Jennifer sat on a bench covered with hides for comfort.

"This is going to be a special night," Jesus told her. "I will be anointed, and I want you to join me in this process." "Why anointed?"

"It is to prepare me for my special journey that is about to happen. You, too, have a separate but special journey that you will make. So, I want you to join me."

"I am honored."

"You are also going to meet some of my disciples. Judas, whom I warned you about, Peter, and John. They will be here soon."

"I'm sure I will like them all."

"Not Judas. He will not be pleased seeing me with a woman, especially one such as you."

Lazarus' sister Mary entered the room. Jennifer noticed that she had a very kind face, and she knew instantly that she could trust her. She had a beautiful loving smile, especially when looking at Jesus.

She gave Jesus a long, fierce hug. "Jesus, the one who will save us all. I am honored."

"I am also honored to be with you," Jesus replied. "This is my dear friend, Jennifer. She is teaching me about bravery and is very special to me."

"Then she is also special to me," Mary replied, smiling. "And such beauty I have never seen. Welcome to our home."

"So, it seems, as everyone who meets her says so," Jesus said with a grin.

"I have everything prepared. Afterwards, we will have a feast. The oil is fit for a king or even a god."

"Mary, I would like to have Jennifer by my side and also anointed."

"Of course!" She paused. "But what is Judas going to say?"

"Like always, Judas will say what he wants to say," Jesus said.

"Sometimes a little too much."

There was a knock, and Mary opened the door for Judas, Peter, and John. Jennifer examined them as they entered the house, surprised over how young they were. Judas looked like a teenager. Peter and John were definitely in their early twenties. She had always envisioned them as being old, but that probably was because all the pictures and statues she had seen of them had depicted older men. The three disciples greeted Jesus as he stood before them.

"Judas, Peter, and John, my special little ones. How are you?"

"We are well, Master," Peter replied. "We are grateful and thank you, Lazarus, for your special invitation."

"You are most welcome. You will all spend the night. I insist." "That is truly generous of you," John said.

At that moment, Judas noticed Jennifer and, in his opinion, she was standing a little too close to Jesus. He instantly did not trust or like her and could not understand why this woman was with Jesus, and who had brought her here. Certainly not Jesus. He was even a little jealous as he did not want to share Jesus with anyone.

"Jesus, who is this woman, and why is she standing next to you, almost touching you, especially considering the occasion?"

John took that moment to really look at Jennifer. "Oy, she is truly beautiful."

Jennifer smiled at him but looked strangely at Judas, since she knew what he was going to end up doing. But of course, she could not tell anybody, including Jesus.

"John, Peter, Judas, this is my special friend, Jennifer. She is from a distant land." "Just how special? Should I be concerned?" Judas asked.

"Pleased to meet you all. I look forward to getting to know each of you." "Why is she here?" Judas demanded. "Why are you with a woman?"

"She was sent from the Father to be strong and show strength by my side for what is about to happen."

Mary entered the room. "It's time. Jesus and Jennifer, please lay on this couch. Take your sandals off and get comfortable. I will wash your feet."

Jesus and Jennifer laid down on the couch and took off their sandals. Mary carefully washed their feet, while Lazarus, Peter, and John went to the dining area and sat on chairs by the table, which had been prepared for the feast. Judas stayed behind, and Mary pulled out a vial of oil that he instantly recognized.

"That is the most expensive oil in all the land. You could feed hundreds of poor for what that costs. Hundreds!" Judas said angrily. But was he really angry about the plight of the poor, or was it simply jealousy?

"The Son of God is worth thousands of hundreds," Mary responded calmly.

Judas noticed that Jennifer's feet were also being cleaned. "Wait a minute. She is getting it, too!"

"Yes, she is with me," Jesus said.

"This is insane."

"Please, Judas, let them be anointed," Peter called over. "Think of the bigger picture."

"Don't worry. You will never lose Jesus," John added. "Much is yet to come. Just love him for what he is."

Mary now went back and forth between Jesus and Jennifer's feet. Rubbing and massaging each foot carefully, while applying a very goodly amount of oil. Actually, to Jennifer the oil did not smell very good.

"Such waste," Judas carried on, refusing to be quiet about the matter.

Jesus looked at Jennifer. "This is the finest oil in all the land. There is nothing else like it."

Jennifer, who was used to the finest salons in L.A. and always having really good oil used on her body, calmly told Jesus the truth as she saw it. Unfortunately, Judas also heard it.

"Sorry, but I've had…better. I mean this is still good, but I am a bit spoiled when it comes to oils. Truly, though, this is still good."

Jesus looked at her and shook his head no, trying to delay the inevitable. Everything changed at that moment, when Jennifer proclaimed that she had had better, Judas changed his attitude, too. He was now angry at Jennifer for thinking that she was too good for the oil used on Jesus and saying that she'd had better. In his mind, that was an insult to both of them.

Judas stared at her sternly. "What did you say? What did you say, woman?"

"I'm not going to lie. I've had better," she replied with a shrug.

"There is no better! How dare you! You think you're just too good. I barely know you, and I can tell that because you are so beautiful, you think you can get away with anything. Not with me. Not a woman."

"I can tell that," Jennifer said. "All I said is that I have had better. It's not an insult, just a simple statement of truth, and it definitely had a better scent. Just a little."

"You think you're too good!" Judas continued ranting. "So, it is good enough for Jesus but not for you. You are arrogant."

"Jesus, you were right about him," Jennifer said, turning to him. "I never said that I was too good. Just that I've had better. Judas, I hope you can hang around long enough to find out."

"Do you have no common sense? Wait a minute. That's a mistake. Clearly, you have no common sense. It is the best oil in the land. There is nothing better," Judas insisted.

"Not in my book."

"Are you out of your mind? You know how much that cost? More than I make in a year."

"Then I would have to say that you are considerable underpaid, by a lot."

Jesus was laughing in the background. He could not remember anyone capable of frustrating Judas this badly.

"I now fully understand why you are here in our land," Judas went on. Surprised, Jennifer asked, "You do?"

"Yes, you were probably cast out of your land for being arrogant and stubborn. Not especially nice traits for a woman."

"Yeah, Judas, that must be it. We all can't be like you. You know, the kind of person you can trust with your life."

"You know, maybe that money should have been used for the poor," Judas said.

"Yes, plenty of silver to go around. I hear you like silver?"

"What a waste you are. If it's good enough for Jesus, it is way too good for you.

Are all the people, who come from your land, as arrogant and stupid as you?"

"Yes! And I thank God for that."

Judas again stared sternly at Jennifer.

"Take a picture, it lasts longer!" As soon as the words left her mouth, Jennifer quickly realized that she had said something she should not have been said.

"What is a picture? Another one of your arrogant sayings?" Jennifer tried to cover her mistake. "Forget it. Just keep staring."

"By the way, what is your land called?" Judas asked.

"California," Jennifer replied without thinking.

"What a stupid name. Sounds like a crazy place. Cal…i.. forn…ia. Sounds like a place where crazy people live."

"Actually, in some ways you may be right. Still, it's home."

Judas laughed. "Land of the insane. I never want to go to that place."

"Like I said. You won't hang around long enough. Don't worry about it." "One more thing that makes no sense, also crazy!"

"It was my sincere hope that you two would become friends," Jesus said with a sigh.

Jennifer shook her head. "No, no way. I have known too many men like him. They can't be fixed."

"I will not lower myself to her standards. It would be lower than hell. Besides, it would take your greatest miracle. And I think that miracle is even beyond you."

"Such words of encouragement. Judas, you really are a peach," Jennifer said.

"What is a peach?" Judas asked.

"Forget it. I meant pomegranate."

"I like pomegranates. Finally, we agree."

"Yes, thick and fruity. No real substance."

"Women such as you are like the wind. Nothing there, but you can feel it. Still empty."

At this point Jennifer had had enough. "You need to get some sleep. Let me help you."

"Oh, no!" Jesus declared.

With her knowledge of martial arts, Jennifer used a karate chop to render Judas unconscious. She gently laid him down on some nearby blankets. "That's much better." She turned to Jesus. "Don't worry. He's fine."

Jesus smiled. "Yes, he finally looks peaceful. Quite a task for him. Let him be. Come, let us enjoy a nice dinner with our friends."

They headed over to the dining table. Mary hurried off to direct the servants to bring the food to the table.

Seeing Judas, John said, "Oh, look, Judas is taking a nap. Good for him."

"I wondered why it was so quiet all of a sudden," Peter added with a grin.

"Actually, Jennifer had a hand in that," Jesus said, smiling at his own pun. "And I must admit. It really did help him go to sleep."

"Glory to Jennifer. You are as amazing as you are beautiful," John said, glad that someone could silence Judas.

"Yes, I am very fortunate," Jesus said. "She is everything and more." "Then Jesus, is she the one?" John asked.

Jesus grabbed Jennifer's hand. "She has always been the one. Now and forever."

"As I am for you," she replied.

"Come, Jennifer," John invited. "Let us talk and feast."

"I have had a very special dinner prepared for tonight," Lazarus declared.

"Lazarus is so nice," Jennifer exclaimed.

"You would be nice, too," John assured her. "Lazarus was dead a while ago, and Jesus brought him back to life."

"What? How is that even possible?" Jennifer asked amazed. In the future, such a thing could indeed be possible sometimes. But back in this time, it was totally impossible. She had read the story, during her studies, but she had thought it was just that—a story.

"With God all things are possible. I am living proof of that," Lazarus said. "Jesus brought me back, and I am eternally grateful and blessed." "Wow. How do to you feel?" Jennifer asked.

"Alive," Lazarus replied joyously with a laugh. "And that is more than enough for me. Jesus is my master and my savior. And I love and adore him."

"This may sound odd, but what was it like being dead?" Jennifer asked.

"I don't know," Lazarus replied. "Except that it was like I had fallen asleep and was awoken by my Lord, which is exactly what happened." "Jesus is eternal life," Peter told her. "His promise is eternal life and salvation, and the love he has for us, and we for him."

"We all love him," Mary said. "Now back to dinner."

"Yes," John said. "Now, Jennifer, tell us all about yourself. Should we wake Judas to join us?"

"I think he has already had more than enough of Jennifer," Jesus said. "Leave him be."

"Yes, there will be plenty of food for him when he awakes," Lazarus assured them.

They sat down and the servants began serving the meal. Of course, bread was the first thing on the table.

The dinner last for hours with wine and plenty of conversation. Judas finally woke up and joined the group, making sure to keep his distance from Jennifer. Actually, Jennifer learned more about the others, than they did about her, as she had to keep her life a secret. Nobody would have believed her anyway. She had a great time.

Later that night, Jesus and Jennifer got ready for bed. And just like the night before, Lazarus' sister, Mary, placed the mats as far apart as possible, just like Jesus' mother, Mary, had done. Judas walked by the door and looked in at Jennifer. Using her fingers and eyes, Jennifer gave Judas the 'I see you sign.' Judas walked away. Once he was gone, Jennifer walked over to where Jesus was and sat behind him. "I want to show you a custom we have in my land." "Show me, please," Jesus replied.

Jennifer started gently massaging his neck, shoulders, hands, and arms. She was astounded at how warm his skin felt.

"What an amazing custom. Yes, this feels very good. Please continue. It relaxes me and makes me feel so much better. You have warm, special hands."

"Not as warm as you. How did you meet Judas, Peter, and John?"

"They are my disciples. There are actually twelve of them. You will meet them all and most will like you. They are just not used to seeing me with a woman, especially Judas."

"Well, they had better get used to it. How did you meet them?" she asked, going back to her question.

"Some were fishermen. Some were farmers. And one was a tax collector. The Jewish leaders really hate him. They asked my disciples, 'Why does he eat with tax collectors and sinners?'"

"What was your answer?" Jennifer asked.

"I came here to call sinners to repent. Those who are healthy do not need a physician. Those who are sick do."

Jennifer nodded in agreement. "I don't know about tax collectors being sinners, but it seems they are hated everywhere. Even in my land."

"Those who became my disciples heard my words and asked if they could follow me."

Jennifer dug even deeper into Jesus' neck and shoulders.

"That is wonderful." He paused a moment before saying, "I told them to follow me, and I would make them fishers of men."

"What about Judas? I think he's jealous of me for some reason. I hope it doesn't make him angry."

"He is always angry but so far, he has proven to be a good person."

"I just don't want him angry at you because of me."

Jesus' expression turned sad. "He will do what he has to do, or what he thinks he has to do. Whether you are here or not, nothing will change. He has been loyal."

"Here, I want to try something on your skin."

"What is it?"

"A special lotion from my land."

In her pouch, Jennifer had brought a few things from her time, placing them in special wrappers so as not to cause alarm. One of them was a high-end body lotion. She rubbed it onto his neck, arms, and back.

She held her hands near Jesus' nose, so he could catch the fragrance.

Before massaging his forehead, "Smell this."

Jesus smelled the lotion and was amazed. He touched the areas where Jennifer used the lotion and was astounded by how it made his skin feel. Jennifer continued the massage.

"What is it? It is what heaven must smell like."

"It's called Chanel."

"I must admit. This really is better, much better. What a wonderful scent. I will sleep well tonight."

Jennifer continued to massage Jesus until he fell asleep. She gently laid him down and walked over to her mat and did the same. She felt safe, especially with Jesus in the same room. Taking a long look at his sleeping form, she smiled and closed her eyes. This time, she quickly fell asleep, and would wake up tomorrow morning ready for a new day.

CHAPTER

NINETEEN

Early the next morning, Jesus approached two of his disciples, saying to them, "Go to the village facing you, and you will at once find a tethered donkey and a colt. Untie them and bring them to me. If anyone says anything to you, you are to say, the Master has need of them and will send them back at once."

The disciples did as Jesus asked. Later when Jennifer woke up, she heard noises coming from outside the room. What she did not know yet was that there were two donkeys outside the front door. At first, she could not remember where she was, but before long, it became crystal clear. They had spent the night at Lazarus' house. Standing up, she noticed that she was alone. *Jesus must be somewhere outside.* She quickly used the outside latrine and returned to find Jesus waiting for her.

"Hello, my angel. We have a special day planned. In this part of the world, it is called Passover. And I would like you to experience it with me."

Jennifer looked out the open door and saw the donkey with her colt.

"I sent John and Peter earlier to fetch them. John always delivers."

"What are the donkeys for?" Jennifer asked.

"It is for an important journey to Jerusalem. We will enter Jerusalem just like King Solomon did many years ago. He had wanted to show the people that he was just as common as they were, so he entered on a donkey instead of a horse. Do you know who he was?"

"Yes, the son of David, the giant killer. David killed Goliath," Jennifer replied.

Jesus turned to Judas, who was standing nearby. "You hear that Judas? Jennifer even knows who King David was and that he killed Goliath. Is there anything she doesn't know?"

"That is wonderful. I am glad you are so enamored with her," Judas said. "But she doesn't know everything."

"That didn't sound very sincere, Judas," John said. "Do any of us really know everything? I don't think so. Otherwise, Jesus would not have to teach us so much."

"Come, we have a great day ahead of us," Lazarus said, hoping to prevent any more arguing. "The people are already preparing for your entry."

"What's going on?" Jennifer asked.

"You and I are going to ride donkeys into Jerusalem," Jesus told her.

Mary approached Jesus and gave him a hug. "You are our savior and Messiah. I love you." Suddenly, she drew back in surprise. "Oh, gracious Lord! What is that amazing scent? I have never smelled anything like it. It is truly divine."

"Chanel, from Jennifer. She brought it from her land. Her land must have many amazing things."

"Judas," Mary declared. "You must come over here and smell this. Jennifer was right in what she had said. It is truly wondrous! Better than anything the best money could buy here."

"I am not smelling Jesus," Judas declared. "That would be disrespectful."

"But I will. If Mary says it is amazing, I must smell it." Peter stepped closer and took a sniff. "Jennifer, we could sell that and make lots of money—a whole lot! It is amazing. Judas, you must take a sniff. It's Chanel from Jennifer."

"I will not!" Judas said, determined not to have to admit that Jennifer was right.

"Then you are truly missing out," Peter said. "It's like nothing I have ever smelled before."

"Come, let us begin our journey," Lazarus said. "I have laid cloaks on both donkeys to make them more comfortable." "Lazarus, you are so thoughtful," Jesus said.

"And you are the giver of life. Nothing could be more. I live and breathe because of you. To say that I owe you my life would be a small statement. I owe you everything including my soul."

Jesus turned to Jennifer. "I have waited my whole life for this, and I am pleased that you are with me. Come let us celebrate. Just so you know, it won't be all good. The Pharisees and Scribes will definitely be angry about what is about to take place."

"Why?" Jennifer asked. "What's their problem? You bring peace and love wherever you go. Why should they object to that?"

"They have forgotten the true meaning of the Bible. I must bring it back to them. Unfortunately, they do not trust me." "Then they are fools," Jennifer said, petting the female donkey, who seemed to like her touch.

"That one is for you," Jesus said. "Up you go."

Jennifer mounted her donkey. Then Jesus mounted the colt.

"Understand that I must lead. What you are about to experienc is crucial to the path I must take on my journey. Just follow me and observe closely."

"Of course, I am just a humble and grateful follower."

They started their journey to Jerusalem followed by Lazarus, Peter, John and Judas on foot. Hundreds of people were already lining the path for Jesus. The placed their cloaks and cut palm branches and flowers on the path in front of Jesus, and cheered his name. Many people were lined up behind them to follow.

"Who is this man?" a person in the crowd asked.

"That is Jesus, the prophet from Nazareth of Galilee," another person replied. "He is here to save us."

"Yes, save us from this terrible oppression," a third person in the crowd added.

Jennifer was excited, as she had never been on a donkey before. Actually, it was a lot of fun. She had not yet realized what all this was leading up to. "This is way better and more fun than walking. Donkeys are great."

"I wanted to use donkeys because it shows the common people that I understand them and know their suffering. They have suffered long enough. The Kingdom of Heaven is upon them, and they should rejoice."

The crowd was getting larger as Jesus drew closer to Jerusalem. They continued cheering their new leader. Some of them believed he was there to free them from Roman oppression. They were desperate to be saved, because the Romans were much harder on the Jews than any other people they ruled over—brutal and cruel beyond compare.

Jennifer was amazed to see how the people loved Jesus. The love these people had for him, and the love Jesus had for them was truly amazing. This was the most remarkable and the purest love Jennifer had ever seen, felt, or experienced. It almost overwhelmed her. The love was so strong that it nearly made her dizzy. She was beginning to understand how Jesus was able to affect billions of people two thousand years in the future from now. He seemed magical and was the absolute beginning of faith. She was only beginning to realize that God's love was greater than anything humankind could ever hope to obtain. The people were so excited to see Jesus that he was almost like a superstar, maybe even more.

"Praise to the Son of David," a man in the crowd yelled out.

"Could this be the Messiah we have prayed for?" another asked.

"Hosanna to the Son of David," a woman shouted.

"Save us from Rome!" a man yelled.

"You are the true son of David. We are with you," another man called out.

"I am with you always," Jesus told them.

"They love you, as do I," Jennifer said.

Jesus looked over his shoulder at her. "They love me now. But in five days, they will hate me."

"I don't believe that," Jennifer said. "How could that be?"

"Because they want me to end the oppression of Rome," Jesus said. "They want me to eliminate the Pharisees and stop the taxes. That will not happen, and they will turn on me. It is not why I came here. My Father did not send me here to start a war with Rome. He sent me to take away the sins of the world—to serve as ransom for many. I told you before that my time here is short. I am pleased that it is with you."

"Could you end the oppression?" Jennifer wondered. "That is up to my father. He has a much bigger plan." "Blessed is the King of Israel," a man shouted.

"If you are the king, nothing will happen to you. Blessed is he who comes in the name of the Lord," Jennifer insisted.

"You understand so much. I do not know how you do it. It is like you already know the future."

Jennifer wished that she could tell him that she did and how. But she dared not. Still, she could not help wishing for a different outcome.

"I know that there is a possibility that future could change."

Jesus shook his head no. "Only my Father knows that."

As they approached Jerusalem, Jesus looked up and noticed that the Pharisees were looking down at him.

"Who are they?" Jennifer asked.

"Our misguided religious leaders, the Pharisees. They are not happy. They think I came here to destroy their way of life, but I came to improve it. I am here to save them, but they do not understand how to be saved. They are hypocrites, and in truth, they don't think a person can be saved. To them, once a sinner, always a sinner, even those born with affliction. They blame it on the sins of the father, but that is not true. My Father does not punish a person for someone else's sins. Yet, many of those they deemed to be sinners are purer of heart than they are."

The crowd cheered Jesus as the Pharisees tried to calm them down.

"Jesus, tell your people to quiet down," one Pharisee shouted. "Their noise is disturbing the peace of the city. You are not recognized by anyone important. You are no decedent of David! You are no Son of God!" "Tell that to God!" Jesus replied.

The people cheered at that last remark.

"Be quiet!" another Pharisee shouted. "You must show respect!"

"I tell you that if they did not cry out, the very stones would," Jesus said.

"Teacher, rebuke your disciples!" another Pharisee shouted.

"God is angry at you and your kind. You must change, or change will happen to you," Jesus told him. "Woe to you, because you load people down with burdens they can hardly carry, and you yourselves will not lift one finger to help them."

That Pharisee then turned to the crowd. "Listen to me. This man is a fake, and he will bring you down with him. Leave and go back to your Passover celebrations. Do not follow false prophets! The Romans will be angry, and you know what happens when they become angry. They will punish you with no mercy."

The Pharisees turned their backs on Jesus and left. Most of the crowd left with them. Also with the Pharisees was the assistant to Caiaphas. He took a careful look at Jennifer and moved closer to hear what Jesus had to say.

Jesus called out to the Pharisees as they were leaving. "Hear me this! Your denial of me and my Father will bring destruction upon you and your city. I predict that Jerusalem will fall soon unless you turn yourselves over to God. There is no other way."

"Give them time," Jennifer said. "You will convince them."

"I have no time," Jesus told her. He dismounted the donkey and helped Jennifer off hers. Handing the two donkeys over to John, Jesus said, "Please return them and gratefully thank their owners for their use."

"I will, my Lord."

"If you don't mind, John, I will accompany you," Lazarus said.

John and Lazarus took the donkey and the colt away. "Peter and Judas, I will meet you later at the Temple." "Do you want me to come back later?" Jennifer asked.

"No, I need you now. Let us go to the Temple so I can pray."

Jesus and Jennifer walked to the Temple where Jesus had taught on a daily basis.

When they arrived there, they saw a large and admiring crowd, waiting to hear his words.

"I must speak to them. Wait here. I will return. They are like sheep in need of their shepherd."

Jennifer was inspired by how the people loved Jesus. They followed him like lost lambs, searching for their home. She was too far from Jesus to hear anything he said, as loudspeakers would not be invented for a long time.

Jesus walked through the crowd as they separated for him. Then he climbed some steps to be higher than the crowd, so that all might see him. He smiled at them and waited for quiet. Soon the crowd had settled down, waiting for Jesus to speak. Everybody looked up at him expectantly.

Jesus raised his hands and looked up into the sky. "Bow your heads, and I will teach you how to pray," Jesus said, and the crowd obeyed. "Our Father, who art in heaven, hallowed be thy name. Thy kingdom come. Thy will be done on earth as it is in heaven. Give us this day our daily bread and forgive us our trespasses, as we forgive those who trespass against us. And lead us not into temptation, but deliver us from evil. Amen."

"Amen," the crowd said in unison.

"Thou shalt love the Lord thy God with all thy heart, and with all thy soul, and with all thy strength, and with all thy mind; and thy neighbor as thyself."

The crowd screamed and cheered. They truly loved this man and felt that he was the savior promised to them.

"My Father is always working to this very day, and I, too, am working." Jennifer looked up at Jesus. Weeping, Jesus looked back at Jennifer. She had nothing to compare this to. The love she felt for him had no limit.

And at that moment, she knew that she would do anything for him.

"You are the chosen one, the true son of David," one person shouted.

"Tell us about heaven," another yelled.

"The kingdom of heaven is for those who humble themselves, those who are teachable, patient, long-suffering, the poor, and the oppressed are promised to inherit the earth."

The crowd again loudly cheered.

"Be ye therefore merciful, as your Father also is merciful." "Jesus the merciful will save us," another cried.

"Yes, there is a need for justice, and it must be the same, whether you are a king or a pauper. Rich or poor, makes no difference. And there must be morality; nothing can be fair without morality. And you must be of service to others as others must be of service to you." The crowd cheered.

"Destroy Rome!" several people yelled.

"Yes, save us from the evil of Rome!" another shouted.

"Love God! Love your neighbor as yourself. Forgive others who have wronged you. Love your enemies. Ask God for forgiveness of your sins. Repentance of sins is essential. I am the Messiah, and I, with the help of God, can forgive you."

The crowd screamed. Jennifer felt like she was at a rock concert only much more intense.

"Remember, the kingdom of heaven is like a mustard seed, which a man took and planted in his field. Though it is the smallest of all seeds, yet when it grows, it is the largest of garden plants and becomes a tree, so that the birds come and perch in its branches. It will give absolute meaning to your life. Both here on earth and after, if you believe."

"We believe. We believe. We believe. We believe!" the crowd chanted.

Jesus continued, tears gently sliding down his face. "I must now tell you this as my Father is calling for me. I will be with you for only a little while longer, before I go to the one who sent me. You will look for me, but you will not find me, and where I am you cannot come. Therefore, you must follow."

"We will follow. We will follow. We will follow!"

"I leave you peace, my peace I give you."

Jesus stepped down and entered the crowd, heading for Jennifer. He grabbed her hand and together, they left the Temple. The people in the Temple hugged each other in happiness. Jesus and Jennifer walked to a quiet part of the city. Jesus still weeping. The assistant to Caiaphas continued watching Jennifer and Jesus. He would have much to report to his master.

"Why are you crying?" Jennifer asked.

"My time here is nearly at an end, and I will greatly miss you."

"Don't think about that yet. Things can change. The future is not written in stone."

Jesus squeezed her hand. "You do not yet understand my Father, but you will," he said sadly.

"All I understand is that I love you."

"And I love you. And that is a parting gift from my Father." "Please, Jesus, give me time."

"Time is not mine to give, but I do love you. Come. I have a friend nearby. We can spend the night there. I look forward to more of your special treatment and of course, Chanel."

"Yes, I will be honored. It's still early. Why don't we walk up to the hill and look at the city as the sun sets? I'll buy us some juice, maybe even wine, and of course bread."

"That sounds like heaven. Where have you been all my life?"

"Always, right in front of you. By the way, who is this friend of yours?" Jennifer asked.

"I will tell you about him later, but he owns a nice house with a large upper room that can accommodate many people, especially for a supper."

"That sounds romantic," Jennifer said.

"Not this time. There will be much to say, which will not make my disciples pleased. Especially Judas."

"You know I have your back," Jennifer said.

"What exactly does that mean?" Jesus asked, his expression puzzled. "It means I will defend you with my life."

"You understand what love truly is. I am amazed at your wisdom. You know so much. It is as if you are aware of things before they are known."

"No, I try to see the whole fig tree, not just part of it."

"I must use that in my teachings."

Jesus put his arm around Jennifer as they walked to the shops to buy food and wine.

*****

Caiaphas sat in his specially made chair at his palace, surrounded by four of his Pharisees or religious leaders that were under his control. He was waiting for his assistant to enter and give his report on Jesus and his new friend. The assistant entered and faced Caiaphas.

"Come. What do you have to report?" Caiaphas demanded.

"I listened at the Temple. And once again, Jesus proclaimed that he was God's equal. I heard it with my own ears. Nothing could have been clearer."

"He must be stopped," the first Pharisee said, angrily. "He is a threat. No human can be the equal of God."

"The time has come to put an end to this," the second Pharisee said. "He is becoming much too dangerous."

"We have to be careful, though," Caiaphas warned. "He is loved by many of the people. We have to make Rome believe that he is a threat to them. They will do the dirty work for us."

"I think the people love him more than us," the assistant said.

"Of course, he is one of them, or at least they think he is," the third Pharisee said. "All we need is for him to make a mistake."

"Does Jesus have a new companion like that woman told me?" Caiaphas asked.

"Yes, my Lord, and she is very different from any woman I have ever seen."

"How so?" Caiaphas said.

"She is a beauty beyond words. She is very light skinned with light hair exactly like an angel sent from heaven. In fact, she may be just that." "And what is that?" the fourth Pharisee asked.

"She may truly be an angel sent from heaven. Only God could create someone as beautiful as she," the assistant said. "I saw hair on her head but nowhere else. Her arms were as smooth as a newborn child." "That is strange," the second Pharisee said.

"What does Jesus think of her?" Caiaphas wondered.

"He is definitely in love with her," the assistant said. "Actually, everybody will be in love with her. There is none like her. No man could resist her. She has to be a siren with a love spell on Jesus."

"This could work well for us," Caiaphas said as a devious plot formed in his head.

"How?" the first Pharisee asked.

"Let us capture and lock her up. Then we will see what Jesus does about it. He is nonviolent, but love changes everything. I want to see what he does. Is she always with him?"

"There are times when she is not with him. That will present opportunities to capture her."

"Have your men use a large net. I want no harm to come to her. If she is an angel, I do not want God angry at me for hurting her."

"If the legends are correct, Angels are fierce fighters and have been known to take out ten fighters at a time," the third Pharisee warned. "They have the blood of God in them, which makes them more than human. So, beware."

"Do not let her put a spell on you," the fourth Pharisee warned. Caiaphas sighed. "She is an angel, not a witch. Get your facts straight." "Sorry," the fourth Pharisee apologized.

"Follow them and take as many men as you need. Remember, do not harm her," Caiaphas ordered.

"Of course, my Lord. I take my leave," the assistant said and left the room.

Caiaphas placed his hand on each of the Pharisees. "We must be together in this. Jesus is a danger to us and our land. He could end it all, and we would be left with nothing but dust. For the sake of our nation, Jesus must die."

"Hail Rome, our savior," the second Pharisee declared.

"Who would have thought that Rome could actually be useful to us?" the first Pharisee said amazed. "But this time they will. They frown upon those who would place themselves above them. As the King of the Jews, they will see him as a true threat."

"Come. Let us have dinner. I have something very special for us. Tonight, we will have beef."

"That is an honor. I have never had beef," the first Pharisee said.

"Trust me," Caiaphas said, rubbing his hands together. "It is way better than goat or lamb, way better. Come, it is ready for us in the courtyard."

"I am ready to eat like a king," the fourth Pharisee declared.

They headed out into the courtyard of the palace, where a table loaded with food and beef was waiting for them.

CHAPTER

TWENTY

Leo looked out the front of the time ship and up at the sky. As his gaze drifted downward, he saw the city of Jerusalem in the distance. So quiet. He did not want anyone to know it, but he would be happy to see a real city again, one with electricity and air conditioning. He was tired of the past and longed for the bright lights of the cities and even the smell of gasoline, which meant he did not have to walk everywhere. There was no noise, except the wind and a few birds chirping from the branches of trees and some bushes. It was just too quiet here. *You hear everything, even whispers.* "There are no clouds, not a one in sight. I would love some rain, even just a little."

"Not much during this time of the year," Elizabeth said. "Actually, not much at any time of the year. Their rainy season here is very short."

Leo walked over to his chair and checked out the view screen that showed the outside of the time ship. "I have to admit that whoever thought of using a house of lepers as the hologram screen camouflage was a genius. Look at them. As soon as people notice it, they scamper away like goats being chased by a lion. See? Look at that one! Hello. Then he does an about face, and he quickly leaves, never to return again. They all scatter and tell everybody to stay away."

"Now Leo, you must remember that there was no cure for leprosy at this time. Those who were afflicted suffered until they died. Only Jesus was known to have cured it, and that was only for a few special ones. There is no such thing as modern medical science right now. You have a serious injury out here, and you are as good as dead."

Leo left his station thinking, *And that's another reason I want to get back to modern civilization. It's just too primitive here.* When he returned to the main cabin several minutes later, he brought four breakfast meals from the ship's microwave with him. They smelled really good.

"Breakfast is ready. Dig in."

Leo, Winifred, Elizabeth, and Keith had a very nice breakfast that a chef had preplanned and prepared for them, just for this journey.

"I'll tell you," Leo said. "You can't say they didn't plan well and put a lot of work into our voyage. I mean this food is as good as first class on an airline, maybe better."

"You're right. I have to admit it is pretty good. Way better than the food out there—way, way better. These people don't know what they're missing," Keith agreed.

"And their ancestors won't know for another two thousand years," Winifred said with a laugh.

"Unless you go to France," Elizabeth said with a sigh. "They always had good food no matter what age."

"I've never been to France," Keith said.

"You should go," Elizabeth said. "It would greatly broaden your horizons and understanding. You need to see the world to understand it. It would open your mind to new and exciting experiences." "I think travel is overrated," Keith said.

"Says the one who doesn't travel but takes the ultimate trip of a lifetime," Winifred teased.

When they were finished eating, Keith continued sipping his icecold drink as he dressed in his Roman outfit, adding the sword and knife last, and making sure they were clean. Elizabeth hummed a song and played with the cross she had brought with her. Leo looked at a map of the area, trying to decide what he would explore today. This time, he would not go alone. He would take Winifred with him. He felt safer with Winifred by his side, since she, like Keith, were their security officers. It was just another beautiful sunny day like most of the days in this time and place.

"I wish I could take this drink with me," Keith complained. "It's so hot and dusty walking around out there."

"You know you can't," Winifred told him. "Enjoy it while you can. There will be plenty more waiting when you get back."

Keith turned and calmly stared at the two empty chairs. They had been bothering him all day. "I wonder why there are extra chairs. I mean the government doesn't usually go overboard. They almost always go under."

"I wonder if they wanted us to bring someone back," Leo said thoughtfully. "Although, I can't imagine who or why. I guess Jennifer is the only one who would know that."

"No, I don't think that's possible," Elizabeth said, shaking her head. "And if we did, I wonder if they would grow old and instantly die by traveling to the future. After all, no one has ever done it before."

"The rifle brought back from the Revolutionary War didn't age," Winifred said. "It looked brand new. So, I don't think they would. Still, there's no sense in bringing someone back from this time. They couldn't really help us. They would be totally lost in our time. And it might be such a cultural shock that it could mess with their minds. It's not like you could send them to college to learn two thousand years of history and advancement."

"Unless that someone was Jesus," Keith said. "He is the main reason why we're here. We are supposed to confirm that he died on the cross. And if he didn't, we need to confirm that as well."

Elizabeth was alarmed by those words. "You don't understand! Jesus must die on the cross to save us all. We are here only as observers. We have our orders. The timeline must not change. It could destroy the world. We have no idea what might happen."

"Yes, we have our orders," Keith said, thoughtfully. "We must save the future. But we also must know the truth, no matter what. That's the reason we're here."

"Come on, Winifred," Leo said. "Let's go. Let these two work out their religion on their own. Let's see now. What's on our list? Will it be Nazareth, The Sea of Galilee, Bethlehem, Jericho, Jordan River, or the Pool of Bethesda."

"I was at the pool yesterday," Winifred said. "Not much to see, not much at all. Just a small pool of water heated by hot rocks. It wasn't very clean either. Even though I could definitely use a bath, I certainly don't want to go into it. There's no filter to keep it clean. And so many people were using it! The Pool of Bethesda is nothing more than a warmed-up fish pond. I'm kind of disappointed so far."

"That is a place of legend," Elizabeth informed her. "Jesus supposedly went there many times, not only to relax in the warm water, but also to heal other people. The story goes that some men brought him a paralytic, lying on a mat. When Jesus saw their faith, He said to the paralytic, 'Take courage, son; your sins are forgiven.' Then he said, 'Which is easier: to say, "Your sins are forgiven," or "Get up and walk"?' And the man got up and went home. There are many other stories of miracles performed there, as well."

"I wish there was a way to confirm those stories," Keith said, his voice clearly filled with skepticism. "Because after two thousand years, nobody really knows what happened. Is Jesus really the Son of God, or just an ordinary prophet, or maybe just a pretender? We even have them in our present time—Pretenders."

"He is real. You can see that for yourself," Elizabeth said. "Maybe if you went out and spent some time around him, you would understand and believe. Anyway, we will find out the truth very soon. God doesn't lie."

"Yes, Elizabeth, I believe you will find out, sooner than you know. However, I think you are worried that maybe everything you heard wasn't true. And that's why you're so adamant about it. For your sake, I hope you're right. I hope most of it is fact not fiction." No one realized that Keith's words had an underlying meaning.

"I'll tell you one thing," Elizabeth said. "It's nice having a large Roman soldier as your escort. The people give us plenty of respect and lots of space. The bad guys stay away from us, and the few that didn't,

Keith set them on a proper course. He likes to teach people lessons." "Oh, what happened?" Leo asked.

"Three young boys gave us a little trouble," Elizabeth said.

"Yes, those boys will never steal again. At least not while I'm around. I taught them a good lesson—that it is a sin to steal," Keith bragged.

"I am sure you did," Leo said. He wondered just what kind of lesson Keith had dealt the boys. He knew what Elizabeth thought, but he was willing to bet that her idea of a lesson, and Keith's were miles apart, and his words were more actions—violent ones, but even he did not think that Keith would murder the boys.

Winifred clearly had not been paying much attention to the conversation. She said, "Oh, yeah, I also went to Bethlehem yesterday. I just completely forgot about it. Not much to remember, considering it was the birthplace of Jesus. You could blink an eye and walk right past it. Nothing much to report there. It's located on the top of a hill with about a hundred inhabitants. Just some tiny huts, small mud houses, and a few goats, actually more goats than people. I couldn't even find the stable or manger where Jesus was supposed to have been born. Nobody could tell me anything. Or maybe they just didn't want to."

"I for one still want to see Bethlehem, just to say I was at the birthplace of Jesus Christ," Elizabeth stated. "It all started there. It's a pivotal point in history. Its name means the house of bread. It's also known as the City of David because the great King David grew up there. So, there is a lot of famous history, especially for this area. I will put it on my list. Got it, Keith? It is a must see."

"Got it," Keith said. "I need one more drink before we go. And this time, I'm making it a beer."

Keith grabbed a cold beer from the refrigerator, opened it, and quickly drank it.

"All the class of a true Roman soldier," Elizabeth said, her distaste for his actions evident. "I don't understand how you could drink that so early in the morning."

Keith burped and smiled. "Easy. One for the Romans."

"Come on, Leo, let's go," Winifred urged. "Get your water."

"On it." Leo and Winifred grabbed their supplies and headed toward the door of the time ship.

"Which way? East, west, north, or south?" Winifred asked.

"It doesn't matter. Everything looks the same out there. Let's cross the city first," Leo said.

"Yes, let's visit the Temple. You know, listen to some music, or whatever they call it. Or maybe just do some people watching. Although everybody looks the same here. No real love of color. I keep wracking my brain. What is that music called?"

"I think it is called hymns," Winifred said. "Onward Christian soldiers marching as to war."

Leo and Winifred left the time ship and began walking toward Jerusalem.

"Well, Keith, where do you want to go?" Elizabeth asked.

Keith thought for a second. Actually, he didn't care about the sights. He wanted to go where he could follow Jennifer and Jesus. He knew his mission, and it had to be done before the Last Supper. He was a man driven by his mission. And whatever sacrifices had to be made would be done. "How about the place of the Last Supper? I'm sure that would be interesting. I mean it's going to happen soon, isn't it? I mean the real thing."

"Yes, I agree. It's one of the most important events in our religious history, followed only by the cross. I believe the room of the Last Supper is located in the complex of Mount Zion, just outside the main gate, near the Mount of Olives. Now it may be vastly different from what we think it is. Rome completely destroyed Jerusalem in 70 A.D., so nothing much was left of the history of Jesus. I believe it was the upper room in a large house owned by a good friend of his. That was where Jesus had his last meal with his disciples and foretold of his betrayal by

Judas. Then the courtyard of Caiaphas, the high priest, was where Peter would deny knowing him three times. All of which came true. There is even a famous painting by Leonardo da Vinci that has been visited by millions almost as much as the Mona Lisa," Elizabeth said.

"Let's find it, then," Keith said. "It shouldn't be hard. There really aren't that many buildings around here, especially with an upper story."

"This is so exciting. Being a witness to the true history of our religion. It all started here. And just think, we are watching it happen," Elizabeth said excitedly. "We will finally know the truth. People have waited two thousand years, not knowing if it was real or not. I know it's real, and we are going to prove it."

"Well, Elizabeth, we'll see if you are right or wrong. At least we know that there is an actual Jesus. If there wasn't a Jesus, Jennifer would be here with us right now. Obviously, she is very busy with somebody. We just don't know if he was or wasn't the Son of God."

"He was and is," Elizabeth assured him. "Don't ever doubt that."

"I never did. I just need to prove it." The lies came easily to Keith's lips.

Keith and Elizabeth left the time ship and began their journey. Keith was determined to follow the President's orders and his own belief that religion was just a farce—a joke played on the masses. Elizabeth, though, had fallen for it hook, line, and sinker. She was now in the way, and he needed to find a way to get rid of her. If he played his cards right, there might be a way to maybe even blame her death on the locals. After all, there were no cameras, except the ones in their clothing. He turned the one in his clothing off, making sure there was no evidence left behind. Once she was dead, no one would remember her existence anyway. Even if there was a witness, no one would dare accuse a Roman soldier of killing a stranger. They would quietly walk away.

"I just realized that there are no cops here to enforce the law. Everybody is on the honor system," Keith said.

"But somehow they still found a way to survive. Give them credit for having some kind of honor," Elizabeth said. "Still, there was a lot of crime here. Most of it went unreported."

"To tell you the truth, it's not much different in our time. I think that for every ten crimes committed, eight go unreported. Nothing much has changed in two thousand years. You can still get away with almost anything."

After an hour, Elizabeth spotted what she thought was the house where the Last Supper was to take place. Just as she had said, it was a large house. Keith couldn't have cared less, but he was pleased that they were now in an area with no people around, a very private spot.

"Not really much to look at. Just a building made out of mud bricks, like everything else," Elizabeth said, clearly disappointed.

"But then, what was I expecting, a five-star restaurant?" "Do you want to go inside?" Keith asked.

"Not really. It's just a house with a room. Maybe we could visit Caiaphas again. Wait, I have a better idea. We could go see Pontius Pilate. Actually, he is the one who sent Jesus to the cross. I will speak with him. He is a very important piece of the puzzle in all of this." Keith grew very concerned by Elizabeth's last remarks. "I can't get near him! He is a Roman commander! He would easily spot that I'm a fake, and instantly put me to death for impersonating a Roman soldier. They would crucify me just like Jesus. No way, it would interfere with my mission. And I won't let that happen."

"Well, Keith, I hate to pull rank on you, but you are under my orders. You can hide in the bushes or go back to the ship, but I'm going to see Pontius Pilate. He must be secretly convinced that Jesus must die on the cross. It can be no other way. I will quietly persuade him. He will not know the difference. Now tell me, what is your mission? Why is it so important to you?"

Keith knew that this was not part of the mission. Elizabeth had been interfering all along. "If history is correct, neither Caiaphas nor Pilate need to hear anything you have to say. Everything went down without any interference from you Elizabeth. The fact that you feel you need to put a bug in both men's ears, tells me you don't actually believe what you've been preaching. In fact, you've been doing the very thing you told me not to do, interfering with history." He suddenly smiled. Now that he thought of it, he actually had a duty to stop her interference. "Well, since you have to know, I'll tell you what my mission is, but this may upset you. And don't worry. It won't last long. Come over here. I need to tell you something very important, and it means everything to me."

Keith walked with Elizabeth to a dark part of a structure, where no one was around. Nobody could see them, and if they did, no one would care. They were too afraid of Rome.

"Okay, just what is your mission?" Elizabeth asked. "And why is it so important?"

"My mission came straight from the President of the United States, and it is to change the course of religion and make sure that Jesus does not die on the cross. He will die in a much different way, and religion will be no more. Jesus is a fake, and it must be proven without a doubt. And that's exactly what I'm going to do."

This greatly alarmed Elizabeth. "You can't do that! I won't let you. I will tell everybody about your plans. You are evil, and you will be stopped. God and I will stop you. I must inform Jennifer immediately. I'll contact her now. Really, do you think God would let you kill his son? You must be crazy."

Elizabeth tried to activate her wrist communicator.

"Maybe God will stop me, but you will not," he said, ripping the communicator from her wrist. "You will no longer be in my way. Only Jennifer will be left. It's time to meet your maker, Elizabeth."

"What? What are you saying?" Fear filled her eyes. She grabbed his arms, foolishly believing that she was strong enough to stop him. Keith pulled out his knife and quickly stabbed into her stomach. Elizabeth grunted and then was quiet.

Keith, who was an expert, knew how to kill people. He quickly turned the knife, slicing upward and then down her stomach, dooming her. Elizabeth died holding onto Keith. Suddenly, a sonic boom was heard everywhere throughout time. As soon as Keith heard it, he realized that he was standing alone with his knife, now free of her blood, out in front of him. Elizabeth and her memory were gone forever. The gold cross she had brought with her was never on the time ship. Jennifer, Leo, Winifred and everybody else forgot that Elizabeth had ever existed, because she never did.

Keith couldn't make sense of what was going on. *Why am I standing here? Why is my knife out? I know the President told me to eliminate any obstacle to my mission. What did I do? And what just happened?*

Keith walked around the structure, trying to put things into perspective. He glanced at his knife, but it was as clean as it was when he had left the time ship. Then his eyes opened wide. *The timeline! Of course, that had to be it. I'll bet if I went back to the ship there would be a third empty seat. I know myself. I know I did my duty. I can't remember who it was, but I know I did what needed to be done.* Keith put his knife back into its sleeve. *That has to be it. If you die in this time you disappear. Like it never happened. Only Jennifer is left, and Jesus will be easy prey. As for Leo and Winifred, they won't be a problem.*

Keith figured that since he was alone, his plan was to follow Jesus and Jennifer and wait for the best time to attack. It definitely had to occur before the Last Supper. He would change the course of history and become the most famous man of all time, except he wouldn't, because no one would remember Jesus or that he had ever existed. The great hoax of religion would never happen. Now he knew for certain that if he killed Jennifer, nothing would happen, and no one would ever know. She would be forgotten, and he would be able to complete his mission.

Keith looked up to the sky and did the unthinkable. He dared God. *There is nothing to stop me. I will kill Jesus and save the world from the evils of religion. People will be free to be themselves. And there is no one up there to hear me. Never has been. I am talking to something that never existed, and I will prove it. Come on, God, if you exist, give me your best shot. But I don't think so.*

Keith walked back toward Jerusalem, looking for Jennifer and Jesus. He had been expertly trained to track. When he walked, people stayed out of his way, and he liked it that way. He was a man on a mission, and he wanted another cold beer.

CHAPTER

TWENTY- ONE

Early the next morning, the sun was just beginning to peek over the distant horizon. Jennifer was still asleep on her mat. It had taken a while, but she had finally gotten used to not being on a comfortable mattress. On the edge of waking up, she felt a very light touch on her forehead. She awakened to find Jesus lightly caressing her forehead. The touch was soft but very warm and comforting. He was just so beautiful. The more you looked, the more you liked. She heard the familiar sound of shofar horns in the background. It was a sound that would remain the same even two thousand years in the future. Some things just did not change. Some things didn't need to.

Looking into his eyes, Jennifer smiled. "Good morning."

"Your skin is so smooth," Jesus said. "How did you get it that way?"

"A gift from God, and maybe a few extra ingredients."

Jesus took hold of Jennifer's hands. "So soft yet so powerful. God did a wonderful job when He made you."

"God and Chanel by Jennifer."

Jesus laughed. "Come, we should leave."

"Don't you want to say goodbye?" she asked him. "Your friends were very nice to give us a place to sleep for the night."

"There is no need. We will be back for Passover dinner in a few days. That will be a grand event. All the apostles will be here to meet you, and of course, Judas. I really wish he would like you. But he is a stubborn man. Once he makes his mind up about something, there is no changing it."

"Yes, your little ones, and you love them all, even Judas," Jennifer said. *Does he know?* she wondered. *Yes. Of course, he does, at least according to the Bible. And yet....*

Understanding escaped her, and she sighed.

"Come, let us walk to the Mount of Olives to see the sun fully rise. I go there a lot. In fact, most days I spend the night there, sleeping under the trees. It is so calm and peaceful, and you can see the whole city from there. It is a very good place to meditate."

"That sounds wonderful. Why don't we stay there tonight, just you and I?"

"That sounds very pleasant. You are truly a gift from my Father."

"I think in this case," Jennifer said, "it was just meant to be." They got up and quietly left the house, walking over to the Mount of Olives. Even at this time in the morning, many people were already out and about. Everyone knew who Jesus was, and they all wanted to greet him.

A young couple with a newborn baby approached them. "Please, Master Jesus, will you bless my newborn child?" the child's father asked. "It would be an honor to have one such as you bless him."

"Yes," the babe's mother agreed. "It would mean that he will have a great future and also give us many grandchildren. You are the great one, Son of David."

"Show him to me," Jesus said smiling. "Blessed are the children. Their spirits are filled with innocence, joy, and laughter." The young couple held the baby up to Jesus.

"I bless you in the name of my Father," Jesus said. "I also bless your parents for having faith."

"Thank you, thank you, thank you, Son of God," the woman said overjoyed. She carefully looked at Jennifer and came to a conclusion. "Oh my God, this woman with you must be an angel. Look at her! I have never seen such a woman. She could only come from heaven. She had to have been sent by God. How beautiful."

"Thank you," Jennifer said. "But I'm just ordinary me."

"No, that is not possible. Only heaven could produce one such as you. Will you please do us an honor and also bless our child?" the boy's father begged.

"Yes, please! A double blessing," his wife added.

"I don't think I'm qualified for a blessing, but thank you for the compliment."

In order to make things go quickly Jesus made a decision. "Yes, this angel will also bless your child. She is very modest but yes, she truly is an angel. Please hold your child up to her. Go ahead, Jennifer the angel.

Give them an angel blessing." Jesus smiled at her.

"I bless you and your parents in the name of Jesus."

"Thank you!" the child's mother exclaimed. "This is the beginning of a grand day. I will never forget this special day."

"Yes, blessed by Jesus and an angel," the child's father said. "This is wonderful!"

Jennifer wished she could take a picture of them, but that technology was many hundreds of years away. A memory would have to do. Then she remembered the camera hidden in her clothing and smiled as the young couple and their child moved on.

She turned to Jesus. "So, you think I'm an angel?"

"What else could you be? What is important is that you arc *my* angel."

They continued walking along until Jesus brought Jennifer to a special spot next to a large olive tree.

"This is my favorite spot. I think, dream, and sleep right here. I feel I am closer to my Father when I am out here. Sometimes he tells me what I must do. Sometimes he tells me what I can't do. And sometimes he tells me nothing."

"It is beautiful. There is so much beauty here."

"From a distance, it does look beautiful until you get closer," Jesus agreed.

"Even close up, you can still see its splendor."

"Sometimes, when I look at Jerusalem, I see all the evil and hatred there. And I feel a terrible presence coming toward me. An ominous presence that even my love cannot save me. I feel something is coming for me very soon, and I am not quite sure what it is. But I know that it is coming from Jerusalem." His expression was one of sorrow. "I do not believe this city will last long."

"It almost sounds like Sodom and Gomora," Jennifer suggested. "We know what happened there."

"Yes, my Father had to completely destroy it. But I believe that Jerusalem's destruction will not come from my Father, but man himself. I need to save Jerusalem before it takes me away."

"Things are different now. You have me, and I will stand by you and for you."

"I don't think any single person could beat you. It would take many. Still… some things cannot be changed."

Jennifer decided to change the subject. She hated to see him so sad. "Where are we going today?"

"We are going to the Temple. It has changed. It is no longer a place of worship, but a common market where people steal and take money from the poor. Each year they want more only so they can have more, while the people have less."

"No matter where you go, I'm afraid that won't change. We have a saying where I come from and that is, money is the root of all evil."

Jesus smiled. "I must use that. I like it. Yes, that is what has happened to the Temple."

"Any idea how?" Jennifer asked.

"The Pharisees want to make money more than anything. They no longer care about the Bible or the people. Now they worship money over my Father. Yet they do not seem to realize what they are doing. They have forgotten the true meaning of the Bible as it was originally written. They try to change it to make it work for what they want, leaving out the people and what they desperately need. They value the words of men over those of my Father."

"You're not alone," Jennifer said sadly. "That happens in my land, too. We're really not that much different. It doesn't matter where you go. All you can do is try to make it better."

"I am not an angry person, but this treatment of my Father's temple has gone too far. Something must be done to make it right. It no longer belongs to my Father, and it must be returned for the good of all. The people must feel that it is a place of worship not a marketplace. The temple has to be God's playground."

"Where I'm from, we call it being taken over by a shopping mall. Everything for added tax dollars and to make a few rich people even richer, meaning less for the people and their real needs."

"You have a great understanding of life. How do you know all this?" Jesus asked. "It is like you have already seen things before they happen."

"No, I just look at life as a circle. Everything is connected with a reason. It seems your Temple is no longer part of the circle."

"I do not yet know what to do, but I must think of something that will have an impact on them. Something they will not forget anytime soon."

"Where I come from, when things get dirty, they have to be cleaned—thoroughly cleaned."

Jesus thought about her words, then his eyes lit up. "Yes! Thank you! That is right. It must be cleaned, so it can become like new again." "A total cleansing."

"A cleansing of the Temple," Jesus agreed. "That is what must be done."

"Hopefully, there isn't a lot of cleansing to do, maybe just a little bit?"

"You have not seen the full extent," Jesus warned her. "But you will."

Jesus looked off into the distance and spotted his favorite fig tree. A tree that he had eaten figs from for years. The figs were always sweet. "Come, my angel. I am hungry. Let me feed you some wonderful figs for breakfast. I have a favorite fig tree, and I have enjoyed its sweet fruit for many years, since I was a child." Jennifer wasn't excited about the prospect of having figs for breakfast, but she did not want Jesus to know. Figs were far from her favorite fruit. "Wonderful, at least it's not bread."

Jesus in his excitement, almost ran to the fig tree, followed by Jennifer. But when he got there, he was disappointed as there were no figs on the tree. He grew angry, because he had wanted to treat Jennifer. "I am sorry, but this tree is a great disappointment to me. There is nothing to feed you. I will curse this tree."

"My love, it's okay. We'll get something else."

"There is nothing else out here. This tree needs to be replaced."

Jennifer thought he was overreacting. She looked at the tree.

"The tree is very old and probably past its fruit-bearing years, but it has been very good to you in the past. Hasn't it?"

"Yes, but there is nothing now. There is nothing for you, and that is what is important."

"Do not curse it, but thank it for what it has done in the past," Jennifer said. "It gave you all that it had, do not expect more from it. Thank it for what it has already given you, not for the instant gratification of now. Like your earth mother, she can no longer bear children, but she is still useful for other purposes. Look there!" she said, pointing to a branch higher up. "See the bird's nest? Would you take away that creature's home? And look, there's another."

"No, I would not," Jesus agreed. "How can anyone not love you? You have the wisdom of the ancients. I do not know how, but you do. Yes, remember the past and do not let it lead you to harsh judgments." He gave her a look of wondering. "You are way too young to be able to understand, but you do."

"Just common sense. But I have a great idea. Come. Let's sit down by this old tree, and I will feed you."

"How can you do that?" Jesus asked, looking around. "There is nothing here." "Just sit, and let me do the rest," she said with a knowing smile.

They sat by the fig tree, and Jennifer opened her pouch. In case of an emergency, she always kept a few protein bars with her. And surely this was an emergency. She opened the wrapper on one and gave it to Jesus.

He turned it over in his hands, puzzled. "What is this?"

"It's from my land and everybody eats them. It's called a protein bar. Try it."

Jesus took a bite and was completely surprised. He had never tasted such a wonderful, yet unusual food. "This is marvelous! It's like a hundred flavors all at the same time. I have never tasted anything so delightful."

"Yes, I figured it would be something new to you, something you had never tasted before."

"This is beyond words. Your land is amazing to have such things. These protein bars are the best food ever. I now thank the fig tree for being barren. For without that, I would have never tasted such a curious yet tasty food."

"All things work out, a lot of times for the best."

"We need to find a way to make lots of these to feed the people. Way better than fish. I have never tasted flavors like these in such a small thing. My Father must learn about them."

"I'm sure he already knows," Jennifer said with a laugh. "He just hasn't told you yet. He may be waiting for a better time."

"Ah, but what better time than now? There are many hungry people, and they would greatly enjoy this protein bar. By the way, what is protein?"

"It's fish, goats, chickens, birds, sheep, eggs, and other things like nuts, all rolled into one."

"It is a total feast, and so small, yet it does so much."

"I have more in case we need them, but now bread sounds pretty good. Believe me, making a steady diet of these would get boring. There's nothing like fresh fruit, vegetables, and of course, meat."

Jesus finished his protein bar and took Jennifer's hand. "Come. We need to clean up. Especially now that I am no longer hungry, thanks to your protein bar. Just leave it all to me. I now know what to do. I love your protein bar. I will call it protein by Jennifer right next to Chanel by Jennifer."

They walked toward the city, where Jesus had serious plans for the Temple. Unknown to both of them, from a distance, a Roman soldier watched them, carefully following along behind. That soldier was no soldier. It was Keith, who was also an expert tracker among many other things. With all other obstacles eliminated, he was singularly focused on Jennifer and the mission the President had given him. Having always completed every task assigned to him, this one would be no different. He would follow them until the time was right, and take them both out together.

*****

Jennifer and Jesus entered the south entrance of Jerusalem, which was closest to the temple. Because of Passover, there were people everywhere—many more thousands than normal. For Jennifer, it was exciting as she watched the people all dressed up for their holiday. It gave her the same feeling she'd had when visiting the Western Wall. When Jesus took her inside the Temple, everything changed. Everywhere Jennifer looked, people were selling and buying. Every single space was occupied in one way or another. Dirty and dusty with loud, animals everywhere. Sheep, oxen, chickens, doves, and everything smelled filthy. The air smelled from pollution, especially with all the animals present. Nothing was being cleaned. This was not a place of worship; this was an overgrown marketplace.

"Uh, you know what I said about maybe needing a little cleaning? You were right, and I am wrong. It needs a lot of cleaning—a whole lot."

Jesus spotted two Pharisees counting money and making sure nobody cheated the Temple. He could not take anymore. It was time for action. He turned to Jennifer. "Please stand out of the way over there."

Jennifer nodded. "Sounds like a good idea. If you need help, just let me know. Go ahead and clean." She moved off to a safe distance, where she would have a good view of Jesus and everything going on.

"The Scriptures declare, 'My Temple will be called a house of prayer,' but you have turned it into a den of thieves!" Jesus shouted. He entered the Temple and began driving out all the people buying and selling animals for sacrifice. He knocked over the tables of the money changers and the chairs of those selling doves. Money fell to the floor, and the people scrambled to get to it. There was confusion everywhere. The people have never seen Jesus so angry.

"What are you doing? Are you crazy!" a money changer shouted. "The Temple will punish you for this grievous act."

"Hear this. I am the Temple! And you are sinning against me and my Father and the common people. You will be punished for this! Leave!"

But the money changer insisted. "We have a right to be here! I have paid my dues to the Temple."

"The Temple is lost, and I am here to return it to its rightful purpose…to worship my Father."

"This is how I make my money to feed myself and my family," the money changer continued.

"To make money from the poor is wrong. You are more friends with the devil than you are with God. You can change and do what is right. It's your choice. Just like heaven is your choice. Do you want heaven or not?" Jesus asked him.

"I do! I want heaven!"

"Then change and follow me and my Father."

"I will, my Lord, I will. Pleases forgive me."

"My Lord Jesus, what do I tell Rome when they want money?" a dove seller asked next.

"Render unto Caesar the things that are Caesar's, and unto God the things that are God's."

"But Master Jesus, how can I tell the difference?" the dove seller asked.

He picked up a coin. "Whose picture is this?"

"Caesar's."

"Then give it to Caesar. The rest belongs to God!"

Jesus quickly made a whip out of cords and began driving the animals out of the Temple. Animals ran everywhere, but mostly out of the Temple, followed by the owners needing to capture them. At this time, the people were in fear and awe of Jesus and did not want to get in his way. They respected him too much to try and stop him. Jesus continued his task.

"You have lost all faith in God. Soon God will lose all faith in you. This is His Temple, pray for His forgiveness!"

Jesus then let the doves out of their cages. Nobody tried to stop him. They just watched. Many left, not wanting the full fury of Jesus or his Father. Deep down inside, they knew that Jesus was doing the right thing for the Temple. Also observing this event were four of the apostles: James, John, Matthew, and Thomas. Each would have a vastly different story of the event. They had never seen Jesus so active. They did not understand what had made him so angry. The two Pharisees also watched with great interest.

"We must inform Caiaphas," the first Pharisee said. "Jesus is truly crazy and a danger. Look at the mess he has created. This will cost the Temple much money."

"I have known him for some time and have never seen him like this," the second Pharisee said. "What happened to him? He has changed."

The assistant to Caiaphas, who was watching Jesus and Jennifer, stood near them. "Do you think it is because of this new woman with him? Has she made him this way? We all know what a woman can do, and often it is not good. Women are troublemakers. Always have been." "Something happened, and it is not good," the first Pharisee agreed. "Jesus is changing. He has never shown anger before. Yes, a woman could do that to a man, especially a cunning woman who is manipulative and evil." "Where is this woman?" the second Pharisee asked.

The assistant, who was watching from a corner, pointed to Jennifer.

"Yes, that woman is too beautiful not to be dangerous. There can be no other reason. She controls Jesus. Just look. That is a look of power and control on her face," the second Pharisee agreed.

"She is definitely not from around here," the first Pharisee said.

"Look at her skin and hair. She is not like anyone I have ever seen. Where is she from? More importantly, who sent her?"

"She reminds me of Cleopatra, and you know how cunning she was," the second Pharisee speculated.

"Yes, she must be the reincarnation of Cleopatra," the first Pharisee concluded. "What else could it be?"

Caiaphas's assistant egged them on. "Yes, I think she is dangerous and a troublemaker. Who else could make Jesus act this way? Trust me, women like her, and there is none like her that I have ever seen, are nothing but trouble. Yet, she is beautiful beyond words."

Still using the whip, Jesus chased the chickens out of the Temple. All of the selling had come to a dead stop. Birds flew everywhere. It was a complete mess. Some people began cautiously cleaning up. Other people were actually cheering for Jesus.

"Thank you, Master Jesus!" a person in the crowd shouted. "The Temple has turned into a cesspool. You must return it to its rightful status."

"Do to Rome, what you did here," another man shouted.

Then the blind and the lame came to Jesus, and he healed them. But the chief priests and Scribes were indignant when they saw the wonders he performed.

And the children shouted in the Temple courts, "Hosanna to the Son of David!" "Do you hear what these children are saying?" Pharisee number one stormed up to Jesus and asked.

"Yes," Jesus answered. "Have you never read: 'From the mouths of children and infants You have ordained praise'?"

"No matter what you say, you are not the Son of God," the second Pharisee shouted angrily. "You will never be the Son of God. Never!"

"I am what my Father tells me I am. Nothing more."

"You are delusional," the first Pharisee declared. "You will be stopped. You are guilty of blasphemy."

The assistant hurriedly left. "I must report this to Caiaphas."

"You cannot stop God. He is everywhere, and the reason for everything. I am guilty of nothing but love for all. I even love you."

Upon hearing that last remark, the two Pharisees turned and left.

Jesus now stood in the center of the Temple. James, John, Matthew, and Thomas surrounded him with a hug. A small crowd stood in attention to Jesus.

"You are a leader among all men. This should be taught to others. It is a great day," Thomas said.

"I am tired of being pushed around," James added. "It is time we started pushing back. I am honored to be your disciple, as we all are."

"Yes," John agreed. "This will go down as the beginning of a new kingdom. The kingdom of Jesus and heaven."

"I will record this for history," Matthew said. "What will I call it?"

"The cleansing of the Temple!" Jesus shouted out to the people still watching. "The cleansing of the Temple!"

The crowd cheered at that last statement. Jesus turned to look at Jennifer. "Please come over and meet my disciples." She approached Jesus.

"Jennifer, you already know John and James. This is Thomas and Matthew."

"Please to meet you both."

"Jesus, where did you find her?" Thomas exclaimed. "I have never seen anyone like her."

"Don't start, she already knows," Jesus assured him.

"Yes, I am sure she does," Matthew agreed. "Good day, my lady."

"We will be back later," Jesus said. "Calm things down here for me, if you can." "Of course, Lord," Matthew said.

Jesus and Jennifer left the Temple.

Matthew turned to John and James. "You knew about her and didn't tell me? What is going on? Our master is with a woman?"

"She just appeared out of nowhere," James said with a shrug. "I don't know. I believe that Jesus thinks she was sent to her by his Father. Look at her, even an angel might be jealous. He now protects her like no other."

"Yes, she does look like an angel," Thomas agreed. "Why is she here?"

"She may be here to help us and Jesus," John said. "Although Judas surely does not like or trust her."

Matthew laughed. "If Judas doesn't like her, that is a good sign—a very good sign. We all know how Judas feels about women, especially any woman next to Jesus."

"For better or worse," John said, "she is here, and we are stuck with her for now. I think Jesus would do anything for her. I mean look at what just happened? Jesus would never have done such a thing before. She has changed him."

"You are right," Thomas agreed. "Maybe this is just what we needed. Especially if Judas doesn't like her. That I want to see."

"Come, we should help clean up," James said. "It will show the people that we care. What a mess."

The disciples started cleaning up, helping others who had already started. The Temple had grown much quieter. Jennifer and Jesus stood outside.

"I think you really showed them today. It was exciting to watch. You do hold a lot of power," Jennifer said, grinning.

"I was very proud of you, as well. You watched everything calmly and reserved, and you did not raise your fist. I am pleased," Jesus said. "You have a lot of control."

"No one threatened you, physically. If they had, I would have responded. At least now they can start the cleaning."

"What is your reaction to how I acted today?"

"To be honest, at first I thought it might be a little over the top. But after seeing what they were doing to your Temple, if anything, you showed great and I mean really great, restraint. You made an excellent point. I agree completely. Trust me, I would have acted much worse. Good job." "Do you think they have learned a lesson?" Jesus asked.

"A few, not all, but a few will wise up. It has to start somewhere and like you said about the mustard seed, it starts small but grows into something big."

"Then I am satisfied."

"Trust me," Jennifer assured him. "No matter what or when, humans will always have the need to learn. It will never end."

"Good, then my purpose will never end."

"Exactly. There is a great need for you everywhere, far greater and vaster than you can imagine," Jennifer said. Ready to move on, she asked, "So, what's for lunch?"

"I am now hungry for bread."

"Goodie, just what I wanted. Can't wait." Her expression, however, told a different story as she thought about all the sumptuous meals she had eaten over the years. What she wouldn't give to share one with Jesus now.

"I'm afraid we have no choice but to wait."

"Yes, I know. That was just an expression from my land." "Some things from your land are truly strange."

Jennifer spotted a bread vender. "Yes, I know. Oh, look, bread, and I have money. My treat, get whatever you like."

"That is so generous of you."

"My pleasure, my love."

"Maybe even some goat milk. It's my favorite," Jesus said.

Jennifer struggled to keep from making a face. "Of course, and maybe fresh juice and some fruit. Whatever you want, my Lord." "You already are what I want. But juice would be nice, especially with the bread," he said, thinking about the kind he wanted.

"Once again, can't wait."

They approached the bread vender, where Jennifer wished they had a croissant, but that was not going to happen. She decided to make the best of it. After all, she was with Jesus and what could top that?

CHAPTER

TWENTY-TWO

Later that day, Jennifer and Jesus strolled down main street in Jerusalem. Jennifer kept her hood up to try and prevent people from staring at her. Yet they still did. Just being with Jesus got you noticed, especially being a woman. Jesus was known to be a loner and was not seen with a lot of women. Many women greatly admired Jesus because he was so good looking. Yet he seemed to not care, so most of them stayed away. But Jennifer, with her unique coloring and features was spectacular to these people and of course, not being from this area or time also made her unique. The people could tell that Jesus was captivated by her.

It hadn't taken long for word to get around about what Jesus had done at the Temple, and a vast majority of the people agreed that he had done the right thing.

Jennifer stopped at a fruit store and talked to the owner. "Are your figs good and sweet? I don't want to buy them if they aren't."

"They are the best. I guarantee it," the owner assured her. "I picked them myself." "Okay, give me some of your best."

The store owner handed her some figs. Jennifer gave one to Jesus.

"Since you're the expert, I need your opinion on the quality and taste of these figs."

Jesus ate the fig. "Very good indeed! As good as the fruit I used to get from my favorite tree."

Jennifer paid the store owner, probably way too much, greatly surprising him. "Keep the change," she told him. "Who knows. I might be back for more."

"Thank you, thank you, thank you! I will take special care of you, beautiful lady."

As they left the seller, she shared the figs with Jesus. Jennifer still wasn't crazy about them, but she had learned to tolerate them because she knew her body needed the nutrients, especially since bread seemed to be their main staple.

Jesus stopped for a second and looked up at the sky. He closed his eyes and seemed to be listening to someone or something. Was it his Father? A moment later, he opened his eyes and looked toward the Temple as if it were calling to him.

"We must return to the Temple. There are people there who need me."

They turned around and headed back the way they had come.

"You spend a lot of time there," Jennifer said. "I sense that it is a very special place for you. You feel like you belong there, and it seems to be your true home."

"That is very insightful, Jennifer. I go there almost every day to teach and sometimes to heal. Now is the time for healing. There are people waiting for us and for the love of God to bring them the peace they so desperately need."

Jesus and Jennifer returned to the Temple area and found it much cleaner now, especially with all the sellers and animals gone. A crowd of people quickly surrounded Jesus. Jennifer stepped back out of the way, but curiosity kept her close enough to see what would happen. She could not describe the feeling. It was as if something special was in the air almost like electricity, although it had not been invented yet, and there were no clouds in the sky that might indicate that lightning was in the atmosphere.

"I'll wait over here," she told Jesus. "Please help your people. I will be overjoyed just to observe and witness the love they have for you."

"Tonight, just you and me and the stars. And nobody to separate us," he assured her.

"How about some bread and wine for dinner and protein bars for breakfast."

"That sounds good and the most wondrous part will be feeling your warmth."

"No, you are the warm one," she told him. "You are like an oven on a cold, snowy winter day. Do you know what snow is?"

"Yes. I have seen it on top of the mountains, but I have not gone there and actually touched it," he said. "I have heard that it can be cold and refreshing."

"Once again, it depends on how you view it. From a distance, it can be beautiful to look at, but if you become trapped in it, it can become uncomfortable and very cold, so cold that it actually hurts."

"Then let there be Jennifer, and bread, and a warm night."

"Can't wait," she said smiling. "Chanel by Jennifer."

Jesus smiled after hearing that last remark as he really enjoyed the Chanel treatment.

The people knew of the many stories about Jesus and his ability to heal people, and they came from all angles, requesting and hoping to be healed. Jesus loved his people and wanted to help as many as he could, but there were so many, and only one of him. It sometimes became difficult to select the most worthy person. But somehow, it always happened, perhaps because it was being directed by God.

A woman with a shriveled hand approached Jesus. "Please, son of David, heal my hand so I can work again and help the Temple and give praised to you and your Father."

"Give me your hand," Jesus told her. "Your faith has saved you, and it shall be rewarded."

Jesus took her hand and kissed it. The hand immediately returned to normal.

The woman fell to her knees and kissed Jesus' ankles. "Thank you, Master. I will always serve you. You are the true king. You are the only one now and forever."

Jennifer's eyes opened wide in disbelief. She could not fathom what she had just witnessed. Nothing in science could back this up. Instant healing was something not possible, even in her time. But she had just witnessed it in real life. Impossible, but it had happened. What wonders could science learn from Jesus? *There is so much he could teach us,* she thought. However, she still did not comprehend what was happening. What Jesus was doing wasn't something that science could duplicate. It wasn't something that could be learned. It was a divine gift from the Father to the Son.

Jesus said to the woman, "You must forgive all who have harassed you. If you forgive, your hand will remain healed." He raised his hands and laid them on top of her head. "I bless you in the name of my father. Go in peace and love."

"I will, my Lord," she promised. "It is amazing to see the love within you. How blessed I am that some of it has been given to me. I am truly humbled. I did not know until now that love could be so pure. Only God could do what you just did for me. You made me whole again, and I feel your love."

"Go and teach others the same love," he told her.

"From this moment, I will live only for you and your love," she promised before leaving.

Jennifer was overwhelmed with emotion. She had not been prepared for this, and it only made her love stronger, if that was possible.

Two men brought a blind man to Jesus.

"My Lord, my Master, and king, I want forgiveness, and I will forgive all who sinned against me," the blind man said.

"Can you forgive and love them?"

"Yes, I can. I also love you, Jesus, and no matter what you do or don't do, I will still love you. I am at your mercy. I will always believe in you. You are the messiah. Even though I am blind, I can feel the love you have for your people."

With tears in his eyes, Jesus spat on his thumbs and pressed them against the eyes of the blind man. The man screamed at first, not understanding the feeling that was rushing from his eyes and spreading throughout the rest of his body, healing his heart, mind, and soul as well. He fell to his knees in front of Jesus. When he looked up to the face of Jesus, his eyes were wide open and clear. Those standing nearby could see the Lord's reflection in them.

"I can see! I can see! I see your beautiful face. It is the most beautiful thing I have ever seen. Thank you, my Lord! Thank you! I am yours forever."

The blind man looked at the two men who had brought him there, and then out to the crowd. There were tears in his eyes. "I can see! Jesus the true Son of David gave me back my sight. It is a miracle! Jesus is a miracle in all ways. Praise be to God!"

The crowd was astonished and more people entered the Temple to experience this man called Jesus. For Jennifer, once more, there was no scientific explanation for what he had done. What Jesus was doing was impossible, or at least thought impossible. Yet, here he was, healing people with whatever strange or unknown power he possessed. No science could explain it. Science would say it was impossible. He had just given sight to a blind man without an operation and taking no more than a second for it to take effect.

"I want you to see what is good and help others to see the true light of my Father. You now know where you have to go. Go in love."

"God is love. Love like no other," the former blind man said. "I have never felt such love. Love for Jesus! I will always follow you." His two friends escorted him away. Several people he passed, reached out and touched him, hoping to receive some miracle of their own. Jennifer realized that even modern science could not do this. It couldn't heal without surgery, medication, or procedures of some sort. How was Jesus able to do it? Once again, the impossible became possible. Jennifer could hardly believe what she had witnessed. She knew the history and the stories, but nothing could have prepared her for the real thing, or how it made her feel. She had tears of amazement in her eyes. Her love and admiration for Jesus knew no bounds.

Next, a woman brought a young boy up to Jesus. The boy was shaking violently and seemed out of control, afraid to get near Jesus. The woman forced the boy closer.

"Jesus, my King, my child is possessed with an unclean spirit. Can you banish it before it kills him? Please, he is my only son. His father is no longer with us. He is all I have left, that and my faith in you."

The young boy broke loose from his mother, ran to Jesus and started to madly hit him with his fists, but he was too small to hurt Jesus, who looked at him and saw the rage within him.

"You are not the savior!" the child screeched in a voice that clearly was not his own. "You are nothing more than an imposter! You cannot save this boy. He is mine and will never belong to you. You cannot defeat the devil!"

Jesus calmly looked at the young boy. And when the demon within the boy realized that it could not scare Jesus away, it forced the boy to turn to the crowd.

"Hear me! Jesus will destroy the world and everything in it. He is great destruction. You will all suffer and die! He is not the Son of God! You will all die with much pain! No one will save you, and you all will belong to Satan!"

Jesus smiled at the young boy and quickly placed his hands on the boy's head, preventing the child from moving. The power of Jesus and God now controlled his body.

"Evil spirit be gone and leave this boy forever! I command you! Never return! Be gone!"

The boy cried out in agony as the spirit that had possessed him screamed in anger and left him. Calm now, the boy smiled at Jesus. It was the first smile he'd had in many days.

Jesus addressed the crowd. "The demon is gone. He will never return to this boy. Do not let it into your lives. My Father will always protect you from him, if you have faith. The devil wants to destroy your faith."

The boy's mother took Jesus by his hands and kissed them incessantly. "You have saved my child and honored us both. I will always honor you. There are not enough ways to say thank you except with all my love."

"That will be enough. Take your boy home and raise him to be a good and loyal son. Teach him the bible and how to be closer to God."

Jesus again looked out at the crowd. "No evil can stand against my Father. The love He has for you will always protect you as will I."

"Glory to God in the highest," someone in the crowd shouted. "And be assured that, if need be, I will die for you. I will most surely die to prove my love for you."

Unfortunately, the people did not truly understand what Jesus meant by those words. They likened them to dying in battle against the Romans. They had no clue that Jesus meant he would die to save their souls.

Jennifer was taken back by that last statement. Of course, she knew the history, but now her love was in the way. If any man deserved to live, Jesus was the one. At this point, Jennifer was so filled with emotion, there was nothing to compare it with. She fully realized that what she had been witnessing were true miracles. Not ones simply talked or written about, but the real thing. She had never believed in miracles before. That had all changed. Seeing was believing.

A woman with a young man approached Jesus, fell to her knees and kissed his feet.

"What is it that you desire? How can God help you?"

"Not for me, my Lord and Master, but for my friend here. He has suffered his whole life and people ridicule and make fun of him for something he has no control over."

"I am pleased that you think of serving him and not yourself. That is the way into heaven. What is his problem?"

"He is deaf and mute, but he shows no hatred to anyone," she told him. "He has been loyal to me for so many years that I want to reward him. But it is not within my power. Only the Son of God can change him. I beg for your love and mercy."

"Then let it be so. Bring him to me and let me show him the love of God."

The woman brought her friend closer to Jesus, who stood calmly before him, hope and expectation alive in his eyes.

And Jesus saw that he was a kind and honest man. Raising his hand, he placed his fingers into the man's ears, and then spat and touched his tongue. "Ephphatha, be opened!"

The man remained still for a few seconds and looked around. Then, his eyes blinked rapidly and widened in amazement as the sounds within the Temple filled his ears for the first time. It filled him with wonder. Turning back to Jesus, he placed his hands on the Lord's shoulders and smiled. Then opened his mouth to speak plainly. "I…love…you, Jesus. Glory to God! I can speak!" His words ended in a joyous shout.

"And do you hear the words of God?"

"I will. I do. I finally do. I can hear." He looked at his friend. "Say something."

She smiled and said, "Blessed be the Lord."

"I heard you," the man said, softly now. "I actually heard you, and all of you," he cried, pointing to the crowd. He dropped to his knees in front of Jesus.

The woman picked him up and kissed Jesus' hand. "You are the greatest man in the history of the world. Thank you for your love."

Jesus touched the man's arm. "You can now hear God and speak to him whenever you want. Tells others to hear and speak with God and learn to feel his love."

"I will, my Lord, I will. Bless you and bless everything that you are. You are all that is good."

The man and woman left. Jennifer was speechless. She had just witnessed the true kindness of God. *If only Jesus could teach us how he does it. Even modern science is primitive and backward compared to him. The stories just don't do him justice. He is way more than the stories.* And now she finally understood why.

The crowd was getting larger, and Jesus was soon overwhelmed. There were just too many of them. They all wanted a miracle. But each time he performed one, it took something out of him. He needed to rest and restore his strength.

He walked over to Jennifer and took her by the hand. "Come. It is time to leave. I need peace and calm, and I need to be with only you."

As they were leaving, Jesus spotted a crippled man on wooden crutches, barely able to walk. Jesus touched him. "Put down your crutches. You no longer need them."

The man did so and suddenly was able to gingerly walk without the crutches. "You will get stronger soon. Walk and spread peace and love and don't stop." "Jesus, my Lord, why did you help me? I did not even have a chance to ask. Thank you."

"I saw a man with a good heart who needed kindness without asking. My purpose in life is to show and give love. Love for all, whether they ask for it or not."

Jesus and Jennifer walked away as the crowd slowly dispersed.

"There are just too many people. They keep coming," Jennifer said, worriedly.

"I know. God made many people in need, and I will love and help as many as I can, no matter what they ultimately do to me. I will still love them."

"I have never felt this kind of love before. It is why I have been alone for most of my life."

"I am pleased. You are special. I, too, never believed that this feeling I have for you was possible. Yet it is."

"I mean, how you are able to do this? I just witnessed the impossible."

"No, it is only impossible because you believe that it was. All things are possible with my Father. If you learn to believe that, you will understand."

Jennifer shook her head. "I have to believe what I witnessed with my own eyes. My love will not allow me to believe anything else. You are who you say you are, and I am lucky that I am here with you. People will never understand how much more there is to you, but I know. You are truth itself, and the way, and the light."

Jennifer and Jesus hugged, knowing that they both loved each other. Hearing a voice come from behind them, they turned to see a heavy man with bad skin, using a single crutch and dragging a leg than could not bend at the knee.

"Jesus, I waited until you were away from the crowd. I have heard so many stories about you. I need help, but I am not a believer. I do not believe in God, especially when I see so many people suffering. Why would God let people suffer?"

"People suffer to be saved," Jesus told him. "I will soon suffer so that even one such as you might be saved. Even you can learn love and change."

The man laughed bitterly. "Look at me. I have to drag my foot, and my skin is covered with boils. As you can see, I am very damaged and in need of mercy. Most nights I cannot sleep because my head gives me pain, and it won't go away."

"I can see where you cannot," Jesus told him. "But what you do not know is that you are more damaged on the inside than you are on the outside. You are rich because of the poor. But your soul is not rich, compared to the people who labor for you."

"How is that possible?" the man asked. "How do you know all this without my telling you? Yes, I have more money than most, but with my money I employ many families so they can live and raise their children. They need me to live. Is that not a good thing?"

"Do you treat them well and pay a fair wage? Do they consider you a kind and good employer? Do they love you?"

"I pay them a wage they can live on, and I do not treat them badly, but they have to follow my orders and do what I say. To be honest, they would not call it a fair wage, while I do. Most do not like me, but nobody really likes the people who pay them for work. I do not feel any love from them, and I do not love them. That, however, is likely my fault as I do not try hard enough. I need to try harder."

"Well, at least you are honest about who and what you are. It seems you have everything money can buy. What do you want from me?"

"I want to buy a miracle. I want to be healed. I will pay much for your powers. You heal people for no profit. Maybe it is time you finally profited from your good deeds. I want to buy your forgiveness. I will give you much money. You can take that money and help others with it. That would be a good thing. Would it not?"

Jesus looked at him with pity. "Miracles cannot be bought. They must be earned by faith and love. It starts by forgiving and being forgiven by others. No amount of money can buy it. That is why it is so valuable. It is beyond money."

"Can I be forgiven?" the rich man asked. "What must I do? Can you ever forgive me for being what I am?"

"I forgive you, but I will not heal you at this moment. You must earn it. You need to heal yourself first from the inside out. Then and only then can the outward healing begin. You cannot buy faith. It has to become the most important desire in your life. You have to open your heart and feel the love of God. These are things money cannot buy. Jennifer, please tell this man about money." "Money is the root of all evil," she said.

"Precisely, so I ask you. Do you want to be saved? Do you want to feel a love that can heal you?" Jesus asked.

"What must I do? Please, nobody yet has ever told me what I must do. I want to be saved. I feel I will soon die unless I change. Tell me how? Please!" the man begged.

"You must do what I did. You must walk into the mountains and survive for forty days and nights with nothing but your soul. And you must show that the devil has no control over you."

"How will I survive without food and water?" Fear filled his heart. What Jesus wanted seemed impossible.

"I did it without food, but that was for me, not you. You will find food and water enough to survive."

"How will that happen?" the man asked anxiously.

"You will survive on the kindness and generosity of others. If you believe, they will save you. Each day and night, you must speak with my Father and learn the way of faith and love. If you do this, I promise you that after the forty days and nights, the devil within you will vacate your body. You will then seek out one of my disciples and tell him that I sent you. And he will heal your leg, your skin, the pain in your head, and your soul. This I promise you. All you need is faith. Faith in yourself, and forgiveness."

Hope entered the man's heart. "My life is empty, and I have nothing to live for. But I want to be saved. I want to live and have faith. I am tired of being a sad, miserable man. I will do what you say. You are now my lord and master, and I can now see this in you. I want to know the love of God. When do I start?"

Jesus pointed to the hills. "Right now. Leave the city. After forty days and forty nights when you return, you will pay a fair wage and treat the people who labor for you as neighbors. Do you understand?"

"I understand, my Lord, and my journey begins now. I feel better even now. I believe you did perform a miracle. You have opened my eyes, and now I see it."

"As your faith grows, you will learn the joys and love of the kingdom of heaven. I see it all in you. I knew it from the first moment I saw you. You were lost. Go and find your way. It is what you desire, and now you know how to find it for yourself."

The heavy man slowly walked away to begin his journey of faith.

"I can guarantee one thing. That man is going to lose some weight. Forty days and forty nights is a definite weight loss program. It will be good for him. Yes, he is going to lose a lot of weight."

"But he will gain the gift of life."

"Come, my love, let's get dinner. That man made me hungry. How about some chicken tonight? I've seen it for sale at one of the shops, and I know exactly where to find it."

"Yes, that sounds delicious, and maybe some bread with it."

"Yes, of course, some bread," Jennifer said with a laugh. "What is a meal without bread? Come, my love, let's go shopping."

Jennifer and Jesus walked into the main part of Jerusalem to buy food.

Later that evening after eating their fill, Jesus took Jennifer to his favorite spot on the Mount of Olives to sleep under the stars. He had borrowed some blankets to make them more comfortable, and they laid down next to each other for added warmth.

"Look at all the stars," Jesus mused. "There are so many."

"Actually, there are way, way more than you think. The scientists in my land have discovered so many that it staggers the imagination." "Do they know what they are?" Jesus asked.

"Yes, they do."

"Please tell me. I've have always wondered about them, and why my Father placed them in the sky."

"In the morning when the sun comes up, what you see would look just like the stars from a distance. Now imagine a lot more suns out in the sky only much, much further away. That is what you see right now. The stars above us are actually many, many suns so far away that they look smaller than the one you see every day."

"I have never thought of it that way, but it makes sense. The night of many suns."

"Actually, they are there in the daylight, too," Jennifer explained. "You can't see them, though, because they are hidden by the daylight of our own bright sun. But sometimes when the sky is dark, you can see them faintly in the distance."

"I know there is a lot more for you to teach me," Jesus said. "There just is not enough time."

"Today you taught me all I need to know and more. Tonight, is a good night as long as I am with you," Jennifer said.

"Yes, a very good night indeed."

"And like I said, I have more protein bars for the morning." She smiled softly at him.

"That will make it a good morning. You are so full of wonders. Till morning." "I still have some bread with me. Here, take some." She gave Jesus some bread."

"The food of life."

"That will change in a few days. You need something special, and I will make it happen."

"You are my something special," he assured her. "There is no one like you, and I am very grateful for that."

"Good. Now, it's Chanel time."

"More wondrous gifts. For the first time in my life, I am enjoying being slightly spoiled, especially by you."

Jennifer smiled. "Who knows? Maybe we can keep spoiling each other."

She applied Chanel to his face and neck. Then Jesus enjoyed the last of the bread.

Later, they both fell asleep under a sky full of stars.

CHAPTER

TWENTY-THREE

It was nearly noon in Jerusalem, and the people were still busy making preparations for Passover. Jesus and Jennifer spent the morning walking around the city, talking with people and generally enjoying being together. Feeling hungry, Jesus sat alone at a small table in the shade of an olive tree. Jennifer had insisted that he wait while she went and bought lunch, as she wanted to pick out the food. Actually, Jesus had come to enjoy being a little pampered. The area where he sat could have been described as an ancient food court.

Jennifer returned with lunch. "All right, lunch is served. Bread, fruit, vegetables, and some pomegranate juice, all for my wonderful king."

Jennifer placed the food down in front of Jesus, who reached up and touched her face to show his appreciation. She sat across from him, and they began eating.

"You have a knack of picking out the best of the best. It is enjoyable to see you take over. Just don't get mad at anybody. I know what you can do."

"I won't," she reassured him. "And if I did, it would only be to defend you. Though after watching you yesterday, I feel if you wanted to, you could defend yourself against anybody or anything. You have powers that people do not understand, and those powers are always good."

"Yes, there are many things I won't show most people. It might confuse them. They would never understand things like what you said about the stars being nothing more than far away suns. That concept would be beyond them." Jesus looked up and stared at the open blue sky. "Now that I know they are there, I can see them even now. They are up there with my Father. You are correct. There are many of them, too many to count."

Jennifer took a bite of her bread. "This bread is actually pretty good. They even put raisins in it this time. Wow, something inventive. Who knows, maybe next time some nuts, the opportunities are endless for bread."

"Yes, a very good lunch indeed," Jesus said, smiling. "I hope the Passover dinner will be as good."

"Oh, I'm going to help out on that, too. It will be an unforgettable dinner. One for all time."

"Sounds like it will be a supper that will be talked about for the ages. But if my Father is correct, it will be my Last Supper with you. And for that I am sad. You have become a very special part of me."

"No, not this time. I believe your Father might just want something else out of you first. Just the start of many. Believe in my love."

"I do, but I also believe in the love and wisdom of my Father, and that is greater. My love for you is very special. I will let nothing happen to you. You will always be in my heart."

"You have been in my heart for way longer than you realize," Jennifer assured him. "I have waited my whole life for you, and it was definitely worth the wait. I do not want to lose it now." She fought off the fear that thought invoked. "I can't."

"When I first looked upon you, I knew that destiny had brought you to me, and I was pleased."

"Yes, I was sent to you. I was born to be sent to you. You are the one I have waited for all this time."

"For that I am honored. We must go to the Temple, now. There are people waiting for my teachings."

"I'll meet you there. I have some errands to do first. It won't take long."

"You have errands already? Even though you have been here for only a few days? What are they?"

"Nothing important, but it's a surprise," Jennifer said. "Please just trust me."

"Of course, my angel. Go do your errands. I will meet you at the Temple later." Jesus grabbed the last of the bread. "And I will eat this on the way. Like you said, it is very good. Soon, my love."

Jesus left and headed to the Temple. Jennifer could not tell him what her errand was, as she needed to go to the time ship to check things out and restock her protein bars, money, and Chanel. She walked past the gate and just for the fun of it, decided to run to the time ship. As she ran, people thought she was crazy. Why run when you can walk, especially in this heat? You only ran when you were running away from something. Jennifer thought to herself, didn't the Greeks start the marathon? Before she reached the time ship, she stopped by a large pile of boulders. The area appeared quite empty.

"Keith! Meet me in the ship!" she shouted at the boulders.

A voice from behind the boulders replied, "Will do!"

Keith had thought that he was well hidden from Jennifer and her prying eyes. Being detected was something he had not counted on. He had always thought he was an expert tracker, and no one knew he was anywhere around. This time, however, he was wrong.

Jennifer walked past the leper colony hologram and entered the time ship. She headed for the refrigerator and removed a cold bottle of cow's milk, which she quickly drank down. "So good!" she said with a sigh. "How I have missed this. Way better than warm goat's milk. I will never get used to that."

She then grabbed some protein bars and put them in her pouch. Next, she helped herself to another bottle of Chanel and more money.

Keith entered and grabbed a cold soft drink. He opened it and drank it down. Then he sat in a seat in front of Jennifer.

"Did you actually believe that I didn't know you've been following me for the last two days?" Jennifer asked him.

"Yes, but I do now. I knew you were good, but not that good. I will remember that." He tried to change the subject. "Sure is hot out there." "Were you following me or Jesus?"

"Does it matter?" Keith asked, trying to sound bored with the whole thing. "I'm just here to observe."

"Yes, and you should remember that, especially if you're following Jesus. Why are you following us?"

"I have my orders, and they come from a much higher source than you." That did not sit well with Jennifer. Her voice hardened. "Listen to me. That source won't be around for another two thousand years. I am the source now."

"Understood," Keith lied. As far as he was concerned, Jennifer would never be his commander. "So, is Jesus the real thing or not? That's what I'm here to find out. I think you already know." He paused. "Or do you?"

Not knowing his intentions or reasons, Jennifer did not trust Keith and was reluctant to answer that question honestly. "I'm not positively sure, yet. I need more time to confirm it. I must be certain. It's a big deal."

"Just so you know. I'm not the only one watching. Someone else is keeping a close eye on you. If I were you, I would be very careful."

"I know. Nothing is truly safe out there. You have to remain on guard. The problem is, they know I'm not from around here."

"What was all the commotion about at the Temple yesterday? I was too far away to really see anything. Was someone causing trouble? Was it Jesus?"

"No, it was nothing. The people love Jesus. God or not, they really love him, and they believe in him. They think he will save them from Rome. Rome is not loved by any of these people, but then, who would love their oppressors? They really believe Jesus has the power to destroy Rome, and they will follow him because of that."

"Yet, if we believe what we have been told over the years, they will all turn on him soon. His cross is waiting. Rome will deliver it to him. He doesn't have much time left," Keith said coldly.

"And I need every second to discover the truth. Do you know where Leo and Winifred are?"

"They left early this morning to explore. They could be anywhere. Leo looks like the perfect slave. He's a funny guy. Actually, if we left him here, he would fit right in, no problem. He would become just another faceless nobody in a sea of humanity."

"It's you that I am concerned about. Especially with you pretending to be a Roman soldier. I really hope you have stayed out of trouble and didn't cause any problems."

"I have. I even taught some young kids the consequences of stealing."

"I don't think I want to know how you did that," Jennifer said. "Too much information."

"They learned a lesson they will never forget. A lesson for all time."

Jennifer could have questioned him further, but she felt certain she would not like what he told her, and there wasn't anything she could do about it now, anyway. "I need to get back; I'm expected. What are your plans? Do you want me to tell you where we're going next to make it easier for you?"

"No, thank you. I think I'm going to stay here and enjoy the air conditioning and some good food and beer. I won't go anywhere until tomorrow. I'm done for the day. The only good thing about this place is that there is plenty of sun to keep our solar panels powered. To be honest, I'm ready to return to our time. There's nothing interesting out there. I can't believe it all started here. It's just too simplistic. I might even take a nap."

"If you change your mind, I'll know it. Take care."

Jennifer walked toward the time ship door as Keith pulled out a beer, opened it, and drank it down. Then he took another.

Jennifer shook her head and sighed. "A slightly drunk Roman soldier. What could possibly happen with that? See you soon."

Jennifer walked back to Jerusalem and headed toward the Temple. Once again, she knew she was being watched. Only this time she didn't know by how many.

Caiaphas' assistant stepped in front of her and put out his hand to stop her. "You need to come with me. You are under arrest by order of the High Priest Caiaphas." When he saw the expression change on her face, he added, "You are surrounded. Do not try to escape."

The assistant placed his hands on Jennifer, but she kicked him in the face, knocking him down, and giving him a bloody nose. She continued walking.

"Get her!" the assistant shouted.

Suddenly, twenty men came out of a darkened corner and surrounded Jennifer. She had not expected this many men to attack at once. She hit a few that came too close, but she knew that this was trouble, and she wouldn't be able to get them all. Looking up, she saw ten more men running toward her. This was an army, and she was one. This was one time she wished she had a gun. It would have come in handy. The only option was to surrender and wait for a better time.

Jennifer put her hands up in surrender.

"Okay. I see that I'm outnumbered. Apparently, it takes an army of men to restrain just one lone woman. I'll go with you peacefully," she told them.

"Take no chance, put the net on her," the assistant ordered.

"I have it!" one man yelled.

"No need for a net. I said I would go with you." She looked at the assistant. "Your nose is still bleeding." She should not have goaded him.

"Use it now! Take no chance!" he shouted.

They covered Jennifer with a net and took her to the nearby prison that looked like a stone cave with rooms and metal bars and shackles on the wall. Jennifer was shackled to a wall with her hands on each side, unable to move.

The head guard in charge was overweight with a large stomach. He smiled a gap-toothed grin at Jennifer. "Look what we got here, an angel of God. The friend of Jesus. That won't do you any good. For a temptress, you are absolutely beautiful, but that won't affect me. I was told not to touch your face but how about a little dirty water. Let's see how that feels, especially to an angel. Do angels like dirty water? Let's see."

The head guard threw a bucket of dirty water on Jennifer, making the majority of the guards watching laugh, while a few were respectfully silent.

"Do you really know who I am? I am Jesus' girlfriend, not just his friend, and he is not going to be happy about this. He will condemn you all to hell. You hear me? Hell! You will never see heaven, never! Think about that. Hell is not a nice place, and it lasts for an eternity. Are you ready for hell?"

The head guard slammed his fist into Jennifer's stomach.

She took it without a sound, not even a grunt and angrily stared at him. "Oh, look at the big bad man, hitting a woman in shackles. Wow, what a brave man. There will be stories written about your bravery. It will be called the coward and the brave woman."

"Forget your face. It needs to be less beautiful. Here, let me be of service to you, my pleasure."

The head guard slapped Jennifer in the face and threw more water on her.

"You will all be wishing for that water in hell. Jesus will send you there. Remember, Jesus is the son of God, and no one enters the kingdom of heaven except through him. How do you think putting me in shackles is going to look? What is it boys, heaven or hell? It's a tough decision. Don't you think?"

There were two men off to one side who were believers in Jesus. They were afraid and decide to leave.

"Please, beautiful lady, forgive us, we are sorry," the first man said. "I do not want Jesus angry at me. We are leaving. We wish you no harm, and we want to be in the kingdom of heaven."

"Most beautiful angel, please forgive me," a second man said. "I want no part in this. We want no harm to come to you." The two men left.

"Now those two have good sense. They want to go to heaven. How about the rest of you?"

"They follow me. I do not believe in your Jesus, nor do I fear him," the head guard said scornfully.

"Good, all the more fun in hell for you and your friends."

The head guard grabbed a whip from the wall and forcefully whipped Jennifer.

"Wow, such a brave man," Jennifer goaded. "Are you afraid of me? A little woman like me. You seem afraid. You are so afraid that you have to use a whip on me."

"I am not afraid of one such as you. Never!" the head guard shouted.

"Good, then come closer. Look, my hands are in shackles. There is nothing I can do. I am just a woman."

The head guard stepped closer to Jennifer.

"A little closer," Jennifer taunted. "Come on. Don't be afraid."

"I am not afraid!"

"Good."

Suddenly Jennifer kicked him in the face, instantly breaking his nose in five places. Blood was everywhere, and he fell to the ground.

"Bitch! You broke my nose! You will pay."

"I'm sorry, come a little closer, and let me apologize. Maybe I can make it better. Actually, you do look better."

"Bitch! I will beat you!" the head guard ground out.

"That's not a nice word to use for a lady. You need to be taught respect."

The head guard grabbed the whip he had dropped and raised it to beat Jennifer. Just then, Caiaphas' assistant walked in.

"Stop! She is not to be harmed, by order of Caiaphas. Leave her be and wait for Jesus. That is who we want."

"I see it now. This is a trap. Just be careful about what you wish for, as you will receive it in abundance. Setting a trap for Jesus will not get you into heaven. You'd better change."

"She broke my nose," the head guard protested.

The assistant looked at the man's face. "It actually looks good. Gives you character. Look at my bruise. She got me too. She's very good at hitting men, very good. Just wait for Jesus. I will return. I must report to Caiaphas."

The assistant left. Jennifer and the head guard stared at each other, but he kept his distance. There was no way he was getting any closer to her feet.

"I'm waiting for you. Come a little closer, please," Jennifer taunted. "Bitch!"

*****

Caiaphas was in his chair waiting for the news.

The assistant entered and faced him. "We have her. All we need is for Jesus to show up and cause trouble. Then we will have him, too."

"Excellent! We will finally have Jesus where we want him. The love of a woman will be his ultimate downfall. How ironic." Caiaphas stared at the assistant's face. "What happened to your face? Who did that to you?"

"She got me. She got me good. She is definitely a fighting angel. She is an excellent fighter."

"I don't want to be disrespectful to angels, especially female ones, but I hear they can be quite the bitches."

"I agree now. She also broke the head guard's nose."

"I know him. He probably looks better now. What else?"

"She did kind of surrender without a fight. Almost like she wanted to be taken." "How many men did I pay for?" Caiaphas asked.

The assistant paused. "Thirty. And I believe we needed them all. You know, to intimidate her."

"Yes, money can do that, especially my money. I should get a discount for such a large number of men. Okay. Wait for Jesus to complete the trap."

"One man's foolish mistake over a woman."

"Just like Cleopatra. I think she was a bitch, too," Caiaphas mused.

"This one is even better. Cleopatra didn't break noses with her feet."

"Cleopatra was no angel that I know for sure, but she was a bitch." The assistant left.

*****

Jesus was at the Temple teaching a small crowd, when he was approached by a young man, dressed very nicely.

He asked Jesus a question. "Good Master, what must I do to have eternal life?"

"You must follow the commandments of Moses and God."

"Please tell me exactly what they are for I know that I am already a good person."

"Love the Lord your God with all your heart, all your mind, and all your soul. Love your neighbor as yourself. You shall not murder. You shall not commit adultery. You shall not steal. You shall not bear false witness. Honor your father and mother. You must follow all these commandments."

"Master, I have followed those my whole life. I have obeyed to the letter every one of them. I have been pure. Surely eternal life will be given to me."

"I see that you are dressed very well," Jesus said. "You must have a life of wealth. You do not know what it means to be poor and humble."

"I have been greatly blessed by God. He has been good to me and my family. I always treat the poor with respect. We pay a lot of taxes. I will pay to get into heaven if I have to."

"You cannot buy your way into heaven. But there is another way."

"Please tell me what it is, and I will do it."

"If you want to be perfect, sell what you own and give the money to the poor. You will have treasure in heaven. Then follow me!"

The young man was taken back by that statement, for he was very rich, and he wanted to stay that way. "I cannot. I want to keep everything as it is. I have too much to lose."

"Yes, you do," Jesus replied. "You will lose eternal life."

Crestfallen, the young man left and headed toward the exit, not looking back. Jesus said to the crowd, "His wealth, status and money are his god. He has a god that is not God."

"Can a rich person go to heaven?" someone in the crowd asked.

"It is easier for a camel to go through the eye of a needle, than for a rich man to enter into the kingdom of God."

"Who then can be saved?" another person asked.

"With men, it is impossible; but with God all things are possible."

Jesus looked up and noticed that John was trying to get his attention. Usually no one would ever try to interrupt him, but this seemed different. John's actions and expression appeared urgent.

Jesus said to the crowd, "We are done for today. Thank you. Go in peace." John hurried over as the crowd quietly dispersed.

"What is wrong, my brother?" Jesus asked.

"Caiaphas has taken Jennifer prisoner. They used many men to capture her."

"Where did they take her?" Jesus asked.

"To the Praetorium. This is a trap. They are using her as bait. Do not take it. Let her be. They don't want her. They want you. Let them have Jennifer but not you."

"This is an insult to me. Of course, I was followed and watched. I am always watched. But this time they have gone too far. Give to Caesar the things that belong to Caesar. Give to God those things which belong to God! Give to Jesus those things, which belong to Jesus! And Jennifer is mine."

"What can you do? They will be watching for you. Do you want us to raise an army and attack them? Of course, if you want to, we will. I will always follow you, even unto death."

"That will not be necessary. They think they are setting a trap for a mouse. They are going to get a lion instead. Wait here. I will be back with Jennifer soon."

"This is going to take another miracle."

"No, Jennifer has already taught me what to do. She did it to Judas. I just need to put them to sleep."

Jesus walked around the building and headed straight toward the place of judgment, where Jennifer was being held. There were four guards standing outside the door and more inside.

Jesus looked at the building and raised his hands above his shoulders with the palms facing the place of judgment. "I command you to dream!"

At that precise moment, all the guards both outside and in fell asleep where they stood. Inside the prison, Jennifer looked around, realizing that everything had become very quiet and that the guards were not moving but standing very still with their eyes closed.

"What's going on?" she asked no one in particular.

Jesus entered the prison and headed straight for Jennifer's cell. He had a glow about him. No one even knew he was there; they were all dreaming.

Walking up to the bars of Jennifer's cell, he said, "Hello, my angel. What kind of trouble did you get into now? I hope you did not hurt anyone."

"No, except for a couple noses. They went after me for no reason, especially that fat one here. I'm going to punish him. He beat me and threw dirty water on me. I smell like the pig that he is. I'm going to take him to the pig market."

Jesus took the keys from the guard and released Jennifer. "Come. Let us go. We do not need any more violence."

"Not before I kick him in the…"

Jesus stepped in front of her. "Forgive your enemies, no matter how stupid they are. If you have a need for revenge, please do it to me."

Jennifer calmed down. "No! I could never hurt you, nor would I ever want to. How about one little thing. I promise. It won't hurt him." Jesus sighed. "Okay, but make it little. And it better not hurt."

Jennifer dumped a water pail of dirty water over the head guard's head and left it there. Then the two of them walked out of the prison.

"What about the guards?" she asked.

"They will wake up, but we will be long gone by then. And believe me, they will be afraid to bother you again. You are safe. They will never know I was here."

"You saved me! You're my hero." She put her arms around Jesus and hugged him fiercely.

"Yes, I know. What else would you have me do? I had to rescue my angel. I am very pleased to see you."

"You are too good for this world."

"Then we must make this world better," he replied.

"I have protein bars," Jennifer said, patting her pouch.

"Good, I could eat them forever."

"Trust me. You would get tired of them after a while. Are we off to our favorite spot? Shall I get some wine, so we can look at all the suns in the night sky?"

"That would be heaven. And more Chanel for the hero." "Yes, heroes get Chanel," she said, smiling gently.

They walked toward the Mount of Olives, stopping first at a wine shop.

*****

Later that evening, Caiaphas' assistant very carefully and slowly went to face his master to inform him about what had happened. The worse part was that he didn't know what had happened, and for the first time in his life, he was actually afraid of what he had to tell Caiaphas.

Caiaphas had a smile on his face when he saw his assistant. "Did we get him? I know we did. He was a fool over a woman. Tell me all. We finally got him. It was so easy. Just one stupid woman."

"My Lord, she is gone. Poof! Vanished from the prison."

The smile quickly left Caiaphas's face. "What do you mean gone?" he demanded. "One moment she was there, and the next moment she wasn't. She is not as stupid as you think."

"That is impossible!" Caiaphas raged. "No one can just disappear from prison."

"Not possible for us, but not for an angel of God. God gave us a message. Leave his angels alone. And I warn you. Do not get her mad at you."

Caiaphas let his anger cool slightly. "This is strange. There is no other explanation?"

"There were ten guards on duty, and not one of them saw a thing. Even the head guard with the broken nose ended up soaked in dirty water with the water pail over his head. He knows nothing. Nobody does. She just disappeared."

"No Jesus? He didn't show up to save her?"

"No one saw Jesus," the assistant said. "She was just gone. She was seen later back with Jesus, so she is still around. What do you what me to do? We can capture her again, though this time I might need even more men."

"No! I will not throw my money away again. Do nothing. Leave her alone. Do not bother her. She is an angel protected by God. This is a warning we must heed. I do not want an angry God, especially with our plans for Jesus."

"What about Jesus? How are we going to handle him?" the assistant asked. Caiaphas sat there thinking. Finally, he said, "We will find another way to get him. One of his apostles will turn on him."

"Which one?" the assistant asked, puzzled. "I cannot think of any of them who would do that."

"One who loves him very much. One who is also a little bit jealous and not fully loyal to him," Caiaphas said, rubbing his hands together.

"They are all loyal to him even unto death," the assistant insisted.

"Which one would possibly turn on him?"

"Easy," Caiaphas said with a smile. "The one who loves silver more than God."

CHAPTER

TWENTY-FOUR

Early the next morning, Jennifer arose as the sun was just starting to come up. Jesus was still asleep, and she moved a short distance away, so as not to disturb him, and marveled at what she saw. There were no clouds in the vivid blue sky, and everything looked so clean because, of course, there was no pollution. She looked around at the beautiful countryside, so pretty, so clean, and fresh. And even at this early hour, people were moving around. *With no TV, cars, electricity, hospitals, police, internet, or phones, nothing was easy. Yet, these people are still very happy. Maybe they are the lucky ones.* Of course, no one here knew the difference. To them, it was their way of life because the invention of electricity was still a long way off. Electricity was the beginning of everything. Without it there would be no modern conveniences, no computer, and no time ship.

She thought about the future and how everything had started right here. Had anything changed back there in her time period? Would it change? One thing she knew for certain. Jesus was real, and her love for him was real. She walked back to where he slept and gazed upon his sleeping form, before lightly touching his face to wake him. He looked so innocently beautiful. And it broke her heart to think that he had nothing but pain and misery in his future. When you loved someone, you wanted to take the pain away, or not let it happen in the first place.

But if she followed orders and did as she was supposed to do, and did not interfere, her hands were tied. She was sad because every second took them closer to the cross, and there was no way to know which was the right path to take. On one side was the history of religion. On the other, she wondered if Jesus could accomplish more good for his people, if he continued to live. Looking at him made her realize that love had no limitations. It just kept getting stronger.

"I was awake," Jesus said, rising to his feet.

"Sure you were."

"I was just playing with you. Good morning, my love."

"And good morning to you, my love. How about we go to the Temple and have some breakfast. Anything you want."

"Anything?" he asked. It never ceased to amaze him when she made such offers.

"Yes! For you, anything. Name it and it shall be yours."

"Bread sound great. We can save your protein bars for a little later. I think I want bread for some reason. It just sounds good to me right now. Bread is the food of life."

"I actually knew you were going to say that. Only the best bread for you. Let's go. Maybe even some figs from one of our favorite shops."
"Yes, that is a journey well worth taking. Shall we go?"

They packed their blankets, and relieved themselves behind some trees, before heading off to find bread and figs. After breakfast, they arrived at the Temple to find the place booming with music and dancing. Hundreds of people were dancing, singing, and playing various instruments, some of which were unfamiliar to her. The music and songs were different from what she was used to hearing. Most of the songs were almost spoken instead of sung, like a chant. No real tunes of any sort. But nevertheless, it sounded good and was performed with lots of energy.

Jennifer recognized harps, horns, pipes, lyres, bells, tambourines, and even an instrument that kind of looked like a guitar. And of course, the shofar, looking and sounding exactly the same as she had heard during her trip to Jerusalem back in the future. Exactly the same she thought. There was even a trumpet of some sort, and it sounded like one, too. The man playing the trumpet had no teeth, but he still smiled at Jennifer. She gave him a coin, which made him smile even more. They moved through the people, stopping and listening to a woman singing a song.

"O come, let us sing to the Lord; let us make a joyful noise to the rock of our salvation; Let us come into His presence with thanksgiving; let us make a joyful noise to Him with songs of praise!" Jennifer also gave her a coin.

The woman bowed.

"Thank you. That was very nice."

"Is there something you are not telling me?" Jesus asked as they continued on. "That money purse of yours seems never ending—always full no matter how much you hand out."

"No, my love, I just plan ahead, as we all should. This is a special trip for me, and I wanted to be ready for anything. Look, there are more singers over here. Let's listen."

They walked over to a group of musicians and singers.

"Look, it's a concert," Jennifer exclaimed.

"A what? That is a term I have never heard before. You seem to have so many."

"It is just a different definition from my land. It means that there are a lot of people all playing the same song. It's the same, even in my land. People seem to love music and being together. It's wonderful. Let's listen."

The musicians were accompanied by singers. They sang:

"How beautiful you are, my love, how very beautiful! Your eyes are doves behind your veil. Your hair is like a flock of goats, moving down the slopes of Gilead. Your teeth are like a flock of shorn ewes that have come up from the washing, all of which bear twins, and not one among them is bereaved. Your lips are like a crimson thread, and your mouth is lovely. Your cheeks are like halves of a pomegranate behind your veil. Your two breasts are like two fawns, twins of a gazelle that feed among the lilies. Until the day breathes and the shadows flee, I will hasten to the mountain of myrrh and the hill of frankincense. You are altogether beautiful, my love; there is no flaw in you."

"That was beautiful! I don't know exactly what it meant, but it definitely moved me. Even children could listen to these lyrics."

"You are so right. Music seems to bring people together. If I knew then what I know now, I would definitely bring music into my teachings. The people love it, and it seems to put them at ease. Yes, music is a good thing. Thank you, my love, for bringing it to my attention."

Jennifer also gave them some coins, and they were grateful.

"Thank you, beautiful angel," one of the male singers said. "For you could be nothing else. Even Jesus is lucky to be with you. Your heart is as beautiful as your soul. You are truly special."

"No one here has ever seen anyone like you. They can sense the good in you, but they have no idea that they should never make you angry," Jesus said. "I would feel sorry for them, if they did."

A woman stepped in front of Jennifer and began to sing. Her voice was beautiful.

"All night long on my bed, I looked for the one my heart loves," she sang. "I looked for him but did not find him. I will get up now and go about the city, through its streets and squares. I will search for the one my heart loves. I looked for him but did not find him. The watchmen found me as they made their rounds in the city. Have you seen the one my heart loves?"

"Thank you. Beautiful voice. And that song had some meaning to it. I like it."

Jennifer gave her a coin. The woman smiled, for it was a silver coin.

"Thank you, special lady. Now it is your turn. Sing us a song from where you come from, even if that be heaven, beautiful angel. Let us hear an angel sing."

"I'd better not. There is no way I could compare to you. It would be a big letdown," Jennifer said.

"This is not a contest, just the joy of music. Sing, sing, and sing!" the woman insisted.

The people around Jennifer start to chant and sing.

"I think the pressure is on," Jesus said, smiling. "It's time. They are waiting for you. You now have an audience."

"I think you mean put up or shut up. I don't even know what to sing." "Whatever your heart tells you," he replied. "As you say, put up or shut up. I think you can put up better than you think."

Jennifer remembered the last movie she had seen before travelling back in time. She didn't know the whole song, but maybe just enough. It was the only thing she could think of.

Jennifer sang, "Jesus Christ. Jesus Christ. Who are you? What have you sacrificed? Jesus Christ Superstar. Do you think you're what they say you are?"

The people were shocked by the foreign sound of the song. Some musicians even tried to play along. Jennifer, too, had a very beautiful voice. The whole crowd listened in as they had never heard such a tune. It was strange but very catchy. Some of them tried to copy the tune. Jennifer walked among the crowd, singing to them, and the crowd loved it.

"Every time I look at you, I don't understand why you let the things you did get so out of hand," she sang. "Why'd you choose such a backward time in such a strange land? Jesus Christ Superstar. Do you think you're what they say you are? Buddha, was he where it's at? Is he where you are? Could Mohammed move a mountain, or was that just PR? Did you mean to."

Before Jennifer could not say the next word, which was die, she caught herself and stopped, realizing that Jesus should not hear this. Better to wait two thousand more years to finish the song.

"Don't stop," Jesus said. "That is a wonderful song, more! I have never heard such music, and I hear everything. It is truly glorious food for the ears. Your land must be truly amazing. I don't know why I never heard of it. You said California? I know not of California."

The crowd was excited. They, too, had never heard such a melody. A man came up to Jennifer and gave her a coin. "That was the most beautiful song I could ever imagine."

"Thank you. I'm afraid that's all I can remember," she fibbed.

"Maybe I can sing a different song some other time."

"Who is Jesus Christ Superstar? We both have Jesus as our name."

Jennifer had to think quick, since she could not tell him that they were one in the same. "A great hero from my land. He lived over two thousand years ago. Yet, he is still revered and respected. A very great man, who loved his people just as you do."

"Maybe I should get to learn about this hero. Is Jesus also a common name in your land?"

"No, not really, but you and he have a lot in common, a lot."

"There is still much about you that I don't know. Sometimes, you have this faraway look about you. And yet, it is not far away but…what is the word I'm looking for? Distant? I just don't know. I want to know more but at the same time, I simply want you the way you are now. You make me happy and lucky just to be alive."

"Come, let's walk. You'll find that I am just a simple woman, who has finally found a reason to have faith. And for me, that is enough for now." "Yes, for me, too."

Jennifer pulled her hood back over her head. The hood almost completely covered her face and hair. She didn't want to be too noticeable. As they walked away from the crowd, Jennifer turned around and gave them the thumbs up signal with both hands. The people in the crowd looked confused, unsure what thumbs up meant. But they smiled at Jennifer anyway and waved goodbye to them. One man looked at his thumbs, and then raised his, too, a big silly grin on his face.

Jennifer and Jesus walked around the Temple and past one corner. On a ledge were two Scribes and four Pharisees, watching the people of the Temple, and of course, watching Jesus. They especially noticed that Jesus had a female companion with him.

"Jesus! Is this another one of your whores you have with you?" the first Scribe shouted. "You have so many; I am beginning to lose count. Please present your new whore to us. I greatly anticipate the introduction. Is she another prostitute?"

"I knew you had to be around here somewhere," Jesus replied, angrily. "Just like all of you, who can see but are blind to the truth. Your eyes are open, but only to the darkness that lies within your hearts."

"Who are these men? What did he mean by many? It's obvious they're women haters. They have no respect. I'd like to teach them a lesson, but of course I won't, as it would displease you."

"For that I thank you. They are the leaders of the Temple. They never think ahead, but only what they want to think." To the Scribes and Pharisees he said, "This woman is not a whore."

"We can see plain and clear," the second Scribe said. "A whore is a whore. You cannot fool us. We know you only too well, Jesus."

"You know me not at all and nothing but the darkness of your own minds. Once again, you judge even before the judgment. You are nothing but snakes and the children of snakes. How can you escape going to hell? How can you judge this woman? You have never seen her. You know nothing about her, yet you think you do. Can you not see your mistake?"

The crowd grew silent and listened to this conversation between Jesus, the Scribes, and Pharisees.

"It is simple logic. Anyone with you must be a whore," the first Pharisee claimed. "She can be nothing else."

"Logic doesn't work on you. You don't even know what logic is. You are not logical enough to even understand what logical is," Jesus told him. "I will prove that I am correct."

"This will be interesting. Show us your proof," the second Pharisee mocked.

They all laughed at that last remark. Jesus took Jennifer's hand. She was still hiding behind the hood as he led her forward to stand in front of them.

"Fools always hide from the truth," a third Pharisee accused.

"Jennifer, please remove your hood and show them," Jesus said. Jennifer pulled back her hood.

Upon seeing her face, the Scribes and Pharisees were at a loss for words. They looked at each other, and then back at Jennifer. They had never seen anyone as beautiful as she. Never.

"Your silence speaks for you. What do you say now? Is this not proof?" Jesus asked.

"This is the one time even God would have to be silent," the first Scribe exclaimed.

"She is definitely not from here. I have seen no one like her," the second Scribe added. "She has no equal, at least not on earth. She is definitely not from here. Look at her hair and her skin. Where is she from?"

"She is from a land far away and has been sent here to help and teach me. You should listen to her, because with her beauty comes the wisdom of the ancients—a wisdom you seemed to have lost."

"Maybe God sent her to you to help teach you some respect," the fourth Pharisee said, cunningly. "Maybe she can open your eyes to the truth. I think she is too good for you. Tell that to your God!"

"My God? Who is he? For judgment, I have come into this world. So, the blind will see, and those who see, will become blind. You have forgotten who God is, and what He is all about."

"How dare you insult us? You have nothing in common with God except a lie," the third Pharisee said angrily.

"My God is the God of Jacob, Isaac, and Moses. He sent prophets, wise people, and experts in the Law of Moses. But you killed them, or nailed them to a cross, or beat them, and chased them out of town. You can no longer see what is important, the life of the common person."

"You never understood," the second Scribe said. "It is difficult to keep the peace, especially with Rome in charge. You do not understand the truth around you. It is not simple to deal with Rome. They are the masters, and we are nothing but slaves to them. We are here to save the people."

"You crush our people with unbearable religious demands, and never lift a finger to ease their burdens. You shut the doors of the kingdom of heaven in the people's faces. You obey Rome over our God." "And you sin and break the Sabbath!" the fourth Pharisee shouted.

"And what did I do that was so terrible? I healed the hand of a man who was hurting, and my apostles picked some grain so they would not go hungry."

"What is wrong with that?" Jennifer asked. "I don't see it as working and breaking the Sabbath. Can you not help people on the Sabbath? Can you not feed them? Or are they supposed to go hungry? You can praise God every day, not just on the Sabbath."

"Be quiet, woman!" the first Pharisee ordered. "How dare you speak to us? You are just a woman with no common sense. Beauty is not wisdom."

"Oh, really," Jennifer said. "I remember now. I saw many of you working on the Sabbath."

"We are saving souls. That is different," the fourth Pharisee declared.

"That is just the definition you use for an excuse. I know the Bible, too. God rested on the seventh day, but he didn't take a day off. That day is for worshiping God, not punishment for not doing so. As I said you need to worship God every day, but you still have to live."

"Who is this woman?" the first Scribe demanded. "Shut her up! Keep her in her place. How disrespectful!"

"Jennifer, please, I will take over now," Jesus said gently.

"Be my guest. They're starting to get on my nerves, anyway."

Jesus turned to the Scribes and Pharisees. "If a sheep falls into a pit on the Sabbath, would the owner not lift it out before it dies? Is not a man even more important in the eyes of God than a sheep? You are empty of religion, because you do not honor the supernatural power of God. It is possible to have justice and mercy even on the Sabbath. You have been writing your own laws and adding them to the Bible. That is a sin."

"You are guilty of blasphemy, and you will pay for that!" the second Scribe shot back.

"Do you think I am unaware of what you are planning? All of you. You will make up new stories and falsehoods, just to see me eliminated.

That is what you want, because you are jealous of how the people flock to me. Look at you, your beautiful clothes, your fancy hair. You want everybody to notice you as if you are special. You are fearful of the truth, and you want to destroy me because I am the truth."

"We are special," the fourth Pharisee said. "And we will have our way. It is our duty to teach the people. Your teachings only give them false hope."

"I give them the hope the Father wishes them to have. You are not teachers," Jesus said. "You are devoid of learning. I tell the people to do what you say. But do not copy what you do, for you do not practice what you preach. You lock people out of the kingdom of heaven. You can't go in, and you keep others from going in, too. You don't save people anymore. You condemn them."

"No, we only condemn you!" the first Pharisee replied. "For you have condemned yourself. When you are no longer here, you will be lost to the world, and no one will ever remember you. You will be nothing but dust."

"No, that is not true." Knowing the truth, Jennifer could not hold back. "You are the ones who will not be remembered. You already know that you are not liked, only feared. The people will never love you like they love Jesus, and that makes you ignorant and angry. You should learn from the love of Jesus. He will be remembered and loved for as long as the world exists." She stopped speaking, wondering if she had said too much.

But she needn't have worried, for the Scribes and Pharisees were deaf and blind to the truth.

"Be silent, woman! A woman like you could only be trouble," the second Pharisee shouted. "I never want to see one such as you again. Go back to where you came from."

"You have murdered the prophets of old, just as you want to murder me. Do you deny that?" Jesus asked.

"We don't need to deny anything," the second Scribe said. "You are but a small thorn in our foot, which must be removed for the injury to heal. You make up stories that are nothing more than dreams. Your teachings are dangerous."

"You are making a big mistake here. You are the true danger. I know what you are planning and so does God," Jennifer said. "God is watching every move you make. You are just puppets, out of control with broken strings."

"Beautiful or not, we are never going to listen to you," the second Pharisee said. "Nobody listens to women. They are not smart enough. They never learn. You were born a woman for a reason."

"Careful, she just might be an angel," the third Pharisee warned.

"And I hear they are total bitches."

"Please, I do not need your thoughts," the second Pharisee said.

"Sorry, but you never know," the third Pharisee said. "Just look at her. I would not want her angry. I have heard stories of angry angels, and they never turn out well for us."

Jesus turned to the crowd. "People of Jerusalem, listen to me. My time is short. O Jerusalem, Jerusalem, thou that killest the prophets and stonest them, which are sent unto thee. How often would I have gathered thy children together, even as a hen gathers her chicks under her wings, and ye would not! Behold your house is left unto you desolate. I will have mercy and not sacrifice."

"You will receive the one and not the other," the first Pharisee promised.

"Then do not listen to me, but listen to the words of God!" Jesus said in a thunderous voice.

"We teach the words of God! You do not even begin to understand what they mean," the first Scribe declared. "You were not sent here by God. You are a carpenter and nothing more. Go back to your work and leave us to ours."

"Is not God a carpenter?" Jesus asked. "He built everything you see, including you. Look around at everything, and tell me that God is not a carpenter. You have sinned using his name."

"Please, O mighty one of false illusions, tell us our sins," the third Pharisee mocked.

"You teach about God, but not the love of God. You preach God, but convert people to a religion that you have twisted with your own desires. For you, oaths sworn by the Temple are not binding, but oaths sworn by gold or sacrificial gifts are binding. You teach the law but do not practice the most important part, justice, mercy, and faithfulness to God. You are clean on the outside but dirty on the inside. Your mark of righteousness has a secret inner world of ungodly thoughts and feelings. You are filled with wickedness. You are like whitewashed tombs, beautiful on the outside, but filled with dead men's bones."

"Anything more?" the first Pharisee asked. "Because we need to go save some souls, and you will never be one of them. You cannot be saved." He turned to the others. "Come, let us do out duties and not be bothered anymore by this false prophet called Jesus."

"And have lunch," the first Scribe whispered to himself.

"You have killed those whom God sent to you, and you will kill me!"

"Good day, Jesus," the fourth Pharisee said.

"Enjoy it while you can," the first Scribe added.

"For what you are about to do, I still forgive you. Can you forgive yourselves?" Jesus asked.

"Not by one such as you," the first Pharisee said. "We will see you soon, and you will not be so proud then."

The Scribes and Pharisees turned around and walked back into the Temple.

"They are a mean group indeed," Jennifer said. "Doesn't anybody around here like or respect women?"

"The religious leaders are the old, and they must leave space for the new. But you have my highest respect. You have taught me much. I wish you could teach them. But yes, women are not respected and that must change, and it will."

"Jesus and the kingdom of God. Everybody is equal in the eyes of God."

"How do you know all these things?" Jesus asked. "Can you read my mind?" "No, but I can read your feelings."

"Come. Let's enjoy the day, more to come later. I've had enough of these people for one day. Unfortunately, I will see them again, all too soon."

"I think we need some wine after all the commotion and stress," Jennifer said.

"Yes, bread and wine sound wonderful."

"Can't wait. And I know right where to go. My treat. Come, my Lord."

"You are definitely my treat," Jesus said. "And after lunch, I have a special event planned that I, of course, want you to be part of."

They headed off toward Jennifer's favorite wine shop. And later, they had a very nice lunch at their now favorite food court.

CHAPTER

TWENTY-FIVE

After a delicious lunch and some very enjoyable wine purchased by Jennifer, she and Jesus left Jerusalem and headed to the Mount of Olives. Jennifer knew that every second that passed, led them closer to the end that had been written about for centuries. But she was having a hard time coming to terms with it, and she still had a lot of decisions to make. Whenever she thought that her love had reached one hundred percent, she was wrong as it continued to grow ever deeper, beyond her expectations.

She was also concerned about Keith. He continued watching their every move, and this worried her more than she would like to admit. There was no way she would ever trust him. She knew that the President had given him a much different mission from the one she had. What was that mission? Her gut told her that it was something that if accomplished, would have serious consequences. Keith was extremely dangerous—a man who did not mind killing. She also knew that their paths were going to cross very soon, and nothing good would come of it. At this time, she wished that Keith had never existed, or at least had never been picked to go on this mission. The world would be a better place if he had not been born.

Something else had been bothering her as well. There were seven seats on the time machine. Yet, only four people seemed to have made the trip. This did not make sense to her. Why only four? It wasn't like the government to leave those seats empty. If anything, they would have wanted to send more. Then her mind flashed back to the two sonic like booms she remembered hearing. Nothing in this day and age could possibly have created them. *Would the death of a team member do it, creating a violent ripple in time?* She wasn't certain, but she would ask Dr. Adams when she returned to her own time. And if that were the case, then two of the team members had been killed. How and by who? Was it Keith? The thought revved up the warning signal already going off in her head.

She also remembered the pilot that had taken the craft back to Colonial Times. Surely, he or someone like him would have been assigned to the mission. Yes, she was capable of piloting the ship, but wouldn't they have wanted someone more qualified on such a trip? That still left one more seat. From her reasoning, she did not believe it had been occupied, otherwise there would have been a third sonic boom. Why not? Then a chill ran down her spine. Was it for Jesus? And if so, was he supposed to be dead or alive? She hoped alive, but she was conflicted. Her heart and mind did not agree. One thing was certain, though. To save Jesus she would show Keith no mercy.

Jesus put his arms around Jennifer and kissed her hair. "Your hair is softer than anything I have ever felt. Softer than any dove, and they are very soft, except compared to you. But tell me. What were you thinking about? It must be something unpleasant to cause the lines on your forehead and between your eyes."

"My love, you have no idea how difficult it is to be me. There is a lot of work involved. Just staying in fighting shape takes a lot of effort and training."

Jesus felt that she was avoiding his question. He wanted her to share her worries and concerns with him, but he would not pressure her. "I would say that you are a master of your trade."

"Best possible response," she replied. "Thank you."

"This is going to be a special time for us. Much is going to happen. It is even better because you are here."

"How is that? What's going to happen?" she asked.

"You are going to meet my entire little family. All twelve of my disciples are waiting for me. You know some of them, but soon you will know them all and of course, they will adore you."

"All but Judas. I doubt he will ever change his opinion of me. There isn't time. But eleven out of twelve is a pretty good percentage. Do you want me to stay behind and wait? I don't mind." It would also show if Keith was following her or Jesus.

"I want you near, but not too close. I have things I need to tell them about that are important, and some of it, they will not want to hear. And I fear they will object to them quite vehemently. But they have to know that the truth is coming and soon."

"I will be your silent loving angel," Jennifer promised.

"Good, I hope," Jesus said. "Try not to knock anybody out. Judas already knows what you can do, and he definitely fears you, although he would never admit it."

"Of course, my love. I will honor all your disciples, including Judas. Maybe I might even try being a bit nicer to him. Who knows?" Her thoughts, however, were quite different when it came to Judas. She wanted to lock him away somewhere, so that he would not be able to betray Jesus.

"That would be wonderful! Afterwards, all of us will journey to Bethany, where we will have dinner and spend the night at Simon the leper's house."

Jennifer grew alarmed. "Simon the leper? Won't he be contagious? I want you to be safe." She wasn't keen on the idea of being exposed to leprosy either.

"Do not fear. He is contagious no longer. I cured him. He is grateful and will serve a good meal for all to enjoy, as he is also wealthy. Now, my disciples do not fully yet believe that he has been cured, so some of them might keep their distance. But rest assured, he is healthy and free of disease. As for me, I have never had a sick day in my life. I am immune to almost everything that mankind is not. It is another gift from my Father."

"For some reason that makes perfect sense. It could be nothing else," she said.

They entered a small shady area of trees and found all twelve waiting for Jesus and his words. The disciples knelt before Jesus. Jennifer sat down nearby but not too close, where she could get a good look at all twelve men. *The stories never got it right. How very young they are.* Most were still under twenty, with Jesus clearly the oldest and maybe Peter the second oldest. The rest were very young. This was a big surprise to her. For some reason, the term wild young kids popped into her head. Some looked at Jennifer with surprise but quickly returned their focus back on Jesus.

"Peter, James, John, Andrew, Bartholomew, James the Lesser, Judas, Jude, Matthew, Philip, Simon and Thomas. How good to see you!"

"Master, we are honored to be here with you. We know you have much to say. We are at your service," Thomas said.

"With all our love for our king and master," Peter added. "We are yours and gladly so."

Jesus pointed to Jennifer. "That woman sitting over there is my special companion. Her name is Jennifer. She is from a faraway land. You will meet her later as we travel to Simon's house. Almost all of you will find her pleasant, unless you make her angry. I suggest you don't. Just ask Judas."

"Let us look at her, Jesus. We did not know you had a new companion. We are surprised and pleased. It is an honor," James the Lesser said.

"We know her," John said. "She is an angel like no other. More beautiful than Cleopatra. Way more."

"As if you would know what Cleopatra looked like. She died before you were born. Jennifer is just a common woman, nothing special that I can see. I do not understand why everybody is so enamored with her," Judas said, disgruntled.

"I will tell her you said that so she can put you to sleep again," Jesus teased.

"I will bite my tongue. I am not sleepy," Judas said. "Please tell her I do not wish for that sleep ever again."

"If Judas doesn't like her, she must be very special," James the Lesser said with a big smile. "We all know what Judas thinks about women. We have known that for a long time. So easy to tell."

"I believe they should know their place, that's all," Judas said defensively. "And sometimes they have to be told where their place is, because they don't know."

"Yes, and we know exactly where that place is," Peter said knowing how the man thought. "Don't we, Judas?"

"Come. The talk to end all talk is here," Jesus said in a tone that told them this discussion was at an end. "My time here is growing short, and I do not have much time left."

He sat on a large rock above the disciples as they sat on the ground in front of him.

"I love all of you here, but you will undergo the greatest tests of courage and faith you have ever experienced. Your faith and lives will be tested, and it will not be pleasant. I will be the first, but you will all follow me and share my suffering. My time is soon."

"How is that, my Lord?" Bartholomew asked, puzzled. "We wish no harm on anyone. Who would want to harm us?"

"The chief priests and elders plot against us. Their minds are closed to the words of God. Because of that, all of you will face and suffer tribulation and persecution. Once I have returned to my Father in heaven, they will seek you out, lay their hands on you, and persecute you, delivering you to the synagogues and prisons, and bringing you before kings and governors for my name's sake."

"We will be strong for you!" Andrew declared. "We will always be with you. We will always follow you."

"You must also be strong for yourself," Jesus told them. "The true test of your faith is coming. For you are my disciples, and you must remain strong. They will test your faith with pain and suffering. They will test you because of me."

"What are these tests?" Judas asked. "Even to the death, your disciples will not fail you."

How ironic that you, Judas, of all people would say that, Jennifer thought.

"If any man comes to me, and hates not his father, and mother, and wife, and children, and brethren, and sisters, yea, and his own life also, he cannot be my disciple. And whosoever doth not bear his cross, and come after me, cannot be my disciple. Whosoever he be of you that forsaketh not all that he hath, he cannot be my disciple. It is very simple. Anyone who wants to follow me and be with me on earth and in heaven must be willing to pay the price to save his soul."

All the disciples shouted in agreement with Jesus.

"We are with you from the beginning to the end and beyond," James declared.

"Is this the end?" Thomas asked. "Why are you telling us this now?"

"The end is not yet," Jesus said. "This is just the beginning. There is more."

"Tell us, Master," Peter said.

"The Jewish people will once again suffer greatly. God is always testing them. For like a tree in the wind, they sway back and forth, never knowing which way to go or which way to break."

"We have always suffered, yet the Temple brought us together," James said.

"I tell you; I now prophesize the destruction of the Temple and Jerusalem!" Jesus said.

"No!" the disciples yelled.

"That could never be!" James the Lesser declared. "The people will protect it with their lives."

Jennifer quietly listened, knowing that what Jesus said was true. Knowing the history of Jerusalem, she knew that in seventy A.D., the Roman army surrounded Jerusalem and completely destroyed the Temple. She very smoothly crept closer as she wanted to hear more. No one noticed her. They were all intently listening to Jesus.

"Not one stone will be left upon another; everyone will be thrown down. There will be nothing left but faith. The Temple will be destroyed down to the bare ground. Many of our people will die and not know why. They will suffer again just like they have already done so many times before. It is their fate to suffer. This is how God will judge them."

"When?" Judas asked. "When will all this happen?"

"When God wills it to happen. It is what He wants, and He will let nothing interfere."

"How do you know all this and why?" Judas asked.

"Judas, my Father knows all, and if He knows I know. I know even you, and I still love you and always will."

"I would die for you," Judas declared. "You are my lord and master."

"I know. As for why, it is a true test of faith. It's what God wants as proof of our love for Him. We must all suffer in order to obtain eternal glory."

"I hate to say it, but it does sound depressing with nothing to look forward to. We are doomed," Philip said worriedly.

"Not so," Jesus promised. "You will live forever in my kingdom. While many that remain will die forever, never knowing the joys of heaven."

"Then we must suffer to enter the kingdom of heaven," Peter said. "It will be worth the price."

"There will be a seven-year tribulation. During that time, there will be false Messiahs, wars, famines, earthquakes, the whole world, not just the tribes of Israel, will face tragedy. The sun will darken. The moon will not give its light. The stars will fall from heaven, and the powers of the heavens will be shaken."

"I do not want to see that," Judas said, shaking his head.

"You won't, but others will," Jesus told him.

Jennifer also heard that part. She knew there would be many wars, but the people would survive and actually thrive. The apocalypse had not happened yet, even after two thousand years. She also knew what Judas would do and how it all would end for him.

"Is there no hope?" Andrew asked.

"I now tell you of my second coming. I will return in judgment to set up my earthly kingdom. The righteous dead will be resurrected, and together with the righteous living will be glorified and taken to heaven, but the unrighteous will die."

"Teacher, tell us, when will these things occur?" Peter asked. "What will be the sign whenever all these things are about to be fulfilled? And what will be the sign of Your coming and of the completion of the age?"

"Look at the fig tree, and all the trees," Jesus explained. "As soon as they come out in leaf, you see for yourselves, and know that the summer is near. So, also, when you see these things taking place, you know that the kingdom of God is near. Truly, I say to you, this generation will not pass away till all has taken place. Heaven and earth will pass away, but my words will not pass away."

Jennifer was taken by surprise upon hearing this. She knew that was not going to happen in the very near future or even in the present generation. Jesus either had the dates terribly wrong or to put it simply, he was mistaken. She thought that if Jesus was wrong about his second coming, maybe he was wrong about the cross, too. Maybe he did not need to die on the cross. She was confused. Maybe her love was not in vain. Maybe Jesus could live and do the world an even greater amount of good. But like the disciples, she, too, misunderstood his words.

"There will appear in heaven the sign of the Son of Man, and then all the tribes of the earth will mourn, and they will see the Son of Man coming on the clouds of heaven with power and great glory. And he will send out his angels with a loud trumpet call, and they will gather his elect from the four winds, from one end of heaven to the other. That is the end. After that, the righteous will shine like the sun in the kingdom of their Father, forever."

"My Lord, how will you know the righteous?" John asked.

"When the Son of Man comes in his glory, and all the angels with him, he will sit on his glorious throne. All the nations will be gathered before him. That is the Day of Judgment. All the people will be gathered together and will be separated into those who have pleased God and those who have offended God, as a Shepherd separates the sheep from the goats. This will not be an easy task simply from outward appearances, as long-eared sheep and goats look very similar. I will lead the sheep, and God will bless those who have fed and clothed the hungry and the poor, but the goats will be rejected from God's eternal kingdom for they have ignored the needs of others. They will go away to eternal punishment, and the righteous will go on to eternal life."

The disciples were silent. They looked at each other unaware of the rough path that lay before them. Unfortunately for them, it would begin very soon. And they would suffer in more ways than one.

This is a very sad week, Jennifer thought to herself. There will be no good outcomes for anyone. The tragedy of love, and the worst part is not knowing why God wants it this way. Only God knows.

"Shall we begin our walk?" John asked, knowing that the sermon was over. "Simon is waiting for us. He will feed us well. It is good that Jesus cured him, we hope."

Everyone stood up and began walking.

Jesus took Jennifer's hand. "Come. It is not too far, just a couple miles. It will give you time to show them how marvelous you are. They will all love and admire you."

"That will not happen," Judas said, sourly. "I will not fall prey to her beautiful poison. I will stand back."

The remaining eleven disciples surrounded Jennifer as they walked, with Judas staying slightly behind. Jennifer smiled at each of them and soon, just like so many other men before, they fell for her charm and beauty. They could not help it, and they were powerless to resist her, except for Judas.

After forty-five minutes, Jennifer and the eleven were like one. Jesus didn't have a chance to say a single word to her as the disciples talked nonstop. She charmed them all without even trying. It was in her nature. They even made jokes. Stubbornly remaining behind, Judas refused to join in.

"Then the goat said, not tonight, I'm busy," James said, delivering the punchline to his joke.

Everybody laughed at that one. When they reached the House of Simon the leper, Jennifer noticed that it was a much larger and nicer house than the ones the common people occupied. There were even a few servants working in the yard. Jesus had told her that Simon was fairly wealthy. Jennifer tried to remember the events that were supposed to happen this night. *Simon the leper's house, what happened? Then she thought, What isn't going to happen?*

Before they reached the front door, it quickly opened, and Simon came out. "Come in, my friends. I have a grand dinner planned for us. It is good to see all of you. Come, wine and food are waiting. Let us eat, drink, and be merry."

Looking at Simon, Jennifer had to smile. He was a thin, older man with a long, coarse white beard. The beard nearly covered his whole face, and she wondered how he was able to eat without getting it in his beard. But he was very friendly, and it was obvious that Jesus was his favorite.

"Thank you, my friend," Jesus said, warmly. "We are all hungry and look forward to your company."

Entering his house, they were led to a room where a large dining table, big enough to seat them all, was waiting. The table was covered with some of the food, along with an assortment of wine cups to choose from. Even though the disciples all knew that Jesus had cured Simon of leprosy, they did not get too close. Instead, they gave him a gentle, friendly wave.

"I speak for all of us," John said. "And we thank you for your hospitality and friendship."

Simon went outside to the courtyard to check on the food. Jesus sat at the head of the table. The disciples sat around him, taking up all the chairs. Jennifer took a seat in the chair closest to the door. She actually liked that one for some unknown reason.

"Jennifer, my love, please come and sit next to me. I want you always by my side."

"Thank you," she replied. "I will join you later. But first there is something I must do. This is the place for me now."

Jennifer entered the kitchen area and grabbed a wet cloth, which she used to wash Jesus' hands. Everyone watched, but no one said a word. At this point, she still had her hood up, but then she pulled it down.

"Thank you," Jesus told her with a smile. "I now feel clean. How is it that you always know what to do, and when to do it?"

"Just proper teaching from my father and mother."

Thomas grabbed the cloth and also cleaned his hands, before handing it to Philip, who did the same. Eventually, all the disciples had cleaned their hands with the wet cloth. Simon returned from the courtyard carrying more food and placed it on the table.

"Simon, why is it that we must do the cleaning of the hands and not you? Are we not your guests? Did you not tell your servants?" Jesus asked.

"I am sorry, my Lord," Simon apologized. "I did not think. Maybe I was just too excited."

"I cured you of leprosy. Hopefully I didn't cure you of politeness as well," Jesus said, teasingly.

"I humbly apologize," Simon said again. "Who is this beautiful woman I see with you? She is soo…."

"Yes, we already know," Jesus said. "She is one of a kind." Jennifer smiled. "Hello, Simon."

Lazarus entered from the courtyard just in time to hear the exchange. "That is Jennifer, the beautiful angel. How are you, sweet lady? Please give me greetings."

Lazarus walked over to Jennifer and received a big hug from her.

"Nice to see you again. I didn't know you would be here," Jennifer exclaimed happily.

"I did not want to miss a chance to see you again. Right, Judas?" Judas frowned. "Apparently, you are under her spell, too. Everybody is."

"No spell, just a warm smile," Jennifer said.

"I heard you had some trouble at the Temple. Do not let it bother you," Lazarus said. "Ever since Jesus raised me from the dead, they have been wanting me to die again. Just because I am alive, they think I am causing too much trouble for them. Too many people are hearing about it and turning to Jesus because of it. It makes them very angry."

"You are too mean and cranky to die again," Andrew joked. "You are safe. I hope."

"As long as Jesus is here, I am always safe," Lazarus said.

The servants began serving dinner. Martha, Simon's wife, who had been busy preparing food in the courtyard, entered the room.

"Please, dinner is served," Simon announced. "Martha, you know everybody but Jennifer back there. She is here with Jesus."

"A woman with Jesus? Are you sure?" Martha teased. "What a beautiful name. This is wonderful. Again, are you sure?" Judas frowned. "We are sure." Jennifer waved at Martha.

Martha waved back. "We will talk later, while the men are busy. I want to know about this, especially with Jesus. I am so happy for him." Once again, the friends were together and having a good time. Jennifer noticed that everybody from this time seemed to like being together and talking. Then she realized that they had no other option, other than to talk to each other, as there was basically no other form of entertainment. Not so much in the future, where people were happier with their cellphones and televisions than each other. It made her sad in a way. Maybe people would get along better and enjoy life more if they spent more time with each other in person, instead of through their phones and social media.

There was one more person coming, and Jennifer was ready for this one, as she now remembered the whole story about the meal at Simons, and what had happened on this night. There was a knock on the door. The arrival of this person was the reason why Jennifer had seated herself closest to the door.

"I'll get it," she said.

"No, the servant will get it," Simon insisted. "Please remain seated." "No, I insist. I'll take care of it. Please, let me handle it."

Jennifer went to the door, which was out of sight from the main table, so that no one standing at the door could see the people in the other room. In front of her was a strange-looking woman with long black hair, holding a small box in front of her. She and her hair did not look very clean.

"May I help you?" Jennifer asked.

"I am here for the special one. I must see him. His name is Jesus, and I will clean him with my hair," the long-haired woman said. "I have brought special ointment."

Jennifer had remembered that this was the woman who used her hair to put ointment on Jesus' head and feet. She looked at the woman and her hair, and there was no way that any woman, including this one, was getting near Jesus. No way. She had already cleaned Jesus.

Not on my watch. Not going to happen.

"Let me in," the woman said. "I must clean Jesus. Look, the ointment is ready as am I."

"Do not concern yourself. It has already been done. I have already done it. No need. Please come back some other time. Thank you, and have a nice night." Jennifer was about to shut the door.

"I will not leave until I perform my service. I will not," the woman insisted. "I must do what I must do."

"No need for your service. Try someplace else."

"I will not leave until this perfume is on Jesus. You will not deter me. I am on a mission," the woman said stubbornly.

"Please wait here," Jennifer said. "I'll be right back." She closed the door and returned to the table. "Judas, it's for you."

Judas looked puzzled. "That is strange. Who would want me and knows I am here?"

"It's definitely for you," Jennifer insisted. "No one else." Judas got up and went to the door.

Jennifer grinned. "Wait for it…. Wait for it…. Wait for it."

Everybody looked up when Judas started yelling from the doorway. "Get out, you slut! You whore, you tramp, get out! Leave now!" He slammed the door and returned to the table.

"Good for Judas," Jennifer said, a satisfied smile on her face.

"One thing for sure. Judas is predicable," Bartholomew said.

"Absolutely, I was counting on it," Jennifer said.

"Who was that at the door?" Lazarus asked Judas.

"A bitch," he replied.

"I think it was some woman just trying to sell cheap perfume. I couldn't get her to leave," Jennifer said. "So, I had to bring out the big guns."

"What are big guns?" Simon asked.

"In this case, it was Judas."

Thomas raised his cup. "Cheers for Judas, the big guns." They all raise their cups and drank.

"Besides," Peter said, "who needs cheap perfume when you have Chanel by Jennifer."

Jesus smiled. "Yes, I must agree."

"And I have more for you later," Jennifer promised.

Later that night, everyone got ready for sleep. Just like in every other place where they had spent the night, Martha put Jesus in one corner of a room, and Jennifer at the opposite end as far away as possible. They were the only two people in the room and as soon as everybody left, Jennifer walked over to Jesus and massaged his muscles from behind, while putting Chanel on his face, hands, neck, and arms. Jesus loved it. "I have been looking forward to this all day. Thank you, my angel. That smells so nice, and you feel so nice. I only want your touch."

"Exactly. But I do have one tiny question, if you don't mind."

"Ask me anything, anything," Jesus told her. "Whatever you want."

"What did that man mean earlier today by saying, is this another one of your whores?"

Jesus was at a loss for words. "I can't keep my eyes open. It's time for sleep. We will talk later. Sleep now."

Jesus fell asleep. Jennifer gently eased him down and covered him with a blanket. Standing, she looked around the room. She was not sleepy yet, and might not be for a while.

"Well, I might as well go find the goat and make friends with him." Jennifer walked out to the courtyard and looked for the goat. In this courtyard, however, she actually found four goats.

"Hey, boys or girls. Need some company? I do. Come, let's talk."

Walking over to the goats, she began petting and rubbing them. The goats surrounded her, wanting attention.

CHAPTER

TWENTY-SIX

Jennifer woke up to another sunny morning in Israel. Before making the trip back in time, she had figured it would be sunny most of the time without a chance of rain. *Funny how I miss rain, and the sound it makes.* She didn't know why. She just did. Surprisingly, she had learned how to sleep better on mats and of course, on the grass in the Mount of Olives, her favorite spot to be alone with Jesus. Looking across the room at his mat, she realized that he was already up and saying goodbye to Simon, Martha, and Lazarus. His disciples surrounded him, waiting for instructions.

Jennifer stood up and rolled up both their mats before joining them and giving Jesus a quick hug. "Good morning. I'll be right back. I need to see a goat or two."

"Of course, my angel. I will be here waiting for you." Jennifer walked past Judas. "Good morning, Judas."

"Why are you saying good morning to me?" Judas asked warily.

"Did I do something wrong? Are you angry at me again?"

"No," she replied with a smile. "I just wanted to say good morning."

"You are not going to make me sleep again. Are you?"

"No, Judas. Let there be peace between us," she said.

"I am not ready yet," he replied. "I still do not trust you."

"Okay, maybe later," she said shrugging.

Jennifer walked past the courtyard over to the goats, who were eating grain that had been given to them. "Good morning. I'm back. Remember me from last night? Of course you do. We had a great time." One of the goats looked up. "Baaaaa."

Afterward, Jennifer returned to the main room to find that everyone had left, except for Jesus. "Where is everybody?"

"I gave them all special errands," Jesus replied. "They will be busy for a while."

"I hope it wasn't me, or anything I said."

"Of course not. Everyone except Judas told me to tell you goodbye, but you will see most of them again tomorrow night for supper."

"Oh, yeah, looking forward to that. I will make it a surprise."

"Let us walk to the Temple. Today will be a long day of teaching."

"I'll tell you what," Jennifer said. "Let's walk to the Temple and once there, allow me to go off for a while and explore some more. That way you can focus on the people you're teaching."

"But I would like you to be there. I always want you there, watching and protecting me."

"I will always protect you. But you need to teach, and today I need to explore. It's part of my mission to your land. I must learn about it in order to teach my people about you and your customs. You need to teach, and I need to learn. You have a special land, and I must find out everything I can about it."

"Then let me go with you, and help you learn. I will teach later."

"No, the people need your teachings, and that is critically important. They rely on you and need you. I will have dinner and wine waiting for us at our favorite place. Plus, Chanel. What do you want for dinner? Anything, just name it."

"Bread sounds wonderful, especially with wine."

"Yes, I knew that," Jennifer said. "But you know. Man cannot live on bread and wine alone. I might surprise you with a few other things as well."

Jesus smiled. "Ah, so you do listen to my words. What I said was, Man does not live on bread alone, but on every word that comes from the mouth of God. Man needs his spirit to be nourished as well as his body. You only think of others. Whatever the case, I will tell my Father to protect you as if you were me."

Jennifer and Jesus had a pleasant walk to the Temple. They were obviously both in love. And Jennifer would do anything for Jesus. Every hour brought him closer to the cross. It was a thought she could not bear to dwell on. There must be something she could do. Approaching the Temple, they hugged, and then separated from each other. Jesus headed for the Temple area. Jennifer continued walking. She blew Jesus a kiss. "See you tonight, my love. Remember Chanel."

"Yes, Chanel by Jennifer," he replied smiling. "As you would say, I can't wait."

Jennifer took her time, walking slowly while watching the people go about various tasks, and knowing that once she returned to her time, all these people would no longer exist. *What a strange thought.* She looked around and spotted Judas standing by a nearby doorway. She wondered what he was doing, but then she remembered. This was where Judas sold out Jesus for thirty pieces of silver to the high priest. She knew that thirty pieces of silver was a goodly amount of money at this time, worth about twenty thousand dollars in her time. She hoped that she could talk some sense into him. She approached Judas, startling him.

"Judas, how are you? What are you doing here?"

"Nothing, just meeting some people. You can go. Go back to Jesus. That is what you want."

"Look, I know we aren't on the best terms, but we both want the same thing. We love Jesus and want others to love him as well."

"He has forgotten me," Judas complained. "I am not in his thoughts. He does not think of me anymore, of that, I am sure."

"No, he hasn't," Jennifer said. "He speaks highly of you. You need to talk to him. You are one of his chosen. I am just a friend."

"You are more than friends, but take heed. It won't last long. Jesus is losing his direction."

"That's up to you, Judas. Look to your heart. Look to your love, and look to your faith."

Jennifer opened her pouch and grabbed some coins. "Here, I want to give you some money. You know, to help you out maybe even help the poor."

"I do not want your money," Judas snarled. "I will soon have money enough."

Jennifer did not realize that Judas had not seen the gold aureus coin, she had for him. It was worth way more than thirty pieces of silver.

"Okay, just sit down and think it over first. Jesus loves you. He has told you that many times. Please don't do anything drastic. Think about your love."

"And I love, Jesus, which is why I must do what I must do. I bid you farewell."

You LOVE him? she wanted to shout. You love him so much that you would betray him to his death for a lousy 30 pieces of silver. You snake! You…you…Judas! Her last words stopped her righteous anger. Yes, that was where that saying had come from.

Judas. Do you understand that when you hand him over, they will kill him? Do you realize that? And do you realize that you will feel so remorseful, as you should, that you will take your own life? Hang yourself? Would you believe it if I told you…? No, probably not. After all, I'm only a woman, she thought bitterly. Knowing that her words would be useless, she bit them back. Instead, she said, "Goodbye, Judas. I am not your enemy. See you at supper tomorrow."

"You are coming even there?" he asked disgustedly.

"Of course, and you do not want to miss it. It will be very special."
"Women!"

Jennifer left and headed through the gate to visit the time ship. She needed more coins and a little more Chanel. And of course, an ice-cold drink wouldn't be bad. Looking around, she figured Keith must be somewhere nearby. She had never trusted him, now more than ever, and she knew that he was going to do something bad very soon. She must be ready. After a short, pleasant walk, she entered the time ship where Leo and Winifred were inside getting ready for another adventure.

"Hey, guys, how you doing? I haven't seen you since we first arrived." Jennifer grabbed an ice-cold soda and quickly drank most of it down.

"Hey, you got here just in time," Leo said. "We're leaving on a grand adventure. It's a big day for us, and maybe history as well." "Where are you going?" Jennifer asked.

"We're going to the Dead Sea and Masada," Winifred replied smiling broadly. "I want to see King Herod's Palace as it really was. I'm so excited."

"That's a long way from here. Are you going to run?" Jennifer asked.

"Not us," Leo said. "We're going first class. I hired a couple camels to take us. Out here, it's like the Mercedes of travel. Nothing better. Sitting way up high, and they can move pretty fast. Only the best for us. By camelback, it's only a couple hours away. Luxury travel in the time of Jesus."

"Yes, we have to meet our camel driver shortly," Winifred said. "Have you seen Keith?"

"Yes, he's always around and close by. Actually, too close. I worry about him."

"I wonder what he's been doing," Leo said. "He never goes with us."

"Seems like he spends most of his time here, drinking beer," Winifred said.

"He follows me around a lot, out of sight, but I agree. He spends a lot of time in here," Jennifer said. "He should never have come on this trip."

"That's odd," Winifred said. "Why out of sight?"

"You tell me. One thing, though, if you're going to witness the main events, you'll need to get back in time. We only have a few days left here," Jennifer said. As she spoke the words, her gut churned. No matter what happened, their time here was coming to an end. What would she do? If Jesus died as he was supposed to on the cross, she would go back to her own time sad and brokenhearted. *But what if he didn't? Then what?* Would he come forward in time with her? Even though he loved her, she doubted it. Sure, he might want to visit her so-called land. But he would want to return. His mission was here with his people. *If that happens, would I go back, or stay here with him?* She honestly could not answer that question.

"Well, take care," Leo said, breaking into her thoughts.

"Say hello to the camels for me," Jennifer said almost absentmindedly.

"Away we go! Camel time, can't wait," Winifred said. "I hope they don't smell."

Once Leo and Winifred had left, Jennifer replenished her coins and Chanel, and drank the last of her cold drink. She took out another cold can of soda and rubbed it against her forehead.

So nice. I wish Jesus could feel this. He would really like it.

Jennifer sighed and replaced the can in the refrigeration unit. Then she left the time ship to head back to Jerusalem. She had only walked a few feet when she felt a strange sensation wash over her. Something wasn't right and danger was nearby. She'd always had a sixth sense for that kind of thing, and those feelings were never wrong. She felt danger for her and for Jesus. The time she had dreaded was finally here. She heard someone behind her, and she knew exactly who it was.

"Hello, Keith, what can I do for you?" Jennifer asked as she turned around to look at him.

"I want you to meet some of my new friends. They're dying to meet you. That was a joke. See? I do have a sense of humor."

From behind some boulders, six men that Keith had hired as assassins, stepped out in front of Jennifer. They were armed with swords, which were drawn, seemingly ready for battle. They stared at Jennifer and smiled.

"Yes, they definitely look like friends of yours," she told Keith.

"I know you like obstacle courses, so I'm going to make one up for you."

"Why, Keith?" Jennifer asked. "Why do you have so much hate? I think you enjoy giving people pain."

"You are the only person who can stop me from my mission—the mission assigned to me by the President of the United States. Therefore, you must be eliminated."

"And what is your mission? You can tell me now. You have nothing to lose at this point."

"I am here to kill Jesus before he gets on the cross. I will end all religion. It will be me. And once you're dead, nothing will remain of you, not even your memory or any memory of you. The perfect murder." "I'd be willing to bet it wouldn't be your first," Jennifer said.

"Why do you say that?"

"Two sonic booms that I'll bet echoed throughout time. I figure we had at least two more people with us on this mission, one of whom was the pilot."

Keith shrugged. "Could be, but I don't remember."

"If you kill me, how are you going to get back to our time?"

"Oh, that won't be a problem. I got one of the pilots to train me as a backup before we left, in case something happened that you couldn't. Anyway, I will achieve my mission and kill Jesus."

"You can't do that! I will stop you! You can't interfere!"

"Good luck with that. After I kill Jesus, I will cut him up and burn his body. He will never come back. And if he does, he will be a freakin' zombie. Just think, Jesus, the first zombie."

"God will stop you!" Jennifer said angrily.

"God doesn't exist. Nothing will stop me. Now, I'd like to make things a little more fair and interesting. I know you're good, actually the top ninety-nine percent. But I am a one-percenter and out of your league. Here, take this. You'll need it," Keith said, throwing her a sword that landed on the ground at her feet. "I borrowed it from a Roman soldier. And don't worry. He'll never need it again."

"I figured that. You don't care how many people you murder." "I tried to buy it at first, but he wouldn't sell it to me. It was definitely a bad decision on his part, very bad."

"How nice of you," Jennifer said sarcastically. "I always knew you would be trouble, and that it would come down to you or me. You never cared about anything but your selfish ego. It will not end well for you. You know the old saying, Live by the sword; die by the sword."

"Here is the obstacle. If you want to stop me from killing Jesus, you have to get through my six friends here first. Each one has been promised a lot of money, and the one who kills you, gets double. You get through them; you get to me. Although it probably would be better if you let them kill you first. Because I won't be so nice. Nothing will save you from me."

"Really? Big, bad you have to have six men to take me on first. What's the matter? Couldn't sneak up on me and stab me in the back like the coward you are? Tsk. Tsk. I should have known."

Jennifer's words hit home and almost worked. Keith's face flushed a deep red. He was about to attack her himself, when he looked at the six louts he had hired. They looked right back at him, and he knew that if he deprived them of the money he had promised, they most likely would kill him and take all his money. Because if he killed her himself, he would not pay them any money.

"Think what you want. You supposed to be so good. You should have no trouble taking these guys out." Keith knew his words would rub the six men the wrong way. And he hoped it would make them all the more eager to kill her.

"I have faith!" Jennifer shouted. "Something you know nothing about."

"Good!" Keith said. "Die with it then, because it means nothing. Once you're dead, Jesus will never remember who you are, and he will be easy pickings for a man like me. Jesus the zombie, maybe a movie someday. Pick up the sword, Jennifer. You're going to need it. Good luck."

Keith walked away toward Jerusalem, leaving her facing the six assassins.

Jennifer picked up the sword. "Now you men listen to me. I don't wound, maim, cut or scratch. I kill quickly and deadly. You will not survive. It will not be nice. Leave now, and you will live to see another day. I will defend the man I love with your lives!"

The assassins laughed and pointed at Jennifer.

"A woman will be no problem," the first assassin laughed. "It's easy money. Where did he find you, woman? Women cannot fight. You can't even hold that sword right. This is a joke." "She is pretty," the sixth assassin said.

"Yeah, pretty dead," the third assassin said.

"Just remember, you can't spend it if you're dead," Jennifer warned.

"I will end this very quickly and get double," the second assassin said.

He stepped toward Jennifer, not realizing how quick she was. Jennifer took a step forward and stabbed the sword through his mouth. It protruded out the back of his skull. She pulled out the sword, and the man fell to the ground, shaking like he was having an epileptic fit.

He died in a pool of his own blood as his shocked partners looked on. Jennifer quickly moved behind some large boulders.

"Surround her! Listen, woman, there is no escape," the third assassin shouted.

"You were first and lucky, but I will not make the same mistake. Come and face me! Die with honor."

The other five assassins looked around the boulders but could not find her.

"Come out, woman," the third assassin taunted. "I will make it quick, just like you did with my friend."

What the third assassin did not realize was that Jennifer was on top of the boulder above him. She jumped from her perch, landing on his shoulders and pushed her sword down through the top of his skull, reaching his esophagus, and killing him instantly. Jennifer quickly moved away as his partners returned.

"Kill that bitch!" assassin number five shouted.

The first assassin climbed between some boulders, looking for her. But Jennifer was hidden below him between some rocks with a shadow covering her. She pushed her sword up through his groin area right to his lungs. The sword pierced his heart, killing him. Jennifer moved to another area out of sight.

The fourth assassin looked at his now dead friend. "Three dead in less than a minute. This is no ordinary woman. What are we up against?"

"Just more money for us," the fifth assassin growled. "Let us attack her as one. I will rape her dead body!"

"And I will join you in that with pleasure," the sixth assassin said.

"I don't think so."

Jennifer picked up the sword from one of the assassins and threw it, hitting the fifth assassin right between the eyes. He remained standing for a few seconds before falling to the ground dead.

Jennifer stepped out to face the remaining two assassins. "Told you. Now it's just us. You want it one at a time or both together. Doesn't matter to me. It will have same end result. How does that money sound now? Dead men spend no money. What will it be, boys?"

The two remaining assassins faced Jennifer with their swords up. Then they looked at each other and shook their heads before throwing their swords down, turning and running away from her.

"Definitely not worth the money," one man said to the other.

She looked toward Jerusalem and spotted Keith moving slowly. Actually, he was walking too slowly, almost as though he was waiting. Jennifer now realized that Keith had a mean, evil streak in him. She would have to be cautious. She started walking after him, knowing that she needed a plan as Keith was super dangerous and a talented killer, far beyond anyone she had ever known. Her mission was to save Jesus, at least for now. It seemed funny as she thought about it. Here she was trying to save Jesus, knowing that he would die in a few days. But even if it cost her life, she would willingly give it for Jesus. She just had to make sure she killed Keith first. She did not hurry, giving herself a few moments to recover from her fight with the assassins. Finally, she caught up to Keith.

"Good, I knew you would take care of them. You just saved me a ton of money."

"Is this fun for you?" she asked. "Why?"

"Trust me," Keith replied. "If there is a heaven and hell, I am a damned man, heading straight to hell."

"It sounds like you want to go there. It's where you belong."

"Yes, probably. I knew those idiots couldn't hurt you. I just wanted to wear you out a little. I'll take any advantage I can get, even if I don't need it. So, now is your chance to save Jesus. To prove that God does exist or to prove that he doesn't."

"He is real!" Jennifer said. And for the first time in her life, she said it with real conviction. Yes, He is real. He does exist. And she believed it with all her heart.

"Look at it this way. If you're still around in a few minutes, you may be right. Don't count on it, though. Let's see how good you are at sword fighting."

"After three weeks of practice, I became the state fencing champion. Let's find out."

"Amateur. Nothing will stop me."

Keith and Jennifer faced each other. Keith was bigger, stronger, and faster. Jennifer knew she had to turn her smaller size into an advantage, but how? Keith swung at Jennifer but she tumbled under his legs and came from behind, slicing a long cut across his back.

He grunted in pain. "Good job, you got me. But as soon as you are dead, it will go away. Now watch."

"Are you sure about that? Even if I disappeared from time, the sword won't. It will still have your blood on it, and you will still have your injuries," Jennifer shot back.

Was she right? He did not know. Yes, she would disappear from the timeline as though she had never existed, but the sword was made in this time. Surely without her to use it…. It was all too confusing. He would just have to wait and see what happened.

Keith and Jennifer sparred back and forth. The blades clanged and squealed whenever one struck or slid off the other. When a thrust or lurch got past the other one's blade, the other did his or her best to sidestep it. Then Keith got lucky. He feigned to the left, then swung back, under cutting her blade and stabbing into Jennifer's stomach. She jumped back before it went very deep and gasped at the burning pain. Stepping back a little further, she tried to regroup.

"That's got to hurt," he said unkindly. "Now you can't concentrate on just me. The pain is biting, nagging at you. You're bleeding. If you continue, will you bleed to death."

Too busy celebrating the beginning of what Keith thought was the end for her. Jennifer swung her sword, slicing his face across the cheek. The injury angered him. If she was right about the wounds remaining, he would be scarred for life.

Keith counter-attacked Jennifer, fiercely slashing back and forth against her sword. Her sword might have been well made for that era, but it was a weak copy compared to Keith's sword, which had been made with the finest 21st-century metal and science possible. Jennifer could do nothing, except defend herself, knowing that she was outgunned, so to speak. She regained her footing and tried to strike back, but her blows no longer had the necessary force to do much harm.

Realizing this, Keith gave her an evil smile. "I guess God loses. I grow weary of this game. It's time to settle this."

Bringing back his sword in a giant swing, he completely shattered Jennifer's weapon. And without a sword, there was no way to stop Keith. She needed to run. It was the only way, or she would die. But she was injured, and she needed a new plan of attack.

Grasping her wound with one hand, Jennifer ran. But Keith brought her down when he threw his knife, hitting her in her right thigh. The blow, as well as the injury, knocked her face down on the ground. She quickly turned over on her back. *If I have to die, it will be facing you*, she thought.

Keith approached her, raising his sword high for the kill.

"It looks like oblivion for you. But you were a good soldier, and in your honor, I will make it quick. The only problem is I won't remember this or you. So sad. I win and religion will never be the same. I would say that God is waiting for you, but we both know that isn't going to happen." Jennifer looked up, knowing that Keith was going to kill her, and there was no way out of it. She thought of Jesus, and the love she had for him. Now he would never even remember that she had existed. She would miss the Last Supper tomorrow that she had made big plans for. She saw Keith's sword, shinning in the sun and knew this was her last moment. God would lose. Her love for Jesus would be lost. He was standing right over her.

"Before you kill Jesus, there is something you need to think about," Jennifer said.

"I told you. God doesn't exist. You're living…no dying proof of that," Keith said.

"It's not that."

"Then what?"

"If you kill Jesus, the reason for our coming here will disappear with him. There will never have been a mission to come back here. What then? Will the time machine suddenly appear in the lab without anyone in it? And what about you and Leo and Winifred? Will you end up back in our time, but doing something completely different, because you would not be needed for a mission that no longer exists? Or will the three of you just cease to exist?"

Keith hesitated, lowering the sword just a bit. He had not thought about any of those possibilities. They were far beyond his pay grade. And he just wasn't bright enough to know what to think. "I'll have to think about that further. In the meantime, getting rid of you won't make any difference whatsoever." He raised the sword high again, ready to plunge it into her heart.

Jennifer took in a deep breath, preparing herself for the pain she knew she would have to endure, even if only for a few seconds. Looking Keith in the eyes, she gave him her most defiant expression. That's when she heard the sound of something flying through the wind. A moment later, her breath rushed out and her mouth dropped open as a spear pierced Keith's back, and protruded out of the front of his chest. Jennifer looked at it in relief. She would know that spear anywhere. It was the Spear of Destiny.

Keith stood in shock looking at the point of the spear coming out of his chest. He dropped to his knees as Longinus approached from behind. Pulling it out, he raised his foot and shoved Keith over to the side, so that the body would not fall on Jennifer.

Looking down at her, Longinus said, "I told you I would watch over you. What are you doing out here? It is dangerous. I can't believe a Roman soldier would try to kill you."

Keith was barely alive, unable to fully understand what had happened. Longinus helped Jennifer up, and she looked at Keith. "He was not a Roman soldier, only a fake. You have done me the greatest love of all time, which will soon be forgotten but remembered for all time."

Her words made no sense to him. "You are injured," he told her.

On the ground, and still puzzled, Keith did not say a word.

"Soon, you will see God, and he will pronounce judgment on you," Jennifer said.

Then he died. At that moment, another giant sonic boom ripped through time. One moment, Jennifer was looking at Keith's body. There was nothing there, no blood, no evidence, no sword, because Keith was never born and never existed. Everyone who Keith had ever hurt or killed, except for Elizabeth, were never hurt or killed by him. They would die when they were supposed to, but not by his hand. The four assassins that Jennifer killed earlier now never happened, because Keith had never hired them. Elizabeth, from the future, who had died before Keith, could never return, because her existence had already been erased. And with his death, Jennifer's wounds disappeared, and she forgot that she had even been injured.

"What are you doing here outside the gates and on the ground?" Longinus asked her, forgetting what had happened before Keith disappeared. "Lucky for you I followed you. Are you looking for something or someone?" His spear was clean and bloodless with Keith's existence erased. It would not be until later that Jennifer would remember the sonic boom and realize that yet another member of their team had vanished, but like the others, she would not remember who. "I don't know, but I am glad to see you. How are you, my friend?"

"Very well. Come, let me escort you back to the city, where you will be safe."

"I'll gladly accept that offer," Jennifer replied. "Why don't I buy some wine? We can sit and talk."

"That sounds wonderful. You are the gift that never ends."

"Actually, where I come from, it is called the gift that keeps on giving."

Jennifer and Longinus walked back to Jerusalem where they sat at the same table, they had occupied a few days earlier. The same shop owner hurried over to them.

"Two of your best cups and a pouch of wine for my wonderful friend here," Jennifer ordered with a smile.

"Coming right up."

"I don't know what I was doing out there," she told Longinus. "I must be confused or something. But my handsome guardian angel was looking over me."

"Where are you from that is so different from here? Whatever you do, don't let Rome find out about it."

"Actually, my land is in no danger of ever becoming another Roman conquest. It's too far away for them to reach, and I'm extremely happy about that."

"Why don't you stay here?" Longinus asked.

"Like you, I have my duties, and I must go back, most likely never to return." The shop owner returned with two cups and a pouch of wine for Longinus.

Jennifer handed him two silver coins, which included a very good tip.

"Thank you! Thank you!" the shop owner said. "Come any time, and I will serve you first."

"I will miss my new friend, Jennifer," Longinus said.

"And I will miss you, Longinus. You have become so special to me. Somehow I know you have a special purpose."

Longinus picked up his cup. "A toast to Jennifer." Longinus drained his cup. "Where is Jesus? Why are you not with him?"

"He's teaching at the Temple. I had some errands to run and thought it best not to disturbed him."

"I watch him from a distance, wishing I could be there to hear his words. But being a Roman soldier, I would scare everyone off. Still, I hear of his teachings, and they are wonderful."

"So, what are your plans, and what do you really want?"

"That is easy. I no longer wish to serve Rome. Rome is cruel and a danger to all. I would like to live a simple life and maybe raise goats, or sheep, or possibly even beef. I hear beef has a great future. Just a small farm, but it is only a foolish dream, especially with my salary. You spend it as soon as you make it. So, my dream will never come true."

"That is a wonderful dream. I think it can come true, especially for one as wonderful as you," Jennifer assured him.

"No, it cannot happen. They have it planned out so that a Roman soldier can't save money, which makes him dependent on Rome for the rest of his life."

"I think that God sent us to each other for a reason."

"Is there truly a God?" Longinus asked. "I hope so. I know there are no Roman gods, never have been. But for some reason, I believe in Jesus." "Yes, Longinus, and God loves you as his own son. He sent you to me for some reason, and now I know what it is."

Jennifer drank some of her wine, and once again, handed her cup to Longinus, who drank it down very quickly.

"I wish you a safe journey back to your land, Jennifer. You will be always be in my thoughts."

"Please do me a favor, as I hate goodbyes," Jennifer said.

"Tell me, and if I can grant it, it is yours."

"Close your eyes and open your hand," Jennifer said. "And please do not open your eyes until I am gone. Please."

Longinus looked puzzled, but saw no reason why he could not grant her request. "Of course, I am honored to do that, and I am honored that I met you. You are the most beautiful woman I will ever meet, and so special. My eyes are now closed and my hand is open."

Longinus thought that Jennifer was just going to touch his hand to say goodbye, but that was not going to happen. Jennifer took out six gold aureus coins and placed them in his hand. She then closed his fingers around the coins. The coins were more than enough to buy a nice farm, and for Longinus to live on it for many years. She kissed Longinus on the forehead.

"I know that God loves you, and he has a purpose for you. Remember, God loves you. Jesus loves you, and I love you. Farewell, my dear friend."

Jennifer left, knowing she would never see Longinus again. She hoped that maybe she had changed his path to a better purpose and happiness. She took one last look at the Spear of Destiny, unable to figure out why it held so much meaning for her.

*****

Later that night, Jennifer and Jesus were at their favorite spot on the Mount of Olives. Jennifer brought an excellent selection of food and some very good wine. After dinner, she rubbed Chanel into Jesus' shoulders, neck, and forehead.

"How was your day, my love?" he asked. "Anything exciting happen? Did you break any more noses?"

Jennifer laughed. "You always ask me that. Believe me, I don't go around doing that kind of thing every day."

"I am glad."

"Actually, it was kind of boring, not much happened, just an ordinary day. I did run into Longinus, the owner of the Spear of Destiny, and we had some wine. He is a very nice man, and I know you would like him. He really hates Rome, and he has a special feeling for you. I think he actually believes in you. I know he deeply respects you. You have touched him, and he is Roman. He told me he doesn't believe in any of the Roman so-called gods."

"He is a smart man. There are no gods, except my Father. I am sure that I could make him my friend, even with the Spear of Destiny." Jesus drank some wine. "Sometimes, it is nice to have a day where nothing happens. It gives you time to relax."

"Maybe," Jennifer said. "I was hoping for a little excitement, but it just wasn't on the menu. More wine?"

"Yes, do we have more bread?"

"Yes, I brought plenty. And I have protein bars for breakfast."

"For having such a boring day, you are so exciting," Jesus said. Jennifer sighed. "I wish this night could last forever."

"Yes, but time is not something we can control. Nothing can stop destiny. Every second I feel closer to mine. Like the Spear of Destiny, we both have a destiny coming soon."

"There might be something else, along with a little love."

Jennifer and Jesus laid down quietly and gazed at the stars. They fell asleep, lying against each other as if one.

CHAPTER

TWENTY-SEVEN

The sun was just appearing over the horizon when Jennifer opened her eyes. The first thing she saw was Jesus, standing a few feet away from her, staring at the city of Jerusalem. He was just so stunning to look at. She could watch him for hours. She wondered what he was thinking about, knowing that he has just spent his last peaceful night on earth. She was pleased he had spent it with her. Tonight, he would have his Last Supper. Then everything would turn to pain from this moment on. She shuddered. *Why? Why does he have to suffer so much? Why does it have to be the worst torture and death any human being could endure?* She knew why. But that did not mean she understood it. Not really.

Jennifer had special plans for the Last Supper. She wanted to make the meal unique for Jesus. He knew what was going to happen, maybe not all the particulars, but he knew it would be horrible. Yet he faced it so bravely. The ultimate sacrifice to save mankind. It was what God, his Father demanded. Jesus was so special; thirty-three years was not nearly enough time. The few precious days she had spent with him would never be enough. Yet, there was nothing she could do to change it. She knew she could not be selfish and keep him all to herself, forsaking billions of people over the centuries, and literally slamming the gates of heaven in their faces. All she could do was try to make him happy for the moment, because that was all she and Jesus had.

Jennifer stood up, walked over to Jesus, and put her arms around him. "Good morning, my special love. A penny for your thoughts." Jesus smiled down at her, his expression puzzled. "With you it is always a good morning. But tell me. What is a penny?"

"It's the smallest denomination of coin. This expression was first said by a man in a different country from mine. And at the time, a person could buy a lot for a penny. But that is no longer the case. A penny nowadays is practically worthless."

"Then did you mean a lot of money for my thoughts, or only a little?" Jesus asked.

"Oh, a lot, of course. Your thoughts are so valuable, they are priceless."

"Thank you, Jennifer. I only wish others thought the same as you," Jesus replied. "I think we still have some juice left over. Shall we have juice and a protein bar for breakfast?"

"Yes, bread can come later. Thank you." He touched Jennifer on her shoulder. "You are the owner of my heart and always will be."

They sat down next to the tree to eat their breakfast. During the entire time, Jennifer continued to hug Jesus. She did not want to let him go or feel the pain he would have to endure. Who would have thought that she would fall in love with the most famous man in history? Talk about picky. There was no way to top this. He turned out to be way better than she ever could have known. She thought about all the pictures of Jesus throughout the ages. None of them even came close. No artist, no matter how good, could capture his true beauty. Even if Jesus was sitting for the picture, it would be impossible. You would have to see him to believe it. "I need to go to the Temple and pray. And I will need to be alone. This is very important."

"Without knowing, I know. I need to do some errands to get ready for later. It is good for both of us to be busy." Inside her mind, though, she did not want to leave his side. But she had to respect his needs. And like he had said, it was important for him to be able to prepare for what he was about to endure.

"Now do you remember where to go and how to get there?" Jesus asked.

"Of course, the house with the upper room," Jennifer replied. "We spent the night there."

"Of course, you would remember. I am sorry I even asked you that question."

"What about the disciples? How will they know?"

"They have been told how to get there," Jesus replied.

"How?"

"They will look for a man carrying a jug of water, and he will guide them to the house."

Jennifer looked puzzled. "Aren't lots of people always carrying water? Everywhere I look, I see water being carried."

"No, in Jerusalem only women carry water. The only men who carry water are the Essene—a mystic Jewish sect, and queer. You would call it effeminate."

"That's interesting, especially around here. You don't see many of them."

"The Essene tend to themselves and train to be priests from a very young age," Jesus explained. "They believe in God but not in me. Their tradition is characterized by strict adherence to Jewish law, and a special concern for the purity of the priesthood. They believe in the imminent coming of a Messiah or Messiahs, who will usher in the Day of the Lord, in which Gentile rule would be vanquished through a cataclysmic conflict between the Sons of Light and the Sons of Darkness."

"Gentile rule meaning Rome."

"Rome and more but right now, mostly Rome. After all, they control most of the world. I am surprised they haven't conquered your land."

"We're just too far away," Jennifer said. "They don't know of our existence." "Better for you if they never do."

"So, if the Essene don't believe in the Son of God, are they dammed?"

"Yes, they are, but they are stubborn in their ways, and because they never have children, it will not last long. They will end themselves, and God will look the other way as they are not bearers of fruit."

"Well, you always get the ascetic ones. I think they will last."

"Yes, they will," Jesus said. "They are the most stubborn of all."

Together they walked to the Temple. Jennifer was still confused and sad. This was the last day, and Jesus would be crucified tomorrow if nothing was done to stop it. Could he be wrong about the cross? She thought he was wrong about some of his predictions. Why not the cross? But by saving Jesus, would it cause too much trouble in the ripples of time? Would it change everything? Was it a curse that she fell in love with the most perfect man of all time—a man she could never spend the rest of her life with? They told each other farewell at the Temple.

"I will see you later, my love. Please stay out of trouble, and do not hurt anyone who doesn't deserve it."

Jennifer gave him a sad smile. "Don't worry, my love. I won't. I will obtain various items for supper. I will also bring clean cloths and a towel, so I can properly wash your feet and hands and even those of your disciples. I will clean them in your honor. It will be my special duty to do so."

"Wait, how did you know about that? I never told you. That is something I must do."

"Isn't it the custom around here? I pick up things quickly."

"Yes, you do, but this has to be my task. I must show them that I am one with them. They must understand that in order to be first, one must be the servant to others."

"Not for the Son of God. I am now your representative on Earth, and I will willingly do it in your place. It's the same as if you did it. Besides you need to tell them a lot of things. You will not have time for washing. If I do it, it means you did it, no difference. I am honored to serve you in this way."

"Your reasoning is understandable. But no, you do not really understand. The lesson I must teach them is important. This is not a task that you can take from me. Please understand." "All right. If you insist," Jennifer said.

"I do. There are some things that must be done in order to prepare my disciples for what they must do once I am gone," Jesus told her.

"All right, my love. I understand."

"There is much on my mind, but I will still miss you."

"That you will miss me, greatly pleases me. What I do now is for you. I want everything perfect just for you, as you are truly the special one."

Jesus left for the entrance of the Temple, while Jennifer walked towards outside the city and back to the time ship.

Even with her head covered, people noticed Jennifer as someone very different and mysterious, along with her amazing looks. People tried not to stare at her, but still ended up staring, embarrassed when Jennifer smiled back at them, which she almost always did.

She thought to herself and spoke softly, "The people here are so nice—just pure and innocent. We have lost so much over the years, maybe we can get it back."

Jennifer continued walking until she heard a voice behind her. "Hello, beautiful lady, I have a present for you."

Jennifer turned around to see a pretty woman possibly in her late 20's, well dressed in a very bright purple dress. In her right hand was a small pouch. The woman placed the pouch in Jennifer's hand.

"What is this?" Jennifer asked. She was curious as to why a perfect stranger would give her a present.

The woman smiled and hugged her. "It is Frankincense, a very special gift for a special lady."

Jennifer didn't know what to say. "I don't understand."

The woman took Jennifer's hand, which was now holding the pouch. "It's the same gift that was given to Jesus when he was born and now you get some."

"Why?" Jennifer asked curiously. "Do you know Jesus?"

The lady laughed. "We all know Jesus. I have been his friend and follower for the last three years. He saved me from seven demons, and I am forever in his debt. He saved me when no one else could. His love is the greatest love of all. I have never seen him so happy until I saw him with you. You have to be sent by the father; it could be nothing else."

Jennifer reached out and took the woman's hand. "No, I was not sent by the father or at least I don't think so. But I do feel very lucky and honored to be in his presence. Are you one of his followers, don't worry you can tell me as I am, too."

The woman then kissed Jennifer's hand. "A few of my friends and I help and support Jesus with whatever we can. I am fortunate enough to be able to give him financial benefits from time to time because, as you probably know he doesn't believe in the concept of making money. And yes, I do follow him."

Jennifer nodded. "Yes as do I, and I know he could be very rich if he wanted to."

"That is not his way, and it is one of the reasons he is the most special person on this earth," answered the woman. "All I know is that you are special and special for him. He needs you. I feel so happy for him because you have found each other. And now, I bid you farewell. Please enjoy my gift, burn it over a fire and everything will smell so beautiful, just like Jesus."

The woman walked away.

Jennifer raised her hand to stop her. "What is your name? I want to thank you."

"What you are doing for Jesus is all the thanks I need."

Jennifer wanted to know more. "At least tell me your name."

The woman turned and faced Jennifer. "My name is Mary."

Jennifer smiled and slightly laughed. "My, there are a whole lot of Marys' around here."

The woman looked Jennifer directly in the eyes. "Yes, and we have one thing in common. We all love Jesus. And you know what? I love you, too." She walked away.

Jennifer thought about what had just happened and speaking to herself said, "Son of a gun. Touché." Jennifer continued her walk back to the time ship as she needed to think and try to figure out the proper course of action she should take.

She entered the time ship and as always, first grabbed an ice-cold drink and quickly drank it down. Sitting in her chair, Jennifer wondered what Leo and Winifred were doing. *They're still on their camels exploring. They should be getting back. After all, the most important part of our mission is to witness what happens to Jesus. To see with our own eyes if everything the Bible said about Him was true.*

All she could think about was Jesus, and what was going to happen tomorrow. For four hours, she sat in the chair. It went by as if it were only a few seconds. She didn't know what to do next, except that she had to go shopping. She grabbed more supplies and headed back to the city, pulling her hood over her head. Armed with a shopping list in her head, she knew right where to go, the rich people's market. Remembering where the man had told her where it was, she entered the main store. It was a much nicer store, almost like an ancient Neiman Marcus of Jerusalem. This time, there was a woman in charge. Jennifer was impressed but not for long.

"Can I help you find anything?" the shop attendant asked. "Wait! You do not look like you belong in this store. Who and where is your master? Bring him here so we can do business."

Jennifer knew that any man would bend over backwards to help her, but this woman was immune to her charms.

"I have no master, just me. I am not a slave. Never have been, and never will be." "Maybe you should shop somewhere else. This is not the place for you," the woman insisted.

"I'm just looking. You never know. I might buy a lot of items from your store. You can't tell just by looking at me. Don't judge me by my appearance."

"I can tell," the shop attendant said, stubbornly. "I shall call the owner to escort you out. We don't want you here. He will make a swift exit of you."

The shop attendant exited through a door that led to the back of the shop. A moment later, a large, fairly fat man came out and walked menacingly toward Jennifer. He stopped in front of her and gave her a stern look, thinking she was nothing but a poor slave begging for food or worse, trying to steal it.

"You need to…," the owner began in a loud voice.

Jennifer threw back her hood and suddenly, everything changed as he saw how beautiful she was.

"You need to be…." Stunned, he changed course. "…personally showed by me anything you want."

"I thought you might change your mind. Yes, I want to do some shopping."

"Of course, my beautiful lady, but this is a very expensive store. It may be beyond your means but not your beauty."

Jennifer opened her pouch and brought out a handful of silver and gold coins, practically giving the shop owner a heart attack.

He yelled at his assistant. "Get out here and wash the feet of this beautiful lady. Now!"

The shop attendant came out with a bucket of water and a cloth as the owner escorted Jennifer over to a chair to sit so the attendant could wash her feet.

"Thank you. You are doing a very good job. I'm impressed." Jennifer handed the woman a silver coin as a tip, which completely surprised the woman as she had never received a tip so large.

"Thank you! Thank you!" the attendant said, nearly tripping over her own tongue. "I apologize for my insincere behavior. It will never happen again, beautiful lady."

"So, where do we start?" the owner asked eagerly.

"I heard that you have the best beef in town."

"Of course, yes I do. I think this is the only place in town for beef, and it is the best."

"Good. I need enough for fourteen people, and I have a list for more items. This is your lucky day. Also, I want some nice washcloths and a large towel."

Twenty minutes later, Jennifer walked out of the store with a large basket filled with food, wine, and drinks, some really nice washcloths, and a large, fluffy towel. The basket was fairly heavy, but Jennifer had carried worse, and she did not have to go far. The shop owner and shop attendant were very happy as they waved goodbye to Jennifer.

Realizing that the basket was heavy, the shop attendant suddenly ran after her. "Please, I would be honored to help you. You treated me so nicely." "Thank you," Jennifer replied. "That would be wonderful."

Together they took it to the house with the upper room where the Last Supper was to be served. They stopped at the front door. "Farewell, there will be servants here to help take it inside," the attendant said. "This looks like the best dinner anyone could ever want."

The shop attendant left, and Jennifer knocked on the door. To her surprise Peter answered it.

"Hello, Peter, how are…."

"Not ready yet, come back later." He seemed distracted and closed the door.

"That was strange. Let's try this again."

Jennifer knocked on the door, and once more, Peter opened it.

"Not again, I said later. We all must wait, and that includes you," he said closing the door once more.

"Hmm, maybe three times will do it?" Jennifer knocked on the door for a third time.

Once again Peter opened it.

"Really, Peter, three times? Is three a special number for you? I think it is. I have food in this basket."

"We have to wait until Jesus is here. I am sorry, but we must wait for the anointed one. No one can enter until he is here." "You're here," Jennifer said.

Before Peter could answer, a voice was heard from behind Jennifer.

"I am here," Jesus said. "Let her enter."

Jesus hugged Jennifer. Then he looked at the large basket that she had next to her. "What is this surprise?" Jesus asked. "It smells wonderful. It is already making me hungry."

"Special food and drink for supper."

"That is a wonderful gift. Peter, bring the food inside and take it to the upper room to be prepared."

"What, Master?" Peter asked.

"I think he needs to be told at least three times," Jennifer said.

"He heard me. Come, Jennifer. Please enter. You have been here before." "Yes, I was, not so long ago. Time is moving so fast."

Stepping through the door, after Peter retrieved the basket, Jennifer looked around, and it hit her as she realized that this was the *real* house of the Last Supper. The house she had visited in modern-day Jerusalem was not this one, which was why she had not realized it when she was here before. *They got it all wrong. It's not even close.* This was just a house with a fairly large room on the upper floor. Nothing fancy, but big enough for a large group.

Jesus and Jennifer walked up the small set of stairs to the actual room. Once more, Jennifer looked around and thought to herself, *This really isn't the same room.* The historians made a mistake. She would have to correct them later. In the center of the room was a large table with fourteen chairs. She noticed that the chair in the center, most likely for Jesus, was a much larger one than the others. Two servants were busy preparing the table for the disciples. Peter carried in the basket that Jennifer had brought and set it down next to the table. One servant looked inside.

"My God, look at this!" the first servant said. "There is beef in here! This is the most wondrous basket of food I have ever seen!"

A second servant helped unpack the basket, and the two of them placed the food on the table along with the original Jewish food that had been prepared for the meal.

The second servant was so amazed, she named all the food as they removed it. "Chicken, fresh apricots, fresh melons, cheese, honey, grapes, fish, and look at that bread! Lettuce, cucumbers, mustard sauce, nuts, wine, very good wine and pomegranate juice. Wow. And beef fit for a king!"

"Even the servants will be allowed to share in this food," Jennifer said. "I insist."

"Thank you, my beautiful queen," both servants said together. "Jennifer, this is a supper, not a feast," Jesus exclaimed. "Although it does look very good."

"For my love, it is now a feast," she declared.

"You will make my disciples fat," Jesus laughed. "They will become too sleepy." "Everybody needs at least one great meal in their life—one they will always talk about."

"Yes," Jesus agreed. "This is one supper that will be remembered for the ages." Jennifer spoke to one of the servants. "Would you bring a large bowl and a pitcher of water here for washing feet?" "Of course, right away," the first servant replied.

At this time, the rest of the disciples entered the upper room. They came in and without saying a word, stared at the table loaded with so much amazing food.

"Look, Jennifer brought beef!" Peter exclaimed, his mouth watering.

"It cannot be. That is only for kings," Thomas said.

"Do not doubt, Thomas. It is indeed beef," Jesus said.

James looked on hungrily. "I have always wanted to taste it."

"There is more than enough for everybody," Jennifer laughed.

"Judas, look, Jennifer brought beef," James said. His eyes were lit with anticipation.

"That is too rich for me," Judas grumbled.

"Suit yourself, more for me," Bartholomew said. "Let me try a taste." Bartholomew took a small taste of the beef. He loved it. "That is a food fit for God. I have never tasted anything so delicious. The stories were all true about beef. I predict that someday everybody will love the taste of beef. Way better than anything else I have tasted, and I have tasted plenty."

The other disciples gathered around the beef, hoping to snatch a taste as well.

"Now gentlemen, we must wait, until you are properly prepared," Jennifer said. "Please, everybody, find your seat with Jesus sitting in the seat at the center of the table, of course."

The servant entered and placed a large bowl and a pitcher of water down in front of Jesus, who got up from his chair. Wrapping the towel Jennifer had purchased around his waist. He poured water into the large bowl and began to wash the disciples' feet. Then he dried them with the towel that was wrapped around his waist.

When Jesus came to Peter, Peter said, "Lord, are you going to wash my feet?" "You don't realize now what I am doing," Jesus said. "But later you will understand."

"No," Peter said, adamantly. "You will never wash my feet."

Jesus looked into his disciple's eyes. "Unless I wash you, you cannot share life with me."

"Then Lord," Simon Peter replied, "not just my feet! Wash my hands and my head, too!"

"A person who has had a bath needs to wash only his feet," Jesus answered. "The rest of his body is clean. And you are clean. But not all of you are." As he said this, he glanced at Judas, but no one noticed except Jennifer.

Once the disciples were clean, they began eating.

James rubbed his hands together. "I want some of that beef. I have always wondered about it."

"Let me show you a better way of eating it," Jennifer said. "First, cut two slices of bread and lay some beef on one slice, then cheese on top of the beef, lettuce, a little cucumber, and some mustard sauce. Finally, you cover it with the other piece of bread and eat everything at once." She handed the completed sandwich to James. "Here, try this."

James accepted it and bit into it, chewing with relish. "This is truly wondrous! It is so good! Come, everyone must try this. What is this called?"

"We call it a sandwich," Jennifer said. "It's a big thing where I come from."

The disciples all began making their sandwiches, passing the ingredients around the table for each one to choose, according to their tastes. Jennifer made another one and gave it to Jesus.

Jesus took a bite. "This is good! You are a wonder upon wonder. I am certain that you are a gift from my Father to aid me in my final days on earth, and you greatly have."

"I am just here to serve the chosen one." Jennifer made her own sandwich and retreated to the end of the table.

"Sand…witch," John said, trying out the word. "I see neither sand nor a witch. But it is the most remarkable food I have ever tasted."

"My Lord," James began. "While you were at Temple, we had a discussion among ourselves, and we wondered. In what order do you regard us?"

"What do you mean?" Jesus asked. Although he knew exactly what James meant, he wanted his disciple to say it.

"Which among us will be the greatest in your kingdom?" James asked.

"You do not understand the true meaning of tonight," Jesus said. "Greatness is never the goal. You know that those regarded as rulers of the Gentiles lord it over them, and their superiors exercise authority over them. But it shall not be that way among you. Instead, whoever wants to become great among you must be a servant, and whoever wants to be first must be the slave of all."

"What is greater than greatness?" Peter asked.

"For who is greater? The one who is at the table, or the one who serves? Is it not the one who is at the table? But I am among you as one who serves. You are those who have stood by me in my trials. And I confer onto you a kingdom, just as my Father conferred it onto me. So that you may eat and drink at my table in my kingdom and sit on thrones, judging the twelve tribes of Israel. My kingdom is not of this world and in order to be great in my kingdom, you need to learn how to serve. Greatest are those who serve others."

"We are sorry, my Lord," Andrew said. "We did not understand."

"The days are surely coming when the Lord will make a new covenant with the house of Israel," Jesus said. "He will put His law within them, and I will write it on their hearts. I will be their God, and they shall be my people. No longer shall they teach one another or say to each other, know the Lord, for they shall all know me, from the least to the greatest."

Jennifer sat at the very end of the table in the last chair, witnessing probably the most famous event in the history of the world. Knowing she could not take part in it, all she could do was watch and observe, for this night was for Jesus only. His last night on earth, and his last time with her. She knew the history, but she had no idea what was coming next or even what she was going to do. She noticed Judas finally sneaking a piece of beef. He went back for seconds.

"Master, you are always with us and will be always with us," James the Lesser said. "You have too much to do to be taken away."

Jesus looked up to heaven. "Father, the hour has come; glorify your Son that the Son may glorify you, since you have given him authority over all flesh, to give eternal life to all whom you have given him. And this is eternal life, that they know you the only true God, and your Son whom you have sent. I glorified you on earth, having accomplished the work that you gave me to do. And now, Father, glorify me in your own presence with the glory that I had with you before the world existed."

"What will happen to us, Teacher?" Jude asked. "What do you want us to do?"

"I have said these things to keep you from falling away. They will put you out of the synagogues. Indeed, the hour is coming when whoever kills you will think he is offering service to God. And they will do these things, because they have not known the Father, nor me. But I have said these things to you, that when their hour comes, you may remember that I told them to you. But now I am going to Him who sent me, and none of you asks me, 'Where are you going?'"

"My Lord, you are too powerful," Judas said. "Nothing can hurt you."

Jesus looked at each disciple in turn. "You, my wonderful disciples, must be prepared to meet a new order of things, new conditions, and accept persecution as will I. But remember, God will always be on our side, no matter how tough the times will be." "God will protect us!" Simon said.

"He will protect you by giving you entry into his kingdom," Jesus said. "No one comes to the Father except through me."

Jesus then took the bread, and after giving thanks, broke it, and gave it to each of his disciples. Jennifer did not receive any bread.

"Take and eat this. For this is my body given up for you. Do this in remembrance of me. For I am the bread of life. He who comes to me shall not hunger. Eat."

The disciples ate the bread that was given to them by Jesus. When they had finished eating, Jesus took his cup, blessed it, and gave thanks, saying, "This is the cup of my blood, the blood of the new and everlasting covenant; it will be shed for you and for all, for the forgiveness of sins. Do this in memory of me."

The cup was passed around for the twelve to drink. Again, Jennifer did not participate.

"Master, we are confused," James said. "What is about to happen?"

"You must keep in mind my sacrifice. For I tell you, I will never again drink of the fruit of the vine until that day when I drink it anew with you in my Father's kingdom."

Unlike the disciples, Jennifer understood what he meant and knew exactly what was going to happen. She knew that his disciples would eventually suffer greatly. None as badly, though, compared to Jesus. He would suffer the most, and she did not want to think about it.

Tomorrow would not be a pleasant day.

"We will not let any harm come to you!" John declared. "We will die first to protect you!"

"The Pharisees and Scribes have conspired with Rome to have me killed," Jesus said. "I must suffer."

The disciples were in disbelief. They believed that Rome was bad, but not bad enough to kill Jesus.

"That will never happen!" Thomas insisted.

"Again, do not doubt yourself, Thomas. I am going to die a sacrificial death for the sins of many. It will be my blood that will pay the blood sacrifice. Only then can a new covenant be established. I want you all to remember this celebration feast and commemorate it in the future to remind my followers of my sacrificial death for them."

Jennifer knew more than anyone that this event would be remembered for all of religious history.

"We will gladly die with you in honor!" Andrew said. "Everyone here will sacrifice for you and your honor."

"No, not all," Jesus contradicted him. "I tell you that one of you here, one who ate this food, shall betray me."

The disciples were shocked at hearing that remark. Jennifer of course knew that it was true, and who would be the one to do it. Poor Judas. Little did he know that he, too, would soon die at his own hand and never be saved, for although he would regret betraying Jesus, he did not repent. "It cannot be!" James said, angrily.

"None of us could betray you," Simon insisted.

"It is not a simple thing to say," Jesus said. "It is a betrayal of death."

"My Lord, who is it?" Philip asked.

"You cannot betray the one you love!" Peter said.

Jesus looked at Peter sadly. "The greatest betrayal of all is love. Love fed by jealousy."

"We have traveled too much with you," Bartholomew said. "You are one and the same with us."

"I must atone for humankind's sins, and this is just the beginning," Jesus said. Jennifer stared at Judas. She knew he was the one who started the wheels turning toward the death of Jesus. Still, she really didn't know why. It didn't make sense to her.

"Master, is it I?" Matthew asked.

"The Son of man indeed goeth, as it is written of him. But woe to that man by whom the Son of Man is betrayed! Better for that man if he had never been born."

"Rabbi, is it I?" Judas asked.

"Thou hast said it," Jesus replied. Then Jesus took a piece of bread, dipped it, and gave it to Judas Iscariot, the son of Simon. "It is the one to whom I will give this piece of bread, after I have dipped it in the dish. What thou doest, do quickly."

Judas stood up and left. The remaining disciples thought that Jesus had sent him on an errand. They did not know that Judas had left to betray Jesus, but of course Jennifer did. Tears threatened to spillover from her eyes, because she knew that this was the actual beginning of the end. Time seemed to speed up. It felt like it had only been a short time ago when she saw Jesus for the first, most wonderful time. And unless the course of history changed, it would soon be for the last time.

That was something she dreaded more than anything in her life. "Where is Judas going?" Thomas asked.

"To do what he must do." Jesus stood up. "It is time for the Son of man to be glorified, and God to be glorified in him. Little children, I am with you a little while longer. You will seek me; and as I said to the Jews, now I also say to you. Where I am going, you cannot come. Therefore, a new commandment I give unto you, that you love one another; as I have loved you, and that you also love one another. By this shall all men know that you are my disciples, if ye have love for one to another. Your brotherly affection will be sign of your apostleship, and the world will recognize you as men set apart." "Lord, whither goest thou?" Peter asked.

"Whither I go, thou canst not follow me now; but thou shalt follow me afterward," Jesus replied.

"Lord, why can't I follow thee now? I will lay down my life for thy sake," Peter said.

"Peter, I know you better than you know yourself. But Satan hath desired to have you."

"That cannot be! I will follow you to prison or even death!" Peter insisted.

Jesus said to Simon Peter, "You are the first of the apostles, my rock. I also say to you that you are Peter, and upon this rock I will build my church; and the gates of Hades will not overpower it. But soon you will be overcome and turned. I have prayed for thee, that thy faith not fail you." "I will never turn against you," Peter insisted.

"Wilt thou lay down thy life for me?" Jesus asked. "Amen, amen, I say to thee, the cock shall not crow, till thou deny me three times." *Three times hits the mark,* Jennifer thought.

"My Lord, I love you with all my heart, and this time you are wrong," Peter said. "I would never deny you." *We shall see,* Jennifer thought.

"I give thanks to God for this meal and to have my true followers with me," Jesus said.

All the disciples stood up and bowed their heads to Jesus.

"And we all thank Jennifer for the beef and the special food she brought," James said.

The disciples turn their heads towards Jennifer and also bowed.

"For God so loved the world that he gave his only Son, that whoever believes in him should not perish but have eternal life. For everyone who exalts himself will be humbled, and everyone who humbles himself will be exalted. I am the Way, the Truth, and the Life," Jesus said.

"When will we see you again, Lord?" Jude asked.

"I tell you that on the third day, I will rise and soon after, you will all witness me for the final time before I ascend into heaven to be with my Father. And I will forgive all."

Jennifer knew that she would not be here to prove or disprove his prediction. But now she was certain that Jesus was the Son of God. Her emotions were tearing her apart. How could you love someone so much, yet witness their death? She wanted to tell Jesus more, but she knew she could not. She wanted to cry but again, she could not. He would be human for just a little while longer. After that, he would be the true son of God, impossible to touch and feel. Her emotions were now getting the best of her.

"We will end with the Lord's Prayer," Jesus said.

Without thinking Jennifer spoke. "Our Father, who art in heaven, hallowed be thy name."

Jesus and the disciples turned their heads toward her in surprise. "How do you know that prayer?" Jesus asked. "I have never taught it to you."

Jennifer at a loss for words said, "I just know it. Maybe God taught it to me." "Please continue, and we will join in," Jesus said.

"Thy kingdom come. Thy will be done."

Jesus and the disciples joined her in the prayer.

Jennifer continued. "…on earth as it is in heaven. Give us this day our daily bread. And forgive us our trespasses. As we forgive those who trespass against us. And lead us not into temptation; but deliver us from evil. For thine is the kingdom, the power and the glory, now and forever. Amen."

Jesus approached Jennifer and put his arms around her. "You have added a few words I did not teach the others. I approve. Come, let us enjoy the evening and walk to the Mount." "And sing!" Bartholomew added.

The disciples began singing from the 'Hallel.' "Praise the Lord, you his servants; praise the name of the Lord. Let the name of the Lord be praised, both now and forevermore. From the rising of the sun to the place where it sets, the name of the Lord is to be praised. Praise the Lord, all you nations; extol him, all you peoples. For great is his love toward us, and the faithfulness of the Lord endures forever." They walked to the Mount of Olives.

CHAPTER

TWENTY-EIGHT

It had been a long dinner, full of talk, but not much hope for the future, at least for staying alive. The sky was clear with many twinkling stars, helping to make the walk to the Mount of Olives lovely. Whatever happened, this would also be the last night for Jennifer. It was time for her mission back in time to come to a conclusion. Jennifer knew the future. And for Jesus and all his disciples here, it would not be good. Looking around, she noticed how happy everyone was, just being together, and she was glad that she had been able to bring beef to the dinner. It had been a great hit. For most of them, it would be the first and last time they would ever enjoy the taste of beef.

The week had gone by too quickly. Had it only been a week? In some ways, it felt shorter, in other ways, longer. So much had happened, and the time she had spent with Jesus felt completely natural and special. It was as though they had been together forever. But they hadn't.

She wondered about how much time had passed in the future. A week here in the past might have been mere seconds or minutes in the future. Maybe everything would be changed when she returned. Maybe it wouldn't. Time would tell. Until she returned, there was no way of knowing how much she and the others had done that might have changed things, even a little. She watched Jesus as he spoke to some of the disciples while they walked. A lot of pain was coming his way, pain she did not want him to experience. If only he would listen. Jennifer knew that this was the last night for Jesus—a night where he would get no sleep, no rest, no peace. Everything was heading toward the cross. Jesus dropped back, so that Jennifer could catch up to him. The only thing she cared about now was her love for Jesus and the amazing man that he was.

When she reached him, he kissed her gently on her lips. "Come. You and I need to talk, and it is a talk I do not desire, but one we need to have. Time is no longer on my side, and you mean so much to me. I must do what I must do, no matter what I want or desire."

"You know me by now," Jennifer said. "I just want what's best for you. The short time I have been with you seems like love forever. I never want it to end."

"Actually, it's like I have known you all my life," Jesus said. "I have never matched with someone so quickly. But like a shooting star, it doesn't last long. It is over way too soon. I know you have much to look forward to, and you will be forever happy. You are a wonderful gift to me, especially now at this time with the events that are about to happen. Your future lies in a different direction. You are a very special shooting star."

"We need a lot more shooting stars. That would make me happy. I want you to have more out of your life. You have so much to give. You are a shooting star with no end. I will never be the same without you." Jesus looked upward to heaven with a strange expression on his face. He stood in silence for a short while. "Father, tell me the secrets I must now know. What do you want me to do? I will do whatever you desire. But no matter what, please protect Jennifer. She is one with me. Treat her special for my sake. That is all I ask, for I know what I must do."

Feeling desperate, Jennifer begged him. "Don't look to him. Look to you. This is your decision to make. Yes, you are the son, but you aren't the slave to do only his bidding. God gave us free will and that includes you. You can decide for yourself. You can change everything, including your fate, if only you want to. You are free to decide."

Jesus took her hands in his. "I know, but this is bigger than the two of us. These events were set in motion long before you and I were born. It's as if they have already happened and somehow, you know what I am talking about. You seem to know or sense the future with great accuracy. Come. Let us walk and enjoy our remaining time together. Even in pain, I will think of you. You will always be a special part of me."

Jesus and Jennifer walked into the Garden of Gethsemane, each with many things on their minds.

"There is so much I want to tell you," Jennifer began. "Things that would amaze and delight you, as well as the feelings I have for you. But there aren't enough words. I don't know or have the right words I need to express what I hold in my heart and mind for you. You are my world, my everything. You are a love I never could have imagined, even if I lived for 2,000 years."

"I know, my love," Jesus said. "Although I do not know about those things that would amaze and delight me, in a way, I almost do. Does that make sense?"

"Yes. Yes, it does."

"As for your thoughts and feelings for me, words aren't necessary. I sense them. I see them, and yes. In my heart I feel them. All have been laid bare to me, as I can see within your soul. And I thank you for your love," Jesus said. "I know that you love me with all your heart, all your mind, all your soul, and all your strength. And because of that, I know that you also love my Father."

Although the words still escaped her, she understood they weren't necessary. He knew what her words could not express, and that filled her with joy. At the same time, she also knew that soon she would have to return to the time ship and her own era. On the other hand, if she could talk Jesus into saving himself, maybe she would stay with him. But staying would also affect the timeline, and change history forever, possibly in a very harmful way. For her, the best outcome would be for Jesus to come with her and live in the future. Jesus would learn very quickly and adjust to a new life. And naturally, he would be the most famous man in the world.

But that, too, could greatly affect the timeline and things might be worse not better. There was just no way of knowing. Would Jesus be accepted if he went to the future? Or would he be once again be crucified, as no one would believe that he was Jesus. They wouldn't even know who he was. Would his Father then rearrange things so that what had once happened in the past, would then happen in the future? It was all so confusing. And if he didn't die, he would be over two thousand years old. Jennifer had another thought. What if no one believed that the government had a time ship, let alone the capability of traveling back in time? The government would deny everything. All Jennifer knew was that she loved the greatest man in history, and he was alive, standing right next to her. Alive for the moment.

"Jesus, I need you to trust me. I am so happy that you realize how much I truly love you. Not just you, but everything you stand for. I have a bad feeling, and I don't want anything terrible to happen to you. As I said before, I love you beyond anything that love can explain."

"I know, for you have been very special for me," Jesus said. "At first, I thought you were sent as a temptation, to distract me from my mission. Being so beautiful and mysterious, I thought that the devil might have sent you."

Jennifer was about to protest, but Jesus held a finger to her lips.

"Trust me. That thought did not last long. I came to realize that you were a true gift from my Father, sent to show me that loving one person is just as special as loving all. Before you, I loved everyone I could reach. Trust me, some of my earth brothers were very difficult to love, but not you. Except for the love of my Father, which is greater than man could ever hope to experience, and the love of my mother and earthly family, I never really knew the full extent of love, until I met you. You have given me a great gift, and that gift is called strength and bravery. And because of you, I am stronger now for what I have to do. I am not afraid to face the devil in front of me. I never knew that women could show such strength, but now I do. You have changed everything. You are everything." "You must leave with me tonight," Jennifer urged. "Don't ask me why. Just come with me. Everything will be better if you do.

Come with me to my land. They will love and honor you, and we can live a lifetime together, just you and me and probably millions of others. You can do so much good. You have so much to offer."

"I know why you are here, and I know your mission. I don't know where you are from, but I know and feel you. You cannot save me. I must do what I have to do. But believe me. What I have to do was made easier because of you. I want my Father to save you most of all. He will protect you for all time, as will I."

"All this isn't necessary," Jennifer pleaded. "Please come with me. I can save you. We can be together."

"You do not yet fully understand my whole purpose for becoming man, but you will soon. You have already saved me in a special way that was so important to me. You have saved me from fear, and I am braver and stronger because of you."

Tears welled up in Jennifer's eyes, threatening to spill over. "I have to save you from tonight. After that, we can take it day by day."

"Yes, I believe that you can save me, but if you do, countless others will not be saved. The gates of heaven will remain closed to them, and I cannot allow that to happen. You once told me to look at the whole fig tree not just one fig. One person is not worth millions. If I go with you, no one will be saved. Do you understand?"

Jennifer fought back her tears. "Yes, I do. We have a saying in my land, which is: 'The needs of the many, outweigh the needs of the few… or one.' Yes, I know only too well."

"I like that saying. I wish I had heard it sooner. I would have used it. It makes a lot of sense."

"I wish there was another way. My love for you grows stronger with every passing day. I thought it would reach a certain point and level out. But it keeps going higher with no end in sight. You could have a new life in a land that needs and already loves you. Don't ask me how or why. I just know." *But they wouldn't know him, her inner voice said. Without the events that are about to happen, Jesus will become nothing more than a prophet, if anyone remembered him at all.*

"You have been such a gift to me. I wish I could return the favor. I wish I could be with you the way you want me to be. But too many souls need to be saved. They are more important than both of us. It is a sacrifice we both have to make. In his ultimate wisdom, only God my Father knows why. The only thing we won't lose is our love, which will last forever. I never thought I could feel what I feel for you. You have made me a better person. You have opened many eyes."

"Are you kidding? You are the greatest thing in my life. I was nothing until I met you. You have made me a true believer, and I want to spread the word to everyone. Before you, I was lost. Now I am found. Found by you and your love. You are the truth I have been searching for all my life."

"Please spread the love of my Father in your strange land. I wish I could see it. And believe it or not, you are now even stronger than you were before you met me. Your land needs you more than it needs me."

"The love of your Father is already there in so many ways."

"For that I am pleased. But the night is here, and so is my destiny."

"I just don't want anything to happen to you. I would gladly die, trying to defend you. I might even try to defy your Father. You are that important to me. I would go that far and beyond. Tell your Father that I can be very stubborn, especially for the one I love."

"That would be a grave mistake. You cannot defy my Father. No one can. What happens to me has to happen, whether it happens now or later. I am at peace with it. My only regret is not having more time with you. These past seven days with you has been more special than many lifetimes. I, too, feel more complete because of you. It will be sad to see you leave. But I have a long night ahead of me."

"Nobody knows the future. Not even the future."

Jesus looked into her eyes. "You do! Of that I am now certain. But what is written in stone cannot be changed. You already know that I have to finish my work here on earth. I must do what is necessary, what is written. It is not for me. It is for the souls of all eternity. Like you said, the needs of the many."

"I'm not so sure. I don't know what might happen. Stones can be broken and new words engraved upon them."

"I also feel that the land you came from is more than just far away," Jesus said. "It is beyond far away. I think farther than the suns in the night sky."

"And in my land, they will love you. Come, make a choice. A choice to live with new love and purpose."

Jesus shook his head sadly. "I must stay, and you must go. My purpose is here. My Father will not change his mind. You have a mission, but I am no longer part of it. You must go. You must return to your people. Your mission is almost as important as mine. I don't know for certain what it is, but I know that it is. You have a special purpose, and that is why God brought you to me. But to fulfill that purpose, you must return to your land. You have no choice. And neither do I."

"Please, then let me stay the night. I guarantee I will not fall asleep on you. I will stay awake the whole night, no problem. You can count on me. I may be the only one here that you can. Let me protect you. At least let me give you more time, a lot more time," Jennifer begged. She was, of course, referring to how the disciples kept falling asleep, when Jesus went off to pray that this cup be taken from him, until he made peace with it and accepted his Father's will.

"My disciples will protect me. They are very loyal. Well, maybe one or two might be a little off, you might say. But still, they will stand by me even to the death."

"Like Judas? He didn't stay by you, and he won't protect you. He's off betraying you at this very moment."

Jesus was floored by her words. "I knew that. But how…. How did you….?"

It was like a slap to her head. She has said too much. "I…. Why else would he leave the meal and go skulking off? You can't fight the Romans. No one will stop them. You just need more time to figure out a new plan. You will win. You will always win. You just need more time."

"I believe you know a lot more than what you're telling me. But it doesn't matter. You cannot change that which is about to happen. It will be done according to my Father, and it has already been set in time. You already know that, I am sure."

"Then let me stay. Just for the night. I only want to be close to you. You are a part of me now, and I never want to lose you."

"No! You must leave. If you stay, you will be harmed, and I do not want that. The Romans and the elders will go after you. They will put you to death, and I will not let that happen. You need to be able to tell the world the truth. Remember, it's what you wanted. To learn the truth from the truth. You have learned what you needed to learn. Now is the time to return to your land. Now you are the teacher. Besides, I do not want your last memory of me to be one of watching me suffer and die."

Jennifer began to cry. She was normally very strong, but these emotions were just too powerful for her. "How will I ever truly believe that you and I were here? Is this all real? Or was it just a dream? When do I wake up? Because I don't want to."

"This is very real, and I will prove it to you. I don't have many possessions. I actually don't believe in them, but there is one. And this one I must give you. Every time you kiss it, you will feel my love for you."

Jesus took off a small gold ring from his left pinkie finger and placed it on Jennifer's left ring finger. It fit.

"Shortly after I was born, three men came from the East to visit. They brought wonderful gifts of gold, frankincense, and myrrh as an offering. This is the one that was saved for me. It has always been with me, and now it will be with you. I am honored that it will forever be with you."

"Three men bearing gifts? That sounds so familiar. When you were born?" Naturally, Jennifer knew all about the magi, but she could not let Jesus know that she knew.

"That is what my mother told me," Jesus said. "She told me many stories about the time of my birth, and all the special events that happened when I was a child. She holds each one dear to her heart. I think the ring proves that. I would never buy one."

"They must had been three wise men to do what they did," Jennifer said.

"Three wise men, yes, I agree."

"Could be a popular saying some day. Three wise men, who knows? It could become quite popular. Might even be made into a song." Jennifer looked at the ring on her finger.

Jesus kissed the ring. Jennifer also kissed it.

"The ring has been blessed. By both of us. Jennifer the angel, or better yet Jennifer the fighting angel."

Jennifer put her arms around Jesus and kissed him. Jesus returned the kiss. They embraced.

"Now, you are blessed," she said.

"I was blessed from the first moment I saw you."

Jennifer cried as she hugged Jesus. She did not want to let him go. Pain was etched into her features and tore through her heart, because she knew that this would be the last time she would ever touch or see Jesus. She felt a loss so great that it was as if every emotion had been ripped away from her. She believed with all her heart that she would never know another love like this.

Jesus gently released her and slowly backed away. "You must leave now. Just go. I command you to not look back. You might be leaving, but your love and strength will stay with me. Go now. Do not look back." Tears formed in his eyes. "I will love you for all eternity. Have a pleasant journey back to your land. Take all of my love with you, for your love has been so special to me. But if you love me, you must go."

"I love you! I always have. I always will," Jennifer told him, biting back a sob. "You must go now. Go with love."

Jennifer looked at Jesus one last time. Then she turned around and walked away. True to his command, she did not look back. She continued walking until she was out of sight from Jesus, her face, fully wet with tears. Jesus continued watching her, until she disappeared from sight. "Father, thank you for this wonderful gift. Please, please protect her, especially on her journey ahead. I am now all yours. I am ready."

Jesus turned around and rejoined his apostles, knowing that his life was no longer in his hands, as he had given it to his Father. He thought about Jennifer. And although he usually was not emotional, many tears formed in his eyes. He already missed Jennifer, as she truly had made him happy, happy for one last time. Jesus knew what was going to happen. He had known from the very beginning.

"Let us walk," he said to the disciples. "For we have a long night ahead of us."

"Where is Judas?" Simon asked. "Have you seen him?"

"He is where he has to be. Still, no matter what, I love and forgive him."

"Only the Son of God could have the strength and wisdom of forgiveness," Mark said.

"I need to pray to my Father. Come, pray with me. The hour swiftly approaches." "Where is Jennifer?" John asked, looking around for her.

"I really like her like no other."

"She is a long, long way from here. Too far for us to ever see. You will never see her again. She is as far away as the stars, maybe more." "Then she really was an angel?" Peter asked.

"Not in the sense you mean, but she was an angel to me," Jesus replied.

"But why did she leave? What do you mean, Teacher?" Matthew asked. "God my Father gave her to me, and God my Father took her away. He knew I needed her for a brief time. She was sent here for a reason and only my Father knows why. She was here as a blessing. She made me realize that women are the same as men. They both should be treated equally."

"No, they are here to serve us and have our children," Luke contradicted. "That is the way it has always been."

"And that way is wrong," Jesus said. "Women are every bit our equal, and now I am going to give a new commandment. Things need to change. Thou now must treat women the same as thyself, a man and a woman are the same. They are both equal. That is my order, and it must be obeyed. Starting right now."

"Thy will be done, Master. I will record it for all time," Peter said.

"As will I," Matthew said.

"Is this because of Jennifer?" John asked. "She did change you. You seem stronger. I think she changed all of us in many different ways. I never knew a woman could do such things, but she did."

"Yes, she has opened my eyes as even I was blind, but no longer. She has given me so many things. She was so wise, her beauty just a small part of her. She was the whole fig tree."

"I really liked her," James said. "She was very special and just so beautiful. She had a glow about her, and it wasn't because of how pale she was. If there ever was a goddess, it would be her."

"Who wouldn't like her?" John asked. "Except of course, Judas, although I think Judas was more jealous of her than anything. And we know how he feels about women."

"I think if she'd had more time, even Judas would have given in," Bartholomew suggested. "She was an angel in so many ways, both inside and out. I think she would have turned Judas. In fact, I am sure of it."

Jesus looked up at the night sky full of stars. The more he looked, the more he could see. Now he knew that they were almost endless, like his love for Jennifer. A night full of suns. "Come, my brothers. Before you know it, tomorrow will be here. We must be ready. The needs of the many."

The disciples surrounded Jesus in a circle of love.

Jesus approached each disciple and gently touched each on the face. "I love you all. You are a part of me, as I am a part of you, now and forever."

All the disciples knelt, not knowing the future.

Jennifer did.

CHAPTER

TWENTY-NINE

Jennifer walked at a steady pace, knowing she could not turn around for one last look at Jesus, but she desperately wanted to. The tears running down her face made it appear as though she was standing in the rain, but the night was clear and warm, almost hot. Every person, action, and incident that had happened the past week went through her mind. Every moment that her love for Jesus had blossomed and grown. She had found Jesus, and she had discovered that he was not only real, but amazing. Everything had changed in her life. She now believed the impossible, because it never truly was impossible, just not understood. For the first time in her life, she had found love—the kind of love one dreams of or reads about in romance novels, only to lose it, and knowing that tomorrow, everything would be gone.

It all had happened way too fast, but love had no speed. It could happen fast or over a long period of time. For Jennifer, it happened almost instantaneously. She knew she loved Jesus from the moment she saw him in the distance that very first day. As Jennifer walked, she pondered over the meaning of love. Could it be that she had always loved Jesus, but just like in her dream, she had not been able to find him until now? Maybe her dream was not a dream, but something bigger.

The night was always dark in a time without electricity. Jennifer could see small fires here and there, but not enough to make any difference. She wasn't far from her time ship, and she wanted to run, but it was too dark. Not a soul in sight. A wave of loneliness washed over her. The loss of Jesus was almost too much to bear. No matter how hard she tried, the tears would not stop. *Is this what happens when you fall in love? Why does it have to hurt so much?*

She knew she would never see Jesus again, but she would have her memories, and finally she knew the real truth. It was a truth that she could tell the whole world. That was her new mission in life. Was it her turn to be crucified? Because most people would never believe her. Was she doomed to the same fate as Jesus?

From out of the darkness, a woman approached Jennifer, carrying a cup with a lighted candle in it. "Hello. Are you lost? Do you need help?"

"Thank you, but no. I'm not lost. I'm going back to my camp, which is a little further from here."

"We have a warm fire and some food just over there," the woman said, invitingly. "Why don't you join us for a while? You look like you are not from around here."

"I would not want to impose," Jennifer said, but the thought of people, light, and some food tugged at her overwhelming sadness.

"Not at all. You would be most welcome, and we would be honored to have you as our guest. Please come."

Jennifer followed the woman over to a campfire, where they were joined by the woman's husband and young son. She sat next to the fire, and it felt good. Amazingly, she discovered that she was actually starting to feel better now. "Do you live here?"

"We are actually from a small place a couple days' travel from here," the husband replied.

"Why are you here?" Jennifer asked.

"We came to hear a great man talk—a man who finally gives us love. I don't think you would understand, but this man gave us so much hope. He made us happy to be alive. Looking at you, you probably never heard of him. We heard him speak at the Temple this very day."

"His name is Jesus, and yes, he is truly a great man. The only problem is there are people who hate him and want to destroy him, and that makes me very sad," Jennifer said.

The woman and her husband were surprised and shocked to hear that.

"How do you know of him? Please tell me," the woman begged.

"Yes, please tell us," her husband added.

"I heard him speak about a week ago. He is much more than we know. He is pure love. The one hope for us all. Only He can save us."

"All I know is that he is our loving savior, and we must follow him," the husband said. "He is wise in all ways."

"Mommy, I am tired," the young son complained. "Can I sleep now?" "Yes, my son, soon," she replied. "But we must respect our guest. Jesus would want it that way."

They sat near the fire with Jennifer sharing food and tea with them. While they ate, Jennifer told them that she was from a faraway land and that she would return there tomorrow.

"I will never be back here again, although I will never forget it." Finishing her meal, Jennifer stood up. "Thank you for your hospitability, but I must be on my way. It was a pleasure meeting you. You were so kind to take a stranger in. Thank you."

"Please do us one favor if you can," the husband said. "Will you tell your people about Jesus?"

"That I will. I guarantee it. Goodnight. May God be with you." "He is and will always be," the woman replied.

Jennifer walked away into the night.

The woman looked at her husband as they watched Jennifer leave.

"I know it sounds strange, but I have a feeling that woman is blessed." "Do you think she understands Jesus?" her husband asked.

"They are one and the same," she replied.

"Mom!" her son complained. He was so tired, he could barely keep his eyes open, but their talking kept waking him up.

"Yes, let's all go to sleep," his mother said, soothingly. "I feel tomorrow will be a very special day, not only for us, but for the world."

Jennifer walked into the darkness. Even though she had a flashlight in her pouch, she knew she could not use it. Then, she stopped and thought, *What the hell. Pulling out the flashlight, she turned it on. If anybody sees me, I'll tell them it's a firefly. I can't wait to have a hot bath and a hot pizza.*

Jennifer started running, using the beam of her flashlight to guide her. It felt good to run. Thirty minutes later, she finally reached the ship. Walking past the hologram of the leper colony, she stepped into the time ship. Inside were the remaining two crew members. In their minds, they believed that there had only been three original crew members. Although they couldn't figure out why there were so many extra seats. Maybe they were for something secret, or possibly a future mission for another team. Jennifer sat next to Winifred, with whom she had become good friends. She calmed down from her run and used a towel to wipe the sweat from her face.

"We are scheduled to leave tomorrow, but we haven't really gotten any positive proof yet. For some reason, our cameras wouldn't work. They wouldn't record anything. It's as if someone was trying to stop us from proving we were even here. This is so strange. Although I do smell like a camel. Actually, they're very nice animals. Very friendly. Would camel smell be considered proof?" Winifred laughed.

Leo tried to smell himself, lifting some of his clothing to his nose.

Jennifer looked at the ring on her finger that Jesus had given her.

She kissed it, and surprisingly, it gave her some small comfort.

"We were here," Jennifer said firmly. "The whole world will soon find out. This is what they have been waiting for."

"All the same, we need proof," Winifred insisted.

"We don't need proof. It is better to believe and have faith. Two thousand years of faith is more than enough."

"Jesus did a number on you," Winifred said. "You spent the whole week with him and yet, he isn't here with you."

"How can you say that?" Jennifer asked. "You know what is going to happen tonight and tomorrow morning. He has a greater mission, way more important than me. But I truly love him." She paused to fight back the tears. "He told me I had to leave. And I know he loves me. He loves us all. He will die for us and everyone who ever was or ever will be."

"You have to believe in your faith in him," Winifred said. "He gave you the right message. For the sake of the world, these events must play out. My belief and spirit cannot believe otherwise. Some things can never be changed, and they shouldn't. Better to have loved and lost than…."

Jennifer threw up her hands to stop her. "I don't want to hear that! Not now, not ever. Just better to have loved, and leave it at that."

"Look, I have believed in Jesus since I was a small child," Winifred said. "I never had any doubt that Jesus was real. I didn't need to come here to find that out, but I think you did. I was more interested in seeing history with my own eyes."

"And now that I have, I am changed forever. I now have the greatest gift of all," Jennifer said.

"And what is that?" Winifred asked.

"Love of life and faith."

"It's so sad, knowing what's going to happen tomorrow. The greatest love of all time is going to happen," Winifred mused. "The biggest event in human history, and we are here to witness it. Love starts tomorrow."

"I know. And at the same time, I will lose mine." Once again tears slid down Jennifer's face. Her grief was nearly unbearable.

"Get some sleep," Winifred told her. "I'll stand watch tonight."

"No, I'll be up anyway," Jennifer said, shaking her head. "Sleep will not happen for me tonight. Jesus won't sleep tonight either. We are in this together."

Winifred looked like she was about to object.

"That's an order. You sleep."

"If you're sure," Winifred said.

"I am."

"Then I bid you goodnight."

"Yes, goodnight," Leo said. "This is the last night I'll have to sleep in this chair. Thank goodness."

Leo and Winifred adjusted their seats to the sleeping position, trying their best to make themselves comfortable.

"I can't wait to sleep in a real bed again," Leo said. "I don't know how these people survived out here without proper beds. Amazing."

Jennifer stepped outside the time ship. She could barely make out the outline of Jerusalem in the distance, where everything would happen tomorrow. She thought about the beating Jesus would have to endure and being nailed to a cross. She knew that even Jesus didn't truly know what was going to happen to him. He didn't know that this was his last night. Jennifer stared at the distant city. She did not want Jesus to die. But she knew she must not interfere. And knowing it, not even a sleeping pill could make her sleep tonight.

*****

The sun finally rose, and the outline of Jennifer's face could be seen clearly. It was a night of tears, a night of thinking, and a night of decision making, and she was more determined than ever to follow her heart.

"I love him, and I'm not going to let him die. I just can't!"

Slipping back into the time ship, she quietly opened a special cabinet that only she could open. A cabinet that Jennifer and no one else knew about what was inside. The others were still sleeping. From the cabinet, she pulled out a double gun holster and strapped it on. From one corner of the cabinet, she reached for two Sig Sauer P226 9mm Legion pistols with fifteen-round magazines. Placing one in each holster, she attached extra magazines to the belt. She then pulled out a MP5/10 Submachine gun with 30 rounds in the magazine, and placed it with a strap over her neck so it laid against her chest. She then added extra magazines to a pouch attached to her holster. Donning a robe with a hood that completely covered the guns, she left the time ship and walked toward Jerusalem.

"I am coming, my love, even though you told me not to."

Jennifer knew where she needed to go. She was heading for

Golgotha, also known as Calvary and the Place of the Skull, where Jesus was to be crucified. She was determined to save Him, the man she loved, and nothing was going to stop her. The quickest way there was through Jerusalem.

How could you not want to save the one you love? It's impossible. I have no choice.

Jennifer entered the city and after a short walk, she was confronted by four Roman soldiers on horseback, blocking her path. She looked behind her to find six more blocking any possible retreat. The soldiers, who were carrying shields, set them down in a line against a mud wall.

"We have orders to find and eliminate you," the Captain said.

"Caiaphas informed Pilate that he believes you are a danger to the Roman Empire. Possibly more than Jesus himself. It is a shame, though, as you are such a beauty. But your beauty is considered a danger as well. We were told you would cause trouble. You will find out what Rome does to troublemakers."

"I am not a danger to anyone, unless you stand in my way. Get out of my way, or you will find out what I do to trouble. Even Rome cannot stand in my way."

"Oh, my, such brave words from a mere woman," the Captain said in a mocking voice. "Do you want to know what my soldiers think?"

All the soldiers laughed. Clearly, they did not see her as any more of a threat than their leader did.

"You are just another foolish, stupid woman," the Captain said.

"When will you ever learn? You cannot stand against us. You will die."

"I think the time has come for you to learn a lesson. Fear a woman! You will bow down before me."

"Never!" the Captain shouted. "Especially to a woman." He threw a knife down in the dirt in front of Jennifer. "Show some honor and kill yourself. Do not make us do it. It would be shameful. We will bow to no woman. I guarantee it. Nothing could make us."

"There is an old saying from where I come from. 'Fools who came to scoff, remained to pray.'"

"What does that mean? Just kill yourself and make it simple. I don't want to get down from my horse in order to kill a stupid woman, too much effort."

"I have always wanted to do this, ever since I saw some old Clint Eastwood movies."

The soldiers looked at her like she was crazy, since they had no idea who Clint Eastwood was or a movie for that matter.

"Now you will know the true power of a woman. Behold!"

Jennifer threw back her hood and opened her robe, pushing it to the side to reveal her weapons. She pointed the submachine gun toward the Captain. Modern man would have been impressed, but the Romans had no idea what these weapons were.

"What is that, a stick or something?" the Captain scoffed. "Look at it, it would not stop a sword. You are truly an idiot—soon to be a dead idiot."

All the soldiers laughed again. There was a human-sized statue right next to the Captain. Using the high-velocity rounds in the submachine gun, Jennifer completely destroyed it to the amazement of the Captain and his men. Pieces of the statue flew everywhere, hitting the soldiers and everything else within range. The horses were terrified, especially from the loud noise of the gun. Jennifer then shot into the shields against the wall, completely destroying them. The soldiers did not know what to do. Jennifer then fired into the dirt in front of them, sending dust particles ten feet into the air. Nobody could see anything for several seconds. The soldiers were horrified. Jennifer quickly slammed another magazine into the submachine gun. Then she pulled out both of her pistols and fired them at the swords the soldiers were holding, thus knocking them out of their hands. The soldiers were stunned and could not move.

"That stick is loud. My ears hurt," the first soldier exclaimed.

"What is this? This can't be real!"

"I know who she is," the second soldier declared. "She is Ares, the god of war. She can be nothing else. She is a god!"

"I thought Ares was a man," a third soldier argued.

"Well, I guess we got that wrong," the first soldier declared. "Look at her! She is a goddess."

The foot soldiers dropped to their knees in front of Jennifer. The mounted soldiers, along with the Captain got off their horses and also knelt.

"Look who bows now," Jennifer taunted.

"I mean look how beautiful she is," the fourth soldier said. "She could be Venus, goddess of love and beauty."

"Take a look at that statue," the fifth soldier said. "I don't think so." "How about Artemis?" the third soldier suggested.

"I don't think she's hunting us," the sixth soldier shot back.

The second soldier disagreed. "Like I said. She is Ares, the goddess of war."

"Now that we have that settled, please part ways, unless you want more of my magic stick," Jennifer said. "Believe me. As easily as it cut through that statue, it will cut through flesh and blood even quicker."

"Yes, wondrous Ares, we are yours to command. I apologize for my behavior, but I did not know. Please forgive me," the Captain begged.

The soldiers stepped aside.

"This is the first god I have ever seen in person. I am honored," the fourth soldier said.

"I think she is the first god anyone has ever seen," the sixth soldier said. "Finally, I believe in them. I thought for a while they were just made up."

The second soldier shook his head. "They are real. They are definitely real. Now, I finally believe."

Jennifer walked past them, pulling her robe closed to cover herself and the guns. She knew it was wrong to perpetuate their belief in false gods, but right now, she felt that she had no choice. She had to get to Jesus, and she would do whatever it took to do it.

"Hail, Ares, goddess of war," the Captain shouted.

"Actually, my name is Jennifer."

"Hail, Jennifer, goddess of war," the third soldier exclaimed.

As Jennifer walked away, she said, "Cute. Tell Caiaphas to mind his own business."

"I will, Goddess," the Captain promised. "I will. I never did like him anyway."

Jennifer stopped and turned back toward him. "In fact, I want to give you an order."

"Yes, my Goddess," the Captain said. "I will do whatever you command." "Good! I command you to break his nose and tell him it's from me." Jennifer smiled. "Let's just call it a parting gift. Got it?"

"That I will gladly do, with pleasure. I hear and obey," the Captain promised. "It will be done immediately."

"Do not disappoint me," she warned.

"I will not, my Goddess," the Captain said, smiling. "I will break his nose with glee."

Jennifer continued walking for several minutes, when she felt a strange sensation—a sensation of death. She looked to her left and in the distance, she noticed a tree near a ledge. On that tree was a body, hanging by a rope. The body did not move and was lifeless. Jennifer immediately knew who it was, and it made her sad.

"Judas."

Why him? He loved Jesus, she thought. What could make him do such a thing, and then take his own life as punishment, the ultimate punishment? How could anybody do that to Jesus, let alone someone who had followed him out of love? Had this been God's plan all along? Why does anybody have to die in order to give us salvation? Do we need death in order to save us? I hope it wasn't because of me, because he was a bit jealous. But then again, Jesus said that no matter what, this was how it was going to happen, and nothing could stop it. Judas wasn't such a bad person. So why did he betray Jesus? Jesus only gave him love, and I know Judas loved him. It wasn't the money. If Judas didn't love Jesus, why would he kiss him at the end? I don't understand God's plan, I don't think anyone can. It is just too complicated. It needs to be plainer, simpler. There is enough killing already, even for God.

"Dear God, like it or not, I am going to save your son! And I have the firepower to do it."

Jennifer continued toward Golgotha. She now believed that nothing could stop her. She needed to get there before the first nails were hammered into Jesus' flesh. As she stepped into an open field not far from her destination, she heard a loud, almost ear-shattering bang come out of nowhere. She covered her ears with her hands. In front of her, a giant wall of fire suddenly materialized. Inside the wall, lightning bolts shot through the entire area. The wall was hot, and Jennifer could not approach any closer. It was a hundred yards high and half a mile wide. There was no way around it, and it continued growing hotter. Jennifer backed up even more. Suddenly words appeared on the wall of fire in front of her.

Go back! You must return to the place you came from. You have given my son the greatest gift. You have given him unrequited love. His destiny is the salvation of all and for all to come. You have a different destiny. You must return to fulfill it. Leave with love. For that is the greatest gift of all.

Jennifer looked around and quickly realized that she was the only one who could see and feel this wall of fire. The people around her continued what they were doing as though nothing was happening. Jennifer felt the heat grow hotter, and it was only for her. This confused her to no end. But she could not deny what she saw and felt.

"Son of a gun. I can't win. You won't let me!" Jennifer looked up at the sky.

"Okay! You win! I see that now. Jesus was right. I can't go against the Father."

Realizing that this message was from a higher source, she sadly abandoned her mission. And at that very moment, the wall of fire and lightning disappeared. Everything was calm. Jennifer kept looking up at the sky.

"Am I a pawn in your grand game of chess? Did I perform my mission? Did I do what you wanted or more likely what you commanded?" she asked, tears streaking down her face.

Jennifer looked up at the hill where Jesus was now on the cross.

"Are you going to let your son die just to prove a point to mankind? Is there no other way? Did you bring me here so that all this could happen? Why am I here? Tell me!"

Dark clouds quickly formed in the sky. Lightning passed through the clouds, resulting in loud, rolling thunder that spread across the land.

"I love Jesus," she cried, raising her hands to the sky in a pleading gesture. "Does that mean anything? He means so much to us. You're taking him way too soon. Let his love flourish and cover the world. It is too soon to end his love."

And in her mind, she heard the words, *Neither his love nor mine will ever end.* Jennifer's hands fell to her sides, and she realized that there was nothing she could say that would make any difference. For the first time in her life, she felt completely helpless. But now, for the first time in her life, she had total faith.

"You can take Jesus away from me, but you can never take away my love for him."

And had she been in the right frame of mind, she would have realized that God would never take away her love. Then Jennifer remembered something written in one of the gospels. It stated that Jesus had obediently went to the cross to ensure the salvation of those who would place their faith in him. This had been God's plan since before time. Nothing was going to derail it. Nothing was going to keep it from happening.

She headed back to her ship. After slowly walking for half an hour, Jennifer turned around, and in the distance, she could see three crosses on the hill. She knew that Jesus was on the center one. Her eyes filled with tears. She knew that he was still alive, but in horrific pain. She would never see him again, at least in this life. But her love would last forever. She thought about the week she had just had and realized that even if she told people, no one would believe her. Falling in love with Jesus? They would tell her that everyone did. That's why he was Jesus. Nobody would know or realize that she was talking about the real man.

"Please, God, have mercy. I love him."

Jennifer now thought about the Spear of Destiny, and why it was so important. It would end the suffering. She was satisfied that Longinus would be the one who did it. He would do it because of love. She walked to her ship and entered. Leo and Winifred were awake and dressed, awaiting instructions. She quickly placed the guns back into their cabinet and locked it.

"Where did those come from? Were you expecting a war?" Leo asked puzzled.

"No, I just wanted some target practice. You know, to relieve my nerves."

"I hope it worked," Winifred said.

"It did." *And I didn't even have to kill anyone.*

"Did you see…?" Winifred began, not wanting to finished the sentence.

"Yes." Jennifer would say no more.

The conversation between the two women went right over Leo's head. "I had no idea those guns were even here. Can you imagine? If the Romans had those, we would all be speaking Italian right now."

Jennifer had no comment for that, but she knew he was right. "It's time to go home. Nothing more we can do here. It is completely out of our hands."

"Yes, Commander, I mean Jennifer. Time to go home," Leo said. "I don't believe we belong here. We're simply visitors from another time and place."

"I definitely could use a shower, internet, TV, driving a car, and a lot of other things," Winifred said.

"Yes, things were much simpler here, because they only had each other. Yet they have love, faith, and kindness. I think our time period has lost a lot of that. There definitely isn't as much love."

"I think we just have more people, billions more, and they each have different ideas and beliefs," Winifred said.

"Way, way more Christians in our time than there are now," Leo agreed. "But it all started here."

"Yes, a small seed was planted here, and it grew into a very large tree. And on that tree was one more leaf, which is now me."

"So now you believe," Winifred said. "That means the mission was a great success. The addition of even one more believer made it worth the trip. I am happy for you, and it pleases me that you now realize the truth."

"Yes, I learned the truth from truth itself, for He is the way, the truth, and the light. And soon, I will tell the world. I know the truth will bring even more people to the faith. Even the ones, who don't believe will at least know the truth. They can still deny what they believe, but they can't deny the truth. The truth is the truth. It's as simple as that."

"I, for one, have a lot more respect for camels now," Leo said. "They can go all day without water, and they're actually pretty comfortable."

"Tell that to my rear end," Winifred said. "It's starting to get sore."

"Okay, everybody, take one last look while you still can. Say goodbye to ancient Jerusalem."

Leo and Winifred looked out the door one last time, gazing at the city in the distance.

"How about you, Jennifer?" Winifred asked. "One last look?"

"I already had mine. I do not need another. Close the door and get into your seats. Time to go home. Time to end the suffering." And in her heart, she knew that home would never be the same again.

"Gladly," Leo said, getting into his chair. "I'm with you."

Jennifer was seated in the pilot's chair. Winifred settled into her seat, and everyone strapped in.

"Engaging in five, four, three, two, one."

The engine roared to life, and the time capsule shot up into the sky with a loud sonic boom. Jennifer was pretty sure that everybody, including Jesus, heard that sonic boom. They would not know what it was, maybe a message from God. Where the time machine had once rested, was now just empty land. In the distance, three crosses stood out against the sky. It was a scene that would be remembered throughout time. Jesus looked up toward the sound in time to see the wormhole open and engulf the capsule. And instantly, he knew that Jennifer was going home, and his heart was glad. It was beginning to rain now, but only Jesus felt it. He looked down and saw the Spear of Destiny held by Longinus, and he knew that his suffering was at an end.

Destiny had been met and served.

CHAPTER

THIRTY

After uttering the word "engage," Jennifer closed her eyes. It had all been so much to handle. Imagine not saving the man you loved, but she had tried her best. The last eight days went by in a flash. At least now, she knew that Jesus was no longer suffering on the cross. She wondered if Longinus was able to change his life and become a beef farmer. All the people she had met were gone two thousand years ago. That was her hope, but she was afraid to open her eyes, not knowing where or when she was. Was she back in her own time? Every second seemed like an eternity. There was a long silence. Was everything the same, or had it been changed by her actions and those of her team members? Was there still a Pope, or had he been changed along with religion?

Finally, she heard a knock on the door outside the time ship. She opened her eyes and glanced at Leo and Winifred. They looked dirty and tired, and they smelled. It was not a pleasant smell, as the camels were never bathed in ancient Jerusalem. There was another knock on the door. Jennifer, Leo, and Winifred stared at each other, not knowing what to expect.

"Are we back?" Leo asked. "I don't think it took very long. Just a few seconds."

"I'm afraid to open the door," Winifred said. "Will they still be human? Have we returned to the right time period?"

"Here's a thought, although I don't really want to think about it," Leo said. "What if we are still in ancient Jerusalem? What if we are trapped there forever? That would change history."

"It would definitely change us," Winifred said. "Now I'm worried about what is out there waiting for us."

"I wonder if anybody back in time even remembered us, after we left," Leo said.

"Maybe Caiaphas," Jennifer said. "But really, no one would write about it. Broken noses happen all the time."

"Well, it has been two thousand years," Winifred reasoned. "People forget a lot of things in that amount of time."

"Only one way to find out. We're here, no matter where here is. Open the door," Jennifer commanded. "This is our destiny."

Winifred opened the door and to Jennifer, Leo, and her surprise, Dr. Adams stood smiling at them through the open door. He waved at a smiling Jennifer.

"Oh my God, it smells like dried-up…I don't know what in here," Dr. Adams said. "Definitely time for a shower or two."

Leo and Winifred looked at each other and grinned. They knew the reason why.

"Camels," Winifred and Leo said in unison.

"Hello," Jennifer called. "So nice to see you again."

"Okay, it looks like all are present and accounted for. Just an extra minute while we do some disinfecting. It shouldn't take long," Dr. Adams promised.

Using a hose, Dr. Adams sprayed a soft white disinfecting mist into the cabin. Everybody held their breath for a second. Then facing the cabin, he held up an air testing meter and checked the results.

"All good. How do you feel?"

"Isn't it obvious?" Winifred asked. "We feel and smell like dirty camels. What else would you expect?"

"How long were we gone?" Jennifer asked. "I am really curious about this one."

"First, how long *were* you gone?" Dr. Adams asked.

"Eight wonderful, glorious, and sad days," Jennifer replied.

"And as you can tell, no showers were available to us," Leo said. "Only a warm fish pond used by too many people."

"Well, you may have been gone eight days, but not so much here," Dr. Adams responded. "Not long at all."

"How long were we gone?" Jennifer repeated impatiently.

"A whole, whopping, fantastic eight minutes," Dr. Adams announced joyously. "It did seem longer. But by the clock, it was exactly seven minutes and fifty-eight seconds. Maybe a new world record."

"Wow. I never would have guessed. So, did anything happen while we were gone?" Jennifer asked. "Anything strange or anything at all? I mean sometimes eight minutes can be a long time."

"Not that I know of," Dr. Adams began. "But wait. There was something, although I'm not sure if it had anything to do with you or not. We had three massive sonic booms during that time, occurring only a few minutes apart."

"I believe I can explain those," Jennifer said.

"I'm sure you can, and you must have many amazing stories to tell. But the President wants to be the first to know. So don't say anything yet. You have to be debriefed and all," Dr. Adams said with a snicker.

"We're under strict orders not to question any of you until you speak to the President. So, say nothing for now. Besides, what can happen in eight minutes?"

"A new love, a lifetime of love, and a lost love," Winifred replied.

"And a new respect for camels," Leo added.

"And ice and anything cold," Winifred continued.

An assistant approached Dr. Adams and spoke to him. "Everything is ready, sir, and the escorts are waiting." "Escorts? Why?" Jennifer asked.

"Ah, yes," Dr. Adams began. "We have to watch over you for a while to make sure you are who you were, and time travel didn't cause you any problems, especially going that far back into the past. They will take you wherever you want. Almost like tour guides, except they will do exactly what you want. We need to cover ourselves no matter what. A lot can happen in two thousand years."

Jennifer, Leo, and Winifred exchanged glances as the realization that this had probably been the greatest event to ever occur in the history of mankind. Finding out the truth after two thousand years of uncertainty. It just staggered the mind. Right now, they were three of the most important people on earth, as long as they were able to remember. Jennifer looked down at the ring Jesus had given her, and she definitely remembered. Not wanting anybody to see, she briefly turned her back and quickly kissed the ring. It wasn't that she was embarrassed or anything, but she did not want to explain the ring or where it had come from. They might want to take it from her.

"Come on out, Jennifer," Dr. Adams called. "You still look really good, really good. You didn't age a second. In fact, maybe you got even younger."

"Thank you," Jennifer replied. "I certainly don't feel any younger, but I appreciate the compliment."

"I guess that makes me nothing but mincemeat," Winifred said quietly.

"Oh, no," Leo assured her. "You look great. I really hope to see you again and not just two thousand years in the past. I had a great time with you. You and the camels were fantastic. I hope you and I can become friends. I mean good friends, really good friends."

"Thank you, but honestly, no one can compare to Jennifer," Winifred said. "Even Jesus couldn't resist her charms. But yes, Leo, I hope we can become good friends, too. To put it as a pun, time will tell."

"Actually, in the end, he did resist me. But for a much larger reason. Bigger than the both of us, bigger than the world," Jennifer said. "And I now know without a shadow of a doubt that there was no one else like him and never will be. He was mankind's greatest gift."

"The President is anxiously waiting to hear everything. For him, it has been a long eight minutes, since he was in charge of the whole project," Dr. Adams said. "In fact, it was his project and only he knows why."

"I definitely need to talk to him," Jennifer said firmly. "There is a lot we have to discuss."

"Each one of you has been assigned two escorts. Two women each for Jennifer and Winifred and two men for Leo. Now, what do you want first?" Dr. Adams asked.

"Duh…how about a shower?" Winifred asked.

Dr. Adams smiled. "Yes, that is number one on the list. Something quick to eat possibly?"

"How about a hotdog and some fries?" Leo asked.

"Pastrami sandwich with lots of mustard," Winifred replied.

They turned and looked at Jennifer.

"Just a protein bar for me. I'll think of something better later. Maybe a hot pizza, but for now, just a protein bar. Oh, yes, and an ice cold drink, anything, just as long as it is ice cold."

"Oh, boy, you must have been spoiled there. The food you ate must have been completely different from what you were used to eating," Dr. Adams said. "I bet they would have loved a protein bar back then—a whole new taste."

Jennifer thought about the ones she and Jesus had shared. "You have no idea." Dr. Adams turned to his assistant. "Get them their food before they really get spoiled."

"Yes, sir," the assistant replied, leaving to fill their order.

"Yes, I was very spoiled," Jennifer said. "But on to the shower. That is a luxury I have sorely missed."

"You can say that again. No showers back then, none," Winifred said. "As you can tell."

Jennifer, Leo, and Winifred were escorted a short distance to the shower rooms. Each one used a different, private shower room that had been assigned to them before the trip and that now held a set of their regular clothes and supplies.

"It was an honor traveling with both of you," Jennifer told her teammates. "We will speak soon. I'm sure we'll have lots more to talk about once we have a chance to relax and think about it."

"Yes, unforgettable," Leo agreed. "It was an amazing eight minutes. Not to be missed."

"Don't forget we have racquetball next week," Winifred said.

"It will be fun kicking your butt," Jennifer teased. "Bye." She waved goodbye to her teammates before heading into her private shower room. Her escorts remained outside. "Relax," she told her escorts. "This may take a while. I need to calm down."

"Of course, take all the time you need," the first escort assured her. "We are at your service."

Jennifer closed the door to her room and turned on the shower. But she did not go in right away. Instead, she sat down on a bench next to it, listening to the sound of the flowing water. There was a lot going on in her mind. *Everything is over, and I'm back. What and how much am I going to tell the President?* The last eight days had been nothing more than eight minutes of a single day, but her memories would last for the rest of her life. She had fallen in love with the most famous man in history. A man then, but a God for all. Removing the clothing she had worn on the mission, she carefully folded them and placed them in a small hamper.

She sniffed herself and to her amazement, she could still make out Jesus's unique scent on her hair and skin. The smell was almost as strong as her love. It smelled like heaven. She looked at the running water and realized that the water would remove that wonderful odor. She did not smell bad like Leo and Winifred, as she had not been around any camels. Looking at her hand, she silently stared at the ring Jesus had given her. She kissed the ring—the ring of love, hoping to feel his kiss in return. She stood up and turned off the shower. Instead, she washed her face, under her arms, and her privates. Then brushed her teeth and rinsed with mouthwash.

"The shower may be a way off. Your scent is staying with me, Jesus. The President will have to take me as is."

Dressing in a clean set of clothing from the ones she had brought in her suitcase before the mission, she walked out the door and approached her escorts.

The one she had spoken to earlier handed her a protein bar and a cold drink.

"Thank you."

"You're welcome," the woman said with a smile.

Jennifer opened the wrapper on the bar and took a quick bite. She then pulled the tab on the cold drink and took a long, satisfying drink. Closing her eyes, she sighed before taking another drink and emptying the can. "Now that was good."

"There is a lot more in the limo," the woman assured her.

"Okay. Time to see President Peck. His wait is over. Mine has just begun." "Who?" the second escort asked. "The President, of course," Jennifer replied.

"Yes, the President is very eager to see you," the first escort said. "Please follow us. The limo is waiting outside."

"I just want to make one quick stop on the way. It's my favorite monument with the Ten Commandments on it," Jennifer said.

"I know what monument you are speaking of and of course, we can stop there," the second escort said. "But you may be a little confused. There have always been Eleven Commandments from the very beginning with Moses."

"Maybe you just forgot," the first escort added. "What's the difference anyway, ten or eleven. Doesn't matter."

"Maybe yes, but I now really need to look at it. Eleven, something to think about. Maybe I'm a little mixed up," Jennifer agreed.

Jennifer and her escorts got into a black limo and drove off. Inside, Jennifer grabbed another cold drink, orange juice this time, opened it, and took a healthy swallow. "So good!" She looked at the bottle. "I will never take you for granted again. Cold is king." Turning to her escorts, who sat across from her, she said, "Excuse me, but I need to make a call."

"Of course, anything you want," escort number one replied. "We are here to serve."

"I'm sure you have other orders, too. Just want to call to my friend, Winifred. I need to ask her something."

Jennifer took out her cell phone and called Winifred, putting the phone on speaker.

"Well, that was quick," Winifred said when she saw who was calling her.

"Let me tell you that shower felt so good. The pastrami sandwich was heaven. And air conditioning is one of the best inventions of all time, that's for sure."

"You bet. Hey, I just have a quick question for you. I forgot something important."

"What is it?" Winifred asked.

"How many commandments are there?"

"I don't know them all, but I do know that there has always been eleven."

"Eleven?"

"Yes, though now that I think about it, there should be a lot more added to the list," Winifred said.

"Thanks, Winifred. Call you soon."

"Bye. Call me anytime."

Jennifer punched off the phone and looked at the gold ring on her finger. A gift from Jesus, but maybe much more. She remembered Ten Commandments, not eleven. Maybe time had not changed her as it had the others. Was the ring protecting her? She was pretty sure that if she called Leo, he would say eleven, too. She wondered what else had changed.

The limo stopped at the monument. Jennifer got out and walked over to it. Sure enough, there were now Eleven Commandments. She looked at number eleven and read it out loud. "'Thou shall not change that which has already happened.'"

Jennifer knew exactly what it meant. She might be the only one in the world who did. And now she realized that some things definitely had changed because of the time ship, and what they had done in the past. They? Or was it more what she had done in the past?

Returning to the limo, she got in, and they took off to see the President.

"See, I told you there was eleven," the second escort said.

"Especially, 'Thou shall not change that which has already happened,'" Jennifer said.

"That is the only strange one," the first escort said, puzzled. "No one had been able to figure out what it means. It's a total mystery. Many have tried, but no one has come up with an explanation yet."

"Yes, I can see that. A total mystery for all time." Yes, Jennifer knew exactly what it meant. Had God created it just for her and possibly other future time travelers?

Before long, the limo pulled up to a building where the President was waiting for her. Jennifer looked at the building. It definitely wasn't the White House. *That's odd. Could this be another office?* But that did not make sense either. Four Marines waited on the sidewalk to escort her to the President. They surrounded Jennifer and walked her inside the building. Once inside, they escorted her to the main office, where the President was waiting, and opened the door. After all, the whole trip had lasted only eight minutes for him. She felt a little sick to her stomach. Was it nerves? She walked into the room and saw a man sitting behind a very nice desk with a large cross around his neck. She did not know who he was as this man was not President Peck. She had never seen him before.

"Excuse me, but I'm here to see the President. Can you tell him I'm here, please?" Jennifer felt a little mixed up as she realized that no one knew the consequences of time travel yet. It would be impossible to fully understand.

"Jennifer, you are quite a joker," President John Thomas said with a smile. "What a sense of humor. I always liked that about you. Please have a seat, and let's talk for a little while. I love our talks. You are just plain fun. And may I say that you look very good for someone who has traveled over two thousand years in time and back. In fact, very good.

How do you feel since our last visit? I'm sure you have many amazing stories to tell me. I am so pleased that I picked you to head the mission. You were the perfect one. In fact, you were the only one."

Jennifer sat down in front of his desk and noticed a large wooden name plate there that read "President John Thomas." She looked up and saw a picture of him with the words "President of the United States." *Did Jim Peck ever exist or did God have a special say in that, too?* she thought. Why did she remember the way it had been? Once again, she looked at the gold ring on her finger. Maybe Jesus had given her a special gift. She had never met this man, yet he knew her. Time was a puzzle that might never be solved. Being a superbly trained FBI agent, she quickly adapted to the situation.

"Yes, Mr. President, I can be just a funny clown. How are you, sir? So nice to see you again."

"Well, for eight minutes I was really concerned," President Thomas said. "But as soon as the time ship reappeared, I was ecstatic. I'm ready to know the truth after two thousand years. Two thousand years of truth, lies, stories, legends, and who knows what else? Many people have died, trying to find out what you finally know for certain. The old saying that the truth will set you free, finally makes sense. That is the reason I sent you on this mission. To find out if Jesus was real and our faith was real. I pray that it is."

"I didn't notice that crucifix before, have you always worn it?" Jennifer asked.

"You are truly an expert. It was a gift from my mother, and I felt compelled to wear it just for this occasion. I wish she were here to hear the words you are about to say. She always believed, and she passed that same determination onto me. They said you were there eight days! I mean for us it was seconds. Time travel is strange."

"I was hoping the cameras could tell us a very interesting story," Jennifer said. "A lot of things we got wrong, very wrong. But some things we got so very right."

"Unfortunately, I was just informed the strangest thing. None of the cameras worked. There was nothing on them. They were the very first things we looked at. There were two super cameras on each of you, and none of them recorded anything. It's almost as if they were erased. Was anything brought back? Even the cameras inside the time ship failed to function. We need some kind of proof."

Jennifer covered her ring with her hand. "Just the smell of the camels. Although I think Leo and Winifred did bring a few small items back, nothing big and nothing special. More like souvenirs, because basically, we were tourists."

"Then I guess it is up to you. You know the answers that mankind has been waiting for. You, my dear, can change the world. A world that has been moving away from religion and even from the blessed Jesus Christ. I feel so sorry for us, but you can change all that. We have lost our meaning. So many people think that God is dead. That Jesus never existed. That faith is no longer real." The President looked sad.

"During my time in the past, I saw people who were hopeless, but they still had hope. I saw people who were treated with hatred, but they still found reasons to express love. I saw the beginning and the end. But the end brings a new beginning. I witnessed jealously, and I witnessed compassion. I saw a simple love that seems to be lost to us. I saw people who would actually talk to each other. But what do I know? I'm just one person."

"The one person who knows the truth and is blessed over the millions who don't," President Thomas said.

"Can one person really make all that much difference?" "Jesus did." "He did," Jennifer said nodding her head. "Yes, he did."

"Just tell me the truth, good or bad, just the truth. Was Jesus real? I repeat, was Jesus real? Are our hopes real? Can we save our planet from the evil surrounding it? Is our love for Jesus and God not lost? Can we be saved and can we be saved with faith? Good or bad the whole world needs to know the truth." "To learn the truth from the truth," Jennifer replied.

"And you are the only one who knows."

"No, sir, millions already know," Jennifer said. "They have for a very long time." "Known what?" the President asked.

Jennifer stood up. "Mr. President, I just returned from an amazing adventure. I traveled over two thousand years in time and back. There is a lot to think about. I need a little time to think everything over in order to give you a proper report, especially to your question about Jesus." President John Thomas sighed. This wasn't what he had wanted to hear, but he knew he had to be patient. "Of course, we have waited over two thousand years. What does it matter if we add more time to it? Just not too much time, please."

Jennifer walked to the main door and opened it. Then she turned around to face the President. "I will give you one response to your question for now."

President John Thomas stood up. "Please, what is it?" Jennifer looked the President directly in the eyes. "Yes!"

Jennifer closed the door behind her as joy lit John Thomas' face, and she was escorted back to the limo, where her two escorts were waiting. Climbing into the limo, they drove off. Jennifer grabbed another cold drink from the refrigerator.

"President Thomas sure is nice," she said after taking a drink.

"Yes, he's been great for the last two years," the first escort said.

"Everybody seems to like him."

"They even like the first lady," the second escort added.

Jennifer was amazed. "Boy, two years can sure go by in a flash. I hardly noticed." "Where to now?" the second escort asked.

"There is a little church I'd like to stop by. I'll tell you how to get there." "Lead on. We hear and obey," the second escort replied. Jennifer directed them to the small church she had visited with Father Davis and the four rough teenagers. She realized then that in reality and true time, that had happened only yesterday. The limo stopped in front of the church. Jennifer got out and walked to the front door. She noticed that the doors and walls were now clean with no graffiti on them, almost as if they were brand new. Could this also be a change in the timeline? She entered the church and spotted Father Davis, along with the four teenagers from last night, who had cleaned the church and put things back in order.

Father Davis looked up at the sound of the door opening and saw Jennifer. He had a big smile on his face. "Jennifer, welcome back! We have great surprises for you!"

Seeing Jennifer, the four teenagers ran to her and knelt down in front of her. Surprised, she said, "Hey! Whoa! What is this? This isn't necessary."

"In their case, it is," Father Davis said. "Whatever you did you, you somehow performed a miracle for these four young special people. You opened their eyes to truth and love." Father Davis walked up behind them. "Jennifer, I want you to meet my four new converts, helpers, and friends. They are from top to bottom, Peter, the tall one, John, the clean one, James, the one who now prays and Mary, the loving one."

"Peter, John, James and Mary," Jennifer said with a grin. "Now where have I heard those names before? How wonderful to meet you. I see you have changed, and I am very pleased."

"We have changed because of you and what you said," Peter told her. "You opened our hearts and our souls, and we owe you a great debt. You saved us. You taught us a lesson about life."

"Please get up. I am honored, and it's only been eight…I mean one day."

"It happened this morning," John said, excited. "We woke up and felt different. Something changed us and that was you. Whoever you are, you are magic."

"You gave us true faith and now we want to believe," James said. "Something wonderful happened. I finally feel like I have a purpose in life."

"You know me," Mary said. "I was for you all along. You go, girl."

"They were here six o'clock this morning with cleaning supplies and a whole new attitude—one of faith and love," Father Davis said proudly. "Something changed them, and it could only have been you."

"We were wrong," John said. "We had no right to do what we did. You taught us that we need to respect others, and maybe forgive ourselves and try to do better. I'm think I want to study to become a priest."

"That would be wonderful," Jennifer said. "We need more people like Father Davis."

"I even learned all Eleven Commandments," James said. "Even that weird one." Jennifer smiled at him. "That is very impressive, even the weird one."

"I actually feel loved, even by my parents," Mary said. "And for the first time, they both kissed me as I left the house this morning. It felt really good."

"I now believe in Jesus and God," Peter said. "I don't know how. It just happened. I'm now so happy. It feels great. I feel so alive, and I want everyone to feel the love, love for all."

Jennifer felt like she should pat them all on the head. "It happened because it's true. All you had to do was to open your eyes and feel the love that God and Jesus have for you. That love has always been there. You just needed to find it again. The impossible is no longer impossible."

Father Davis looked closely at her. "Jennifer, I sense something different about you. Something special. Something we have all been waiting for, but we don't know what. There is a special light about you. What has changed?"

"I am the same person I was last night," she said. "My stomach feels a little queasy, but not bad."

"No," Mary said. "Even I can see it. You're different and the same, but different in a special way. I can't explain, but it's there. There's something special about you."

"Yes, you have powers we don't understand," Peter said. "You changed us, and you made us believe."

"I'm just Jennifer."

"Yes, Jennifer, the chosen one," Father Davis said.

Jennifer was puzzled. She had thought that when she returned to her own time, she had left that title behind her. "I have a few more errands to do, but I'll stop by in a few days. I'm very pleased at this outcome. It makes me feel really good and happy, and I need to be happy right now. Thank you all."

"Thank you and bless you," the four teenagers said in unison.

Father Davis cocked his head slightly and said, "I think you have already been blessed and from a much higher source than us." "Goodbye. I will see you all soon. Thank you for the new love you now have." Jennifer again looked at the ring on her finger and wondered what was next? Returning to the limo, she got inside and took another drink of her soda. "Okay, just one more stop. The big church downtown."

"That's the one I attend," the second escort said. "I know exactly how to get there."

The limo drove off heading for the cathedral. Jennifer kept staring at the ring. The limo stopped at a red light, and she glanced out the window, noticing a large billboard. A huge smile came to her face. The billboard read:

LONGINUS BEEF

**throughout history, the finest beef in the world,
now available in fine markets everywhere.**

Jennifer's smile went from ear to ear as she realized where that name had come from. Here was actual proof that she had changed at least one life for the better. "Son of a gun. It worked!" "What was that?" the first escort asked.

"Oh, nothing, just talking to myself."

Thirty minutes later, the limo stopped in front of the Sacred Heart of Mary church in a no-parking zone.

Seeing Jennifer's questioning look, the first escort said, "Don't worry. We can park anywhere we want and nothing will happen to us. We'll wait here for you."

"Actually, you might want to go home and come back. I could be a while. Don't worry. I won't mind. I can call you when I'm ready."

"Yes, but we would," the second escort said. "We would be fired and sent to Alaska."

"Oh, dear. We can't have that," Jennifer replied. "But I'm warning you. You might still be here to see the sun come up."

Her escorts looked outside the limo window and noticed that it was still daylight, actually only midday.

"But it's just past noon," the first escort said, a quizzical look on her face.

"Get my point. There are bathrooms inside the church, and there are stores everywhere," Jennifer said. "You have been warned."

"All I can say is that I will see you when I see you," the second escort said. "Have a pleasant night."

"Take care, ladies."

Jennifer stepped out of the limo and entered the church. Walking down the center aisle, she sat down in the front pew across from a large cross that hung on the wall behind the altar. The cross held an image of Jesus carved in wood on it. She looked at the image and shook her head back and forth.

"Not even close. Not even remotely close. You have no idea." But then how could it look like him? The artist that had carved the image had never seen the living Christ.

Standing up, she left the pew and entered the sanctuary, walking up two steps and crossing to the marble altar, which was empty, since morning mass had ended hours ago. She knew there was something she needed to do, but did not know what, until she remembered a Catholic wedding she had attended. Jennifer genuflected and made the sign of the cross. She wasn't Catholic, but having gone through and witnessed what she had, she felt it was not only necessary, but important—a powerful protection, as her friend had explained to her.

Her emotions were tearing her apart, but her stomach felt a little better, especially being right here in God's house. Being inside the church, she no longer felt so alone but closer to her lost love. Was he watching her right now? She felt a presence, but she was uncertain what it was. Looking to her left and then to her right, she examined the stained-glass windows. Each window depicted one of the stations of the cross. A wave of sadness washed over her, but true to her word, she decided that she would not leave the church until the sun rose in the morning. She would do this for Jesus and her love.

Three nuns, who were talking quietly, entered through a side door that led to another part of the church. Seeing her, they nodded. But when Jennifer acknowledged them, they were mesmerized, unable to take their eyes off her. Then all at once, they smiled. The sisters seemed to know something that Jennifer did not. They were overjoyed and happy, as if something wonderful had happened, and they hurried over to her.

"It's very unusual to find a parishioner in the sanctuary," the tallest one said. "Usually, they are seated or kneeling in the pews."

"Oh, I'm not a parishioner, for now at least," Jennifer replied.

"You are the most beautiful pregnant woman I have ever seen," the oldest of the three said. "There is something very special about you. We knew it the moment you smiled at us. Watching you, we had no choice but to come over."

"Sorry, no way," Jennifer said with a shake of her head. "I have to disappoint you as I have not been with anyone for quite a while. Actually, a whole while, like my whole life. I am definitely not pregnant, no way. It's impossible."

"Oh, yes, you are," a petite nun said. "Maybe you just forgot."

"No. Believe me, you wouldn't forget something like that," Jennifer reassured her. "Like I said, impossible."

"Maybe impossible for you, but not impossible for God," the older nun reassured her.

The third nun, a cheerful, slightly overweight woman said, "Sisters, this one may be special indeed. I think you are the mother of hope. The one we have been praying for. The one we have needed for a long time. The one who will open our eyes and save us. Our hope for the future."

"It happened once. Maybe it can happen again," the older nun said firmly. "God works in mysterious ways."

"I know in my heart that God wants to save us," the third nun said. "This could be the answer we have all been waiting for. God has always loved us. We just needed to love him back. That is all he has ever wanted."

All the nuns hugged Jennifer. And as they walked away, they kept glancing at her.

Jennifer touched her stomach. She felt different somehow, and it certainly would explain the problems she had been having with queasiness. She thought about the wonderful, blessed Mary, conceived without the stain of original sin, thanks to her immaculate conception.

Mary was the immaculate conception, not Jesus, born without sin so that she would be pure enough to give birth and become the mother of Jesus. Could it happen again? But how? That would mean that Jennifer would also have been born without the stain of original sin.

For hundreds and hundreds of years it had been foretold that a new messiah would appear. *My God, can the new messiah be a child from the original messiah? Can lightning strike twice in the same way? Why can't I remember? I don't think so. But no! I was not visited by an angel with an announcement. And one thing I am certain of is that I am still a virgin. Aren't I? Is this the plan God had for me? To be the mother of the new messiah just like Mary. God, are you there?*

"Oh, by the way. What is your name?" the petite nun asked. They had stopped about ten feet away from her. "We want to know what to call you, other than the chosen one, so we can remember you."

"You know, I have always gone by my first name, Jennifer, but I think I'll start using my middle name for a while."

"And what is that name, beautiful lady?" the older nun asked.

"You can call me Mary."

"Ah, Mary, just like the blessed mother. What a beautiful name! It becomes you very much. We will pray for you and look after you, special mother named Mary."

The nuns left, and Jennifer returned to the front pew and sat down to gaze at the cross. She thought about what the nuns had said and what could have happened and how. It was hard to remember, after all it was over two thousand years ago. Two thousand years was a long time, but her tears were still fresh. Fresh with love for an amazing man, who was no longer a man but divinity itself. The love she felt for Jesus was only getting stronger, more real than she ever thought possible. It was the most real emotion she had ever felt. She knew he would always be a part of her. Love was timeless. Jennifer kissed the gold ring given to her by the most amazing person to ever live. She raised her eyes to look up at the cross with the image on it.

"I love you! I love you! I love you!"